MISFIT MAGE

MISFIT MAGE

Fledgling God

Book 1

Michael Taggart

This is a work of fiction. Names, characters, places, and incidents are the
products of the author's imagination or are used fictitiously. Any
resemblance to actual persons, living or dead, business, companies, events,
or locals is entirely coincidental.

Cover by Michael Taggart

Editing by Beth Dorward
www.reedsy.com/beth-dorward

Detail editing by Jessica Lack
www.reedsy.com/jessica-lack

Additional editing by Conor Welter
www.reedsy.com/conor-welter

Micro editing by Steve DeHart

Print Copy, Book Spine, and Back Cover by Cynthia D. Griffin
www.CynthiaDGriffin.com

ISBN Number:
9781709666094

Printed in the United States

First Edition

This book exists because of the encouragement and support of one person—Judi. She listens like a wise monk on a mountain top and encourages like a mother duck. If everyone had a friend like her, then the world would feel loved, safe, and emboldened to be all they can be.

Judi, thank you for laughing at all my jokes and pretending all the book ideas I had were good ones. In short, You Rock!

To my nephew Shane, thank you for listening to all the mechanics of magic in this world. It's a much better place with your input and support! It's also been a lot more fun.

To my editor Beth Dorward, thanks for taking a chance on a new author! This book is sooooo much more readable with your help.

To my detail editor Jessica Lack, thank you for proofing this on such short notice! All my verb tenses are now lined up nicely.

To my cover artist George Long, you nailed it! It is everything I wanted and more.

To Bermuda Moses, you are my furry muse! All the loving looks, purrs, standing on the keyboard, sleeping on the keyboard, and bird watching has somehow gained a life in these pages. Love you little fella.

To my husband Harold, you are the soundtrack to my world! You give me the life that lets me follow my dreams. Here's too many more happy years together!

Table of Contents

1

Run for Your Life

Sprinting while naked is not an easy thing. I've seen streakers before, and while I've admired their desire for mischief, I've never thought of it as a painful undertaking.

I was running for my life down the hall, and despite the motivation to maintain top speed, Captain Winky and his two first mates were voicing a loud, painful protest of their mistreatment.

The human body is a wonderful thing, and normally it would have responded to a fight-or-flight situation by compacting all members. A tight package makes for minimal jostling, and I think I could have even enjoyed the feeling of air flowing over my nether regions. However, I had been interrupted in the middle of some fine nookie, and nothing about my rather upbeat member was compacted.

Two men in black suits pounded down the hotel hallway behind me. They were built like ass-kickers, and as such they would surely give me a hurtin' if they caught me. However, I'm lean and nimble and I was able to put some distance between us.

I wasn't sure why they were after me—neither one was acting like a jilted lover. But right now, getting away seemed like a good use of my mental powers. I'd leave figuring out why for later.

It's hard to create an escape plan when you're starting from, "Oh baby, that feels good!" but I had the beginnings of one. I figured I'd get to the stairway and either take it to the bottom floor and out an emergency exit, or maybe duck onto one of the other floors and hide. It wasn't much of a plan, but a chase is fluid and quick. Hopefully it would be enough.

I made it to the end of the hall with a good lead on my pursuers, burst through the door to the stairway, and right into the arms of another big, suited ass-kicker.

It startled the heck out of me, and I think it startled him too. He was expecting to catch me, but he wasn't expecting me to be naked. He must have been a straight guy because he did what all straight men do when suddenly holding a piece of man ass: He backed off.

That gave me enough room to maneuver, and I hit him with everything I had. I had about six seconds, ten tops, before Thing One and Thing Two came through the door after me.

I went into hyper mode, punching him three, maybe four times at full speed, which ended up being a mistake. His training kicked in and I went from, "naked dude, back off," to, "hostile dude, maim and destroy."

I weigh about 150, and although I'm mostly lean, hard muscle, I still lack the power of a more massive frame.

Mass wasn't a problem for my opponent; he must have weighed in at a good 250 pounds, and he shrugged off my punches. I'd fought bullies as a kid, so I knew to aim for his chin or nose. A chin shot might stun him, and a nose shot would hurt like hell, making his eyes water. Either one would let me slip past him. He had good training though, ducking his head and raising his shoulder.

He was close, really close, and I knew I wouldn't have time to sprint up the stairs before he grabbed me. Wrestling with this guy would be a bad idea. Instead, I did the unexpected and slightly insane move of jumping toward him, grabbing him around the head and neck, and throwing myself over the railing.

My 150 pounds might not have been enough mass to knock him out, but with a gravity assist, it was plenty of mass to whip his head around—and where the head goes, the body goes. He toppled over the railing after me.

The stairs were like most flights you would find in hotels: They went back and forth between floors, so he didn't have that far to fall. However, they were made of concrete and that is a rough landing. It also didn't help him that we continued to rotate in the air, and I landed on top. He hit the concrete with a crunch, and I rode his body like a toboggan as it thumped down the steps to the landing.

For a second, I thought he might be dead—I didn't want to be a killer—but then I saw him breathe.

I hopped off of him and flew down the next flight of stairs. I had just reached the next floor when I heard Thing One and Two burst through the stairwell door a few floors above. I checked out which floor I was on—eleven—and made a quick decision that I was still too high to make a mad dash for the ground floor.

I was sure they would hear me if I stayed on the stairs, so I took the door onto the eleventh floor. Nobody was in the long hallway, so I started jogging to the other end. I figured there should be another stairwell at that end; hopefully I could use that to escape. I really needed some clothes, though. I couldn't move around the city and blend in the way I was.

At that moment, two thugs appeared at the end of the hall.

My God! How many guys are after me?

One or two meant I just ticked someone off. Five bruisers meant this was a full-on hunt by someone with resources. My smart mouth and easy loving were always getting me into trouble, so this wasn't the first time I'd had to run to save my hide. This was my first manhunt, though, and it was starting to scare me.

At least the two guys on this floor weren't as big or professional as the others. Things One and Two had looked like professional hit men or mob enforcers. These two looked like smaller sidekicks that were trying way too hard to look tough. One had a shaggy mop of hair that was supposed to be casually cool, but instead just looked unwashed and greasy. The other had a tiny goatee—classic villain style—that he probably stroked while saying, "I will keel you aaand your leetle friend!"

I couldn't go back to the stairwell behind me and I didn't want to try getting through Shaggy and The Villain ahead, so I cast out my senses looking for another way.

For as long as I can remember, I've always been able to do things that were special. Not short-bus special—magical special. Maybe magical isn't the right word. I don't mutter incantations or call on gods or anything like that. Rather, I have talents and insights most people don't.

Anyway, I needed a way out, and I could see what looked like another hallway branching off to the right. My extra senses told me it wasn't another hallway; it was a small area containing a vending machine and two elevators.

Escape by elevator works great in the movies, but in real life the timing usually sucks, and it ends up being a trap. I didn't have much choice in this case. I needed to call an elevator to this floor now. Delicate magic was beyond my concentration at this point, but I'd used my little Punch Rocket many times before and the image came to me easily.

I pictured the base first—four fins sitting against my chest, ready to use it as a launching pad. The body was fire-engine red in the traditional rocket shape topped off by a white fist. It was more cartoon than NASA, but the magic didn't care, and it was fun to visualize.

I fed it power and my little rocket blasted off, trailing perfect puffs of white smoke. It flew down the hallway, turned right with a cartoon *skreeeeee*, and wooshed off again. The little white fist smacked into the elevator call button for "up," then the Punch Rocket backed up and smacked into the "down" button. Both call lights lit up as the feisty little spell gave a toot and was gone.

Now I just needed an elevator to stop. I didn't care if it was going up or down; I just needed to get off this floor.

The two thugs at the other end of the hall were walking toward me. I guess they figured they didn't need to hurry; I was running toward them after all, and they couldn't see my magic. I slowed down a bit. I could see with my magic sight that an elevator hadn't arrived yet. The closer I got the more nervous I felt. If an elevator didn't show, I was going to be trapped in a small space with two guys that were a lot bigger than me.

Okay, make that four guys. The stairwell door slammed open behind me and Thing One and Thing Two barreled through. I was screwed!

I sprinted toward the little hallway, arriving just as the elevator dinged and the door slid open. The arrow said it was going up, so I slipped inside, punched a button for one of the top floors, and held down the "close door" button.

I heard shouts out in the hallway and the sound of running feet. The Things and their sidekicks were coming to get me.

The elevator stayed open for what seemed like forever, but it finally slid closed and I slumped back against the wall in relief. That's when I realized I wasn't alone.

A tall, older lady in a blue dress was enjoying the heck out of my naked show. She kind of reminded me of Blanche Devereaux from *The Golden Girls*.

"Is that what all the kids are wearing these days?" she asked with a twinkle in her eye.

"Umm, no," I said intelligently, as I tried to cover up with both hands. I found out very quickly that two hands don't cover up much.

"Oh, don't bother trying to hide the naughty bits. It isn't anything I haven't seen before." She smiled, then cocked her head to the side. "Although, you are definitely the nicest looking man I have seen in a long time!" She gestured at my abs. "Those are especially nice."

I started blushing. Then I tried not to blush, which only made me blush even more. I had always thought blushing just happened in your face, but I was managing to do it all over.

"Oh dear! Now I've gone and made you all nervous. How on earth did you end up like this?"

For a moment I almost opened my mouth and told her everything. I'd met this cute guy in an exclusive game of poker, and afterward we had gotten a room. I was discovering he was way better at shagging than he was at poker—what he could do with his *real* hands was divine. His poker hands? Not so much—when the door flew open and two guys jumped me. Now I'm here, running for my life, and doing a one-man stripper act.

"I'm being pranked by my roommates, ma'am. They think it's hysterical that I'm running the halls naked."

"Well, you tell them that is not nice! It is kind of funny, but you could get into trouble running around like this." She thought for a moment. "Do you want to wait in my room while I call housekeeping and get all this straightened out?"

I was tempted, but I didn't think the presence of an older lady was going to stop these guys. They would just deal with me and then deal with her too.

"Thank you very much, but I think we can work it out." I gave her a smile as the elevator slowed down.

"Oh, I need a picture!" She was quick. She had her cell phone out and clicked away before I could tell her not to. "Bridge club would never believe me without this!" The doors slid open and she gave my butt a friendly pat on the way out.

"You be careful!"

She cheerfully waved as she disappeared down the hall and the doors slid closed.

The elevator started ascending to its next stop, floor 23, and I only had a few moments to figure out what I was going to do. They knew I was on the elevator, so I couldn't ride it down to the first floor. They also had both stairwells covered, so going down that way wasn't an option. What I needed to do was hide out for a while. Hopefully they would get tired of the chase and just leave.

The elevator arrived at floor 23. I pressed a bunch of the buttons for the other floors—might as well confuse the trail a bit more—then stepped out and just listened. Everything was quiet—no sound of running feet—so I peeked down the hallway. It was empty.

What I needed was a vacant room that would stay unrented for the rest of the night. Rooms with a view were given out first, so I picked a room at random that faced the back of the building.

I put my hand on the door and let my awareness seep into the room. Using my talent to look through things is really difficult. It took a few moments before the room started to form in my mind. Since I wanted to make sure the room was empty, I just needed to scan for large human-sized forms. It would have been really challenging to see anything smaller than that.

Nobody was inside, so I switched my attention to the latch. No matter how you lock a door—and this hotel had those fancy card readers—the actual part that keeps the door shut is the latch. It's the spring-loaded piece of metal that fits into the door frame, and it's impossible for most people to mess with without tearing it apart.

However, I can do things most people can't. I gathered my energy and *flicked* the latch. I could hear it bounce back, but it wasn't enough to open the door. The hotel had good locks with strong springs. I gathered my energy and *flicked* it again. I did better, but it still wasn't enough.

I put both hands over the lock. Sometimes it seemed to help if I was as close as possible to whatever I manipulated. I gathered all my energy, held it, took a deep breath, gathered some more energy, and *FLICKED*.

This time the door opened. I stepped inside just as I heard the ding of the elevator. I closed the door quickly, softly, and stood in the dark with my heart racing.

How in the hell were they finding me so quickly? It just didn't seem fair. I'd been chased before, and contrary to what the movies show, it's actually pretty easy to lose someone if they aren't right on your tail.

Of course, the elevator could have been bringing anyone to this floor, not just my hunters.

The room had a deadbolt, which I set, as well as one of those metal catches you use to keep everyone out, even the maid. I set that as well. Then I put my hands on the door and *looked* into the hallway.

It felt empty, but I stayed there, letting my awareness expand to include a sizable chunk of the hallway. I was about to let it go, when a being of pure power stepped off the elevator.

I say it was a being because the power was so bright that I couldn't tell anything about it. I didn't know if it was a guy, a girl, or even human.

I do know I'd never seen or felt anything like it before. I wanted to squeak and cower in fear. I jumped away from the door, hoping that whatever it was hadn't sensed me.

I was suddenly aware I was shaking. All that adrenaline and emotion was starting to catch up to me.

What the hell had I gotten myself into? How did I end up being chased by five guys who looked like bouncers and now there was this being with god-like power out there? I didn't know this God Dude was after me, but I didn't know he wasn't either. (I decided to call him God Dude as that is a lot less scary than Giant Powerful God Thing That Can Squish You Like A Bug. It's also much shorter.)

The smart-ass voice in my head was still making jokes, but I was starting to get scared—really scared.

I took a deep breath and started walking up and down the room, swinging my arms, letting the fear out. Runaway emotions were not going to change the situation I was in. Instead they might make me do something stupid.

After a few minutes, I felt better and began to think through the situation. The only thing I could think of that could have caused any of this was the poker game. Maybe one of the players was a sore loser and connected to the mob or something like that. I'm a good judge of people, though—you have to be, to be a good poker player—and the game had finished without anyone getting fighting mad. Sure, some of the men were upset, but I don't think anyone lost more than they could afford.

I'd pocketed thirty-five thousand from the night, and I wasn't even the biggest winner. Fortunately, I'd learned to secure my winnings immediately; I'd already mailed the cash to myself.

Maybe my lover from tonight had a jealous partner? That didn't seem to fit either. He was just as surprised as I was at the interruption, and none of the suits had been ranting or raving about vengeance and hurt feelings.

Instead the whole thing felt very professional, even clinical. The thugs didn't hate me. They were just doing their job. Well, they might hate me now that I'd dropped one of their own down a stairwell, but it was still a job for them.

If I was reading this right, then getting out of here was going to be more difficult than I hoped. If this had started in anger, then there was the chance that they would cool down and just leave. They might be cursing my name, but they would tire of this and go home. If it was a job, however, they would stick around and do their damnedest to get me.

Their payment and reputation would be on the line. I had no idea how God Dude figured into this. Maybe he was here for some other reason that had nothing to do with me. This was a hotel, after all. Maybe God Dude just wanted a good night's sleep. I could only hope.

2

Death Experience

After several minutes of thinking and pacing, I decided to look into the hallway again and see if anything was happening. When I did, I almost jumped out of my skin.

Shaggy and The Villain were on the other side of my door. How were they finding me so fast? Did I have some type of tracking device on me? I was totally in the buff, so that seemed really unlikely.

Just to be sure I did a quick self-scan—nothing I could detect.

They seemed to be hanging around waiting for something—the door was still locked and latched so maybe I had a few minutes to try something. It seemed like hiding wasn't an option; I needed to go on the offensive.

Using my talent on people, or anything alive, is a lot more difficult than manipulating regular things—a person's natural energy gets in the way. I'd found a way around that, but it took time to work.

Instead of dropping a full enchantment on them, I'd start with a tiny, seed-like hex and let it grow using their own energy. I still couldn't do anything big, but there are parts of the body where a tiny disruption can make a huge difference.

I began by imagining a tiny little man in front of me. He was super small, barely the size of a speck of dust. I needed him to do lots of work, so I dressed him up with a pair of overalls, a miner's helmet, and gave him a pickaxe. He needed to fly, so I added a tiny jet pack as well as a GPS so he knew where to go. Last, and most important, I placed a glowing green ring on his finger that he could use to make an exact duplicate of himself.

With that, I dubbed him Bob One, and gave him a bit of power to wake up. He blinked, stretched, swung his pickaxe a few times and then flew through the air going, "Wheeeeeeee!"

What can I say? If I had a jetpack I'd probably fly around going, "Wheeeeeeee," too.

Bob One quickly settled down, ready for work. The first thing I did was have him trigger his magic ring and make a Bob Two. Then both of them triggered their green rings to make Bobs Three and Four.

The leaders of my work crew were ready to go. I loaded in the coordinates on their GPS, wished them lots of luck, and sent them on their way.

The four Bobs flashed me a thumbs up, triggered the lights on their miner's helmet, engaged their jetpacks, and *wheeed* their way toward the top of the door. For normal-sized people there was no way through, but when you are a tiny speck even a crack in the door frame seems like a superhighway to the outside.

Bob One made it out to the hall, over to Shaggy, and into his right ear. On his own, Bob One couldn't do much damage, but once inside he began using his magic duplicator ring and soon there were two, then four, then eight determined little workmen. Some of the Bobs started hammering into the ear canal while the rest continued making reinforcements.

The other Bob leaders had flown into Shaggy and The Villain's other ears, and the same process was going on there. At some point my two assailants were going to have a nasty surprise—all I had to do was wait.

I was feeling pretty good about what I had done when Things One and Two showed up. That must have been what the two sidekicks were waiting for. Thing One took something out of his pocket and held it up to my door. For a long moment nothing happened. I'd already started on new Bobs for the two Things when the entire door lit up and I felt power, like an electric shock, shoot up my hands and arms. I jerked my hands away and jumped back as the door glowed. All the light slid to the locks. One by one they disengaged, and the door opened.

That was not good—not good at all.

Shaggy and The Villain entered first, followed by the Things.

Suddenly the room felt very small.

Thing Two put the "Do Not Disturb" sign on the outside handle and closed the door. The room had gone from feeling like a safe place to feeling like my tomb.

I needed to slow the action down—give the magic time to work—and somehow come up with another plan.

"Hey guys! I'm glad you could make it! It wouldn't be a party without you."

I flashed my brightest smile and waved like I was inviting them into the room. The aura of menace they were projecting faltered as they looked at each other in confusion.

"I'm sorry I don't have lots of party food but there are a few things in the mini fridge and some complimentary chips and candy bars by the TV. No sense in kicking my ass while you're hungry."

I tossed two candy bars over to Shaggy and The Villain and grabbed a bag of chips for myself. To keep the show going I opened it and started munching.

"What would you guys like?" I asked the Things as I got into the mini-bar. "Maybe a drink to help you get in the mood for a nice smack down? I have a single serving of a nice white wine, or– oooh, some Jack Daniels!"

Shaggy had just opened his candy bar and was getting ready to take a bite when Thing One reached over and smooshed it in his hand.

"Don't ever take anything from the sups," he growled. "They're tricky bastards. You never know what they are trying to do to you."

Sups? What the heck was a sup?

"It's just a candy bar," Shaggy whined, until Thing One really clamped down on his hand. Then he turned white and shut up.

Thing One looked over at The Villain, who quickly threw his chocolate away. It seemed pretty clear who was in charge.

"Now, we are going to guard the door so he can't get away again. You two have first crack at kicking his ass. It's a small room so he can't go far."

Shaggy started to scrape the chocolate off his hand.

"Pardon me, guys, but what is a sup?" They all looked at me like I was stupid.

"Well, you are. You're a sup," The Villain spoke up.

"But what is that? A supervisor? A superintendent? I was a shift supervisor at Yum Burgers once, but I can promise you I wasn't mean to anyone. Well, except for a few customers, but they were the assholes first."

"You're a supernatural." My face must have registered how shocked I was. "Don't look so surprised. Even a young sup knows they are special."

I'd never told anyone since I moved to Louisville what I could do, and I'd never met anyone else who seemed magical. Well, other than tonight. Tonight seemed to be full of magical surprises. Were there other people like me?

Shaggy chuckled. "I think we might have a real case of Ugly Duckling, fellas. This sup doesn't know who he is."

"Not that it matters," Thing One spoke up. "A job is a job. Remember, no knives, no guns, he is to be beaten only. Take your time—the client wants his last hours to really hurt."

"Go have your fun. Just don't kill him yet. We'll do that when it's our turn."

The casual discussion about my demise and what was going to precede it sent a chill through me. They were so matter of fact. It seemed to put the stamp of truth on the next few hours. I was going to have a horrible, painful death.

Shaggy and The Villain started to move toward me. They were moving slowly, carefully, keeping me at one end of the hotel room.

The dresser/desk with the TV was on one wall, the bed on the other, with a path between them. The path was comfortable enough for one person but a bit cramped for two. Behind me were a table, two chairs, and a standing lamp. There was more space to maneuver, but that would benefit them more than me. Hopefully I could work it so I would only have to face one of them at a time. My odds of getting through this still sucked, but they sucked less than dealing with all the goons at once.

I pulled over the TV. It landed with barely a clatter on the soft carpet. It wasn't much, but they would need to step on or over it to get to me. Their footing wouldn't be solid and hopefully I could use that to my advantage.

Adrenaline poured through me again and I trembled with nervous anticipation.

The anticipation was getting to Shaggy too. He hovered on one side of the fallen TV, not quite ready to make the first move. The Villain was right behind him, trying to look menacing, yet obviously happy he wasn't going first.

I used the lull in the action to quickly visualize another Flying Miner. The image was fresh in my mind from the previous enchantment, so he formed quickly. I filled him with energy, duplicated him, and was starting to give out GPS coordinates, when Shaggy worked up the nerve to attack. It was awful timing. I lost my concentration and all four miners popped out of existence. I had hoped the Flying Miners would be working on the Things as I was dealing with these two.

Shaggy gave a battle yell as he screwed up his courage, stepped on the TV, and lunged in with a left hook. I didn't want to give any ground, so I threw up both arms to block it, as well as the right hook that followed.

He threw a left hook again—not much imagination there—then did what I'd been hoping and waiting for. He staggered and the next punch went wild.

My enchantment was finally working.

The human ear is a sensitive collection of bones, nerves, and fluids. Mess with it, and you can cause phantom sounds, headaches, loss of balance, and nausea. It's really hard to fight when the room is tilting like a carnival ride and your head is pounding like a ten-shot hangover.

Shaggy staggered toward the bed, then back toward the desk. He tripped, fell, and smacked his head on the side of the desk. It was a solid hit; his skull emitted a solid thunk and bounced a bit. It hurt just watching it.

The Villain wasn't having any fun either. He was down on all fours doing a passable imitation of a pub crawl. He smelled like it too when he threw up.

Two goons down. Two to go. Unfortunately, it was the harder two and I didn't have any enchantments on them.

I was just starting to work on another round of Flying Miners when Thing One launched into action. He operated like a pro: no hesitation, no sarcastic comments, just quick efficient action.

He dove onto the bed, rolled, and came up in the clear space by the table and chairs. With one smart move he'd gotten to the only open spot in the room, leaving me trapped against the wall, the desk, and the two guys on the floor.

Reaching into his jacket pocket, he pulled out two collapsible metal batons and flicked his wrists to activate them. They snapped out to a good two feet of military grade steel. Then he charged.

The batons gave him reach, power, speed. My magic was small and slow. I had no chance to stop him.

The first blow smacked onto my right arm, and the pain hit me like a bath of ice water. I didn't know one hit could hurt so badly. The second, third, and fourth blows showed that it was no fluke— they all hurt that bad.

I tried to move, to cover up somehow, but the beating was relentless. He turned my naked flesh into a mass of deep bruises. He beat my chest, thighs, back, arms—whatever part of me he could reach. He left my head untouched, or I would have quickly been unconscious.

It seemed like this went on for a long time. When he finally stopped, I was a quivering, huddled mass of flesh pressed up against the desk for the tiny bit of shelter it offered.

Someone was screaming. It just went on and on.

Then I realized it was me.

I stopped, drew in big gasps of air, and huddled, shivering, trying to make myself as small as possible.

I didn't know why he stopped, and I didn't care. My world was one of hurt and pain.

I was in shock that something so horrible and awful had happened to me. I just couldn't comprehend it.

Finally, I looked up.

He was sitting on the bed looking at me. A faint smile played on his face.

I couldn't see Thing Two, so he must have still been guarding the door.

"I'm sure you're wondering why I stopped."

I was, actually. I was deathly afraid of the answer.

"I'm giving your mind time to catch up."

WTF?

"Your body will discover all kinds of new sensations this evening, but all that will be wasted if your mind can't keep up. In order for you to get the most out of your last hours, we will take a few breaks, to reset what is normal for you, before we take it to the next level."

I really, really did not want to go to the next level.

"Speaking of breaks . . ." He left the bed and sat beside me. He then started gently touching me, running his hand over my arms and body, pausing to point out an area of skin that still had normal coloring instead of blue or purple.

"Looks like I missed a spot." He smiled.

This was super creepy. I flinched when he touched me and tried to shrink away, but there was nowhere to go. As he kept touching me, I relaxed a bit.

He held my right hand, gradually extending my arm.

Then he stood, pulled me up by my wrist, bent my arm over the desk, and snapped it in two.

I just stared. My arm left my shoulder in a normal line, then, just above the elbow, it hung straight toward the floor.

Arms aren't supposed to do that.

And someone was screaming again.

There is something about a broken bone that makes the world stop. I wanted to call time out, I'm finished, the end.

I wanted to go home.

I wanted my Mommy.

I wanted an adult to walk in and make everything all right.

Nothing like that happened. The room didn't reset. The men didn't go away.

Thing One peeled me off the desk and held me against the wall. He began touching me again. Working his way down, until his hand was cupping my balls.

"Stage Three," he said, and squeezed.

I discovered there were different flavors of pain. The pain from the baton whipping was sharp and urgent. The broken arm felt deep, consistent, crippling. The pain from my testicles was a mix of the two. It was deep, powerful, and yet urgent in its intensity.

Thing One had the powerful grip of a farm hand and the sensitivity levels of a surgeon. He varied the crush and focus so the pain was constantly changing. Sometimes he would focus on one testicle, and sometimes he would mash them both together.

Sometimes I howled. Sometimes I begged him to stop. Sometimes I just said, "Please," over and over again.

I would like to say I'd planned to vomit all over him, but I hadn't. It was a lucky accident.

It wasn't a little bit of puke, either. It was like demon possessed, pure projectile, hurl everything in your guts, type of vomit.

It poured down his shirt, inside and outside his suit, and splashed up onto his face.

I wish I could have enjoyed his look of revulsion and horror, but as he stepped back and let me go, I just sunk to the floor in relief.

Thing Two started laughing.

"Shut the fuck up!" Thing One yelled at him as he started toward the bathroom. That really set Thing Two off, and he started laughing so hard he snorted.

The bathroom door slammed closed, and for a while all I heard was the laughing. He finally quieted down, then Thing Two came over, squatted down, and looked at me.

"You gotta forgive my partner. He really gets into the artistic side of his work. He calls it the Death Experience, and really tries to give sups like you something special before you pass on. Think of it as your last chance to do penance, or build character, or something like that."

"I just keep it simple. The client says to beat you, so I do. Life is hard. Sometimes leaving it is hard too."

With that, he punched me in the face. My head snapped back and bounced off the wall, only to meet his next punch.

We built up a nice rhythm, him punching and me bouncing.

The nice thing was that my brain started rattling around and my world got foggy. A foggy world didn't hurt so much and that was appreciated.

My eyes swelled shut pretty quickly. That was fine with me. I didn't want to see what was happening anyway.

"Move along people, there's nothing to see," I said in my best Leslie Nielsen voice. Or I think I said it. Anyway, it was hysterical, and I just laughed and laughed.

Actually, I don't think I could have been laughing on the outside, because my jaw shattered and my mouth just hung open.

My mind drifted.

Maybe it wouldn't be so bad if I died after all. All I did was hurt people. Like my dad. I hadn't meant to harm anyone. He just made me so angry sometimes.

And then there was the fire. I could still hear my sister screaming.

I worked so hard not to hurt anyone, not to get angry, not to get attached. I just let go. Moved on.

I liked poker tournaments. I was good at them and made a lot of money. Right now that didn't seem like enough reason to live, though.

Maybe the universe was doing me a favor, stopping me before I killed someone else.

There was yelling. Thing One was back and he was yelling at Thing Two for ruining his Death Experience.

Even though my eyes were closed, I could still *see* the room. Thing One was glowing a bright red in anger.

I *looked* at myself. My light was dim and dirty, with small cracks of dark blue and black running throughout. As I watched, my glow faded a bit, the cracks got a bit bigger.

Thing One stomped off to the bathroom and came back with the ice bucket filled with cold water.

He dumped it on me and went back for more.

Around the third bucket the world started to come back into focus. It wasn't so funny or existential anymore.

In fact, it sucked. Waves of pain crashed against my mind. I felt broken on a fundamental level. I just wasn't working anymore.

One element clearly came into focus, though.

I wanted to live.

Now that the alternative felt so close, I was very clear. I wanted life. I wasn't sure how that was going to happen, I felt way too fuzzy to have a plan, but my light was not going to die out.

I must have given some sign I was thinking again, because Thing One stopped and knelt beside me.

"This isn't exactly how I would have wanted it, but we are going to skip to the end of this evening's activities."

He laid me on my back and began pressing on my lowest right rib.

"It is now time for you to drown."

He pressed, relaxed, pressed again, and then—SNAP.

"Drowning isn't so much about water, although that is the most common way it happens."

He began pressing on the next rib.

"People drown in their own blood. Sometimes, they get too drunk to turn over and drown in their own bile."

Press. Press. SNAP.

Oh God, please stop.

Next rib.

"The thing about drowning, though, is that you just can't get air. Breath is our greatest need, more than food or water, and so it is also our greatest fear."

SNAP.

Stop! Please! Stop!

"You are going to face that fear tonight."

I don't want to die.

SNAP.

"The basis of breathing is being able to expand and contract your chest. The muscles open your rib cage, forcing your lungs to fill with air."

SNAP. He switched to my left side.

"Then your muscles contract, pulling in your rib cage, and the smaller space causes your lungs to exhale."

Stop! Stop!

SNAP.

I couldn't draw a full breath.

"Without your ribs being strong and sound, your muscles have to work very hard to get any oxygen."

SNAP.

"You will experience the sensation of drowning."

SNAP.

I don't want to die!

"Eventually your muscles will tire."

SNAP.

"You will stop breathing."

SNAP.

"You will die."

I DON'T WANT TO DIE!

For the first time in my life, I fully embraced my power. It had always felt like a different side of me. There was this part of me I didn't understand, hadn't wanted to understand until now. It only caused pain, anger, loss.

For the first time I truly accepted myself, power and all.

My mind expanded.

I felt and saw with extreme clarity.

I could define every loop in the carpet, the dust in the air, the texture of the walls.

I could feel the moisture in his skin, the fabric of the suit, the hairs on his arm.

It was like I had never seen before. Now I could see everything.

He also glowed with light—healthy, powerful life.

My light was small, pale, almost out.

I needed his light.

I would have his light.

So I took it.

All of it.

I didn't just take his life. I took the warmth of his body, dried the liquids that gave him tone and shape, drained the energy of his mind, and sucked every bit of useful power out of him.

He hit the floor, a dried-up withered husk that looked like it had been dead for years.

Thing Two cried out in alarm and reached for his gun.

With my added power, I *reached* and drained him too.

My light was brighter, but less than I hoped. I struggled to breathe. I could feel the darkness closing in on me.

I reached again, draining Shaggy and The Villain. Then I drained everything in the room. I left the walls and door alone, but everything else was fair game.

The wood of the desk and table warped and splintered. The bedding crumbled to dust. The wallpaper faded and peeled. I even drained the spores and microbes in the air.

It still wasn't enough.

I had life, but the darkness was coming faster.

I didn't have long. I had to fix this. Now.

In desperation I tried to imagine something, anything, in front of me.

My mother appeared.

She was only about 12 inches tall and strangely dressed in a brown robe, but it was her. She looked young, healthy, even happy in a solemn way.

I knew she was dead, that this was just an image, but I was so glad to see her. My mom was here. She could fix this.

I filled her with energy.

"Help me," I begged. "Heal me. Save me. Make me better."

I realized my mom's feet were bare. Then they changed into roots and sunk into the ground.

"Heal me."

Beautiful green leaves grew out of her robes.

She extended her arms to me. Vines shot out of her hands.

"Save me."

The vines reached me, took root, started growing around my chest.

"Make me better."

I felt roots inside me, burrowing, meshing, supporting.

"Heal me."

The darkness closed in. The vines grew, encasing me.

"Save me."

I drew a breath. It felt just a little bit easier than the one before.

"Make me better."

I was cocooned in darkness. I could sense nothing but my mother and the vines. I knew if I stopped giving my mom power then her image would fade.

The darkness would win. I would never know life again.

So I hung onto my mom.

Ignoring the pain.

Ignoring the panic that wanted to creep in.

Ignoring the darkness.

I looped the chant.

"Heal me."

"Save me."

"Make me better."

3

Cocoon

Going into shock is nature's way of easing the transition from life to death. It takes the edge off the pain and keeps the mind from focusing on how mangled the body is.

I didn't want to transition, so I couldn't let the peaceful oblivion take me away. Instead I stayed as alert as possible, pouring magic into the enchantment. The darkness was soft, subtle, inviting. It kept asking to come in. It promised peace and rest.

Ironically, I found the best way to resist was to focus on the pain, to focus on what was wrong with me. The vines and roots continued to grow through me, supporting my broken bones. It wasn't just my bones that were affected, though. They were somehow helping to renew every part of me.

I wasn't sure exactly how the enchantment was working—it was born more from a cry of desperation than a clear plan. The magic was working, though, so I let it continue and hoped it would be enough.

The vines broke out in leaves. Little white flowers bloomed. Then they all withered and died, leaving behind a rich dark soil. The second generation of vines were smaller but much more prolific. They filled up every part of me like a dense spider web. These vines flowered constantly with large yellow blossoms which gave off a pungent musty smell. The shock was long gone by this point and the pain was overwhelming. The smell of the blossoms somehow helped dull the intensity, so I just breathed in life and held on.

Finally, the little vines died too, and a heavy thick moss took its place. It was soft, peaceful, and quiet—like I was wrapped in the coziest blanket in the world. Lavender plants sprung up all around me; the beautiful smell reminded me of home.

It was at that point I noticed I wasn't in the hotel anymore. Instead, I seemed to be in a graveyard on the top of a hill. This world was a bit different than I was used to; everything seemed more dramatic. The colors were more saturated, the smells more powerful; even the sound of the breeze in the tall grass sounded high definition. It was like I had been transported into a filmmaker's fantasy world. I knew I was still in the hotel room and this was some sort of hallucination, but it seemed so real.

In contrast to the beautiful trees and waving grass, the graveyard itself was gray and lifeless. The earth looked scorched. A few shattered headstones littered the ground and four dried husks marked where men used to be.

As I used my *sight* to look around, I noticed I had a headstone behind me. It read:

"Here lies Jason Cole. He's still alive, bitches!"

The epitaph had a lot more bravado than I was feeling at the moment—but it was still pretty cool. It looked like my sarcastic humor had crossed over into fantasyland just fine.

The moss was leaching away the pain, and for the first time I felt like I could start to relax a bit. The sweet lavender, the soft warm moss, and the murmur of the wind lulled me into a peaceful trance. I felt the warmth when the sun came up, and it gradually faded away as the sound of the evening crickets rose.

I could have stayed here forever, until I heard the wind singing. It was a haunting melody that spoke of loss and hope. There weren't any words, but somehow I knew it was singing, searching, calling, just for me.

The wind rolled over me, seeking everywhere. It kept calling and calling; finally, I whispered a reply.

I didn't have the strength to do more than whisper, but it heard me and swept my words away. The melody changed from loss to cautious excitement, and after a long time I heard the sounds of someone approaching.

It ended up being two someones. They looked a bit familiar. The lady was dressed in a travel cloak that shimmered and glowed in the night. She was adorned with a silver necklace strung with charms. There were so many I could hear them rustle as she walked. Her hands sparkled with rings, most of them set with precious stones that glowed with power. She was either an enthusiastic spokesperson for Tiffany, or a well-equipped magical badass.

My vote was on badass.

She was also quite beautiful, with flowing dark hair, smooth pale skin, and long lashes. She looked a lot like my landlady, Sandy—if my landlady had undergone a fantasy makeover.

Hoping for a hot shirtless warrior, I checked out her companion. He was huge, easily seven feet tall, with rough craggy features and skin that looked like stone. If I had to guess I'd say he was some sort of mountain troll. He wasn't a hottie, but he sure fit the role of warrior. Even warriors have to do manual labor, though, and I noticed he was pulling a small wooden cart behind him.

He also looked a lot like my maintenance man, John. We called him Big John, or sometimes just Big. Mr. Big if you were nasty. He was that big in real life, but he wasn't made of stone.

It occurred to me that if he hit me, I could consider myself "stoned." That seemed so funny, and I just laughed and laughed inside. The moss was making me feel good. I could *see* some mushrooms growing on me. I probably really was stoned.

"Oh my goodness! What happened here?" Sandy looked around at the blackened grass and shattered headstones that made up the graveyard.

"It looks like a hell of a fight—four on one." John left the cart and started taking a look around.

Sandy came straight over to me.

"He's alive, John. He's alive!" She sounded so happy.

If this really was Sandy and John—and it seemed to be—then I was really happy to see them too. I'd been concentrating so much on staying alive, I hadn't thought about what came next. To have someone here to take me to a safe place sounded like the best thing in the world.

"He's wrapped in some sort of spell, and it looks like he's hurt pretty bad, but he's alive." Then she burst into tears.

I was surprised by that. We had always had a good time together, but we didn't hang out a lot, and we weren't what I would have called close. I didn't let anyone get close.

John hurried over and wrapped her in a hug.

"It's okay. It's okay. He's not Jennifer. This is not going to end up that way. This time it will be okay."

She nodded. "I know. It's just so much like last time. It still hurts. I miss her."

John just hugged her and didn't say anything.

It wasn't long before Sandy regained her composure and dried her eyes. A weepy maiden, Sandy is not. With a final sniff, she stepped back, smoothed the front of her outfit, and adjusted her charms. The strong, confident woman was now back in control.

"Let me see what I can do here, and then we'll take him back to the House." I think she was talking more to herself than John as she sorted through her charms.

Selecting one, she unhooked it from her necklace and waved it over me.

Nothing happened.

She frowned, unhooked a second one, and waved them both. I felt a small bit of heat, and the air between us glowed red for a moment.

The heat must have felt a lot more powerful to her, because she yelped and jumped back.

"Well, that didn't go as planned." She hooked both charms back onto her necklace.

"Whatever he's cocooned in is very defensive and certainly not ready to let me help. If I push too hard, it might hurt him even more, and that's not what I want to do. I guess at this point, let's just do a general camouflage and head back to the House. John, see if you can pick him up without hurting him or disturbing his cocoon and load him onto the cart."

John nodded but he had already moved away and started examining one of the bodies. "Before we go, let's have a look around first. We won't come back here again, and this situation is so similar to what happened with Jennifer, but with a very different ending. Maybe there is something here that will help us figure out who was behind all this."

Sandy obviously didn't want to stick around, but she agreed anyway. John poked around at the bodies and then began to walk the graveyard. He was quick and thorough, occasionally stopping to pick at the ground or look at something closer.

Sandy was also trying something, although I couldn't see any obvious results. She'd selected another charm and was pacing the perimeter of the graveyard.

After a couple laps, she stopped.

"What are you finding out, John? I don't want to stay in this realm any longer than we have to. It's not safe for us."

"Well, it looks like all four of the stiffs are mundanes. I can't find any supernatural involvement at all. There are no marks for a containment circle, no magical constructs, nothing like there was with Jennifer. The only thing I came across was this small charm."

He handed it over to Sandy.

"I'm not an expert on those things, but it seems a bit mangled and out of juice."

Sandy held it in her hand and concentrated for a moment.

"Yes, it's completely drained. And not just drained like it's too low to function—I'm talking drained like the original magical construct is gone. Without that, this isn't a charm anymore. It's just a piece of metal."

"Can you tell what it did?" John asked.

"Not reliably. If I had to guess, it was primarily a tracking charm, but it seems like it had a couple other layers as well. I just can't tell anymore."

"This also matches what I'm sensing with the rest of the graveyard. With the exception of Jason and the small patch of ground around him, this whole place is magically dead. There isn't the smallest bit of power anywhere."

"This is only somewhat similar to Jennifer's scene. It had a containment circle and everything inside of it, including Jennifer, was drained. Someone went to a lot of time and trouble to get her power. This seems raw, unfocused, like wild magic."

John looked around and sighed. "This place is depressing. I'll get Jason and we can discuss this on the way home." He came over and gently scooped me up with his two massive hands. I was afraid my cocoon would somehow react with him like it had with Sandy's charm and they wouldn't be able to move me. That didn't happen, and he easily picked me up and carried me over to the cart.

I was also afraid my bones would rub together, or I'd fall apart, or something like that, but nothing of the sort happened either. The mushrooms were still making me feel wonderful and trippy, and my body seemed to be holding up okay.

When John set me into the cart my enchantment took over. Vines quickly grew out from me and covered the inside of the cart. Yellow blossoms unfurled and their earthy smell mingled with the lavender. I'm sure John hadn't planned on pulling home an injured man covered in potpourri.

The vines anchored me to the cart, though, and I felt safe.

"That was unexpected." Sandy looked at John, who just shrugged. "Do you have any idea what kind of supernatural he is? I'm not even sure if he is a natural or a spell-slinger."

"I don't know. He always seemed like a mundane at the House. I never saw him use any spells or abilities. If the House hadn't put out the welcome sign, I would have thought he was just a normal person. This cocoon thing he's got going on is really powerful and complex. That seems more like a natural ability to me."

"I'm not so sure," Sandy said thoughtfully. "What if this is his Waker Moment? First castings are often instinctive and very powerful. It's true what they say: Power is born from necessity and necessity is born from tragedy. My guess is he's a slinger."

"A Waker Moment would also trigger the best of his inherent abilities if he's a natural," John countered. "I'm just getting a vibe from him that says he's a natural. As a natural myself, I'm claiming him for our side."

"My intuition is saying spell-slinger. As a slinger myself, I'm claiming him for my side." Sandy sounded playful but pretty sure of herself.

"Sooooo, you want to bet on it?" John sounded playful too.

"That works for me. The usual?" Sandy replied with a grin.

"Absolutely! I think I want chicken pot pie for the first day, roast beef and Yorkshire pudding for the second day, and I'll let you have loser's choice for the third one."

"Ha! I won't be spending any time cooking. Instead, I'll be the oh-so-beautiful Countess of Huntingdon and you will be my naughty coachman. For the second night we'll take to the high seas and I'll be the pirate captain and you will be my captive. Prepare to be boarded!"

John blushed and rolled his eyes.

"The third night will be, how did you put it? Loser's choice."

John just shook his head and started pulling the cart. "You can be so lusty sometimes. The guys are supposed to be the horny ones and the girls are supposed to be elegant and refined."

"Oh, John, you are so cute when you get old-fashioned on me." Sandy batted her eyes at him. John tried to look exasperated, but a smile tugged at his lips.

"Besides, not every girl gets to make out with someone called Mr. Big."

John growled at her, which just made Sandy burst out in laughter.

"Since you're the captain and all, I'm sure you'll be remembering to cast a cloaking spell before we hit the rough seas?" John said.

"That's the spirit! One cloaking spell coming up for my first matey."

"It's First Mate, not matey." John sighed as Sandy pulled out a charm and went to work.

A thin sphere of magic lifted around us, and the outside world took on more muted tones. It looked darker, but I could still *see* fairly well.

"Alright then, spell is cast. Now damn the torpedoes and full steam ahead!"

"That's hardly very pirate like," John rumbled. "At least you stayed with a nautical theme. But enough about the sea. Let's talk about flakey crusts, rich golden sauce, and just the right amount of carrots and chicken to make the ultimate pot pie."

He drew in a deep breath. "Ahhhhh. I can just about smell it now."

"Whatever." Sandy smacked him on the arm, which had about as much effect as smacking a tree.

"Have you thought about what you're going to make me for my third meal?"

"I'm thinking a slice of humble pie with some Ain't Never Gonna Happen gravy."

"Now, now, woman, don't be bitter."

"I'm not bitter. I'm just right."

"Oh my." He rolled his eyes to the heavens. "Why do I always get the feisty wenches?"

"Because you're Mr. Big," Sandy replied happily.

And with that we trekked on down the hill.

4

Gotta Pee

The first time I woke up it was dark, and I really had to pee.

The bed was different than I was used to: fluffy, comfortable, and way more pillows than a person should have. My body ached in a deep throbbing way, and I tried my best not to move.

Nature's call cannot be denied, and eventually I stirred and tried to get out of bed. The ache doubled in intensity, and it was all I could do to roll over.

"Oh, hey, now. Let's not rush things," a cheerful voice chirped at me. A little round lady hopped out of her chair and came over to me.

"Bathroom," I croaked and shifted closer to the side of the bed.

"Are you sure you are up for this? Maybe you should just rest for a while longer." She sounded concerned and yet so happy.

It pissed me off. Nobody has a right to sound that happy.

I used the emotional energy to drag my legs over the side of the bed, and she helped me sit up. The room spun, and I felt cold. My bladder was demanding, though, and I tried to stand up. That didn't work so well, and I collapsed back onto the bed. Little Miss Sunshine put my arm over her shoulder and helped lift me to my feet.

It occurred to me that this was a strange bedroom and I had no idea where the bathroom was. Sunshine knew, though, and we slowly made our way there amidst a constant stream of encouragement.

It wasn't until I was peeing (oh what a relief!) that I realized I was naked. The little lady holding me up didn't seem to mind, so I figured I didn't either, and we slowly made our way back to the bed.

I was exhausted. I didn't know such simple things could take so much energy, but it wore me out.

I managed to smile and say something that hopefully sounded like thank you, before falling asleep.

When I woke up the second time it was daylight, and again, I had to pee. This time John was my sitter, and he had no problem hoisting me to my feet and getting me to the bathroom.

I had a few more times like that—where I woke up, did a little business or drank some water, and fell back to sleep. I tired out so quickly that all I wanted to do was rest.

One time, I looked up enough to see this guy in the bathroom mirror. He looked like he had lost a fight with a brick wall. I didn't even realize that it was me until I was hobbling back to bed. I looked that bad.

Every time I woke up, I had a sitter helping me out. Sometimes it was John or Sandy, but mostly it was Little Miss Sunshine. They were like my guardian angels, helping me out when I needed it most. I felt safe knowing they were there. I hadn't been taken care of like this since I was a little kid. I didn't know these people well—I'd only been living at the House for a few months—but I was touched by how much time they were spending with me.

When I collapsed back on the bed and started to drift off to sleep, I felt the warm moss blanket and smelled the sweet lavender scent. The spell was still working, healing me.

Then came the morning when I woke up and everything was clear. The enchantment was complete. My eyes gently opened on their own and I saw sunlight coming in the window. Little dust motes sparkled and drifted in the light. A long-haired white cat lay on the floor sunbathing. I realized I had another cat in bed with me. She was a dark brown short hair with green eyes that blinked at me lazily. She stretched out, gently touching me with one paw, before closing her eyes and getting down to the serious business of napping.

I went back to watching the sunbeam, existing in a quiet peace. The serenity of the moment stretched on. It seemed the perfect counterpoint to the recent chaos.

About the time I realized I didn't have a sitter, John came back into the room. Apparently, he'd left the door open and the cats had slipped inside. He was going to shoo them from the room, but I was happy for them to stay.

Sandy brought in a bowl of tomato soup and it was the most amazing thing I had ever eaten. It was rich and creamy, and the flavors danced on my tongue. I finished my first bowl and had a second one.

I was awake, alive, and it felt so good. I still ached and felt weak, but it was better than before.

After the soup, I slept for a bit, but it wasn't the long hibernation of before. When I woke up, I had some of my clothes laid out for me. Sandy had used her master key to raid my apartment.

John helped me take a shower as I still didn't have any stamina. I'm not into the big furry guys but, OMG, John is a perfect specimen. He's got big strong hands, muscles for days, and a deep voice that made me shiver. I ran out of energy about halfway through, and ended up just holding on to him while he finished soaping me down. I tried not to think about it, but the image of all this man making crazy deep love to me popped into my head, and my other head stood up to attention.

I couldn't believe it. I get beaten almost to death, my balls are crushed, I can barely stand, and yet my Mr. Happy was very ready to be happy.

John saw my boner and chuckled. I told him it wasn't me, it was him. He was too much man for anyone to resist. He laughed and kept washing.

After giving me a whole new fantasy for my dreams, we toweled off and he helped me get dressed.

It felt different wearing clothes again. I was beginning to feel human. Sandy asked if I was ready to start discussing what had happened. I suggested we do that the next morning and, with two cats on either side of me, promptly fell asleep again.

I woke up to the happy sound of purring and a paw in my face. Snowy, the white long-haired cat, was giving me an intense look from about three inches away. That was a little much for me so early in the morning, so I gave her a quick scratch and rolled over. Love doesn't give up that easily, so she followed me to the other side of the bed and began purring and patting my face again. I scratched, rolled over, she followed. At that point, I figured I was awake so why not give her some real love. I started out rubbing her ears and ended up several minutes later with all four feet in the air, belly proudly laid out, and some serious tummy stroking going on.

Snowy was purring so loudly that Sandy poked her head in the room to see what was happening. She gave a big smile, came over and sat beside me on the bed, and we both gave Snowy all kinds of fuss. Two on one was just too much and the happy feline wandered off to get breakfast.

I felt good enough to get up for a bit, so I went into the kitchen and had breakfast. The kitchen was one of those open-style spaces, with a double oven and huge double-wide stainless-steel refrigerator. The counters wrapped all the way around and there was a place I could sit on a bar stool and watch Sandy cook.

I'm used to Sandy the landlord; she is all business. Sandy in the kitchen, though, is pure poetry. She has a natural Zen and rhythm, her long black hair flowing with the movements. I found myself drawn in, staying in the moment with her until the plate of food landed in front of me.

She started me out with blueberry pancakes topped with real whipped cream, fresh blueberries, and locally sourced syrup that had a smoky flavor.

It was yummy. I couldn't remember the last time I'd had homemade pancakes, much less ones this heavenly.

John found a reason to stop by. Said he smelled smoke and wanted to make sure everything was okay. Yeah right; I'm sure it had everything to do with concern for the building and nothing to do with the savory smells making him hungry. He plopped his large frame down on the stool beside me—making me feel tiny—and Sandy expanded the breakfast to include thick-cut bacon and scrambled eggs with feta cheese. She made the bacon crispy; you could snap it in two and nibble on it like a potato chip. So good.

Little Miss Sunshine came around too (something about bacon and eggs being magical ingredients) and sat on the stool on the other side of me. Suddenly I felt big. From a distance, we counter sitters must have looked like a row of those Russian dolls that keep getting smaller.

For a while we just ate breakfast and chatted away. It felt nice to be here, to be included in the easy conversation. Just good times, good laughter, and an odd sense of belonging.

Usually my time was filled with smoky tables of poker players trying to outmaneuver each other, followed by relaxing in an empty apartment or maybe a quickie with someone I thought was cute. Casual times like this didn't happen often for me. This felt like home and it felt good, really good.

5

Orientation

As breakfast was winding down the conversation turned to me and what had happened. I found it hard to start, so Sandy took over the conversation.

"Your recovery has really been remarkable, even with magical means. It looks like your broken bones have knitted back together already, and that normally takes six weeks or more. It can take several months for a full recovery. I have a charm that would cut the healing time in half, but you've managed it in a couple days. How are you feeling?"

"I feel better. A lot better," I replied. "Not that I'm perfect or anything. My whole body feels sore, my bones ache, and I still feel a bit shaky. I'm alert, though, and very happy to be alive. It feels really nice to do something normal like eat breakfast." I smiled at Sandy. "Although I would hardly call this a normal breakfast! This qualified as a feast! I don't think I've had a breakfast like this in forever."

"And what a fine feast it was, too." John pushed back his plate with a regretful sigh. "I only wish I had more room to continue to enjoy it."

He waved a finger at me. "Don't expect this all the time. She's just trying to get you addicted. Once you're hooked on the Sandy Special there ain't no going back. You are her slave forever."

Sandy laughed. "Aww. Thanks, John. You make such a nice slave too. Now move all those muscles and get me some more sweet tea before I beat you and throw you in the dungeon."

John took her glass as he looked at me tragically. "She's been promising me that for years. I get my hopes up, but somehow, it never happens."

"Oh, whatever," Sandy said with a playful smile.

Sunshine gave her glass to John as well and looked over at me. "These two can go on like that for hours. I usually ignore them and let them play."

"Let's get back to you and how you are doing," Sandy said. "When you first came here your jaw was shattered and your arm was broken, along with all of your ribs. You were so bruised you looked like an extra in a zombie movie. I know you are feeling better, but I don't want you to start overdoing it. Give yourself time and you will be fine."

"Having a Waker Moment can be tough, and yours was a real doozy. Just go easy on yourself for a while. You have time to keep healing."

Sandy and John nodded in agreement as I just looked confused. "There is so much I don't know about all this, so I'm going to start asking. What is a Waker Moment?"

Sandy gathered herself. "I guess this is as good a time as any for your orientation. Annabeth, John, I would appreciate it if you would help me out." She turned to Annabeth. "I did Annabeth's orientation on my own, and it was a disaster. A complete disaster."

"Oh now, it wasn't that bad." Sunshine reached over and patted her hand. "It was all just a bit much to take in. In all fairness, I was hurting so much from having to leave my family that I needed someone to be mad at. You let me be pissy with you for a while, and that was what I needed. I've adjusted to this new magical life, accepted my new beginning, so all's well that ends well."

I couldn't imagine Little Miss Sunshine being mad at anybody. I guess everyone has a darker side. I also realized I knew her name now. I'd been calling her Sunshine for a while now and that just seemed like her name. Annabeth. It was nice. It fit her. I'm not that great with names so I repeated it three times in my head and used it in a sentence. I'd learned that little trick from a guy in a poker game. He'd remembered everyone's name right off the bat, and after I'd remarked on it, he let me in on his secret. He had other secrets too, as I remember; I'd lost the game to him.

Sandy turned back to me and continued. "A Waker Moment is the defining event of great need that causes a supernatural's ability to appear. Something happens that causes great mental or physical distress, often to the point of dying, and your power breaks free to save you. Once your power is free it's the start of a whole new life. You aren't a mundane anymore. You're a supernatural."

"Think of it like having sex for the first time. It's messy, awkward, and often embarrassing, but it changes your life and opens up a whole new world. All those urges make sense and you don't feel as weird anymore."

"I've always liked the sex analogy, but it's more like having sex underwater and you can't surface until the deed is done," John interjected. "You figure it out fast or you don't figure it out at all."

"So are all Waker Moments as bad as mine?" I asked.

"Some are," Sunshine said kindly. "Some are even worse. Some sups can't recover like you have and they go through months of rehab and trauma. You still look like you got bitch slapped by a herd of ugly sticks, but you will be back to your normal self soon enough. The important thing is to accept what happened and start looking ahead to what is next."

"So, you guys are supernaturals?" I asked.

Everyone nodded.

"I know you guys, or I thought I did, but obviously I don't know the special side of you. Maybe we could go around and you guys could tell me what I need to know about you—from a magical perspective."

"That's actually a good idea. I'll have to remember that for future orientations. I'll start." Sandy settled back in her chair. "My name is Sandy Felton and I first awoke as a mage about seventy years ago."

My eyebrows shot up.

"What, you thought I was younger?"

"Oh my God, yes!" I said. "I figured you were a bit older than me. Maybe late twenties or early thirties, but I didn't think you were ancient!"

"First, I'm not ancient," Sandy said primly. "Comments like that will NOT get you invited to dinner."

"Oh, sorry. I didn't mean it like that at all. You just look so young!" I stammered. I was going to say she looked so young for someone so old, but I shut my mouth in time.

"Now that is much better. Some mages like to cultivate the wise old crone image, but that is not me. I'm actually quite young when you consider the magical community as a whole. Beings with real power can last for a thousand years or more. You will find that you settle into a certain age and look that feels good to you. You won't have to worry about getting old."

Now that sounded nice. Not having to worry about wrinkles, those weird spots on your skin, and seizing up from arthritis would be wonderful. Surely there has to be catch, though.

"So, if we don't age, then how do we die?"

"There are lots of ways to die other than old age," Sandy said. "You could get hit by a truck or some other accident and die that way. Some sups get risky with their powers and something backfires and kills them. Sometimes we get tired of life and look for a way to end it. Sometimes we are killed in battle."

"Really?" I looked around to see if she was joking.

"The supernatural world is a lot more like the wild west or the mafia," Sandy instructed. "For most of history, it has been about who has the most power. The old saying is still true, 'Might makes right.' Civilization as we know it is a relatively new concept. Laws and fairness often do not have a place in the supernatural world. The supernatural world isn't just humans either. There are lots of creatures from other realms that end up here and we have to either orient them or send them back. Many times, they don't want to be sent back and they fight. Sometimes the fights get big and deadly. You can't take on a pack of wargs without some injuries. Those things are tough, and it always seems like they end up here in Louisville."

"How does the world not know this?" I asked. "How do I not know this? I've had magic all my life and I always thought I was alone. I figured there had to be others, but I've never seen or heard anything that made me think other people had talents too."

"You've already had magic?" Sandy was clearly surprised. "Magic talent doesn't show up until you have your Waker Moment. Near death is what forces us to transition from mundane to supernatural. Before that we are just regular people. No talents, no magic. I've never heard of anyone having powers before Waking."

Sandy seemed distressed about this for some reason.

"That would explain why the House let him stay here before Waking," John said. He turned to me. "Have you noticed anything physically about yourself that you thought made you different? I am part mountain troll. I'm what is known as a natural. That means I don't have freeform magic like Sandy and Annabeth. Instead, I have specific attributes and abilities that belong to a mountain troll. I've had the abilities all my life, and instead of learning about magical runes, I've worked on learning how to best use my natural abilities. There are lots of naturals in this world and the realms, and we are still learning about new types."

John's question made me want to go into the bathroom and check myself to see if I suddenly had an extra appendage or wings growing out of my back. If John wanted to come and examine me all over, that would be fine too. I felt a bit flushed just thinking about it.

I pulled back from that line of thought. "I don't have anything physically different about me that I know of. Mom never said anything about that when I was a kid. I've seen other naked guys and I seem pretty normal compared to them. I met one guy that had an extra toe and another guy was so double jointed he could bend his arms backward. You've seen me in the shower, John, do I look normal to you?"

John laughed. "I must admit I was looking! Everything about you seems human and normal. Well, except for your package. Mother Nature was feeling kind and generous the day she handed that out."

I could feel myself flushing. I'm sure I was bright red.

"Oh, stop!" Annabeth looked a little embarrassed, but she was laughing too.

"Come on now. We've all talked about it. There's an elephant man in the room!" John said.

"A fireman with his very own hose," Sandy pitched in.

"The mighty python of the jungle," John said.

"Thor has a mighty hammer!" Sandy said.

"If you're bringing that sausage, I'll need to bring more biscuits!" Back to John again. The two of them were having way too much fun.

"Oh, guys. Stop. You're embarrassing him." Annabeth was really trying hard for the scolding look, but her grin was breaking out.

I was feeling really self-conscious. I'm sure I was blushing all over. They were just having fun, though, and I didn't want to bring the mood down.

"That's okay," Sandy said. "It's better to be blessed in that area than the alternative."

"True that." John toasted me in the air with his sweet tea.

"So, tell me more about your magic," Annabeth urged. "I'm learning so much from Sandy and the concept of charms and how to make them just fascinates me."

"Oh no," John groaned. "If these two get to talking about magic it can take all day."

"Oh hush," Sandy scolded him. "If you get bored then go fix something. You are the handyman after all."

She turned to me. "Okay, tell us about it. How does magic work for you? Just tell us at this point; don't show us. You haven't worked magic since your Moment and it may have changed for you so let's be careful."

"Well, I just decide what I want to do. Then I make a little cartoon creature that can do the job and give it interesting tools or machines to get it done. Next, I add some power and send it off to work. It seems like the clearer I make the image, the better it works, so I try to make it really colorful and interesting. My creations are really tiny, though, and they don't have much power. I have to make several of them just to move a penny, so I've gotten creative on how to do as much as I can with just a little bit of force."

"So, you can just make up a spell on the fly?" Sandy and Annabeth shared a look. "You don't have to say anything or use a charm or focus?"

"Until I met you, I didn't know anything about charms. I just make up what I need when I need it. Of course, I do have some little guys I like a lot. I give them different tools depending on what I need them to do. It's easier than trying to create a whole new character from scratch. One of my favorites, Bob, looks a bit like Mario, from the game, and he gets a jetpack, or super glue, or light saber, or whatever I need for him to have. It's actually pretty cool."

"Wow. That is pretty cool!" Sandy was clearly fascinated. "My magic requires a structure to work. It has to be crafted ahead of time and each charm only does one thing."

She didn't have her big necklace of charms on today. Instead she had a bracelet strung with tiny pewter figures.

"I take something that is solid and normal, like a piece of metal or a gem, and create a magical rune inside it. Different runes do different things and you can layer them for different effects. It can get really complex. If I do something wrong the results can be unexpected, or it just blows up.

"Learning runes, triggers, and constraints and how to layer them is a skill that takes many lifetimes to master. Once I have a charm with a good matrix, I still need to fill it with power and that takes a circle. The circle takes the static magic in the world, gets it spinning, and funnels it into the charm for use. I can then use the charm until it runs out of power."

"We are hoping you will be part of our circle," Annabeth said. "It takes at least four people to anchor a circle, although more is better. Right now, we're down to three of us, and not being able to charge anything has left us pretty tight in the magic department."

She looked over at Sandy, "We would have had access to lots of mages if someone was a bit more diplomatic and kept their mouth shut."

"Being diplomatic never was my strong suit." Sandy grimaced. "Who would have thought it would be so hard? I only called Isobel a bitch and set her hair on fire. That's at least more diplomatic than saying she's an old drooling ass-wipe with delusions of power and a fetish for peeing in public. I should have made her boobs droop and her nose hair grow like barbed wire." Her eyes flashed as she relived the moment. "How she ever got to be Coven Master I will never know. If I wasn't already running this House, I'd challenge her for leadership, and believe me, I would win!"

Sandy looked grim and powerful, and I resolved never to piss her off if I could help it.

Annabeth nodded. "That woman was a hussy. I don't say that much as I was raised right. But, bless her heart, she was a brassy bitch. So, needless to say, old burnt-and-smoky banned us from the local charging circles and forbade any mages to work with us on pain of banishment. We haven't had a circle since Jennifer passed on."

I was afraid to ask what had happened with the coven and get the full story. Sandy was getting so worked up, I starting to wonder if the breakfast silverware was going to start zooming around the room at lethal speed.

I was also afraid to ask about Jennifer. That was obviously an emotional topic.

It was wonderful to talk about magic, though. I hadn't told anyone about it before and it was so good to hear that I wasn't the only person with power. The idea of charms fascinated me and I wanted to learn more.

6

First Magic

"Can you show me how a charm works? Maybe do some magic?" I figured that was a safe topic to segue to.

"Oh, of course!" Sandy pushed her dark thoughts aside. "Let me see . . ." She began sorting through her charm bracelet. "Most of these give me information or protect me, but they don't do anything visible I can show you. This one will raise your core temperature until you burst into flame, but I don't think that is the kind of demonstration you're looking for."

I looked at Annabeth to see if she was joking. Annabeth just patted my hand and gave me a big smile. That didn't really answer my question.

"Ah, this will work," Sandy said. "It's a charm that is fairly simple. It has a rune to add kinetic energy layered with a directional constraint that makes me the center. Put them together with a bit of power and you have this."

She stretched out her hand and the saltshaker skated across the counter and into her palm.

"With most charms it's easy to add an inverse switch. If I trigger the same charm, but as its opposite, I get this."

The saltshaker gently slid along the kitchen counter for a few feet and stopped right in front of Annabeth.

"Look at that control." Annabeth smiled at Sandy. "One day I'll be able to move it like that." She gave me a wry look. "When I try it, either the shaker doesn't move at all or it shoots across the room like a bullet and makes a hole in the wall. Want to see?"

"Oh, no." Sandy quickly took the saltshaker away from Annabeth. "I don't need any more salt in my walls. It has plenty already."

"Can you try that again?" I asked Sandy. "Sometimes I can see inside things and I'm curious to see what your charms look like when you're doing magic."

"So, you have the sight?" Sandy said. "Some magic users are extra sensitive to magic in certain ways. Magic has different sounds for them; some smell it or feel it. I can see it as colors. It's a bit hazy but I can tell if something is magical or not and generally what type of magic it has. Annabeth can hear magic."

"For me it usually has a certain tone or note," Annabeth said. "If it's a complex piece of magic it can have a whole tune. Sandy has this old artifact in her workshop that sounds like an entire orchestra. Mostly I just listen to hear if a new charm is good or not. If it sounds tortured, it's probably just going to blow up."

"That is useful," Sandy said. "I can't see if a charm is good until I start to fill it with power. At that point it's too late."

"I'm not sure if I can see magic," I said. "That's why I wanted to see you use the charm again. When I turn on my sight, I can see just about everything, although it can take a while to come into focus. I can see all around me, and if I really focus hard, behind doors and around corners."

"That sounds useful," Annabeth said. "You are just full of surprises." She held her hand behind my head. "How many fingers am I holding up?"

It was pure reflex, I *looked*.

"Two fingers," I said, and then gasped.

The room was so clear. I could see everything in the kitchen down to the finest detail. I could *see* all the grooves in the cutting board in its rack in the far wall. I could not only *see* them; I could *feel* them.

I could see every line and swirl in the hardwood floor and the small crumbs on the plates in the sink. Extending my awareness even further, I looked inside a closed drawer. It held four hand towels, an oven mitt, forty-three bread ties, and three clips to put on a bag of potato chips to keep them fresh.

I'd used my sight all my life, but this was amazing! It was like I had viewed the world through an old black-and-white 13-inch TV, and then suddenly it changed to a huge high definition widescreen. I just couldn't believe how detailed and crisp everything was.

A memory surfaced: This is what it was like in the hotel room after I started drawing in my power.

I shuddered and felt the cold inky blackness start to swirl. With a mental shake, I let the memory go and pushed the darkness away.

Annabeth was still giving me fingers behind my head, so I quickly caught up.

"Three fingers."

"Your thumb."

"A fist."

"Now you're just waving your fingers around."

Sunshine let her hand drop. "That is so cool! What do you think, Sandy? Have you heard of anything like this?"

"Not really. Maybe it is some type of natural ability?" She looked at John, who just shrugged.

"If you could really see inside a charm, that would be handy. So much of what we do when making a charm is laying down mental patterns. But I can't actually see the final result and that makes it so difficult. It's like trying to make your way through a room in total darkness. You might have a good idea of how the room is laid out, but you are still going to run into the furniture."

Sandy looked so excited I thought she would just jump into teaching me right there. I must have looked a little overwhelmed because she reined it in and asked, "So now that you have opened your sight, how are you feeling?"

All the detail was a bit much. I wasn't used to everything being so sharp; it was giving me a headache. I was also worried about the darkness I'd sensed. That seemed real somehow. I wanted to keep going, though.

"I'm fine. It's a lot to take in right now, but I want to see what I can sense when you use your charm. Can you do that again, but slowly?"

Sandy held the charm in her hand for a moment. To my *sight* it had a bright core of yellow light. From that nugget of energy, there were lots of small lines that led off and formed various shapes. One led to a wiggly shape in the center and then to a circle surrounding it. Next there were a series of shapes around that were encased in a larger circle. One of the shapes around the circle looked like a strange arrow. As Sandy activated the charm, I saw the nugget of magic pulse and the lines fill up with energy. The center wiggly shape changed color first to a bright orange. That spilled over the first circle, lit up some of the shapes around it including the arrow, and then exited the second circle as a tight beam. The beam hit the saltshaker, encased it, and slid it along the counter to stop in front of Annabeth.

"Wow! I saw it all. That is just cool! You are going to have to show me how to do that."

"Certainly," Sandy said. "Learning magic can be so much fun. Even though life changes a lot as a supernatural, being able to do magic makes up for some of that. I don't think I could go back to being mundane again. Now, since everyone perceives magic differently, let me know exactly what you saw."

"I saw a hard core of magic, like a battery, then there were all the lines with circles and shapes, and they intersected with each other. I'm assuming that was the rune you were talking about. The middle part changed to orange, got through the first circle, and then hit the arrow. That seemed to focus the magic and it then shot out to hit the saltshaker."

"Wow!" Annabeth said. "That's it. That is how charms work. You have the power source, the rune, and the constraint. Being able to see a charm in action is going to really help you learn to make them. You are going to do so well at this!"

She leaned over and gave me a big hug.

It made me happy.

I looked around at Sandy and John. They were smiling at me and I felt so included. I'd kept my magic a secret for so long. It was freeing to be open like this—to find others like myself that practiced magic and loved doing it. This must have been what the ugly duckling felt like when he discovered he was a swan.

I had so much to learn and now I had a teacher—three teachers actually. Sandy and Annabeth could teach me about magic and John could teach me about the rest of the supernatural world.

"If you feel up to it, can you show us a bit of your magic?" Sandy asked.

"Oh, I don't know," Annabeth said. "He's just started to get better. Should we rush things? It may not be safe."

I was a bit apprehensive myself. What if my magic didn't work anymore? What if it did work but I couldn't control it?

"I think I want to try it," I said. "I'm nervous. I haven't done any magic since that night. Sandy, you said my magic may have changed, and my sight is certainly different than it was before. I feel like this is a safe place, though, and I want to try something small. I used to levitate a penny all the time. I started doing it because it was neat and a fun way to practice. Then it got to be a habit, like tapping my feet or chewing on my nails. If I got caught doing it, I'd just tell people I was working on a sleight of hand magic trick. Nobody ever thought it was real magic."

"That sounds like the perfect thing to start with," Sandy said. "Plus, a penny is small. If it gets out of control it won't make a big hole in the wall." She gave Annabeth a look. "Until I can charge up my charms again, I don't want to be spending a lot of power fixing up my living room."

"Hey, I haven't trashed your place that badly," Annabeth said. "I'll admit the levitating incident was pretty bad, but I've been much more careful since then."

"You mean your 'Hulk Smash' moment?" John said. He started laughing. "You should have seen it. Annabeth freaked out and waved her charm around like it bit her. Meanwhile all of Sandy's furniture followed the charm, smashing into the walls, the ceiling, just about everything."

He flexed like he was the Hulk. "Me Annabeth. Me smash things."

I looked over at Annabeth, as short and sweet as she was, and started laughing too.

"What can I say?" Annabeth said. She was trying to be indignant but then she gave up and flexed like the Hulk.

"Me Annabeth. Me smash things."

Seeing her do it was even funnier, and I cracked up. Then both of them started trying to out-Hulk each other, and the whole thing took on a life of its own. I couldn't remember the last time I laughed so much.

Sandy was having a good time too, although she was quick to point out it was her furniture that had been smashed. There is a saying that the difference between tragedy and a great story is two years. I'm not sure how long ago this had happened, but Sandy was still in touch with the tragedy of it all.

After the laughter died down, we all refreshed our sweet tea and Sandy walked over to a design painted on the wall. It was a series of interlocking lines and she started tracing it with her finger.

"Jason, since this is your first time doing magic after your transformation, let's take a few extra precautions," Sandy suggested. "After the whole 'Hulk Smash' incident, I asked the House to come up with better safety measures, and it gave me this."

With a flourish, she finished tracing the lines and they began to glow a deep red.

Then the furniture started moving. All of it. The sofa, end tables, rug, lamps, everything started sliding across the floor and lining up against the far wall. As the rug slid away, a circle was revealed, etched into the floor. It looked very magical, with a large outer circle, a smaller inner one, and lots of mystical looking symbols and lines in between.

It was pretty cool.

Sandy walked over and touched the outer circle. Light raced out from her finger and lit up the whole thing like a Christmas tree.

Double cool.

I wasn't sure what it could do yet, but I knew I wanted one.

Sandy took my hand, her grasp firm and warm, and led me over to the circle. The light had risen and now shimmered in the air. I reached out my hand to touch it; the light was firm, like a wall. Sandy gestured and the resistance vanished. Together we walked to the center of the circle.

"This is a training circle," Sandy said. "You should be safe here to test your magic. There are protections for you and us woven into the spells that shape it. If your magic gets out of hand, just try and let it go, and the circle will do the rest. It naturally dampens the power levels and keeps you from getting harmed.

"I'm going to leave you here and close the circle behind me. Remember to go slowly and test your magic lightly. You'll have lots of time to grow and learn. Let's focus on staying safe and having a good test."

She gave me a penny and then left. I could see the light in the air again and that made me feel better.

My magic had been small. It could only affect small objects and sometimes it took a while to work. I put the penny in my palm and held out my right hand. I'd done this so many times before, it was almost habit.

Every night I would test myself to see if I could make the penny go higher. Most nights I could make it rise a couple of inches or so. Sometimes I could really feel the flow and do better, but not by much.

The small weight of the penny felt familiar and calmed my nerves a bit. I usually imagine a fountain of water flowing up out of my hand and the penny balancing on the crest of the fountain. With a gentle push, I let my magic go. It surged out of my hand and the penny shot a foot into the air.

I was so surprised I let the magic go and the penny dropped. I caught it, and with a flick of my magic sent it back up again.

The power was wonderful! It flowed so smoothly and easily compared to before. The penny danced in the air and I felt a big grin coming on.

John didn't look impressed—I'm sure he'd seen many more wonderful things—but Sandy and Annabeth looked awestruck.

"Such control!" Annabeth breathed.

"And without using a focus. That's amazing. Just amazing," Sandy agreed.

For a while I just played with the penny, switching it from hand to hand, loving the extra power I had.

The magic flowed so easily. I played with the intensity, letting the penny drop way down and then tossing it up in the air again before catching it.

This was how magic was meant to be. All those years with just a trickle of power, I'd known something was off. Something wasn't right. There was more to my power. Now the block was gone, and I was free for the first time.

This was like a kid who had been in his room all day and was finally let outside to run and play. I wanted to jump up and down with happiness. I felt almost dizzy with excitement.

Actually, I *was* feeling a bit dizzy. I figured I'd better back off the stunts for a bit until I'd recovered more.

I let the penny settle onto my hand again.

"I can tell that felt good," Sandy said. "I take it that was a successful test for you? It looked great from here."

"Oh yes," I said. "I never had enough power to make it dance like that before. I could make it float and spin but never jump in the air like this time. The power is so strong."

"You'll discover the power only gets stronger from here," Sandy said. "With time and practice you'll learn to do some amazing things."

My power already felt wonderful. I couldn't imagine it getting even stronger. Well, actually I could. I wanted to start doing fun things with it right now!

"Let's talk about your process for a moment," Sandy said. "Walk us through what you do to levitate the penny."

"I put the penny in my hand and then I feel the magic," I said. "It feels like water inside a hose. It's like the water is turned on at the spigot but the nozzle has yet to let the water flow. There is a pressure there. Then I imagine a fountain of water, like what you would see at a water park, coming out of my hand and I let the magic loose. It flows out of my hand and raises the penny. It takes a lot of control to keep it balanced. When I first did this the coin would slide to the side and fall out of the flow. I learned to shape the flow so it would cushion it and generally keep it in the center."

"That sounds a bit like how a charm works," Sandy said. "There is a power source, the caster releases the pressure with a trigger, and the charm shapes the magic to do various things. In this case, however, you are the power source and shaping the magic on the fly. That is pretty incredible. I've heard of that being done before but it's usually by a natural and their powers are mostly instinctive and limited to a specific set of skills. I can't wait to teach you and see how much you can grow. If you can shape magic yourself, then you'll have a big advantage when you start working with the structure of charms. It's like you've already learned to compose songs with a little whistle. Imagine what you can do with a grand piano."

7

Losing Soul

I was feeling better, so I started making the penny dance again.

"There is one big difference between what you are doing and using a charm. You are using your own personal energy as the power source. What visualization are you using to reabsorb the power?"

"Ummm, I'm not sure what you mean," I said. "I just let the energy flow and it floats the penny. The flow seems to disappear on its own."

"Oh my goodness," Sandy gasped. Her eyes got big and she started waving her hands at me. "Stop! Stop what you are doing right now." She looked like she was ready to jump through the circle and smack the coin right out of the air.

I cut off the magic and caught the penny.

"What's wrong?" I asked.

"When you made your little people, the ones you were telling us about earlier, did you keep control of them? Did you bring them back to you?"

"No," I said. "I just gave them directions and sent them on their way. After they were done, they would give a wink or salute or something and disappear."

What had I done wrong? Whatever it was must be pretty bad.

"Oh my," Sandy said. She was pacing in agitation. "Oh my. This is dreadful. All those years. Oh my."

Now I was getting worked up too. If the circle was larger, I'd have been pacing also.

"You are doing this with your own personal energy," Sandy said. "It's magic that is keyed to you. It's your magic in a way that no charm will ever be. It's as personal to you as the blood in your veins. In a way it is your soul, your life force. And you're just letting it go into the air.

"Magic is everywhere and in everything, but it is at a low concentration. What we do is condense magic, gather it, store it and use it. Think of it like water. The air has humidity so there are little water molecules all around us. It's not concentrated enough to drink, though. If we had the right equipment, we could take the moisture out of the air and turn it into a glass of water. That is what we do with a magic circle. We take the magic around us and concentrate it into a charm. Sticking with the water analogy, you are using the water in your body to make the little guys and make the penny float. You need water to live, though, so by doing so you are dehydrating yourself. If you lose enough water, you will die. Now that your powers have awakened, you have the potential to use a lot more of your personal energy than before. That also means you can drain yourself a lot faster. I noticed you stopped earlier and looked a bit pale. Did you feel anything?"

"Yes, I was feeling dizzy," I said, "so I stopped."

This sucked. What had I done? I punched the wall of the training circle in frustration.

What she said made sense. I had thought of my practice as training. I usually felt drained at the end but it's normal to feel tired after completing a workout.

I never thought I was losing my essence, my soul! The one thing I thought I was doing right had actually caused me to stay weak all these years.

The room started to tilt, and I leaned up against the circle. I felt kind of sick and weak, like when I'd gone too long without eating.

It took too much energy to stand so I just slid down the wall to the floor. I'd never taken drugs before, but this must be what it was like to crash. I must have lost a lot more of myself than I thought.

I was angry and sad. Angry that the practice I thought was right had been so wrong for me. Somehow, I always messed things up.

I'd messed up my family. My mom was dead because of me. Dad had kicked me out of the house. I hadn't lived on the streets; I was cute enough and there always seemed to be another guy willing to take me home. I got food and a place to sleep in exchange for some nookie. Eventually, they would tire of me freeloading and I'd move on to the next guy. Poker was one thing I was good at, and I'd even messed that up too.

I wasn't good enough to go pro and yet I was getting busted in the underground circuit. I'd been through three cities already and Louisville was supposed to be my fresh start. This time I was going big and going pro. Instead I got beaten to death—well not to death, but pretty close—and now the one thing that had always been mine, my magic, was messed up too.

Life sucked.

Maybe it would have been better if I had just died. Then I wouldn't mess anything up anymore.

While I was holding my pity party of one, the analytical side of me woke up and realized this wasn't normal.

A big part of poker is sticking with the odds regardless of how you are feeling in the moment. It feels so good to go all in and take out another player, but if you do that when you feel like it instead of when the odds make sense, then you'll end up a washed-out, broken player. One of the reasons I'm good at poker is because the dry analytical side of me speaks up and keeps me from doing anything stupid.

"You're being an ass," my analytical side said in a snooty British accent. *"You've hosted pity parties before, but this time you've gone all weepy faster than a teen on prom night. Something is wrong. Very wrong. Now snap out of it."*

I made an effort to focus, to let the emotions go like butterflies in the wind. It wasn't easy, but I sucked it up and looked around.

When I did, I realized Annabeth was banging on the circle. Every time her fists hit the wall it threw out a spider web of light across its surface. It was pretty, and for a moment I was lost to the sparkles.

Then my thinking side smacked me across the face. *"Wake up,"* he said. Just to make sure I got the point he smacked me again.

I snapped into focus and waved at Miss Sunshine. My hand felt so heavy. It was hard to move.

Annabeth stopped pounding on the wall and all the pretty lights stopped. I felt sad about that.

"Use your sight." I realized she was yelling at me. The circle kept magic and physical stuff separated but sound came through just fine. I wondered how long she had been yelling. I must have really been out of it.

She was yelling again. "Use your sight and tell us what you see."

I wasn't sure where she was going with this, but I opened my magical peepers.

There was magic everywhere. My magic. It was a dense fog surrounding me and filling up the space in the circle. It was so thick I could barely see. The magic was an emerald green with sapphire blue running through it. The colors were richly saturated, and they looked so beautiful.

I waved my hand through the fog and the colors swirled and danced. Once again I was lost, but Annabeth was still yelling at me.

"I see dead people," I said, and she looked at me in shock. "Nah. Just kidding. I've always wanted to say that."

"This is not the time for jokes," she scowled at me. "This is serious. Now tell me what you see."

Sigh. Apparently this wasn't the right audience for my humor. Killjoy.

It occurred to me that I was feeling like I was drunk. More than just drunk. I was hammered. No wonder I wanted to be funny. I'm usually a happy drunk. Unless I'm crying, then not so happy.

Focus! Smack. Smack.

"The magic is thick in here, like a fog. I can tell it's my magic. It feels comforting and cozy for some reason."

"Okay. You are doing good," Annabeth said. "Just stay awake and hold it together." She gave me one of her sunshine smiles. She has such a happy smile with dimples and pretty eyes. She made me feel like everything was going to be all right.

She walked around behind me, and she and Sandy started talking. I wanted to drift for a while, but they started talking really loudly.

Sandy was feeling this was all her fault and she didn't know what to do. She was feeling like she failed me and now it was going to be months until I recovered, if I ever did.

"Now listen here," Annabeth growled. "You are the most creative mage I know. You break the rules, you question why things are done the way they are. You explore. You discover. Basically, you rock. You may not have foreseen this happening. We don't know anyone like Jason, so no one could have known this was coming. But you were smart enough to ask questions and figure out what was wrong."

"Most mages wouldn't have had a clue what was up. But you had an idea of how he might work. And you're going to have another idea of how to fix this. You are beyond good. You're great. And you're going to prove it right now."

Go Annabeth! I felt motivated from her pep talk, and it wasn't even directed at me.

"So, let's review what we know," Annabeth said. "Jason has leaked a crap ton of his magic into the circle and left himself drained. The circle is keeping it contained or else it would have already dissipated. We can't take down the circle and get in there to help him or the magic is gone. He is going to have to fix this from the inside without our direct help. Fortunately, he is conscious. Unfortunately, he's loopy as an Irishman at a pub crawl."

I lost the conversation and just drifted again.

I felt so heavy. Gravity seemed to have doubled, and it took so much effort to move. Even breathing seemed labored and hard.

Annabeth was banging on the circle wall again. "Jason. Jason, honey, just focus. Stay with me for a moment. We have an idea."

I blinked to let her know I was listening.

"You said you can make little people who can do things for you. Try making a little person who can collect the magic in the air and bring it back to you. Can you do that for me?"

That was actually a pretty good idea. That's something I should have thought about trying. I must be really out of it.

I smiled and nodded to let her know I heard. I got an anxious smile and a thumbs up in return.

Now I just needed the right little person to do my bidding, someone to clean up this mess. The image of a little granny popped into my head. She had round glasses, a roly-poly shape, and a frilly apron. Her gray hair was pulled back into a bun and her weapon of choice was an old-fashioned vacuum cleaner. She was a happy little granny with a can-do attitude. Just what I needed. I formed her in the air in front of me and was about to fill her with magic when I realized I didn't have any way to give her directions. So, I added a walkie talkie to her outfit as well as a duplicator ring.

With a gentle push I filled her with magic. It was so easy. I'd made her much bigger than my usual creations; she was almost an inch tall. Even as wasted as I was, she still went from image to full creation in a few moments. The old me would have taken an hour to fill someone her size.

<beep> "Ok, see if you can gather up this magic in the air and bring it to me. Over." <beep>

<beep> "Of course, dear. I'll be back in a jiffy. Over." <beep>

She gave a twirl and then kicked on her vacuum cleaner. Immediately it began filling up with magic. I could see light trails as it picked up the emerald and sapphire swirls.

"It's working!" I exclaimed to Annabeth. After a few minutes the bag on the vacuum cleaner started glowing.

"The magic has been collected," I said. "How do I absorb it? I've never done that before."

"We haven't done it before either," Annabeth said. "Just try pulling it back in. Maybe have your little character stand on your hand as you pull in the magic. It would be the reverse of what you do to float a penny."

That was a good idea too. Team Annabeth and Sandy were on a roll.

I directed my helpful granny to land on my hand and tried to pull in the magic. Nothing happened. I could see the power in the bag, but I couldn't feel it.

I had her dump the contents of the vacuum cleaner on my hand. Then I could feel the magic, but I couldn't absorb it. It just swirled away and joined the fog.

Granny vacuumed another full bag again but this time I cupped my hands around her as she dumped the bag.

The magic felt dense, thick, but again I couldn't absorb it.

For the next attempt we emptied the bag into my mouth and I swallowed it. I thought it might be working but after a couple swallows, I let out a huge burp and it all came back up again. It was kind of nasty tasting too. Burping magic gas is not a fun experience.

This was frustrating.

I kept Annabeth posted about what was going on and I could tell she was getting discouraged too. She left her spot on the floor in front of me and had a conversation with Sandy.

I kept on trying different ways to absorb the power, but nothing worked. I could feel the concentration of magic, but I couldn't connect to it.

Annabeth was back. "We have an idea but it's risky. We think the solution to this problem is for you to make your first charm. When you create one it becomes an extension of your magic. Charms, by their nature, are designed to absorb and release magic. We're hoping that it can collect the magic from your little granny and then you can pull the magic from the charm. We are in untested territory here. We use neutral magic to power our charms and we don't pull that back in. Sandy has read something that makes her think this was how they did it back in the old days, before they had charging circles. If it worked back then, it should still work for you now."

I didn't have a lot of experience with charms—only what I had seen this morning—but the idea sounded good. The hard core of magic I'd sensed in Sandy's talisman was very similar to the way the magic looked coming out of the vacuum cleaner. Maybe this would work.

"So, what's the risk?" I said.

"Well, there are two risks really," Annabeth said. "The first is you need to make a charm that is a pure power source, like a battery. In theory it should be much simpler than making a full charm, but neither of us has tried it before.

"The second, and much greater risk, is that it takes power to make a charm. You are already running low on magic, so if you attempt this and fail you are going to be in a much worse situation than you are now."

"So, what happens if I don't do this?" I asked.

"Sandy will take down the circle and the power in the air will flow away. You're low on magic and your body still needs a lot of healing," Annabeth replied. "Instead of being able to heal and regain your power like normal, it may take a long time for you to recover."

"How long?" I asked.

"Well, we aren't sure." She looked away and bit her lip. "You haven't moved much at all and based on the way you're acting we think you are running really low. Our best guess is a couple years."

Years? Did she say years!?

"I'm guessing if I try this charm thing and it doesn't work, it will take even longer than that," I said.

Annabeth just nodded.

So, in poker terms, I could either fold my hand and cut my losses or go all in. The gambler in me loved to go all in. There's a thrill in pushing all your chips to the center and daring your opponent to match. It takes a good hand to do that, though, and there has to be a good chance of success in case your opponent goes for a showdown. I usually review the odds, read my opponent, and then decide.

In this case I was betting against myself. Did I have what it took to make a charm for the first time? If I did, would it work? If I didn't do it, was I okay with the years it would take to recover?

There were too many unknowns.

Annabeth scooted over and Sandy came into view. It occurred to me that these two were having to sit on the floor to be in my field of view. I wasn't even moving my head. That said a lot about my condition. It also wasn't fair to them. I made an effort to focus and include both of them.

"Jason, I know this is scary right now," Sandy said. "We are here for you and will support whatever you decide. Years of recovery sounds like a lot right now, but you are going to live a long time. A few years now compared to your whole life really isn't that much. You can stay in the House and we will protect you until you get your power back. You can choose to stop now and eventually everything will be fine."

"On the other hand, making the type of charm you need should be pretty simple. It just takes power, and that is the gamble. I don't know if you have enough power to make it. If not, then you will have expended more power and will be in worse shape. If you can make the charm, then I feel pretty confident you'll have what you need to start collecting your power again."

So, basically, I would be an invalid and a shut-in unless I got my power back. Sandy was making it all sound nice, but the reality was a long, long recovery time. I hated lying around. I'd go crazy. Not only would it take a lot of recovery time, but it would take a long time before I could defend myself. Sandy said most supernaturals died in battle. That sounded pretty brutal to me. I'd already gotten the crap beat out of me once, and I wasn't anxious to have that happen again. With my powers, with training, I would be able to defend myself. I'd be safe, or at least safer.

On the other hand, if I tried to make the charm and it didn't work, I'd be in even worse shape.

"It sounds like there is risk and reward with either decision," I said. "I'm so new to all this. What would you do?"

"I would try it," Sandy said without hesitation. "Of course, I'm more of the warrior type. I'm okay with taking risks. Losing that much time to recover would drive me crazy. I'd have to risk it. Even if it didn't work, at least I'd know I tried everything." She looked at Annabeth.

"And I wouldn't do it," Annabeth said. "I would take my recovery time and learn all about magic. I'd practice with small amounts of power, and as it grew, so would my skill. When I fully recovered, my skill would match my power and I'd be in good shape. If you keep going now you run the risk of draining yourself completely and taking a long time to recover. That is too much risk for me."

Well that didn't help me much. One aye and one nay. So much for consensus.

Maybe there was one more person to ask, a little person. I looked up at my gray-haired vacuum cleaner wielding granny.

<beep> "I don't know that I have ever asked one of my little people a question before. I guess you would know my magic better than anyone. As you know, I can't seem to recycle my magic and Sandy and Annabeth are thinking a charm would work. What do you think? Will a charm work? Do I have enough juice left to make a charm? Over." <beep>

My little creation just looked confused for a moment and then froze with a blank look. She stayed like that, unmoving, for a long time. I was afraid I'd overstepped her abilities and she might not recover. I had just given up on getting a reply when she relaxed and animated again.

<beep> "I don't have any experience with charms, Sweetie, so I can't help you there. I'm also not connected to your power anymore so I don't know how much is left. There is a branch of the All Rune here, though, so I asked it for help. It doesn't speak in words. It just gives impressions and emotions. I got the feeling that something is coming here. Something dark. Something viscous and rotten. It sounded like broken glass being dragged over pavement. I don't know when it will arrive, but I got the impression it will be soon. Of course, the All Rune is ancient, so its idea of 'soon' may seem like a long time to you. I'm sorry I can't help you more, Sugar. I'm sure it will all work out, though. Just do what you feel is right." <beep>

Well that was certainly interesting. I wasn't looking forward to whatever this thing was heading my way. It sounded like a nasty piece of work.

I focused on the girls again. They were giving me a strange look. They couldn't hear my conversation with the little granny, so it must have looked odd from their perspective.

"At the end of the day this is your decision, Jason," Sandy said. "What do you want to do?"

That was the big question. What did I want to do?

"Let's try making the charm," I said. "I can't stand the thought of taking that long to recover. I've already spent most of my life working with a small amount of magic. I'm ready to learn how to do more."

"You're sure?" Annabeth asked.

"Let's do this," I said. "I even have the base to begin with." I held up the penny.

"That's a good choice," Sandy said. "You're already familiar with manipulating it. What year is the penny?"

"1992," I said. "It's not shiny or anything, but it just feels right."

"Well good," Sandy said. "Having the right feel is important. Although the penny looks like copper, it's mostly zinc. Zinc is a good conductor of magic and stores it well. Both are properties we need right now."

"So, what do I need to do?" I asked.

"The type of charm you're going to make is really simple. It's going to become a small bit of storage for your magic. Sort of like a battery. You don't need to worry about runes or discharge patterns or call triggers or anything like that. It's a power source only, and making a power source is really simple. You just fill it with your magic until it wakes up."

"It wakes up?" I said. "What does that mean?"

"Right now, the penny is just a penny," Sandy explained. "It's got a tiny trace of power in it. Everything does. But it doesn't have anywhere near enough to be infused with magic. I don't know any better way of saying this, but when something is filled with magic it sort of wakes up. Really powerful objects even have their own personality and a limited amount of awareness. You don't need anything approaching that level of power. You just need enough to fill the penny until you feel a connection to it."

"How will I know when it's awake?" I asked.

"You'll feel it," Sandy said. She settled into teacher mode. "It will stop being just an object and start being a part of you. Think of it like wearing a watch. When you first put on a watch it feels heavy and different. You're not used to it. After you've worn the watch for a long time it feels familiar. You're used to the weight and you don't even notice it as you move your arm around. It becomes so familiar that if you leave home without it your arm feels bare. The watch is now a part of you. Making a charm is like that, only more so. You could hide my charm bracelet anywhere in the room and I could tell you exactly where it was and what all the charms do. They are that personal to me."

This whole process sounds a lot like what I did when I created one of my little people. I would visualize what I needed and then fill them with magic. This seems to be the same type of thing except I'd be starting with a real object.

"That sounds fascinating," I said. "So how do I begin?"

"Which hand do you usually use to float the penny?" she asked. I held up my right hand. "Put the penny in that hand and then close your other hand over it." I did that. The penny was now sandwiched between both my palms.

"Can you feel the penny with both hands?" Sandy asked. I nodded. "Okay. Now what I want you to do is let magic out of both palms and force it into the penny. The magic is going to try and roll around the object and escape out the sides, but you aren't going to let it. You don't have any magic to spare so you need to make sure all of it is going in. Start off with just a trickle, until you're sure you are doing it right, then slowly turn up the power. Once the penny is saturated with power, you'll feel it change. When that happens, you can stop, and we'll start practicing moving power from you to the charm and back again."

I was nervous. I was taking the chance and trying something very new for me. Sandy thought it was simple, but this was my first time and the stakes were high.

Annabeth gave me a big smile. "You can do this, Jason. I know you're nervous and that's okay. You'd be crazy not to be nervous. You've used a trickle of magic all your life and that is all you need to succeed. Just go slowly and carefully and you'll find it's easier than you think. You got this!"

That little pep talk was just what I needed. Little Miss Sunshine was sending lots of support and positive thoughts my way. I'm sure if the circle walls were down, I'd have been getting a big hug.

With a gentle trickle of magic, I started.

The power swirled around the coin and then tried to leak out, just like Sandy said it would.

I clasped my hands together firmly, trying not to leave any sort of crack for it to escape.

The pressure gradually built up as the magic had nowhere to go. It still wasn't going into the penny, though, and that was a problem.

I was afraid to really turn up the pressure in case the magic started leaking out. I didn't have any extra to spare.

It occurred to me that maybe I should be working smarter and not harder. I was following Sandy's directions and trying to do this by brute force, but I had a whole level of sight she didn't have access to. Actually, looking at what was happening up close might provide me a whole new course of action.

My sight was already on, I'd been using it earlier to look at all the emerald and sapphire colors swirling in the air, so I honed in on the penny to see what was going on.

I usually *look* at the object as a whole, but this time I needed to see inside the coin. It took me several tries. My mind was still thinking of it as one piece, but when I thought of it as a bunch of molecules, my awareness slipped inside.

I could easily see what Sandy was talking about as far as it being made of two metals. Most of the coin was made of zinc, with a very thin coat of copper over the top of that. What surprised me was the layer of something else on top of the copper. It wasn't a metal or grime or anything like that; it was a layer of color. My magic was green and blue. This layer was a mish mash of colors mixed together with all the beauty gone from it. It was like a box of crayons has melted together and ended up a dirty brown.

The layer was thin but dense, and that was what was keeping my magic from getting in. If I had to guess, the layer was the little bits of power it had picked up from everyone that handled the penny. It had been around since 1992 and who knows how many people had touched it.

What I needed was a way to clean off or get through the dirty layer. My current pressure was pushing on it evenly, and all that was doing was compressing it. The layer was thinner but just as strong.

My analytical side spoke up. *"Well then, old chap, why don't you apply pressure unevenly. That would seem the logical thing to do."*

I'm freakin' brilliant sometimes.

I formed power like a nail, creating the sharpest microscopic point possible, and drove it through the muddy colors.

They parted like hot wax, and my nail of power passed right through the penny and out the layer on the other side.

I'd done it! I now had a column of power lanced through the center of the coin. It only took a moment to expand the column and push the muddy layer off. Without something to anchor it, the mix of colors flared up in my magic and burned away.

The penny was now mine.

The only thing left to do was stuff it full of magic. The penny absorbed power like a sponge, and as it filled up, it began to sparkle. It seemed so shiny and new, like it was being re-minted all over again and given a new life.

The coin also began to give off a tone, like a bell, and vibrate slightly.

The two metals had a different feel too. I could almost taste them. The copper had a bitter undertone, but the zinc had a nice salty touch. Next time I got some fries maybe I'd sprinkle some zinc on them. "*Just kidding,*" I told my analytical side before it started giving me health warnings.

The penny absorbed everything I'd started with and everything I was giving it now. It glowed a bit, but it didn't seem to be full of magic by any means, and it certainly wasn't what I would consider awake.

I cautiously turned up the power, but the coin was thirsty and easily drank in the extra flow.

It was certainly glowing now. The zinc gave off a pretty white-blue color and the copper was, of course, copper colored. I could see the magic packing in there, and it was starting to get dense. It didn't seem as dense as the core of Sandy's charm, so I still had a ways to go yet.

The girls were banging on the circle wall, but I didn't want to lose my focus. I wasn't sure how much power this was going to take, so I put my output on what I thought was a medium flow and just let it go.

Time passed and the magic in the penny got denser and denser. It also began to get harder to maintain the flow.

The penny wasn't just glowing anymore; it was shining. It was a full beacon of light and power. It matched the level of what I remembered from Sandy's charm and then surpassed it.

The penny still wasn't awake.

It became too much effort to flow out magic at the current pace, so I cut back. I felt like I had to be close to waking this thing up. How much more could it take?

Moments turned into minutes. Every minute began to feel like an hour. I was well beyond the easy flow of magic. Now it was torture, wringing myself out to deposit every drop of magic I could find.

It was like I had fully exhaled, and then held my breath. My body was screaming for magic. My temples throbbed and sweat poured out of me. I panted for air and still I hung on.

This was a do-or-die moment. I had to win this. Failure was not an option.

The magic no longer flowed. I could only gather it and push it out in little spurts.

The penny glowed like a small sun, and still it didn't wake up.

I started seeing spots in the air. I wondered if I was going to pass out, and then I realized it was the darkness forming.

Like the specter of death, it formed fast and started to close in. I could feel its icy breath on me, hear its maniacal laughter. It started to pounce on me, and the circle walls flared to life.

Somehow it grabbed the darkness and pulled it outside the circle. The darkness billowed and grew, looking for a way in. It got so thick I couldn't see the room anymore.

The circle's protection had given me a few more moments of reprieve. I had to win this.

I dug deep, deeper than I ever had before, and squeezed out the last possible speck of power. I offered it to the coin.

Please. Please wake up.

But nothing happened.

I just lay there, with the penny shining like the sun in my hands, wondering what went wrong. That was it. I had nothing left to give. I'd failed.

I had thought I was in bad shape before I'd started trying to make this charm, but that was nothing compared to now. My magic would take years to recover now. I felt totally empty.

There wasn't any magic left to keep healing my body. That was going to take a long time to recover too. This was the worst-case scenario.

The penny was glowing many orders of magnitude brighter than Sandy's charm. How could it not be awake? What had I missed?

The girls were still banging on the circle walls, but I couldn't see them. That was probably a good thing as I couldn't bear to see the pity in their eyes.

Instead I looked up and saw my brave little granny.

I didn't have anything left, but maybe she did.

"Help me," I whispered.

"Oh, Love, I can only try." She did a little twirl and started vacuuming. She pulled the magic out of the air until her little vacuum cleaner was glowing like before. This time, however, she kept going.

She kept pulling in more and more magic until the bag looked like it was going to explode. My little creation wrapped her arms around the bag to give it support and kept going. The vacuum cleaner started to emit a high-pitched whine. The bag was glowing so brightly I could see right through her. I could also see she was starting to come apart. I hadn't designed her to handle this level of stress.

My brave little cleaner gave me one last brilliant smile, then she dove out of the air. I cracked my hands to give her room to pass. She made it to the penny before the bag exploded. The penny absorbed most of the blast, but it still tore her up pretty badly. Her construct was badly frayed, and she was starting to fall apart.

Brave until the end, the little granny gave me a final wave, and with the last of her life, she directed all her magic into the coin.

It woke up.

It woke up like a supernova. There was a huge flash of light and a bell-like tone expanded in volume until I could feel my bones vibrating.

The whole penny turned liquid, and the copper and zinc swirled together. It spun into a ball and floated in the air like a small star.

Sandy didn't mention anything about this! Making a charm was a truly impressive event.

The light and sound show continued for a few more moments and then began to settle down. The luminescence changed from star level to a pleasant glow. The tone died down, for which I was very grateful. The little orb stopped spinning and settled into an oblong shape, almost like a little metal egg.

That seemed appropriate. An egg for a new beginning.

I could feel my new creation. It was a part of me in a strange and wondrous way.

It seemed happy. Can an amulet have feelings? I didn't sense anything like that from Sandy's amulet, but then it was her amulet, not mine. Maybe her charms had emotions too.

I was happy too, but I was so drained I couldn't really enjoy the success. I felt cold and hot at the same time. I was shivering with exhaustion. I needed some of my power back, but I didn't know how much I could pull from the amulet.

If I took too much power right after it woke up, I might shut it back down again. That would really suck. I had nothing left for a second attempt.

It felt strong, though. Really strong. It was small but I could feel the power coming from it, like a warm glow.

I opened myself up to it and the warm glow filled me. Power flowed back into my tired body and it felt so good. I'd never really felt my magic before to this degree. I knew what it was like to flow the power and play with it, but I hadn't known before this how it was the foundation for my life.

Magic was warmth, light, life. It was the color and sparkle in a gray world. Without magic, I was a dry, brittle husk. I didn't ever want to get that low on magic again.

The power I'd pulled from the charm didn't seem to hurt it at all, so I pulled a bit more. I'm sure I was still low on magic, but compared to the power level I had been at, I felt like I was swimming in energy.

It felt so good. I laughed out loud and realized I was crying a bit. The girls probably thought I was a mess. I sat up and looked for them.

The darkness was so black I couldn't see anything outside the circle at all.

It was just me, the walls, the fog, and my new amulet.

"Annabeth? Sandy?" I called out.

"We're here!" Sandy said. "Are you okay? What happened?"

"I think I'm okay. It was touch and go for a while there. It took everything I had though." I thought of my little granny. "Actually, it took more than I had."

I'd made hundreds of constructs before. I hadn't missed them when they left, as they just seemed to have fun doing what they were designed for. They always waved and cheered or tooted before vanishing. This time, though, the granny had talked to me, had gone way beyond the call of duty to help me, and in the end had given her life for me.

I was humbled and grateful for what she had done. I'd known her for such a short time, but I would miss her.

"You're sitting up now," Annabeth chimed in. "Are you feeling better? How are you?"

"Yes, I'm better now," I said. "It was really rough there for a while. I wasn't sure I was going to make it. The amulet is awake, though, so it was all worth it."

"I don't know what that amulet is, but it is way more than just awake," Sandy said. "Didn't you hear us banging on the wall?" She sounded kind of peeved.

"Yes, I heard you, but I didn't want to break my concentration. The amulet wasn't awake yet and I needed to keep the flow going. What did you mean the amulet is more than awake? It just now woke up. I can feel it too. It seems happy."

I looked at my little charm fondly. It spun in my hand and let out a happy tone.

"That's just it," Sandy said. "Charms don't have feelings. They have a certain feel and you are connected to them, but they don't have feelings."

"I thought you wanted me to keep going until it was awake?" I said, bewildered.

"Awake, yes. Aware, no," Sandy said. "That charm was awake a long time ago. Back when you were first applying pressure, you stopped for a while. When you started up again the penny was awake and had turned into a charm. Then you kept going, and we were freaking out!"

"Don't ever do that again," Annabeth interjected. "You scared me so badly. I'm too old for surprises like that. Next time I'm pounding on the wall you better stop and pay attention. I may be small, but I can still box your ears, young man!"

Little Miss Sunshine sounded fierce. It was nice to know she cared.

Thinking back on what Sandy said, the penny must have woken up when I cleaned off the layer of dirty colors. That was when I could put power in it for the first time. I could feel the power I was putting in the coin at that point and I did feel connected to it.

I was used to my little constructs, though, and that didn't seem awake to me. It just seemed neutral, fresh, ready to begin. No wonder they were freaking out.

"So, if this little thing is more than a charm, what did I make?" I asked.

"I have no idea," Sandy said. "I've never made anything like that before. It's small but the power is so bright. I don't see as clearly as you do, but even to me it seems like a little piece of a sun. Annabeth, what do you hear?"

"It sounds pure," Annabeth said. "It has a perfect tone, like you struck a master bell in the middle of a concert hall. The notes are round and clear. It's mainly one note but sometimes there are these quick little trills."

At that moment the charm emitted a little melody with a pulse of rainbow light. It was like the little egg knew it was the center of attention and wanted to show off a bit.

"Jason, are you sure you're okay?" Annabeth said. "You're not looking right at us. It's like you can't see me."

"Actually, I can't. There was this darkness, like a black smoke, that showed up the night I was . . . the night that, you know, it happened."

"You mean the night you had your Waker Moment?" Sandy asked.

"Yes. That's a nice way to say it. The night I had my Waker Moment." That sounded much better than the night I got beat to death and somehow saved myself by draining the life out of four people. "Anyway, the darkness came back. It felt real, like I was back in the hotel room again. The circle sucked it all out, though, and now it's outside the wall trying to get in. It's really thick and I can't see anything past the circle, which includes you two."

"Oh my," Sandy said. "That's a new one to me too. I haven't heard of anyone experiencing anything like that. Hang on while I scan for magic."

I heard her charm bracelet jingle and a few moments passed. I spent the time playing with my new charm, or meta charm, or whatever the heck it was. It was so cool. I liked the warmth of the glow and how solid it felt rolling around in my hand.

"I'm not getting any sort of magic reading," Sandy said. "It must seem weird to you not being able to see outside the circle. Regardless, let's handle this one problem at a time. You have made your charm, however unique it is, and the next step is to see if you can pull power back from it. Let's try that now."

I reached out to the metallic egg and pulled a bit more magic. It came to me easily and I immediately felt better. I checked the power of the charm. It was glowing like I hadn't pulled anything at all. The last thing I wanted to do was pull too much and shut it down.

"I'd already pulled some power, and I just pulled a bit more," I said. "That doesn't seem to hurt the charm at all."

"Good," Sandy said. "At least one thing is going right tonight. Now, have your little person collect some of your energy in the air and see if you can absorb it through the charm."

I couldn't use my granny because she was no more. I opened my mouth to tell them, and then stopped. What happened to her seemed personal. I would tell them the whole story later. Right now, I didn't want to talk about it.

I didn't want to make another construct either. It just felt too soon. Maybe there was another way to solve this problem.

I'd been so focused on the charm that I'd stopped paying attention to the magic fog in the air. When I did, I noticed that the fog near my hand was much less dense. Up by the ceiling, the fog was thick and the colors were clear. Near the charm it was almost nonexistent.

I know my brave little collector had been pulling energy out of the air, but this seemed like a bigger change than could be attributed to that. She'd also been vacuuming up in the air, not down by the charm, and yet the fog by the charm was clearest.

I looked around the charm but didn't see anything. It might be easier to examine any effects the charm was having if it wasn't on my hand. With that thought, that little egg just floated up in the air.

I wasn't pushing it with power or making it ride a wave of magic. I just thought about it moving and it did. It was like the charm knew what I wanted and made it happen on its own.

That was seriously awesome.

Now it was up in the air, I looked all around it. I still didn't notice anything, so I looked in closer. I could now see a very slight movement of the fog toward the egg.

The drift was very slow, though. It was like the fog did a lazy turn toward the charm and fell into it. I zoomed in really close, as close as I was when I found the layer of dirty colors. Now I could see the action happening.

The emerald and sapphire colors got almost all the way to the surface of the charm. Then it was like they were caught by the gravity of the orb and pulled in. The egg was absorbing the power, but at a very slow rate. I would be here for a few days waiting for the egg to do its thing.

I relayed what was happening back to the girls.

"That charm is a wonder," Annabeth said. "I wish my charms floated around and had power like that."

"Me too," Sandy said. "I can't wait to study it and see what you did. In the meantime, it looks like the main problem is solved. The charm is pulling your power back in and you can pull from the charm. At the end of the day you will have your power back. We just have to figure out how to speed up the process before you have to pee. I still can't take the circle walls down until you are done."

I wished she hadn't said that. Now I really did have to pee. This was going to be a long day. Still, I was very grateful to have a working solution. Getting my magic back felt awesome.

"Can you make the charm flat? Like a dinner plate?" Annabeth spoke up. "It seemed pretty fluid earlier and it's already changed shape once."

"Oh, that a good idea!" Sandy said. "With more surface area it should absorb your magic faster."

Could I do that? Anything seemed possible at this point.

I pushed out the idea to my little orb and got a flash of light and a happy hum in return. It slowly flattened back to its original penny shape and then seemed to turn liquid. It kept flattening until it was a disk as big as a dinner plate.

I focused my sight back to the surface again. It was still absorbing all the excess energy in the air but at a much faster rate. Now that I knew the process was still working, I started to rotate the disk in the air. The fog swirled around and gradually became more and more faint.

I noticed Annabeth was always deferring to Sandy, but she had some good ideas herself. She just needed the confidence to go along with her thoughts.

I gave the girls an update and then spent the next little while spinning the disk and listening to Sandy and Annabeth chat. As the disk absorbed power, I pulled it back into me again.

It was amazing how I felt with my magic back. My head was clear, and I didn't feel like an emotional basket case anymore. I just felt happy and energized. Losing my magic was no joke. I'd always had a sense of my power, but now I had a whole new awareness of what it did for me. It was like eating watermelon on a hot summer day. When you're thirsty and sweaty it takes a normally bland fruit and makes it taste like nectar from the gods. It is so juicy and refreshing, and you can feel your body begging for more.

My body tingled a bit from all the power. It loved it. Despite how good it felt, I was only sipping the power from the charm. I'd worked so hard to make it alive, I didn't want to reverse the process.

As the magic fog cleared, I became more aware of the darkness. I could feel it pressing up against the bounds of the circle. There was nothing neutral in the blackness. It was alive. It knew me. It wanted to finish the job and consume my soul.

Sandy and Annabeth sounded happy, unconcerned. They couldn't see the darkness like I could.

"So . . . any progress working on this stuff outside the circle?" I asked. "I'm almost done in here and I'm scared of what's coming next."

"I've scanned everything, multiple times," Sandy said. "And I'm not getting a reading at all. I can sense the House, of course, and the training circle, and Annabeth and John. But that's it. Everything is normal."

That wasn't want I wanted to hear. If Sandy couldn't sense the darkness, then she couldn't give me advice on how to fix it.

"For what it's worth, I've scanned too, and I can't sense anything," Annabeth said. "I can hear magic, Jason, and I don't hear any new tones or anything out of the ordinary. I'm sure it is real for you, but we aren't getting anything."

"Maybe your power reacts differently with the power of the training circle. It could be the training circle is cutting off your sight somehow. You've been in sight mode for a long time now. Try turning it off and let us know if it is any different."

"Hang on," I said. "I'm almost done collecting my energy. I'll switch it off then."

The blue and green fog was no longer thick and powerful. Now it was just a few wisps floating around. After it absorbed the last of the energy, the charm gave a little happy note and floated back to my hand. As it moved it changed from a big disk back to its little egg shape again. It sparkled and spun and then dropped into my palm.

Now that that was over, it hit me how tired I was. I was exhausted. This was my first real time out of bed, and instead of taking it easy, I'd almost died doing magic again. I needed to stop doing that.

I wanted to get this whole thing over with and go to bed.

The little charm was still in my hand and I wasn't sure what to do with it. I needed a charm bracelet like Sandy had. I went to put it in my pocket for the time being, but the little object had other ideas. It transformed into a thin band and wrapped itself around my index finger.

I was surprised but happy. I wasn't going to lose a ring or accidentally put it through the wash. If I was a charm, I wouldn't want to sit in a dark pocket either.

Magic collection was done. It was time to stop stalling and deal with the darkness. Before, it had churned like black smoke from an oil fire, and I'd felt an aura of menace. That was also when I'd been out of my mind trying to wake up a charm and losing my magic.

Now the darkness just seemed flat and opaque. It was like someone had coated the walls of the training circle with black paint. It was weird, but it didn't feel menacing or anything. Maybe Annabeth was right, and this was just something with the training circle.

With a deep breath, I turned off my sight, and the room snapped into view.

"Oh wow! I can see you," I said. I didn't realize how much I'd missed them. I'd felt lonely and cut off in the circle.

John was still sitting over by the kitchen counter being quiet as usual. Sandy looked lean and badass even in her kitchen apron. Annabeth flashed me a rosy-cheeked smile and turned up the happy wattage as I looked her in the eyes and she realized I could see her.

Everything was going to be okay. I sagged in relief. Sandy could take down the training circle, I'd give everyone big hugs, and then I was hitting the sack.

"I can see you," I told Sandy. "I can really see you. Oh, this is so nice."

"Good." Sandy looked relieved. I'm sure it was all hard on her too. "Are you ready for me to take down the circle?"

I nodded, and she went to the wall and touched the rune.

The circle collapsed, the walls vanished, and the darkness pounced.

I saw red glowing eyes as the room filled with rolling smoke. It wrapped around me, hoisted me into the air, and I slammed against the ceiling.

I heard Annabeth scream as it reversed course and I slammed against the floor.

John jumped on me to hold me down, and my newly healed bones did some hollering of their own.

The smoky ropes tried to haul me around some more, but with John holding on I wasn't as easy to move.

The ropes morphed into something man-shaped, with two pits of darkness where his eyes should be. His arms ended in sledgehammers and he began beating on John, trying to get him to move.

John turtled over the top of me and held on. I could feel the vibrations of the hammers through his body.

Sandy cast a spell, but it went right through Smoke Man and exploded the furniture behind it.

Annabeth cast something and the room filled with a deep bass tone. The effect was so powerful I could feel it in my teeth.

The smoke lost cohesion and the man thing staggered around the room. Then, the spell ran out and Smoke Man reformed. He rushed Annabeth and knocked her across the room. She hit the wall and stayed down.

He reformed in Sandy's direction and rushed her next. She dove to the side, rolled to her feet, and kept going. Sandy was obviously no stranger to battle. Instead of casting more spells, though, she began banging on the walls and yelling, "Help," at the top of her voice.

Smoke Man chased her, and he was quick. Really quick. It helped that he didn't have to step around anything. His misty form just flowed over any obstacles.

When he caught Sandy, he enveloped her for a moment, and she dropped to the ground.

John surged to his feet with a roar and grabbed the coffee table. I thought he was going to throw it at Smoke Man, which wouldn't have done Smoky any harm. Instead he started waving it like a large fan, trying to create a wind that would blow the smoke away.

Coffee tables are heavy, but John was waving it like it was made of paper. I knew John was strong, but this was insane.

His idea sort of worked. Smoke Man tried to close in on him more than once, but the coffee table kept destroying his cohesion. They ended up in a stalemate. John couldn't harm Smoky, and he couldn't harm John.

The stalemate didn't last for long. Part of the smoke split off and came for me. John was too busy defending himself to help, and the evil was coming fast.

My instinct was to run, and that is exactly what I did. I ran around the room screaming like a girl with her hair on fire.

I dodged furniture, including John's wild coffee table swings, jumped over the kitchen counter, slid along the floor, and did whatever it took to be somewhere the smoke was not.

The problem for me was the same as it had been for Sandy. The smoke flowed over obstacles, cornered like a race car, and just never slowed down. The living room and kitchen were a pretty good size for an apartment, but it wasn't anywhere near big enough for me to get away and hide.

It had already been a long day for me, and I wasn't in top shape anyway. Fear kept me moving, but soon it wasn't enough and the smoke caught me.

It collected around my head like a fishbowl and sucked all the oxygen away from me. Suddenly, I couldn't breathe. I gaped like a fish out of water. No amount of hand waving or rolling would get it away from me long enough to get a breath.

Sandy was awake again, and she was pounding on the floor and screaming, "Help me," along with a few choice profanities.

I had no idea who she was talking to. Did she think a little magic man was going to pop out of the floor or something?

Then I felt him. Thing One. The author of my Death Experience. He was outlined in smoke, sitting cross-legged on the floor by my head. His elbows rested on his knees. His hands were clasped together. He looked at me in a calm detached manner.

I felt fear. Not the normal scaredy-cat fear; I'm talking the freeze-you-in-place, can't-look-away, body-starts-to-shake kind of fear. The kind of fear that leaves you with wet pants and puke on the floor. Thing One was trying to drown me again. This time with smoke.

I heard a crash as a bed landed in the middle of the room. Under normal circumstances I'm sure I would have been surprised, but my ability to process this situation was already overloaded.

A cute guy with tousled sleepy hair sat bolt upright in bed and looked around wildly.

Dark spots filled my vision and the last thing I saw was a smoky Thing One, his eyes flashing red, looking at me. Then the lack of air took its toll on me and I blacked out.

8

Snuggle

Sleepy snuggles are the best. I liked his arm around me. It felt like half of a long hug. His warm chest and body curved around mine. We were spooning and I was the inner spoon.

I put my hand on top of his and pulled him in even closer. I could feel his breath on my neck. I was mostly asleep and didn't want to wake up.

This moment of calm—this moment of peace—was what I needed. I wanted to stay here for a long time.

The next part, when we woke up a bit more, was usually not a lot of fun. Sometimes my hookup would politely try to figure out how to get me out of the house, while I tried to figure out how to get breakfast before I hit the road. The hard light of morning usually put a big ugly stamp on the guy I'd gone home with. Club lighting hid a lot of sins.

My usual rule is that non-club lighting adds ten years and takes two points from a person's hot index. The old saying about going to bed at two with a ten and waking up at ten with a two was often true. I know that sounds a bit harsh, but I'm sure they felt that way about me too.

I'd been in this situation a lot. Dad had kicked me out of the house for being a homo. Well, he'd really kicked me out for burning the house down but being a guy-lover didn't help.

I hadn't been homeless exactly. I'd just been permanently residentially challenged. I had enough good looks to get picked up by someone, so I wasn't living on the streets. Morning time brought out the hustle to get some food and maybe some cash.

It wasn't much of a living, but it got me through until I started learning poker. There were a few guys that actually enjoyed my company enough to let me hang around for a while. I'd been living with Ben for a few weeks when he had a poker night with the guys. I was fascinated. Once I learned the rules, I started to see the patterns in the cards. I won that night and every night afterward. I read Dan Harrington's Texas Hold'em poker formula, all three books, in two days. I was hooked.

I played the legal tournaments and then graduated to the high-stakes backrooms. I won too much too fast and thought it would be best to relocate for a while. Ben was starting to get restless too, so I cooked him dinner, gave him a long sweaty night to remember me by, and left.

After that I'd had just enough money to have my own place without having to trick all the time. It takes money to make money, so I had to be really careful with what I spent and how I played. It wasn't a glamorous life, but it could be once I got good enough to go to Vegas. That's where the real money started. If I could win there, the final destination was Monte Carlo, where the ultra-rich played. I could win a million in a few nights if I was lucky.

For a while I just breathed, enjoying the dream of success and the warm man behind me. I cracked one eye open. The last light of the day filtered through the blinds and lit up my bedroom with a rosy glow. There wasn't much to light up, just the old dresser and the white walls. I didn't have much here. The dresser looked beat up, but it had been cheap and the drawers slid easily. We were lying on a mattress on the floor, no official bed. It was super comfortable and that was all that mattered to me. So what if it was lying on the floor?

Why was the sun setting? I must be really out of sync. I usually wake up in the afternoon. I closed my eye and pushed the thought away.

Why was I in my bedroom? I didn't like bringing anyone back here. This was my space, and simple as it was, I didn't like sharing it. I must have been really drunk, although I didn't remember having anything to drink. Poker and alcohol don't mix. Well, they do, but only if you like to lose. It only takes one sloppy "all in" to end up slinking away with nothing.

I pushed that thought away too. Focus on the snuggle.

I trailed my fingers over his hand and up his arm. He felt strong. I liked that. He must have been more awake than I thought as he took his hand to do some touching of his own. He began rubbing my chest and then trailed his fingers down my side. I loved that. It made me feel long, lean, sexy.

He nuzzled the back of my neck. I couldn't help it. I let out a sigh and arched my back. It felt that good. Things were heating up fast. I could feel myself responding. What was his name again? I couldn't remember.

I rolled over to do some exploring of my own. I kept my eyes closed. I wasn't ready to face reality yet. I would let my hands create the image.

And what an image it was! I was feeling smooth skin, defined muscles, and broad shoulders. I slid my hands down to his ass. What an engine. Wow.

He was back to kissing my neck again. It sent shivers down my back. I moaned. Something more than his hands reached for me and pushed against my aura.

It wrapped around me and started to tingle. It teased me, trying to find a way in. His mouth and hands were keeping me occupied. I was thinking with my little head and it was quite happy with how things were going. Then the power squeezed, and I felt an anger that wasn't my own wake up inside.

The Thing One flexed and the cold power of the grave pushed back.

My spooner flew out of the bed and slammed against the wall. His head bounced off the drywall, hard enough to leave a dent. As he fell to the floor I jumped out of bed and scrambled to the other side of the room.

What the hell!?

I flicked on the light and looked around for a weapon.

Nothing.

Note to self: Get some weapons. The dresser was the only thing in the room other than the bed. I'm sure John could have picked it up and swung it around like a claymore, but I'm nowhere near his size.

Lover Boy was much closer to the bedroom door than I was. I could've made a dash for it, but I was sure he would get to me before I made it out the door.

Speaking of Lover Boy, I got my first good look at him and paused in awe. Nutty brown skin, shaggy dark hair. Everything rippled as he got off the floor. Not in the 'I spend all my time in the gym' kind of way; more like a panther flexing. He had abs for days, broad shoulders, and chocolate brown eyes that would make you believe it when he said he loved you.

"Wait! Stop!" I felt a push of something, but it slid off me. He held up a placating hand. "Just give me a minute."

He shook his head and blinked his eyes hard. I'm sure the smack against the wall must have scrambled his brains.

I took that moment to notice his light blue underwear, which he filled out very nicely. Wait, did he have underwear on before? It seemed like he didn't. I remembered touching his ass and it was bare at the time.

"I know this is a bit sudden for you, but did you have to throw me into a wall?" He grimaced and shook his head a bit more.

He looked upset. Not hugely upset, more like annoyed. Maybe he got thrown into walls all the time. Now I was thinking about it, how had I done that? It takes a lot of force to throw someone. I didn't think I could have even done that physically. I might have knocked him over, but not actually thrown him. My magic was just small time, like lifting a penny . . . wasn't it?

I started to stutter out a reply when I felt the touch again. It was a light poke, like it was trying to get inside me. I waved my arm and batted it away.

"What are you doing?" I demanded.

"What do you mean?" He sounded defensive.

"I felt you do something," I said. "You tried to get inside me somehow. Stop it."

He sighed. "I'm trying to speed up the process."

"What process?"

"Having sex."

"What?" I can be pretty direct sometimes, but not that direct.

"You know. Doing the nasty, knocking boots." He gave me a sexy smile.

"I got that part," I said sarcastically.

"Heels to Jesus. Taking the hot dog bus to taco town."

"I got the picture."

"Bumpin ugly, naked wrestling, the horizontal mambo."

By this point he was making some very suggestive hip gyrations. Part of me was tantalized. Part of me was pissed.

"I got it," I shouted. The pissed part of me was winning. "Where do you get off showing up here with your perfect body in my bed just thinking I'm going to roll over for you."

I was gesturing wildly. Although part of me was hearing what I was saying and, actually, he probably did expect to show up and shag just about anyone. I just wished I knew how I'd met him. Where had he come from? How had he ended up here?

"Easy there, Mary," he said. "I was just having a bit of fun. Trying to lighten the situation and all. You probably don't remember me, but I saved your life the other night."

What was he talking about?

"You know. The smoke. Trashing Sandy's apartment. Trying to kill everyone including you. Ring a bell?"

It all hit me. I remembered everything. I also remembered him. He was the guy in the bed that suddenly appeared in the living room.

"Ahhh. All coming back to you is it? I stopped the smoke last time, but I'm not sure when it will be back again. It's better if we hit the sack now and then you'll be right as rain."

"So, I'm supposed to have sex with you and then I'll be all right?" I asked.

"Yep." He beamed at me like that explained everything.

It explained nothing. Was this 'have sex with a handsome stranger for your health' day? A shag a day keeps the doctor away? Like eating an apple only more fun? I still wasn't clear how this was even supposed to help.

"You've got riders. I've seen it before. It's like having a ghost inside, only in your case it's a poltergeist. They live in your spirit and hijack your magic."

Say what?

"I've never seen anyone have more than two before, but they are all churning and seething inside of you."

I remembered the sheer malevolence of the darkness. Stalking me. Oh yes, they were mad as hell.

"So, what are you? Some sort of exorcist?"

"Sort of. I absorb emotions. I get power from giving and receiving emotional energy. Makes me the greatest therapist in the world." He said that last part rather smugly.

I'm sure he was, although most therapists didn't run around naked and screw their patients. Or maybe they did, and they were just more discreet about it. I've never been to a therapist before.

"A rider's construct is nothing but emotion. Once I absorb that, it will unravel and fade away. Anyway, I have a life far away from Louisville, Kentucky and I'd like to get back to it. The House just dumped me here to solve your problem. Once you're fixed, I can go back home. So be a good boy and do what the doctor orders."

"I thought you were a therapist?" I said.

"Whatever," he said as he walked toward me. Damn, he did look fine! He moved like a dancer. A poem in motion.

This guy was all business, and obviously in a hurry to get home. I guess I didn't blame him. I wouldn't appreciate waking up in someone else's house and having to fix their problem.

"I'm not a prude or anything," I said as he moved into my personal space. He ran his hand over my chest. I could feel the heat coming off of him. "I like a good wrestle in the sack as much as the next guy, and you are certainly attractive enough. It's just, the whole thing seems rather . . . cold, calculating."

I was struggling to keep my big head doing the thinking.

"I'm sure it does. That's because it is. Well, maybe not cold and calculating. More like clinical. This is fast therapy. You'll enjoy yourself. I'll enjoy myself. You'll be rid of your death wish and I'll be home."

"Did you say death wish?" This was a whole new level of scary. What was going on?

"Yep." He nodded. "That's what these remnants do. They destroy their host. They get their vengeance."

Oh, crap.

"You've actually got four of them. Three of them are pretty low grade and kind of muddled, but one of them is strong. Really strong. He's almost got an entire personality in there."

I was pretty sure I knew who that one was. I was scared. Thing One, the Death Experience guy, was a monster in real life. And now he was living in me.

"Sandy told me your story. I'm assuming they were the four guys that tried to kill you."

I just nodded. I felt like the room was closing in on me. I couldn't breathe.

"Hey! Take it easy." He touched my arm and then gently pulled me into a hug. "I'm here. It's going to be okay."

It felt nice to be hugged. In the middle of freaking out I noticed he smelled nice.

"We just need to have sex for several hours and this will all work its way out."

"For real!?" I laughed in disbelief and pulled away. "You tell me I'm going to die and then you hit on me?"

"I have an ability," he said, giving me my space. "I can consume negative energy. I can see it, sense it, and pull it out of people. In your case it is going to save your life. That's why the House brought me here."

I held up a hand and he stopped talking. I needed to process this for a moment. I was remembering everything from last night: the feeling of the grave and the powerful smoky figure throwing people around and then choking me. It was no joke. I had thought I was going to die. I still wasn't sure how I'd been saved. If this guy was telling the truth, then he had probably stopped it.

I wanted the darkness gone. It scared the crap out of me way more than this guy did, and I'd made out for a lot less reward than this.

I dropped my hand and nodded. He casually stepped over and kissed me. It felt strange, and awkward. Now that I had to do this, it felt like I was at the doctor's office. I half expected him to tell me stick out my tongue and say, "Ahhhh."

For some reason that struck me as funny and I started to laugh. The nervous energy was there and even though I tried to stop, I couldn't.

Then I felt embarrassed. This guy was just trying to help, and I was laughing at him.

"I'm so sorry," I said trying to get myself under control. I felt my face getting red and I just wanted to run from the room.

"It's okay." He took my hands in his and just smiled at me. He kept telling me it was all right until I calmed down and could look him in the eye again. He really was beautiful. I didn't know what his story was, but I could have ended up with a lot worse supernatural therapists than this.

I took a deep breath and let it go. I gave myself a mental shake. I was ready.

"Good?" he asked.

"Yes."

"Let's try something a little different this time. A bit of a warmup before we go to the real thing." He kept holding my hands and closed his eyes.

At first, I felt nothing, just his warm hands in mine. Then I felt a gentle pull. It was so small it was almost nonexistent, but I felt something. There was an energy that was moving from me to him. It didn't feel like the grave. It felt like a tiny trickle of water.

I switched on my magic sight and saw something that made me very happy. There was a faint misty blackness coming off of my arms and flowing to him. It was such a small amount, like a smoky shadow, but it was there. When the shadow got to him it let off a tiny sparkle and then sunk into his skin.

We stood like that for a few minutes, then he pulled me in closer. He let go of my hands and began stroking my sides. It felt so good. I felt wanted, needed. He felt warm, alive, human.

The last few weeks had been so catastrophic. My whole life had changed. I'd been hurt on a level that I still didn't comprehend. I was dealing with it and pushing through, but I hadn't emotionally processed it yet. His touch, somehow, said it was okay. I was going to be okay. I was going to get through this. He wanted me. For that moment in time, I was wanted, and my body responded.

Lust surged through me. I wanted him, all of him, right then and there.

I heard an evil roar, and suddenly there was a black flash and smoke was everywhere. My sexy savior was blown through the wall.

I'm talking through the drywall, through the studs, through the wall and into my living room. I wasn't going to get my security deposit back. I was so shocked I couldn't move. The darkness roared so loud I could feel my bones shake, then it all collapsed inside me again.

Everything was quiet and still except for the white drywall dust in the air. I stood there. The darkness scared me so badly I was shaking. These remnants were no joke. I wanted them gone and they might have just killed the one person who could help me.

With a groan, Lover Boy sat up. I picked my way through the debris and went over to help him. He stood up before I got there and dusted himself off.

"Well, that didn't turn out quite like I wanted," he said with a wry smile. He stretched, popped his back, and dusted himself off. From what I could see he looked fine. My respect for him went up. If I'd been knocked through a wall, I wouldn't be getting back up again.

"Are you okay?" I asked, unsure of what to do. "I'm so sorry."

He just waved it off. "Not your fault. Remnants don't like me, and this isn't the first time I've been knocked around a bit."

He looked at the giant hole in my wall. "Although, this is the first time I've been thrown into a completely different room. Your remnants are powerful."

"You're not giving up, are you?" I asked nervously.

"No. I'm fine. This will be fine." He waved in my general direction. "This is just going to take longer than I thought. I'm Tyler, by the way." I realized we had never really met. I'd just woken up with him and the action had happened from there. I went to shake his hand, but he waved me off.

"Your remnants are going to be touchy for the next few hours. Let's give them time to settle down and then we can try again."

My face must have shown my alarm because he laughed.

"No. No. We won't be going for the full cure for a while. We will have to go very slowly and drain them of their power. When there is a wisp of them left, we can try again. I'm sure it will work then."

That sounded like a much better idea and I told him so. He said goodbye and headed out. As he left, I noticed he had jeans on. How had that happened? I didn't remember him putting on any clothes. Oh well. One more mystery in my new crazy life.

With Tyler gone, I got out a broom and cleaned up the mess on the floor. There was dust and drywall everywhere. It hurt to move. I was a mass of bruises and aches from the death experience I'd gone through. It felt even better, though, to do something for myself and just have some time alone.

I really appreciated staying with Sandy and all of her pillows and cats. John and Annabeth had stayed with me around the clock to make sure I was going to be okay. Now, however, it was so nice to have a quiet moment by myself in my own space.

I put on some shorts, warmed up a can of SpaghettiOs, sat on the couch, and started playing some Sudoku on my phone. I'd discovered that getting the numbers lined up just felt right. It had become my own personal meditation. My sister said I was like an idiot savant with the game. Although she would add I was more idiot than savant. Even the really hard ones only took me a few minutes to solve. I could see the patterns in the numbers, and I knew where they were supposed to go. I'd felt the same thing with poker, although that was a more complex game. After sitting at a table for less than an hour I'd know exactly when to push and when to fold. I found it strangely restful and fulfilling.

After several grids I felt much better and switched over to Netflix. I'd binge-watched half a show, eaten a whole can of potato strings and two candy bars, when I heard a light tap at my door.

Maybe it was the time alone, or maybe it was all the food, but I was feeling much better now. I ambled over to the door to find Annabeth looking up at me all cheerful and happy. I marveled again at how much sunshine could fit into her short, chubby frame.

"Hi Jason," she said. "I heard what happened and I just wanted to check on you and make sure you are okay." She spotted the hole in my wall. "Oh! Wow! That is big."

That's what he said, almost made it out my mouth. I clamped my lips shut. I wasn't sure Annabeth would get the humor.

I stepped aside to let her in, and she puttered past me to get the full view. "That is such a big hole," she exclaimed. I couldn't help it; I started laughing.

"What?" She looked at me, then realized what she had said. "Oh, stop it." She laughed as she smacked me.

I flinched. I had so many bruises that even a playful smack hurt.

"Oh! I'm so sorry." She started fussing over me. "Look at you. Just a mass of blue and purple and I go and hit you. Even a bit of green over there. I'm so sorry."

I shooed her away while letting her know it was okay. I was fine. Everything hurt a bit, but I was fine.

Once she calmed down, she started looking around.

"Oh honey, is this all you have?"

My living room was basically an old couch, a TV stand, and a TV. It wasn't much, but it was all I needed. Annabeth poked her nose into the bedroom, where my one dresser leaned against the wall and my mattress sat on the floor.

"You need some color, some pictures, something to make this place look like a home." She looked around in distress.

I hadn't really thought about it, but the room was pretty bland. The walls were a traditional beige with white ceilings and dark floors. The old couch was gray, so it didn't do much to liven up the room, and the TV and its stand were black. I didn't have any pictures to hang up or anything personal to put out.

Traveling light was a real advantage. It meant that I could pick up and leave at any time. Most of my personal stuff had been destroyed in the fire anyway.

When I had gotten here, it hadn't even occurred to me to decorate and do all the normal move-in things I assume other people do. I'd actually been pretty proud of just getting the little bit of furniture I had. The dresser and the couch were nice but used. I'd splurged on the mattress. It was brand new, just the right amount of firm, and oh-so nice to snuggle on.

Add in a medium-sized TV, used stand, and cheap microwave, and I was good to go. It wasn't much but it was a start. I told all that to Annabeth who said that sounded nice, but her tone said that wasn't nearly enough for a start at all. I had a feeling I was going to be gifted some colorful decorative items soon.

"Anyway, I stopped by to see if you would like to go for a walk," Annabeth said. "You've been inside for days. Some fresh air would do you good."

I pointed at my face. I still looked like I'd lost a bar fight with a gang of Hell's Angels. I imagined little kids getting one look at me and running away screaming.

"I thought of that. It's night right now, dear. No one is going to really notice you. People keep to themselves when it's dark." Getting outside for a bit did sound nice. I wasn't up for a long walk, though, and getting all sweaty didn't sound like fun.

"It feels nice outside right now. With the sun down it's cool but not cold. We'll take a stroll in the park outside and we'll be close to here when you feel tired." All five feet of her just beamed at me. She was impossible to resist. Somehow her sunshine overcame my gloomy mood and I agreed.

9

Walk in the Park

One of the things I loved about my apartment was how close it was to Louisville's Central Park. It covers two city blocks and has a small amphitheater for local plays and bands, tennis courts, playgrounds, and lots of walkways and benches. It's the perfect place to spend a summer evening, or night in this case.

We walked out the front door, crossed the street, and picked up a trail that wound through the trees. We took it slow and it felt good to stretch my legs. Annabeth was quiet, just letting me enjoy the moment.

"So. How did you become a super?" I finally asked. I was tired of my own story. I wanted to hear something new.

"Well, first of all, it's not polite to ask that of another supernatural," she said.

"Oh. I'm sorry," I stammered. I hadn't meant to get on her bad side.

"It's okay," she waved it off. "I don't mind telling you. Maybe it will make you feel better about what happened to you. Misery loves company after all. I just made the mistake of asking some others when I first came here, and they were a little touchy. I guess everyone has a difficult time of it, and some just want to forget and move on."

She seemed lost in thought for a moment.

"This is rather hard to tell," she said softly. "I haven't been a super for very long at all. I guess I'm used to everyone already knowing my story."

She took a deep breath and shook off whatever was holding her back.

"I had a car accident. That was my near-death experience. I was getting older and losing my memory a bit. My son was with me and tactfully trying to tell me I should be in a home."

I looked at Annabeth in surprise. She didn't seem that old to me, maybe late fifties? And she was still very spry, active, and cheerful. I couldn't imagine anyone wanting her to be in a home.

"We went through an intersection just as a truck ran a red light. It hit the car on my side and knocked us fifty feet down the road. It crushed my side of the car and knocked my son around a lot. We stopped, upside down, and I remember looking over at my son with blood dripping the wrong way up his face. He was looking at me in shock. I felt myself slipping away and I knew we were both going to die. I just couldn't let that happen. I couldn't let my son die."

Her hands clenched, reliving the moment.

"I looked down and discovered the car door had crushed my chest and legs. I couldn't feel my arm at all. Somehow, I felt myself inflating, like I was a balloon. I pushed the car back and everything popped back into place. Then I reached over to my son and somehow inflated him too. There was blood everywhere, but I knew he was going to be all right."

"They had to use the Jaws of Life to tear apart the car and get us out of there. We only suffered cuts and bruises, no broken bones, and the paramedics said it was a miracle. They had never seen anything like it."

"That sounds amazing!" I was caught up in the scene. "So, your son is alive? He's okay?"

"That whole event was very traumatic, as you can imagine, but unfortunately my story doesn't end there." Annabeth was walking faster now. Caught up in the emotion of it all. I was hanging on every word.

"We both recovered physically, and for a while things were okay. My son was having problems emotionally, getting over the accident. He kept having flashbacks to the event and he stopped sleeping at night. He got moody and irritable and started pushing his wife and kids away.

"Then the strange stuff started happening. I had gotten better not only physically, but mentally as well. Not only did I not have any residual aches and pains from the accident, but I started feeling better than before. My arthritis was gone. I slept better at night. I was looking and feeling younger."

"All this is sounding good so far," I said. "Who doesn't want to be young again?"

"If that's all it was, then it would have been okay. The problem was my son started forgetting about the accident, and then he forgot about me. I wouldn't hear from him in days, and then I'd stop by. He'd open the door, looking good, looking happy. Then he'd see me, and it would all come back. His eyes would get this haunted look, and he'd suddenly look hunched and miserable.

"It wasn't just him either. I'd say something about the accident to his family or my friends and nobody remembered it. I didn't know anything about the Fog of Jonah at the time, so I began to think maybe it was me. Maybe I was going crazy."

"Fog of Jonah?" I interrupted her.

"It's one of the few global spells that protect supernaturals. In this case, it makes all evidence and memories of supernatural events disappear."

"For real?" I said. That seemed like a really powerful spell to do something like that.

"Yes," she replied. "You could be a troll, walking down the street, and nobody would pay any attention to you. Even if something happened—like say a car ran into you—the spell would find a way to make it seem normal and explain it away. In a few days, everyone would forget there even was an accident."

"What about video?" I asked. "Cell phones are everywhere, and it seems like people would get a picture or video of someone hitting a troll."

"It takes care of that too." She shrugged. "I'm not sure how. I didn't have anything to do with making the spell. That happened a long time ago. I just know it works. Believe me, I know it works," she said bitterly.

"I didn't mean to get you off track," I offered. "What happened to your son?"

"The Fog of Jonah really messed him up," she said angrily. "He would see me and remember the accident and getting healed. Then the Fog would do its thing and wipe his memory. Then he'd see me, remember, go through all the trauma again, and get wiped again. I didn't know what was going on. I just knew that I was causing him a lot of pain and I could see it was driving him crazy.

"He began avoiding me and I stopped going over. I just couldn't stand to see him hurting. This was happening to a lesser degree with my friends. They couldn't remember anything happening and it just seemed strange to them that I looked and acted different. By this time, I was starting to look a lot younger. I looked like my son's sister, rather than his mom. I started staying away from everyone. I stayed in the house and didn't go anywhere or talk to anyone.

"I think that was the loneliest time in my life. Years earlier, when I lost Richard, my husband, I thought it couldn't get any worse. I was just starting to recover from that when we had the accident. Then I lost everything and discovered just how bad it could get."

Tears were running down her cheeks. The loss was so real it broke my heart. I pulled her into a hug and just held her for a while.

I'd been lonely myself for a long time, but I couldn't imagine how it must be to lose your husband, your son, and your grandkids. She was always so cheerful too. I couldn't imagine how much strength it must take to face the world with a smile.

Finally, Annabeth pulled back and dried her eyes. We just walked for a while, finished our first loop of the park, and started down another one of the paths.

"The Fog got even worse," she continued. "Not only did it erase any memory of the accident, it erased any memory of me. Sandy thinks it did that because I was looking so different, and without the accident there wasn't any way to explain it. I don't know for sure—I guess I'll never know for sure—but I discovered it when I went to the grocery store. I'd been shopping there for years and it was just a little neighborhood store. The people working there weren't close friends, but they knew me. I finally ran out of food at the house, stopped by the store, and nobody recognized me. I knew a few of them by name and I said, 'hi.' They just gave me clueless looks. It seemed so strange that I deliberately crossed paths with one of my old friends. She didn't know who I was either. I didn't know how this would affect my family. I thought maybe, if they didn't remember me, I could find a way to meet them as a stranger and end up being their friend. It wouldn't be the same as being a mom or grandmother, but at least it would be something. So, I set up a chance meeting on the street. I was just going to pass by and see if they would say anything. If that went well, I was going to find a way to interact with them somehow."

Annabeth fell silent again, lost in her thoughts. I'd been so caught up in my own story of transition I hadn't thought how it must be for others. No wonder it was considered bad taste to ask about how people became a super.

"I had imagined all kinds of outcomes to this meeting and I was so nervous. My son, his wife, and their two girls were walking up the street, talking and laughing. Not a care in the world. Just being the amazing family they are. Then my son saw me. I felt this pressure in the air, like it suddenly got very heavy, and then my son screamed. He screamed in such pain, like someone was ripping his guts out. Then he collapsed. Without thinking I started to run over. My baby needed me. Then my granddaughters saw me, and they screamed too. Except they didn't stop. They just kept screaming over and over again until they fell on the ground shaking.

"It was me. I didn't understand it, but I was causing all this. I stopped running toward them and started running away. I went to my house, packed a bag, and just left. They were the world to me, and I couldn't see them anymore. I had to get out of there. I'd been thinking about a fresh start anyway. Loneliness gives you a lot of time to consider your life. I've always lived with someone or for someone. That's just the way it was when I grew up. I'd never really gone out on my own and lived my own life. As I drove away, I was so upset. I was mad at the world, angry at the loss of my family, and furious at myself for somehow letting all this happen.

"I drove for a long time. I don't know how many days. I didn't know where I was going. I took roads at random, stopped when I was hungry, and slept in my car. I was like Forrest Gump, just running and running and running. Somewhere in all that I left my anger behind. One day I was driving by this field and the sun was shining through the clouds. The light was leaving these rays in the sky and it seemed spiritual and celestial somehow. I pulled over and walked into the field. I could smell the grass, feel the breeze, feel my little small place in this big world.

"I stopped resisting the changes that were happening to me. Instead I accepted them. The universe was pushing me to start over, to create a new life. That day in the field I gave up my old life and resolved to start over. I had no idea what that would look like, but I was going to accept it as it came.

"I drove to the nearest city, which happened to be Louisville, and started driving around. These older homes are just beautiful, and I thought it would be nice to live in one. About that time, I saw the 'For Rent' sign, so I pulled over and went inside. Sandy knew what I was right away and helped me start a new life. Of course, it wasn't that easy to do. The old world had forgotten me so selling the house and getting my retirement account was rough. She put me in touch with a supernatural lawyer and he got it all worked out. Not his first rodeo, I'm sure."

"I am so sorry," I said and gave her a hug. "I can't imagine how hard it must have been. I've been feeling like I had it rough, and you've lived through a Lifetime Original Movie." We started walking again. "Starting over is not easy. I've started over from scratch a few times and I never did it with acceptance like that. After hearing your story, I'm wondering how you're so cheerful all the time."

"I heard a saying long ago that what you resist, persists. If you want something to end or you want something to start over, you gotta go through acceptance. I've lived by that all my life. My new life is good too. I have a store on Etsy, I have new friends who understand me and accept me for who I am, and I'm learning magic from a kickass mage! How cool is that?"

"Very cool," I said. "Sandy does seem like a nice person."

"She's that and much more. Get her to tell you about some of her battles sometime. The woman kicks ass. She's always willing to help others too. That's probably why the House picked her to be the HOH."

"HOH?" I asked.

"Head of Household," she said. "Sorry. There is lots of lingo with the new life. I'm still learning myself. Normally the HOH is picked by the House council, but sometimes the House picks them itself. In this case the House showed up here, and then Sandy woke up in the head suite. John followed her, of course, and Jennifer came down from Chicago as well."

"There is so much I don't know yet," I said. "How did the House just appear here?"

"Well, the House is like this big interdimensional thing. I don't really understand it myself. I just know that parts of the House exist all over the world and in other realms. Sometimes, for some unknown reason, a new part of the House will open up. This one started here in Louisville about a year ago. The one up in Chicago is apparently much bigger and has been open for more than a hundred years."

"How long have you been here?" I asked. I had been thinking of Annabeth as an old timer to this supernatural thing. Now I was realizing she was a newbie like me.

"I've been here about six months, I guess," she said. "Long enough to get settled in and start learning magic. That is one of the best things about my new life: learning that I'm a mage."

When I think of mage, I think of a stiff gray-bearded man with a staff and a blue robe, like in the movies. Annabeth was about as far away from that as possible. She was short, plump, and full of life.

I didn't want to get into discussing magic. I'd had it for a long time, and it seemed like a bit of curse to me. I really appreciated Annabeth telling me her story and I wanted to leave it at that. I didn't want to throw my story of fire, death, and exile into the mix. Time to change the subject.

"So, what do you sell on Etsy?" I asked.

"I sell little charms that put out good vibrations for those that wear them. John got me turned onto the whole Etsy thing. He takes flawed gemstones and makes these amazing rings and pendants out of them. He sells them in his own shop, but he takes the leftover metal and makes little charms for me. I tried to pay him for them, but he says that working with metal makes him happy."

"So, you make all the money?" I asked.

"I feel guilty, but, yes, I make all the profits off the charms. I'm trying to figure out another way to pay him back, but nothing has shown up so far. Let me know if you think of anything when you are talking to him."

"Sure," I said. "So, what do you do with the charms? Can they do real magic like Sandy's?"

She laughed. "Oh, no. My charms aren't like hers. She makes powerful stuff with runes and everything. She's given me some of her old ones, so I know just how good they are. No, my little charms just put out happy vibes because I sing to them."

"You sing to them?" I asked. That seemed like an interesting way to do magic.

"Actually, I hum to them. Singing just sounds more exciting." She laughed. "I did a magic assessment with Sandy and she found out I interact with magic through sound. I hear magic rather than see it. Apparently, that is kind of rare, and not a very good way to work with magic. Sandy says I just need to get creative and make my own path, but right now it just feels frustrating."

I felt like I was missing something. I did my magic with little animated cartoons. I'm sure most people would consider that strange as well.

"Why is singing so bad? Lots of people sing. And we hear stuff all the time. How is this holding you back?"

"Because so much of magic is visual," she said. "Runes determine how the magic takes shape and I can't see them. Magic is usually directed at something and I can't see to direct it. I'm like a blind person. I can still interact and get around in the world, but I bump into things and need a lot of help. I really want to make charms like Sandy, but I can't draw the shapes like her and force them into a vessel. I'm sure I'll get better, but right now it's frustrating."

I thought about my little cartoon characters. I'd already figured out that the clearer I could make them, and the more detail I gave them, the better they did. I relied a lot on seeing where they went and how they interacted with the world. Not being able to see them would be awful. I'm not sure I could do magic without that.

"I see what you mean," I said. "If you compare yourself to sight-based magic, I'm sure there will be things you can't do. Different doesn't always mean worse. Sometimes it's just different. Maybe you can find other ways to get the same effect."

I kicked into problem-solving mode. I have always been good at figuring out new things to try.

"Let's talk about the charms you are making now. You made them with sound instead of sight. What does Sandy think about them? Can she make charms like that?"

"I . . . don't know," Annabeth said thoughtfully. "I've told her I was making these, but I've never shown them to her. I just figured they were too simple for her."

"I'm sure Sandy would like to know you are progressing so I'm sure she would like to see them. For that matter, I'd like to see them."

"Sure! I have one right here," Annabeth said. She pulled a small charm out of her pocket and gave it to me. It was in the shape of an elephant and the detail was exquisite. Most small items like this stopped at getting the general shape right. This had so much more. You could see the bulge of muscle under the skin. The skin had texture and even the toenails were there.

"John made this?" I asked incredulously. Annabeth nodded proudly.

"He's mega talented," I said. I had no idea what types of tools he used or how he did it, but John was an artist. I switched on my magic sight and the little elephant lit up with a soft pink glow. It was more than that, though. It kinda sparkled a bit with touches of dark red and flashes of white.

I told Annabeth what I was seeing and how pretty it was. She loved it. As we were talking, I realized I could feel something too. The charm was giving off a feeling, like a warm cup of coffee on a cold morning, or a cat napping in the sun. It felt lazy, comfortable, and somehow happy.

Annabeth was beyond tickled with all the stuff I was telling her. She'd been making these pendants, but she wasn't a hundred percent sure they were really magical. She'd been worried that maybe her mind was playing tricks on her. Maybe she was hoping for it so much she was imagining it happening. She hadn't wanted to show these to Sandy because she had her on such a high pedestal. You never want to look bad in front of your hero.

Since I could see magic so well, she wanted to know what I saw when she was making them. I was curious too. What did audio magic look like?

We stopped by the side of the path and she took back the pendant. No one was around so it was the perfect time to experiment. Putting the little elephant on her hand and after clearing her throat self-consciously a few times, she began humming to it. Nothing changed that I could see, and I told her so. She just nodded and kept humming.

I could tell she was having problems getting into her usual mode. She was shifting her feet and kept looking at me. Performance anxiety, it's not just for boys.

To put her more at ease I took her other hand in mine and began humming too. Then we started walking again but humming while we did so. Annabeth looked relieved then started to relax. I looked around at the trees and the grass. Even at night they were beautiful. There is something about being in nature that soothes me. I feel serene, happier. More at peace with myself and the world. The shadows from the leaves on the trees danced and a light breeze caressed me. I saw a picnic table off the path ahead of us that was hosting what looked like a million fireflies. In that moment, I just felt right with the world.

I looked over at Annabeth to tell her how happy I was, and my jaw dropped. She was lighting up the world with bright pink sparkly energy. It was just beautiful. The little elephant pendant was throwing off sparks like a Fourth of July sparkler. She was humming to more than the pendant. It seemed like the world was lighting up in her happy glow. I realized that I was glowing a bit also. No wonder the night seemed so special and beautiful. If her charms could make me feel like this, then I wanted one!

I stopped humming and had started to tell her what I was seeing, when I felt a tremor through the ground and heard a dull booming sound. What the heck was that? I felt it again, and then a dark hulking shape came out of the shadows. It wasn't lit up in a happy glow. It looked vaguely human, but wrong somehow. There were glowing dark purple bands around it with some sort of pattern. At first glance it looked some sort of hieroglyphics or letters. It wasn't anything I'd seen before. When it moved, I could feel the ground shake a bit. That thing must be heavy! As it came into the light, I realized it was made of stones. There were larger stones making up its main shape with smaller rocks and gravel filling in the space between them. It had two arms and two legs, although it didn't have enough definition for hands. It had a head, although there wasn't any sort of face on it. Even though it didn't have a face, I could feel it was locked in on Annabeth and coming right at us. Annabeth saw it too, and her happy glow faded.

"What the heck is that?" she shouted. I had no idea, but I knew enough to get out of the way as it dashed toward us. We both dove in different directions as the rock monster barreled between us. It had so much mass that it took it a few moments to stop.

"What do we do?" I yelled to Annabeth.

"I don't know," she yelled back. She looked a lot less panicked than I was. "We have to defend the park. There is a realm gate here." She didn't get to say much more than that before the rock golem was back.

Once again it was focused on Annabeth although it was moving slower this time. It wasn't going to overshoot its rush again.

"Fire!" Annabeth flung her hand out toward the golem. I saw she had a fistful of charms in her other hand. The air distorted and dust motes briefly burst into flame as the heat wave rolled toward the golem. When it impacted him, he briefly caught fire, but it quickly went out. His momentum stuttered, though, so at least it slowed him down for a moment.

"Try cold!" I yelled. Rocks don't burn, at least not without a huge amount of heat. Cold typically slowed things down. Maybe it would freeze in place.

"That's Sandy's charm," Annabeth yelled. "I don't know how to do the opposite."

"Just try it!" I yelled back.

"Cold!" Annabeth commanded. Nothing happened. The golem had made it to her and swung a massive arm at her head. She ducked and dodged to the side. It didn't hesitate at all as it shifted and followed her.

"Take the heat!" Annabeth commanded as she made a pulling motion. It worked. This time the heat ripple moved from the rock monster toward her. She yelped and dove out of the way again. For an old lady, she could move. She came up sweating and red like she had been left in the steamer too long, but Rocky was covered in frost and not moving.

I ran over and tried to push it. If I could knock it over then maybe it would stay down. It must have weighed more than a car; I couldn't budge it. Annabeth ran over to help me, but we couldn't even rock it.

"I'm not sure what else to try," Annabeth said as the frost started melting. We both backed up to give us some room. If this thing started swinging, I didn't want to be close.

We didn't have time to discuss it as the golem started moving again. The next few minutes turned into a cat-and-mouse game. The golem wasn't fast enough to hit Annabeth, and she wasn't powerful enough to stop it. The hot/cold charm was out of power according to Annabeth so freezing it again was out. The golem wasn't slowing down, though. It was only a matter of time until Annabeth slipped up and got hurt. I had to do something, but what?

I felt a strange burning around my finger. It was my little penny that had changed into a ring. It was trying to get my attention. I looked at my hand and the charm had changed. Now it only had a thin band around my finger and the rest was sticking up like a tiny knife. It had at most only about two inches of blade. It only had as much material to work with as a penny, so it looked ridiculous as a tiny cutter. There was no way it could hurt something as huge and dense as the Rocky. The blade was shining with power, though, and I could feel the ring growling, so clearly it had something in mind. What it could do, though, I had no idea.

Then it happened: One of the golem's arms clipped Annabeth, and she staggered. It swung again, and this time she wasn't ready.

"STOP," Annabeth commanded. This time there wasn't a ripple, or anything I could see magical at work. The Golem just stopped. The command had been forceful, powerful, and the world had obeyed. This was her voice magic at work.

As Annabeth sighed in relief, the purple bands around the golem flared and started to turn. I yelled a warning as they spun faster and faster, but it was too late. The golem broke through her magic and kicked her.

It was a powerful kick, catching her right in her center of gravity. It picked her up and hurled her through the air a good ten feet. When she hit the ground, she rolled to a stop and didn't move.

The golem started stalking toward her. She wasn't moving, and it was going to crush her. That couldn't happen.

I ran forward yelling, trying to get its attention, but that didn't work. In desperation I slashed at one of the purple bands with my little knife. To my complete surprise, there was a flash of light and the band snapped.

The whole golem shook, dust flew, and some of the smaller rocks holding it together fell away. It dug into the ground, coming to a complete stop. It didn't even turn around; it just reformed itself so it faced me. It didn't have a face, but its body language conveyed rage. I'd pissed this rock monster off. Faster than I thought possible, it was after me.

I'm sure a great hero would have stayed and fought. I turned and ran. I was still recovering from a major beating and I was in no shape to duck and dodge this thing's attacks. I had to get it away from Annabeth and just hope that she was okay.

I really wasn't in any shape to run either, but that's all I had, so run I did. I wasn't fast, but neither was the golem. I made it to the edge of the park and took the street heading south, away from downtown. I couldn't take the thing where there were a lot of people. They might get hurt, and I now knew the Fog of Jonah would mess with their minds.

Having that thing thundering behind me was intimidating as hell. I ran for a block and then tried to put on some speed and lose it. That didn't work. I was a bit faster on a straight sidewalk, but I had to slow down at the intersections where it would catch up again. It didn't slow down for anything. I didn't think even a car would stop it. The car would be crushed, someone would get hurt, and it would just reform and come after me again. Fortunately, there wasn't anyone on the sidewalks and there was only light traffic on the roads.

After three blocks the panic subsided a bit, and I found my rhythm. I couldn't run forever, but I did have a moment to think. I wasn't completely helpless. I had my own magic. It just took a while to work.

My magic had gotten a boost since my Waker Moment, but it was still small and weak compared to what I had seen others do. I had been able to snap a magic band off the golem, but that had been using my little supercharm. I couldn't cut more bands unless I stopped, and if I stopped it would crush me.

I didn't think one of my little magic cartoon creations could take on the purple bands either. The bands looked pretty powerful and sophisticated. What I could do, though, was take out the stone. It was using its stone body to run and fight. If I took that away, then maybe I could survive this thing.

What I needed were my little Flying Miners again.

With a touch of magic, I created my little guy in front of me. He had blue overalls, a miner's helmet with a light, and work boots. He was just a little fella, about a quarter of an inch high, but I was amazed at just how real he seemed. My magic upgrade was really working. I knew that the more detail I gave him and the more physical he seemed, the better he would work for me. Hopefully it would be enough.

Since he would be working with stone, I gave him goggles to keep his vision clear, and a mustache because he was going to be doing some butch work. Next came a GPS to find his way and a jetpack to get there. In a burst of inspiration, I added a little walkie talkie. That way I could continue to give him orders once his mission started. Finally, I added his green duplicator ring. It would collect what magic it could from the golem, and once it was fully charged, the miner could use it to clone himself. Maybe I couldn't break the purple bands directly, but with the duplicator ring I might be able to weaken them.

Finally, I gave him his weapon of rock destruction, a diamond and adamantium pickaxe. Guaranteed to chop through anything! I brought up its spec sheet, just like an RPG game, and gave it +10 strength, +10 dexterity, +10 against earth and +1000 against golems. That didn't really mean anything in the real world, but I wasn't in the real world. I was in the magical world. I needed this pickaxe to be amazing and in my mind that worked.

I pumped magic into my little guy. I made him as solid and bright as I could without getting dizzy, then sent him off. He gave a happy, "Wheee," because that is what tiny Flying Miners do, and did a test lap in the air. Then he took off for Rocky, trailing little puffs of white smoke from his jetpack. I followed him with my magic sight as he landed on the golem's shoulder and set to work.

He wasn't big, but he started chipping off tiny bits of rocks with ease. It was working!

Or maybe it wasn't. The tiny bits of rock stayed inside the bands of purple and continued to be part of the mass that was the rock golem. A finely pulverized golem was probably just as bad as a blocky rocky one was. What I needed was a way to shoot the rock away from the golem.

What I made was the Ass Blaster 2000.

I started with a worm body, then gave it a big gaping mouth for the rock chips to go into. The middle of the body would crush the rock down and make rock pellets. On the back side of the worm I gave him powerful legs. They would be used to move the worm's body around, but mostly to point the back of the worm into the sky. I made the back end of the little guy a bit like a shotgun. It would cock itself, then pwew—shoot the rock pellet at high velocity into the sky. I added a duplicator ring, walkie talkie, goggles (safety first), and GPS. As a final touch I added a mustache as well, because this little fella was also going to be doing very butch work, even for a worm.

My Ass Blaster 2000 was now complete. I pumped him full of magic and sent him off. He didn't go, "Wheee," but his mustache wiggled and his little legs pumped the air. I think he was happy. He landed next to the miner and started munching on freshly chipped rock. Nothing happened.

The miner duplicated, so now there were two little guys chipping away, and the Ass Blaster 2000 was still eating, but nothing was going out the back end. Finally, the legs got to work and it assumed the position. The ass pumped, and *bam*, a little rock pebble shot away from the golem. For a moment, it looked like the purple bands would pull it back into orbit, but it made it away and clear. Now Rocky had just a tiny bit less stone as part of its makeup.

Success! Now I just needed that to happen like a million more times.

It was disorienting using magic sight to see the golem behind me and still paying attention to what was happening in front of me, so I let the magic sight go for a little bit. I thought I had a winning solution and I didn't want to foul everything up by stumbling and falling.

So, for a while I just ran, feeling the cool night air and the hard sidewalk beneath my feet. I was in a part of the city I'd never been in before. I had no idea where I was or how far I'd gone. I just knew I couldn't stop.

I heard the difference before I saw it. The steps behind me had been a solid booming sound as the golem hit pavement. Now the booms didn't sound as loud and the pitch went up slightly. I switched on my magic sight to check the progress.

And what progress it was! There must have been more than a hundred miners working all over the golem's arm. Each miner was paired with an Ass Blaster, and a rain of rock pellets was shooting off Rocky.

A few blocks later there were two hundred and then four hundred pairs working on the golem. They covered his head and most of the other arm. They were taking him out from the top down.

The bands were shrinking too, and they started shifting the rocks around to keep the golem whole and running. Rocky had started out more than seven feet tall. Now it was about six feet and shrinking.

The miners were still doubling in number, so the work was happening much quicker. In only two blocks it was down to five feet, then four, then three. Its stride was much shorter, and I didn't have to run as fast anymore. I could have outrun it at this size, but there wasn't any point. I'd let my little guys do their job.

The last rocks went super fast, and the purple bands faded away. Finally, the only thing left was a smooth round black ball that rolled to a stop on the sidewalk. There was no light coming off of it, and the miners ignored it.

Instead, there was a spontaneous celebration in the air. All the little miners and Ass Blasters fired up their rockets and took to the sky. The night was filled with puffs of white smoke, wiggling mustaches, and more, "Wheees," than I could count. It was indeed time to celebrate. Ding, dong, the wicked rock golem is dead.

I just stood there for a long moment, breathing in the cool air, basking in the glow of life. Somehow, I'd won. I was going to be okay.

Following close on the thrill of victory was the realization that I'd just run a long way. I was sore, tired, and I had no idea how long it would take to get back home. I needed to wrap this up and head back to Annabeth.

The League of Flying Miners was still celebrating and tooting in the air. I'd learned my lesson back in Sandy's living room; I wasn't going to just ask them to vanish. They were filled with magic. It had started as my magic, but most of them were created from borrowed golem magic and had a slight purple cast to them.

I didn't want to absorb all that magic directly. Partly because I wasn't sure what the golem magic would do to me (maybe I'd turn into a stone monster myself; that didn't sound fun) and partly because I wasn't sure how to absorb them in the first place. I needed to talk to Sandy before doing anything rash.

I felt a burning around my finger. My little penny was trying to get my attention again. I held up my hand and it uncoiled off my finger. It wiggled to the center of my palm and turned into a little egg again. It occurred to me that I couldn't just keep calling this thing my little super charm anymore. It had pulled off some amazing work for me so far and it needed a proper name.

I held it up so all my little creations could see it. "I now dub thee Penny!" I said formally. Then, since it didn't have any shoulders to tap with a sword, I breathed on it, like I was giving it the breath of life.

Penny burst into light and all the miners and Ass Blasters paused in midair, turned as one, and bowed to the little charm.

"Penny, do you have a way to absorb all these creations?" I asked. I felt a little strange talking to my charm, but it seemed to be listening.

It gave a little chime which felt like a yes.

I made a quick walkie talkie and then addressed the assembled host. <beep> "Penny feels like she can be a home for you and your power. Do I have a volunteer to test this?" <beep>

Instantly all hands and tails raised and the, "Wheeeing," started again. They seemed excited by the idea. I was winging things at this point, so a cautious experiment was in order. I pointed to a little miner close to me. He flew over, perched on my palm, then put his hand on Penny. There was a little pop and he was gone.

"Are you okay, Penny?" I asked. She gave a little trill in reply. It sounded happy, so again I assumed it was a yes.

I didn't want her contaminated with the purple golem magic either, even if she thought she could handle it. I had an idea.

I addressed all the little people and worms again. <beep> "I don't want any purple magic getting into Penny. Can you see if you can clean this up and get rid of it?" <beep> In Sandy's living room I'd talked to the granny like she was a real thinking person and her reply had shocked me. She'd understood me and found a way to help when I couldn't imagine one. Maybe there was more to my little guys than I knew.

There was a murmur of voices as all the miners and Ass Blasters started talking to each other. I couldn't pick out anything individually as they were all talking so fast. Then one Ass Blaster 2000 flew to the front, opened its mouth as wide as it would go, and seemed to take a deep breath. Then it closed its mouth and I saw a tiny bump of air moving down its length. It reached the back end, which made a cocking motion, and then blew off some foul purple gas. For its size, it was the fart to end all farts, and it even made a high-pitched flatulent sound.

I couldn't help but laugh. Potty humor at any size is still funny. It seemed to have worked, though. There wasn't any purple aura around it anymore. Now that one was successful, the others joined in, and soon the air was filled with thousands of purple farts.

I backed down the street to get away from the purple haze and the crew followed me, tooting all the way. Finally, it all died down and the Ass Blasters were all cleared of tainted magic. They moved off to the side and now it was the miners' turn. Again, there was a round of high-pitched conversation and then two miners flew forward.

They lined up with each other, and then slammed their pickaxes together. Where they locked together the diamond started shining with a purple light. It flared brighter and brighter and as it did so, the light became clearer. Finally, it died out and the miners were left clear of any stone-magic influence.

Now that there was a successful way to make it happen, the other miners squared off and soon the whole street glowed with purple and white light. I made a mental note to make this easier next time. In addition to communication and flight, I needed a way for my little peeps to decontaminate from any hostile magic.

Penny flared up with light again, and any of the creations that had pure magic started flying over and merging with her. This went on for several minutes. I hadn't realized how many thousands of magical constructs had come from this and it took a while to process everyone.

Finally, the last of the little people merged, and Penny wrapped herself around my finger again. She seemed slow and sleepy. She had just absorbed a huge amount of power and I was worried about her. I hoped she was going to be okay.

"You did good, Penny," I told her. "Thank you for all your help." She gave a single trill. "Go to sleep, or whatever it is you need to do to recover. I got it from here."

She seemed to give a little sigh and then I felt nothing more.

After all the activity, that street now felt very quiet. There were a few streetlights providing illumination, but suddenly I was aware of how many shadows were around me. I'm not afraid of the dark, but after what had just happened, I was a bit on edge.

There was one more thing to handle before heading home, and that was the dark orb lying on the sidewalk. That was all that was left of the once hulking rock golem. It was a shiny black sphere, about three inches in diameter, and it didn't appear to have any sort of power at all.

I kicked it lightly with my foot and jumped back. Nothing happened other than it rolling a few feet. I examined it with my magic sight, but it seemed completely inert. There wasn't any glow or magic to be found. I didn't want to touch it with my bare hands, and I didn't want to leave it on the sidewalk, so I took off my shirt and wrapped it around the orb.

Nothing happened, so I decided to look closer. I thought the surface was dimpled, but really it was covered with runes. They looked like the strange writing on the purple bands around the golem.

I took a peek at the inside of the orb and gasped in shock. I'd seen the inside of Sandy's rune. It had a few magical symbols that filled with magic and caused it to work. I wasn't sure exactly what I was looking at, but the inside of this orb was filled with hundreds and hundreds of symbols. They were laid out in neat patterns and tiny lines connected them in a maze. This had to be a charm on a level that was beyond anything I'd seen yet. Of course, I'd only seen one other real charm before. I was so new at everything and I wondered what Sandy would make of this.

I made sure the orb was bundled safely in my shirt, still not wanting to touch it directly, and started heading north. I'd stayed on one street running south, so I just needed to keep heading north and eventually I'd be home.

I didn't recognize the neighborhood at all, and after a half hour of walking, I still didn't. How far had I run? Obviously being chased by a giant stone monster will cause you to lose track of distance. I walked another half hour and I was getting tired of it all. Winning the battle had felt amazing, but now I was off that high and just wanted to be home.

That's when I felt the cold dark breath of the grave.

I knew that feeling. It meant a remnant was getting ready to cause problems. I was out on my own, at night, in a strange neighborhood, and the last thing I needed was my personal poltergeist to make an appearance.

I picked up the pace to a medium jog. I needed to get back to the House before this thing hit. It felt different than the last time. This one felt a bit weaker, and it was taking longer to manifest. It didn't feel like a hurricane of force like the previous one. Instead it felt like a whisper of evil. Like someone was stalking me, and they were in no hurry to pounce. After a few minutes I could see the smoke in the air, keeping pace with me.

I also recognized my first landmark. I knew where I was, and I wasn't that far from the park. I picked up the pace even more. If I could make it back to the House then Tyler could take care of this thing. As if it knew its time was limited, the remnant manifested faster. The night got cold, and I could see my breath. Then it got colder still. I was freezing.

I didn't know it was possible to shiver and run, but that was what I was doing. The smoke was thick now, and I could feel it sucking the life out of me. I was shaking too much to run when I saw the park ahead of me. I just needed to get Annabeth, make it through the park, and then I would be at the House. I was close.

I dropped out of the run and began stumbling through the park. If anyone saw me, they'd think I was drunk as a skunk. I looked like a hammered freshman coming back from a frat party, but I was on my feet and still moving.

I got to where Annabeth should have been, but she wasn't there. Hopefully she had regained consciousness and headed home. I could see the lights of the House through the trees when I fell. I tried to get up, but I was shaking too hard. The smoke whispered to me, "*Stay down. Just relax. This will all be over soon.*"

There was no way in hell I was letting that happen. My only option was to crawl, so crawl I did.

Hand over hand, I dragged myself closer to safety. The analytical side of myself noted that crawling wasn't so bad. At least I wasn't going to fall over.

This struck me as funny, and I started laughing. It sounded a bit crazy to my ears, like the Joker had hit me on my funny bone. This had been a rough night, but there was no way a remnant was taking me down now. I only had about ten yards left, then the road, then I would be in the front yard of the House. I was going to make it.

Then I heard a strange chattering noise. I looked up to see a huge groundhog glaring at me. I'd seen groundhogs before, and I usually thought they looked cute. Not this one. It was at least twice the size of a regular groundhog, and it glowed. This thing was magical. The chattering noise was the sound of it grinding its teeth together.

"That's not scary at all," I thought sarcastically. Usually groundhogs are defensive little creatures, and they run and hide. They only fight when they are cornered, and then they fight viciously. They have long claws for tunneling through the dirt and powerful teeth to bite through nuts and roots. I did not want to mess with him, especially in my condition.

I could see the smoke circling around it. I guess my remnant figured it couldn't win on its own and was calling in reinforcements. Maybe it was making me seem like a tasty nut or a troublesome predator. Either way, I clearly had Mr. Hog's attention. I kept crawling as he made a barking noise and two more mammoth groundhogs showed up. They were magical too, and just as big.

At first, they just watched me. Then the smoke started circling around them, and they started moving toward me. Crap. There was no way I could out-crawl them. I did NOT want to get mauled by giant magical groundhogs right now. I just wanted to get home.

I crawled faster and tried to get to my feet and run. I was too weak and shaking too badly. The cold was seeping into my bones, and I couldn't feel my hands or feet anymore.

They were just a few feet away when a little hissing ball of fur jumped over the top of me and got between us. It was a kitten, actually a tiny kitten that still had its baby fur. It was fuzzed up, tail out straight, and hopping sideways. It was mad. It was pure attitude. It was going to rip those groundhogs limb from limb if they took one more step.

It was so unexpected that everyone froze. The little black and white kitten probably only weighed about two pounds. It was facing off against three powerful groundhogs who were easily ten times its size. They looked at all that attitude and looked at me like, *"What the hell is this?"*

I had no idea what this was or why I suddenly had a teeny ferocious protector.

The darkness moved first. It sent a patch of inky blackness to take over the cat just like it had the groundhogs. I didn't want to lose my little guy. He was on my side and I didn't have a lot going for me at the moment.

I don't know who was more surprised, me or the remnant, when the darkness reached the cat and he slashed it with his claws. It shouldn't have affected smoke, but the remnant let out a shriek and the patch of darkness vanished. The kitten pounced on the next column of smoke, which happened to be the one connecting me and the groundhogs. He tore it up.

The remnant screamed bloody murder and the smoke around the groundhogs vanished. They looked at each other like, *"What the heck are we doing here?"* and turned and ran into the shadows.

The remnant was weakened, but not done with me yet. It curled around me and doubled down on the cold. I was shivering so badly I couldn't even crawl. I closed my eyes and tried to get control of myself. I had to beat this if I was going to live.

I was still fighting hard when I felt a warm raspy tongue on my face. The kitten was licking me in fast urgent strokes. Then he paused, and I felt his little paw touch me. The darkness hissed and retreated. It didn't retreat a lot, but it was enough.

I got my arms and legs under me again and started crawling. We made it to the road, and I didn't stop. I just hoped that someone wouldn't run me over as I laboriously made my way across the pavement. My black and white companion followed me the whole way, whining and licking everywhere he could reach. He beat back the cold and kept me going.

I made it to the sidewalk and then to the front lawn of the House. I could feel when I pushed through the House wards and a few moments later Tyler ran out and got me. He picked me up in his strong arms and carried me to my room. Once there he undressed me, got naked himself, and then crawled into bed with me.

I started bawling. This night had just been too much for me to handle. Now that I was safe, all my emotions started leaking out of me.

His body heat felt like the sun on a warm summer day. I basked in his natural glow, so very glad to be home again. He held me close, rubbing me and making soothing noises, until the shivering stopped.

I meant to say thank you and find out what had happened to Annabeth, but when the tears finally dried up, I just fell asleep.

10

Perfect Morning

I love waking up slowly. It's the perfect way to start the day.

One moment you're sleeping, the next you're aware of your warm safe space and a bit of the world around you. Then the day slowly loads itself into your brain and when you get up it seems a natural thing to do. It beats waking up with an alarm clock any day.

This morning it was the sun that tipped me over to wakefulness. I could feel my bedroom was filled with light, happy to start the day. Actually, it might not have been morning. The sun seemed to be really bright. That was okay; a late start was fine too.

I had strong arms around me, and I kept my eyes closed, enjoying the snuggle. A few moment later it occurred to me that it was probably Tyler, doing his incubus thing. I touched my magic, and I could feel him very slowly pulling something from me.

Thank goodness he was here. I couldn't imagine fighting the remnants on my own. Suddenly I remembered the night before. That had been crazy. I must have tensed because Tyler kissed the back of my neck and gave me a squeeze.

I felt something on my nose too, something soft. I let my eyes open gently, to be greeted by the sight of a kitten on my pillow. He was white belly to the sky, one paw on my nose, and head thrown back, fast asleep. It was the cutest thing I had ever seen.

I took it all in for a long moment, just breathing and being in my safe place. Then the cuteness was too much for me and I had to rub the belly. There was only room for two fingers, but I lightly stroked his tiny tummy. He gave a big stretch, yawned like his head was folding in half, and then latched onto my hand. His little claws were sharp. I switched from the belly to his head and his eyes closed in contentment. A throaty purring filled the room. It got even louder as I worked my way down his back. Clearly this cat was loving my lovin'.

"I think he likes you," Tyler said.

"This little guy saved my life last night," I replied. I scooched around on my back so I could talk to Tyler. He was as close as the kitten, and just as cute, although in an entirely different way. I found myself studying his face. It was perfect. Warm chocolate eyes, long brown lashes, full eyebrows that arched just right without looking like they had been plucked. A nose that was cute, but not feminine, and lips that curved up slightly in the corner so it looked like he was always smiling. If someone had sculpted the perfect face, this would be it. He was the Mona Lisa of men.

I must have been studying him too long because he poked me. I'm ticklish so I jumped. This disturbed the kitten who glared at both of us. I picked it up and sat it on my chest. I started rubbing it again, and its eyes closed in contentment, loud purring on full blast.

"So, what happened last night?" Tyler asked. I told him everything: Annabeth's charms, her getting kicked by the golem, my mad run through the city, the remnant attacking, and the kitten showing up to save me. I thought he would be shocked by how crazy violent it was. Instead he reacted like it was an adventure.

"Does crazy stuff like that happen all the time?" I asked. I was new to this supernatural thing, but it seemed to me that my life shouldn't constantly be in danger.

"It seems to go in waves," he said. "Sometimes it's one adventure after another. Sometimes a whole year goes by and nothing much happens. You'll learn to roll with it. As long as you don't die you can recover from just about anything."

That was sort of comforting. I was looking forward to life being less exciting. Hopefully that would happen soon.

"So how long have I been sleeping?" I asked.

"About twelve hours or so. I've been here, working on your remnants the whole time. Want to hear some good news?"

"Of course."

"Your escapade last night made one of the lesser remnants come to the surface in a big way. I was able to completely clean it out of your system. I've also been working on the weakest one, and it's almost gone."

That was awesome news. Life would be so much better without these poltergeists stalking me. One down, three still to go. Without disturbing the kitten, I gave Tyler a gentle high five.

"I found your shirt and the golem core. I didn't want it rolling around, so I put it in your dresser drawer."

I thanked him. The last thing I wanted was for someone to find it and activate it somehow.

"You should probably show that to Sandy as soon as possible. I'm a natural, not a mage, so I don't know how dangerous it is. She'll have a better clue of what you are dealing with."

That sounded like a very good idea. I didn't want to activate it and have the golem coming after me again.

"How is Annabeth doing?" I asked.

"She's okay. She was worried about you, of course. Sandy is taking care of her. Last I heard, she was up for a while and now she's sleeping again. Sandy said she's got some big bruises and she's sore, but nothing is broken."

That was great to hear. I was afraid the golem kick had done more damage. Thank goodness it hadn't kicked her twice.

Tyler's naked body was still resting up against me and his hand was absently making little circles on my abs. My body was liking this—liking it a lot.

"Where are you from?" I asked, attempting to keep my mind occupied with innocent things.

"I'm from another House," he said, and left it at that.

"What other House?"

"It's probably best that you don't know." He smiled to take the sting out of his words. "I have clashed with a lot of supernaturals over the years and it's probably best that people don't know too much about me. If they don't know where I live, then they can't find me."

That made sense. I'm sure he'd been asked it a lot, but there was one thing I really wanted to know.

"Are you with someone? Do you have a boyfriend?" Then a thought occurred to me. "Or a girlfriend?"

He smiled and gave me a half hug. "Sort of. And no, I'm not going to tell you about them either."

Sort of—what did that mean? Did he have someone or not? He was so far out of my league, though. He was just here to do a job. I'm sure anything more than that was just wishful thinking on my part.

"They don't mind you doing all . . . this?" I gestured at our naked bodies together.

"Nope. I'm an incubus. That's what I do. It's how I contribute to the House and gain my power. I couldn't be in a relationship with someone that wanted to keep me all to themselves. That just wouldn't work." He paused. "I can tell you that I've spent more time with you than any other person for a long time, and it's driving me a bit crazy."

"Oh, really?"

"I eat negative energy, usually through sex. It's what I'm good at. In your case you have a huge heaping lot of it, but I can only take one little sip at a time. It's like being at a huge buffet and only having a tiny spoon."

He was driving me crazy too. My body was awake and ready for some man time, and there was a perfectly good one lying right next to me that I couldn't touch.

"I can promise you this, though." His beautiful eyes locked on me intently. "There will be a time where the last remnant is too weak to resist, and when that comes, I'm going to shag you like you have never been shagged before. You're going to be screaming my name and begging God for mercy before I am through with you. It will be the single greatest night of your young life; I promise you that."

His words sent a shiver through me. I wanted that to happen, and I wanted it now.

"In the meantime, I'd better go." He gave me a quick peck on the cheek and hopped out of bed. "I don't want to take down the wall again."

That reminded me; I realized my bedroom wall was back to normal.

"The wall. It's fixed!"

"Yep. I'm sure the House took care of it," Tyler said on his way out the bedroom door.

That seemed like such a strange thing to say. I'm sure he meant that John had taken care of it.

Also, was he just going to walk out of my apartment naked? You just don't do that. This whole place was a bit strange.

"Oh, by the way." He walked back in again. "You need to think about food and water for your little friend. Sandy has cats so she probably has something you can use short term."

He was fully clothed. Blue shorts, white shirt, sandals. Looked like he walked right out of a J.Crew catalogue. How the hell did he do that?

"Bye for now, little fella." Tyler waved at the kitten on my chest, who blinked back with lazy eyes. He left and then I heard my apartment door open and close.

I lay there for a few more minutes, absorbing the last of the perfect morning. Finally, I got up and started the day.

My little companion followed me everywhere. He sat on the top of the toilet and watched me shower. The toilet paper that was resting there quickly landed on the floor. He found the stream of water fascinating as I was brushing my teeth and shaving. He must have been thirsty too because he drank for a good while.

For Netflix and breakfast, he climbed up the back of the sofa and rested on my shoulder. Then he played Swat the Spoon as I tried to eat cereal. It made for a messy, milky time. I really wasn't used to this level of attention. My time was quiet time. I just wanted to chill.

He was so freakin' cute, though. Clearly he liked me and wanted to spend time with me. I found that oddly flattering.

After breakfast I dressed, grabbed the golem core and my little guest, and headed up to see Sandy.

11

Saving Penny

Sandy instantly fell in love with the kitten. There was lots of
cooing and kisses, and the little guy was clearly having a good time.
Sandy put him down by the food bowl, and he ate like he was
starving, which he probably was. Sandy's two cats, Snowy and
Biscuit, weren't exactly sure how to handle him. Finally, they just
decided to ignore him, and that seemed to work.

Sandy said she had some spare litter, food, and a couple plastic
containers to use for food and water. She didn't have an extra litter
box, though, and suggested I visit John to see what he could
repurpose.

I started telling her the story of the previous night while she
made me a sandwich. It wasn't just any old sandwich either. She had
homemade raisin bread, which she sliced thick, then added ham,
turkey, cheddar, and mayo. I'd had breakfast already, but this was
amazing. I didn't realize how hungry I was until I wolfed the whole
thing down.

When I got to the part of the story with the golem core, I pulled it
out to show her. Her eyes lit up.

"Oh wow!" She took the orb from me very gently and began examining it in detail.

"This is just amazing! I was sure charms like this existed, but I've never seen anything like it before. Just look at the size of it."

"I thought you would like it," I said. "I don't know anything about charms, but this one seems pretty special."

"It's in a whole other class from the types of charms I make or that I've seen," she said. "Mine are single-use charms that only do one thing and rely on the caster to determine the final result. For example, let's say you have a charm that makes light. You need the right rune for the kind of light you want. For example, do you want a blue light or a white light? Do you want light and heat or just light? Once you have the right rune and power it, the caster has to shape the result. So, do you want a soft glow for a while? A harsh, blinding flash? A directional light like a flashlight, or a general radius of light like a lantern?

"A charm that makes light sounds so simple but there is a lot that goes into it once you start thinking about it. The golem was on a whole different level. It actually had a limited intelligence and performed on its own without the caster being present. That meant it had runes that could detect Annabeth's magic. Then it had runes that allowed it to have arms and legs, and to move around. I guess it also had runes that pulled the rocks together. Once it had a target, it knew to move toward that target and attack it.

"Whoever made this not only knows a lot more runes than I do, but they also know how to link charms in a stable way. I've tried to link charms before, but even two links make everything very unstable. When it blows up, it really explodes. This thing must have hundreds of runes all linked together, and somehow it all works. That is sophistication that I haven't seen from a charm before.

"The other thing is that charms have to be made in one shot. You form the image of what you want in your mind, and then cast it into a vessel. If you get the image or casting wrong by even a little bit, the whole thing could blow up. Given the size and complexity of this core, I'm very sure that whoever made this couldn't have cast it in one go. They have to have done it a piece at a time. If I can figure out how they did that, then I could really make some powerful charms."

That was a lot of information, but even with my limited magical knowledge it made sense. Sandy was going to be the rare type of teacher that made learning look easy.

"This might be a dumb question, but isn't there a book or something that you can read to learn about all this?" I asked.

Sandy shook her head. "I wish there were. The supernatural world is built on power, and knowledge is power. The more power you have, the safer you are, and the more valuable you are to your supernatural family. Everyone is looking for an advantage, and once you find one you don't share it with the world. If you do, then everyone has it and it's not an advantage anymore.

"The magical community is built on the apprentice system. Masters hoard their knowledge so that they have lots of apprentices working for them and doing whatever they want. I've seen masters use their students as sex slaves, assassins, soldiers, or servants for their mansions. There are no real rules, so if you have power and someone else wants it, then you can ask for just about anything and get it.

"I was very lucky. My teacher saw how eager I was to learn and instead of using that against me, she taught me what she knew. The more I see of the world, the more grateful I am to her. Whenever I find out something new for myself, I always make sure and pass it back to her."

"Wow," I said. "She sounds like a remarkable woman."

"She is," Sandy replied. "She not only taught me magic, she got me out of my funk after my transition and showed me how to be a better person. She's the reason I'm head of this branch of the House today. The House picked me, but she molded me into the right person for the job. When everything settles down here, we'll have to travel to Chicago and you can meet her."

I hadn't had a home in a long time, but Sandy, Annabeth, and John seemed like such happy and warmhearted people. I liked being here. Sandy was doing for me what her teacher had done for her. Maybe someday I'd be strong enough to help someone else. I hoped so.

"So, do you recognize any of the runes in the core?" I asked.

"I don't recognize any of this stuff," she said. "It looks like some sort of writing rather than runes. I'll do a search on it and see if it is some sort of old language. Google image search has helped me out more than once."

"I didn't mean the writing. I meant the actual runes on the inside."

She stared at it for a long time, then put it down frustrated. "I can see there is something in there, but just don't have the ability to see it. It's all fuzzy, like I need glasses."

"How are you going to get to the runes then?"

"I'll have John break it down for me later. He can probably take it apart without destroying much of it. Then I'll take pictures of the different parts and reconstruct it as best I can."

I'd planned on giving the orb to Sandy to keep it safe, but I didn't really want her breaking it apart. If this was such a great find I didn't want even a part of it ruined.

"I can see all the details inside it, so how about we figure out a way to duplicate them? That way you have something to study and the orb doesn't get torn apart?"

"That could work." Sandy sounded much happier about this option too. "I have an idea. Let's try modeling clay and see if that will work."

She fetched a block of clay from her workshop along with some modeling tools and I got to work. I picked what I thought was one of the easier runes, but I quickly discovered I was not a sculptor—not even close. The lumpy misshapen thing on the table looked nothing like the beautiful, graceful rune I saw in the orb.

After ten minutes I gave up, at least on the sculpting. I could tell Sandy was disappointed, so we kept talking about materials we could use. I was pretty sure I was going to have to use my little magical characters to do this, so to conserve magic we needed to keep the result as small as possible. Sandy didn't like the idea of using my personal magic for this, but she really wanted to study the results. Apparently, finding new runes and triggers was like finding gold. Maybe even more valuable than that.

We talked materials and finally settled on wax. I needed something that could be molded fairly easily but would keep its shape and all the details. At least until Sandy could take a picture of it. I'd suggested just using one of my little guys to morph into the shape of the interior, but Sandy vetoed that right away. That would put my magic in the shape of all those runes. Who knew what would happen then? It needed to be something detailed and non-magical, so wax it was.

Sandy laid out some wax paper on the counter, put away the modeling clay and tools, and then brought out a block of wax. I wasn't sure how much energy it would take to shape wax, so I decided to just do a small part of the orb. I examined it for a bit and noticed that part of the core was broken down in layers of runes and lines. I picked one layer that seemed to have a good variety as our test subject.

Sandy got her phone ready to take a video and we were good to go. For some reason I was nervous. I took a deep breath, let it out, and began.

First, I made my master sculptor. The runes themselves were tiny, only about an eighth of an inch, so I made him double that height. I gave him a white beard since he was a wise and skilled old man. Next, I added jeans, a plaid shirt, a leather apron to keep him clean, and nice work boots. I started to add a work belt and tools but ended up taking that back. I needed him to work quickly and he needed to see into the orb, so I went with more of a cyborg feel. I replaced his right eye with a scanner that looked right out of Terminator. It would be able to see inside the orb, scan it, and then outline it in 3D in the wax. I gave him two metal arms, both of which had Edward Scissorhands blades on the end. Then, I gave him two more arms that had glowing hot hands for fine details and shaping. Finally, I added a cold cannon on his shoulder for cooling the wax down. I didn't add a duplicator ring or anything like that. The wax wasn't magical, and all the power had already been sucked out of the core, so there wasn't anything to absorb to power the duplication. If I needed another master sculptor, I'd make a new one, maybe with a few more modifications depending on how this one did. I did add a belt of levitation so he could precisely maneuver around the wax, as well as a necklace of communication. He didn't have any normal hands so using a walkie talkie just felt wrong.

I looked over my little master artist. Was I missing anything? I realized I needed him to act quickly, so I modified his boots so that they had little wings on them. Now he was as fast as Hermes. He seemed good to go, so I filled him up with magic and turned him loose.

He was a serious cyborg artist, so there wasn't any *wheeeing* this time. Instead he flexed all his arms and tested his tools. Then, his cyborg eye scanned the layer of the orb I indicated and he got to work. As he started drilling into the wax it quickly became clear he needed another helper. The loose wax was getting in the way and I hadn't given him anything to clear out what he'd already chipped off.

Keeping with the cyborg theme, I made a little motorized wheelbarrow with lots of mechanical arms. It could pick up anything from a large chunk to the finest speck of wax and dump it into its bin. I thought about adding thrusters for movement, but the final sculpture was going to be pretty fragile. I didn't want the cyborg wheelbarrow's turbulence to cause any problems. Instead, I added antigravity wheels, because in my world, anti-gravity works. I love my magic. The final touch was a communicator in the handle. It seemed good, so I filled it with magic and turned it loose.

The cyborg wheelbarrow was perfect. It cleared up the loose wax in a precise and careful way. It wasn't that fast, though, so I made four more of them. That seemed to be enough to keep up with the cyborg sculptor. Sandy was videoing the whole thing and my part was done so I got to sit back and watch.

This was so much better than my attempts with the modeling clay. The runes were tiny, but perfectly formed. They looked almost as elegant in the wax as they did in the golem core. Even the tiny lines connecting them together were represented. They were so fragile that bumping the counter or any shaking at all would probably shatter them.

"This is amazing! Just amazing!" Sandy said over and over. She was like a kid in a candy shop. One thing that surprised her right away was that the runes had protrusions. They were in 3D. All the runes she had seen had been from drawings, so they were in 2D. This was rocking her world.

Everything ran smoothly for about five minutes. The level was about a quarter finished when the master sculptor stopped, turned to me, and bowed as he faded out. I was shocked. That had never happened before.

I made another one and he started working again. This time I kept a close eye on him and noticed that four minutes later he was starting to slow down. He also didn't look as solid. I pushed more magic into him and he picked up the pace again. Just to be safe, I pushed magic into the cyborg wheelbarrows too. I'd never had a creation of mine just fade away before. Of course, I couldn't remember using one for such a detailed and time-consuming task either. If I couldn't use the duplicator rings, then there was definitely a limit on how much magic I could use.

I was a bit worried about how much magic this project was taking up. Before becoming a supernatural, I used to only be able to make one little guy. Now I'd just made five of them and I was refilling them with magic. I didn't want to get into low magic problems again. That had majorly sucked. I was really glad I'd decided to just do a small part of the core. I certainly didn't have enough to do all of it.

After about twenty minutes, the project was done. I was feeling a bit lightheaded from the power loss, but the layer of runes was carved into the top of the wax block in fine detail. It was a work of art and Sandy had the whole thing on video. She switched out her phone for a real camera, one of those high-end ones with the removable lenses. Then she took lots and lots of pictures from every angle she could find. In the meantime, I had the cyborgs merge with Penny. She wasn't talking to me or communicating in any way, and it was starting to really worry me.

Inevitably, Sandy's cats showed up to see what all the fuss was about. Sandy grabbed a charm and sent a wave of power toward the wax block. It encased the block and froze it somehow. It looked murky, so further pictures were out of the question for now. Sandy assured me it would keep the wax structure safe until she unfroze it again. Kitten was too small to get up on the counter, so he sat at my feet and chirped at me until I picked him up. Then he snuggled in my arms and purred.

We went over the pictures on her camera. She had plenty of photos from lots of angles to recreate these runes. I thought she wanted to run off to her workshop right away and get started but I needed her help with Penny.

I finished up my tale of the previous night. How Penny had absorbed the League of Flying Miners and the Ass Blaster 2000s and then went quiet, how I met my kitten, and how Tyler had completely taken out one remnant.

Sandy decided that deserved a celebration, so we poured some wine and toasted to: one down and three to go. We also talked about the kitten for a bit. I couldn't see any sort of magical power around him. Sandy tested and couldn't find any either. If he could hurt a remnant, though, there was something special about him.

I didn't have a name for him. Sandy suggested several, but nothing seemed to really click. For now, he was just Kitten. I'd never had a pet before, but Sandy said it was easy. Just take care of food, water, and number one and number two. Other than that, the cat adopts you and they will let you know what you can do for them.

The kitten sensed we were talking about him, and he looked up at me adoringly. I'd stopped loving on him while we were talking, so I started up again. Sandy said he was training me already. We laughed about it, but secretly I started to wonder if it wasn't true.

Finally, I got to talk about Penny. It wasn't until she stopped communicating that I realized how much I missed her presence. Previously she had mostly made little happy sounds about what was going on and I could feel her presence on my finger. Now she just felt like a regular metal ring and it felt weird. It was like leaving the apartment without my phone. I'd only had her for a little while, but it felt wrong.

"I have an idea of what is amiss, but first let me ask you a question," Sandy said. "Have you added more of your magic to the charm after you created her?"

"No," I replied. "It never even occurred to me to do that. I knew I didn't want to take too much magic out of her in case she went back to just being a regular charm. Come to think of it, no one specifically said not to do that, but it just felt like a mistake to pull too much."

"I don't have a fully aware charm myself," Sandy said. "Sometime soon we will have to talk about your experience and I'll have to make one. In the meantime, I do have an idea of what might be going on." She thought for a moment. "I have the perfect idea for an analogy for all this. Hang on."

She disappeared into her workshop again and returned with a large glass vase. I was curious to see her workshop. It seemed to have just about everything in there. She then went to the kitchen cabinet and took out a clear shot glass. Out of a drawer came some food coloring.

"You don't have to go to all this trouble," I said. "You can just tell me what you're thinking. I'm sure I can figure it out."

"Oh, this is no trouble at all," she said. "I love a good analogy and it's rare that one this perfect comes along. Now listen, learn, and let's have some fun."

I felt like we were putting together a science experiment for school. It was kinda fun.

"In many ways magic acts like water. Not always, but it in this case it will be just fine." She set the shot glass in front of me. "Let's say this shot glass is you, and the water is your magic." She filled up the shot glass with water.

"What color did you say your magic was again?" she asked.

"It's emerald green with a sapphire blue running through it," I replied. "It's mostly green, though."

"Let's just stick with one color for now. Green it is," she said. She added several drops of food coloring to the shot glass until the water was a nice dark green.

"Let's say the vase is Penny. You only need a little bit of magic to infuse a charm." She poured a tiny bit of green water from the shot glass into the vase. "However, you kept going until the charm was aware." She dumped most of the water into the vase. It didn't fill it up very much. I didn't know if Sandy had planned on this being to scale. If so, she thought Penny had a lot of capacity to store magic.

"You survived the evening and your magic reserves gradually filled back up again." She filled up the shot glass with water and then added more food coloring until it was back to a dark green.

"Everything was good until a thousand or more of your little creations merged back with Penny. The very best possible news is that it was only pure magic that merged with her." Sandy put the vase in the sink and filled it most of the way with tap water. Then she put it back on the counter in front of me.

"Analogies are great because they can give us insight into what the problem is and how to fix it. So now it's your turn. What do you think the problem with Penny is?" Sandy was in full-on teacher mode.

I looked at the vase and it was pretty clear to see. The water in the vase only had a hint of green in it. Sandy had added so much clear water that the green was diluted down and barely visible.

"Penny doesn't have a concentration of my magic anymore," I said. "She's mostly pure magic which doesn't have any personality or connection to me."

"You got it in one," Sandy congratulated. "Now, how are you going to fix it?"

Hmmmm. How was I going to fix this? My first thought was to find a way to get rid of the extra magic in Penny. Then she would be back to the normal concentration of magic as before. If I suggested that, though, Sandy would just pour some of the water down the drain. The remaining water would still just be a light green. If this analogy held true, then the energy had already mixed in Penny and there wasn't any way to get the pure energy back out again. Plus, it seemed a waste to get rid of pure magic.

I picked up my shot glass with rich dark water and poured it into the vase. Immediately the water in the vase got darker.

"That's a great first step," Sandy encouraged. "It certainly helps the problem. But it doesn't completely fix it. Now what?" She looked at me intently. Obviously, I was being judged here. I felt like I had messed up the other night, so this was my chance to make a better impression.

The good news was I liked problems like this. Figuring out the best solution was why I was good at Sudoku and in the cutthroat world of poker.

Obviously, I needed to get more green into the vase. The only source of green was the shot glass which was now empty. I could fill up the shot glass with water, add food coloring, and then dump it into the vase. That would be like giving Penny everything I had, waiting until I felt better, and then doing it again. I remembered how gray and cold the world had seemed without magic. I didn't want to go through that again. Actually, the vase was a lot larger than the shot glass. I'd be doing it again and again and again. Not fun.

There was another option, though.

I picked up the vase and poured some of the water back into the shot glass. Then I added green food coloring until it was dark and pretty, and then I poured some of that back into the vase. I kept that up and soon the water in the vase was much darker. It still wasn't the same dark green, but it was a lot better.

"Excellent solution!" Sandy beamed at me. "I know this is an analogy, but the solution is pretty close to the real thing. Let's give it a try. First, pull in some magic from your charm. Don't pull too much on your first go."

I concentrated on Penny. I couldn't really feel that she was awake, but I could access the magic inside her. I gave a gentle pull and absorbed some of the magic.

"How does the magic feel?" Sandy asked.

"It feels . . . bright," I replied. "I can feel that it is new magic and doesn't match mine. Keeping with the water analogy, it feels cooler, like it's not at body temperature."

"That sounds right," Sandy said. "Keep in mind this is new territory for me too. I have the theory of magic, but I haven't pulled in magic this way before myself, so let me know if you feel anything is off."

"Sure thing," I agreed. Sandy might not have personal experience with this but what she was saying made sense.

"Okay, now push some magic back into Penny. Keep the transfer small until we make sure there aren't any problems."

I nodded and pushed some magic back into Penny. I didn't get any response from her, but we had just started. If the color of the water in the vase was any indication, I had a long way to go before she was back to normal.

"Now how do you feel? Can you still feel the magic you pulled?"

Feeling magic like this was new to me. I didn't think of it as something separate from me. It just was.

"I feel good," I said. "Magic seems normal. I don't feel dizzy or weird or anything like that. I can't feel the magic I pulled anymore. It all just feels like my normal magic."

"Good," Sandy said. "Let's try it again, but this time pull a slightly bigger amount of magic."

We did the routine of pulling and pushing magic several more times, each time with a greater amount of magic. I quickly got to the point where I could feel the new magic sticking around a lot longer. When I pushed magic back into Penny some of that new magic was going back into her again, which wasn't the point of the whole thing.

Sandy then asked me to pull the new magic through me and all the way to my left hand. That didn't work so well. The new magic kept breaking up and getting lost in transition. I tried a couple different ideas, but nothing really worked until Sandy suggested spinning the new magic into a ball, then moving it. That did the trick.

That still wasn't great, though, because it then left me with a knot of cold, white magic in my other hand. Going into lecture mode, Sandy decided to teach me an advanced magic technique.

"There are two things you want to do as a magic user," Sandy instructed. "You want to have access to more magic for spells, and you want to be able to cast from the area of your body that will give it the most affect. Both of these aims can be achieved by creating several loci of magic.

"A locus of magic is a compact core of magic that can be used to activate charms or give you a boost to your physical abilities. Most magic users create one automatically in their dominant hand. You are right-handed, and Penny is on your right hand, so I'm pretty sure you already have the start of a locus there. Let's keep this simple and create one in your left hand."

"Feel the magic in your left hand. Feel it pooling in your hand like you were going to levitate a penny."

I used to do penny levitation every day, so this part was easy. I'd usually started with my right hand, but I would often switch the penny back and forth. I nodded at her to let her know I had it.

"Now take that energy and start swirling it, like it's a whirlpool."

That was pretty easy too. I'd imagined my energy like a fountain before so making it swirl was no big deal. I nodded again to let her know I was good to go.

"Now imagine the center of the whirlpool getting very dense. See if you can feel the difference with this denser magic."

I could! The magic felt more solid. Magic felt less like water and more like smoke to me. Maybe that is why the remnants were all dark and smoky.

It was hard to concentrate on this and keep it going so I just nodded at Sandy again. Was there more to do?

"Do you still have access to the ball of new magic you moved earlier?" Sandy asked.

I hadn't kept track of the new magic as I'd been working on my new locus, but now I was looking for it, I could still feel some of my Penny magic in a ball close to my left hand. I nodded at Sandy.

"Take the new magic and gradually unravel it. Think of it spinning in the opposite direction to your new locus of magic. As the magic unwinds from the temporary core it flows to your new core. Keep spinning your new locus and layer the white magic with your regular magic."

That was a lot to keep track of. Fortunately, I knew what Sandy was going for and I had a good imagination. I gradually unwound the knot of new magic from Penny and fed it to the locus I was creating. I was wondering if the new magic would dilute the magic in my new core, but it seemed to merge just fine. When I was done, my new locus felt dense, powerful, and all mine. This was cool! I let it keep spinning and turned my focus back to Sandy.

"Done!" I said. "Now what?"

"That's it," Sandy replied. "Now you just keep it going. Once you have mastered one locus, then you can make more."

"You say that like it's so simple. How do I keep this going all the time?" I asked. Even while talking to Sandy I could feel the locus starting to slip away.

"The idea is simple, but it's not easy," Sandy laughed. "It's one of the hardest things you'll do. It took me months of constant practice to get my first locus down pat. Just keep working at it."

I must have looked as dismayed as I felt because Sandy gave me a hug. "It will happen. I promise. You'll forget about your new locus of magic a lot at first. That's okay. Just get it spinning again and try to condense the core even more. The more you condense it, the more it sticks around. One day you will realize it is always there with little effort on your part.

"Try setting up little reminders for yourself to think about your new locus. For example, brush your teeth left-handed while concentrating on your magic. It takes longer, but you will certainly remember to spin your magic. In the short term, you need to be exchanging a lot of your magic with Penny's magic anyway. That's what this is really about. Creating a magic locus is just a bonus."

She's right. This was really about getting Penny back to being awake and aware again. Creating my own magical core was just something to help facilitate that.

Feeling much more hopeful and a bit overwhelmed, I was ready to take my leave when Sandy stopped me.

"There is one thing I really need your help with," Sandy said.

"Sure! Anything," I replied. She had already helped so much. I was just glad there was something, anything, I could do for her. Well, except give up a kidney. That would take some serious thought. Or kill someone. I wouldn't do that either.

I had some strange thoughts sometimes.

"As you know, I use my charms for magic. What you don't know is that charms are recharged in a charging circle. Since the House and the local mages are not on the best of terms, I haven't been able to recharge my charms, and now most of my charms are completely out of magic."

Sandy sighed and absentmindedly patted the charms on her wrist. "The charms for me are a lot like you and Penny. I'm used to feeling them there, charged and ready to go. I've been careful with how I use them, but still, there is only so far you can ration their power. At some point they are out of juice."

I could tell she was not happy about this. I know I wouldn't be if the situation were reversed. To be a mage without magic would suck.

"I'm happy to help any way I can," I said sincerely. "What do you need me to do?"

"Well, a charging circle is usually made up of at least seven and up to thirteen mages. Any less than that and the circle doesn't work well. Any more than that and there will be too many charms that need to be recharged. A circle can take a while and when there are a lot of mages with charms it can take forever."

"So how many mages can we get?" I asked.

"There's me, Annabeth, you if you will join, and John. Even though he's a natural, he can still stand in as a placeholder."

"Of course I'll join!" I said. "I have no idea what to do, but I'll do it to the best of my ability."

Sandy smiled at me warmly. "Thank you. We were able to make it work, although barely, with Jennifer. Annabeth is still new and not able to really push the magic. John can't feel the magic at all."

She looked at me with both resignation and hope. "You seem to have a good sense of magic flow already. I'm hoping that you can help me like Jennifer did and we can get at least a few charms back in working order.

"I feel like the mages are up to something. I'm not sure what it is, but I feel like cutting us off from a full magic circle was more than just pettiness. I feel like they are waiting for us to get weak enough and then they will do something." She shook her head. "I sound a bit paranoid, I know, and I'm not sure what they are planning. Maybe it's nothing. But my gut tells me something is up. I still need to prepare, but I would like to do it tonight. You need to see John anyway about a litter box, so have him bring you to the circle. He knows where it is."

I agreed and Sandy started bagging up some spare litter, cat food, and bowls for me. I looked at the vase and shot glass of green water and realized I'd just had my first magic lesson. It had gone well, I thought. I'd learned more about how magic worked and how to save my special charm, Penny. Sandy didn't seem disappointed in me, so I guess I'd done all right as a student. Overall, it was a very good afternoon.

She came back with a few bags of stuff and a sleepy kitten. I took it all, thanked her again for her help and support, promised to see her soon, and headed out.

12

Few Drinks with John

All I really wanted to do was spend a few hours working with magic. I had to get my kitten settled in, though, so instead I went back to my apartment and put him in my bed. He passed out like a baby. I made him a little nest in the covers and kissed his head. He felt so soft.

I got his food and water bowls set up and then set out to see John about a litter box. I headed downstairs to the basement. It seemed strange that John didn't have one of the premium apartments—or that's what I thought until I saw his door. It was massive. Solid wood with huge ornate iron hinges like you see on old castles. His door had presence. I guess he needed a big door for a big guy.

I knocked on it, heard nothing, and knocked again. I was about to leave when it opened and John greeted me with a happy smile, and almost nothing else. He was bare-chested, bare-legged, and wearing a pair of gym shorts that were obviously designed for a much smaller man. They were skintight, straining to provide some sort of decency, but also making it very clear he had nothing else beneath them.

He looked like Thor, only bigger, hairier, and even more manly, if that was even possible. He towered over me with his seven-foot height, and his arms were as big as my waist. I felt like I was in the presence of a god. Part of me wanted to kneel; part of me wanted to do bad, bad things to those shorts.

My brain was still trying to catch up to my hormones when Tyler slipped around John and out the door. He was only wearing a pair of shorts too. My brain shorted out and I think I started drooling. Two perfect men in their own way and I didn't know where to look first.

"Thanks for the good times," Tyler said, and hopped up to give John a kiss on the cheek.

"The pleasure is all mine," John said, and ruffled his hair.

"Hi Jason," Tyler said and kissed me on the cheek too. "Bye for now." He waved and disappeared down the hall.

I was in shock. Did these two just do what I thought they did?! I was speechless. Like literally, I couldn't say a word.

"Come on inside. Let's have a pint." John put his arm around me and pulled me inside. He smelled like sex and rain and fresh cut grass. I felt like I was being herded along by a thunderstorm as he guided me to a table and put a mug of beer in my hand.

I took a sip, because that is what you do, and my senses were hit with the taste of summer and sunshine. It was cool, refreshing, and delicious.

"What is this?" I asked.

"It's my own special lager," John replied. "I've been working on my own process for several years now." He went on for a bit about yeast and fermentation times and how much easier it was with all the new-fangled equipment these days. I tried to follow it all but I'm a beer drinker, not a beer maker.

It did give me a chance to look around his place. It was nothing like I thought a basement apartment would be. It was more like a Hobbit hole from the Lord of the Rings, or an English pub, although on a scale big enough for a seven-foot man. It was all wood arches, nooks and crannies filled with stuff, and thick rugs over hardwood floors. I felt like I was on a movie set or something.

I lost myself in watching John flex as he talked about his hobby. He liked to talk with his hands, and I liked to watch him talk with his hands. Before I knew it, my pint was empty and he poured me and himself another.

"I know you didn't come down here to hear me talk about beer, so what can I do for you?" John asked.

"Well, couple things," I said. I was still hung up on seeing him and Tyler together. The beer was making me feel a bit bold too, so I just came right out and asked.

"I guess first of all I'm kinda floored that you and Tyler . . ." I gestured. "You know . . ."

John threw his head back and roared with laughter. "That Tyler sure is something special. I haven't felt this good in a long time. I mean, sure, it's what he is, but he's damn good at it."

John gave me a wink. "You're driving him crazy too."

"What?" I said. "Me?"

"Yep. I think he is someone that usually has fun and moves on, leaving them better than before. He's stuck with you, though, and I think he's gotten to liking you a bit."

Tyler was starting to drive me crazy too. There are only so many times you can wake up with a naked god of a man in your bed before you have to do something about it. Hopefully the remnants would be gone soon.

"So, what's it like?" I asked. "I didn't even know what an incubus was before all this."

"There really aren't words," John said, staring off in the distance for a long moment. "His magic gets hold of you and suddenly you are in heaven. You know that feeling you get when you finally tell someone a secret that has been weighing you down? Or you cry yourself out and all you have left is hope?" I nodded. "It's like that, only times a hundred. Or maybe a thousand. You just feel good. Like you woke up to the best possible morning and there is nothing but adventure before you."

I could see that playing out right before me. John obviously felt good, happy, relaxed—almost giddy. We toasted Tyler and his health.

"So are all incubuses like that?" I asked.

"I tell you lad, if you see another incubus you'd best run away as far and as fast as you can. They are mean sons of bitches and they will drain you dry and leave you a husk."

I was shocked.

"Tyler is special. Like, House special. He only takes negative emotions and leaves you better than before. Normal incubuses take all your emotions and leave you a shell of what you were. They are crazy hungry too. I've seen a village after one of them went through there. It wasn't pretty."

We toasted Tyler again: May he always be on the side of what is good and right in this world.

"What do you mean by 'House special'?" I asked. "I'm new to all this so right now everything seems magical and different."

"That's just it," John said. "The House invites who it wants, and it seems to pick up the sups that are different. Special, if you will. I'm part mountain troll but I haven't already merged with the earth. Annabeth only hears magic. You have been doing magic since before you were a super. Sandy has crazy power levels. And, Tyler is a good incubus."

We toasted to being special.

"Don't get me wrong, not everyone in the House is a nice person. There are some right arse holes. I can tell you that."

We toasted arse holes: May they fall over in their own shite.

"Oh, by the way, I wanted to say thanks for taking care of the wall in my bedroom," I said.

"Oh that. It wasn't much," John replied. "The House took care of it. I'm called the handyman around here, but really the House doesn't need much help. I'm really here to provide moral support for Sandy and a strong hand if she needs it."

We toasted the House: To its health, or whatever health a House may have.

"So, are you and Sandy together?" I asked.

"Oh no, lad," John said. "She's way too independent for that. Having someone else to answer to just brings you down." He then gave me a broad wink.

I was confused. "So, you aren't together?" I said.

He tapped his nose. "You are on the money, lad. Don't want any of that around here." He then gave me another broad wink.

"I'm confused," I said. I really was. I didn't know if it was the beer, how close John was to me, or how he was sending mixed signals about Sandy. My brain was feeling a bit like mush.

"No need to be confused," John offered. "Sandy is a strong woman and head of this House. I'm her good friend and faithful companion. Both of us have had our pains in the past and we want no part in any sort of romantic entanglement." He looked all serious and shook his head solemnly. Then he nodded at me knowingly and gave me the broad wink again.

I gave up. Whatever was going on with him and Sandy was none of my business anyway.

We toasted strong women. Then toasted strong women that were something more. We laughed uproariously. Somehow this was very funny.

Something was rubbing up against me. I looked down and it was my little kitten. How had he gotten in here?

"Oh, I'm supposed to ask you about a litter box," I said. "I have a food and water bowl from Sandy but no litter box."

John reached way down and picked up the little ball of fur. It looked like quite a contrast, this tiny kitten and this huge mountain man. They bonded instantly, though. The kitten rubbed his head against John's furry chest and purred like a motor. Then he ended up on his back, chewing on John's fingers as he rubbed his belly.

We toasted kittens and furry bellies.

John stood up and moved farther into his apartment. "Let's see what we have. The House is always bringing me stuff so I'm sure I have something here we can use."

Sure enough, there was a huge pile of metal items in the back. I got up to follow him and somehow the floor wasn't steady. In fact, it was moving like the deck of a ship. Doing my best sailor imitation, I staggered after him.

John started sorting through what looked like junk to me. There were pieces of pipe, pocket watches, a highchair for a little kid, a stop sign, a metal lion that looked like it was ready to pounce, and even a potato peeler. The list went on and on.

John rooted around in the mess for a while, then finally held up an old metal pot looking thing. "Ah ha. This should do the trick."

"What is it?" I asked. It didn't look like anything I'd seen before.

"It's an old bed pan. They used to use these in hospitals when old people couldn't get out of bed and needed to poop. This will be perfect."

It didn't look perfect to me. I wasn't sure what a litter box should look like, but it certainly wasn't like that.

"Let's see now. We need the same function, just a different form." John began running his hands over the bedpan and talking to it. I just swayed and let him do his thing. It occurred to me that I'd normally think he was a bit crazy. All of life seemed to be crazy recently, so I just let it go and accepted that John was doing what he needed to do.

Sure enough, after a few moments, the bedpan started flexing. Then it folded on itself a few times, flattened out, and assumed more of a box-like shape. The front of the box was lower so the kitten could get inside, but the sides and back were higher to stop any random streams that might be flowing out. He put the box on the floor for Kitten to test it out. He hopped inside and seemed happy and curious.

John didn't stop there, though. He kept going and soon the top was decorated with a fine scroll work. He added little statues on the back. They were two Greek women pouring water out of a vase. It was like a statue you'd see in a fancy European garden. When he finished it was the most beautiful litter box I'd ever seen. It looked like a beautiful antique by a famous artist.

Kitten didn't care and proceeded to lie down and start licking his privates. I guessed this was as good a place as any to do that. John picked up the ornate litter box and we headed back to the beer table.

We got fresh pints and toasted litter boxes: May they always be clean; and being able to lick your own privates: It's a guy thing.

I gave John a very heartfelt and slightly soggy thanks, and he assured me it was no problem. One of the best things he loved about being part mountain troll was his ability to shape metal. As far as he knew, he was the only one who had it.

Apparently, his dad had befriended a mountain troll back in Scotland. They would eat rocks together and listen to the wind and the earth. It was his quiet place away from his wife and his six sons and seven daughters.

We toasted quiet places: May they always be . . . quiet. For some reason that was so funny.

The troll's magic and the rocks gradually changed his dad into a troll too. Before his dad finally walked into the mountain, never to return, he and his wife had one last fling and John was born soon after. The mountain was strong in John and it only became more so as time passed. Because he was so strong in mountain-troll magic, he couldn't have kids. He had married for love but lost his wife. She wanted children. This was a painful experience and he had vowed never to marry again.

He paused and we didn't toast anything. Instead he was just lost in his memories for a while. Finally, I took his hand in mine and squeezed it. He gave me a sad smile. I slugged him on the arm, because that is what guys do to say we understand. He slugged me back to say thanks for understanding and I flew across the room. We laughed until we cried. I was feeling no pain from all the brew, and John finally got back to his story.

He had lived with lots of his clan children until he broke his great, great, great nephew out of jail (framed for murder) and became an outlaw. They left Scotland and had lots of grand adventures together. His nephew eventually died, and it was much more emotionally painful than John thought it would be. John found a House in Chicago and just sat for more than a hundred years grieving. He was there so long that everyone thought he was just a statue.

One day this beautiful but annoying woman came to him. She got in the habit of just sitting and talking to him. She was passionate, forceful, sad, lost, and couldn't have kids as well. That touched something in John, and he related for the first time in a long time. When she started to go into battles, he went along with her as he didn't want her to get hurt. She pulled him out of his shell and one day after a battle they became lovers. Both of them agreed they were not relationship people. They liked each other and spending time with each other, but that was it. Sandy would live for a long time, and they bonded on things that he understood. He would do anything for her and would defend her with his life. He was earth to her fire.

I was weeping at the end of his story. It was so beautiful and tragic and romantic.

We toasted his mountain home and the rocks he ate as a child. We toasted his dad and his mom: May they rest in peace. We toasted earth and we toasted fire.

John showed me a ring he was working on. It was an emerald ring with a band made out of white and yellow gold. It was mostly white gold, with a vine wrapped around the ring and little, tiny leaves on it. The veins of the leaves and the vine were in yellow gold and the rest in white. The detail of it all was stunning. There was even a tiny ladybug on one side and fly on the other. At the top of the ring, the leaves made a nest for the emerald. It still had the dark non-emerald rock at the bottom and the top had been cut away to reveal the dark green stone. The way it had been cut suggested the petals of a rose.

I think it was the most beautiful thing I had seen in my life so far. John said there was a flaw in the emerald, so it really wasn't worth much to the rest of the world. To him, it had seemed like a flower, and that was the start of the ring.

We toasted the ring and we toasted flowers.

This moment was perfect, and we toasted all the beauty in the world.

Somewhere in there the floor got very rude. It jumped up at me and smacked me in the face. John thought that was hysterical and so did I. He picked me up, put me on my feet, and the floor jumped up and smacked me in the face again.

I decided that maybe I'd better hug the floor for a while so that it would behave. John thought that was a good idea and maybe he'd hug the floor with me. We crawled over to a thick rug and I snuggled up to him. The kitten joined us like a cherry on top of a sundae.

I told John I loved him and that he would be my brother forever. John said he loved me too and we would eat rocks together. In fact, we would go rock hunting soon and listen to the earth and the wind. I wasn't sure about that but he was now my brother so I guessed it would be okay.

We laughed and talked about things I don't remember, and finally fell into a peaceful sleep.

13

Painted to Circle

I was running through an old subway tunnel. Water dripped from the walls and I heard the trickle of water from a small stream. I had to pee, but I could see the water was hitting the third rail. Occasionally it let off a shower of sparks. I couldn't pee here without shocking consequences, so I ran further down the tunnel, looking for a dry spot. It seemed like I ran forever until a conductor showed up under a spotlight. He grabbed me by my shoulders and shook me. He kept telling me to go to the light. He shook me harder and harder. Finally, a snake came down from the ceiling, wrapped around my leg, and hoisted me into the air.

I woke up to John holding me in the air by one leg and shaking me. That is not the best way to begin a morning.

I mumbled something, and John dropped me back on the rug again. "Wake up lad! We don't want to be late for Sandy's circle. She's a good lass, but she doesn't take kindly to be being kept waiting. No sir. Not at all."

Oh my God! It wasn't morning. It was now evening, and time for my first magic circle. Sandy was depending on me.

I looked at John in a stupid panic, and he had to shake me again. What the heck was wrong with me? Then it all came back: the pints, the toasting, and passing out on the floor. Oh God.

As I staggered off to the bathroom, I realized I was still foggy. My head pounded, my mouth tasted like week-old socks, and I was having problems thinking. I peed long enough to put out a small fire and made it back to the kitchen, where John pulled me a pint.

I waved it off with a look of disgust. I'd already had way too much of the stuff. The last thing I needed was to show up more drunk than I already was.

"Now see here, lad. You need this," John said. "Sandy isn't going to be happy, you showing up like this for her circle."

"I know that," I said. "That's why I'm saying no to any more of your stuff. I need water, not beer."

"That's where you are wrong," John said sagely. "Just a touch will do you. It will give you confidence, clear your head, and take that hang dog look off your face."

I said no a few more times, but John wasn't taking that for an answer. I finally drank his pint, and surprisingly, it did make me feel better. After the pint of beer, I then drank a pint of water.

John got a call from Sandy; she and Annabeth were almost ready. I ran to pee again and I noticed I was feeling a lot steadier now. John was looking worried about the time.

"You're not ready, lad. I let you sleep a bit more, figured it would do you good. Now I'm afraid we are going to be late and you do not want to make Sandy wait." He was practically dancing in anxiety.

"What else is there?" I asked looking around wildly. I thought I was just supposed to show up. Was there some sort of magical something I needed to do to prepare?

"You need to get painted," John said. "Get your spirit totems on." He pulled out a set of paints and brushes. They were basic colors, like red, green, white, and brown.

"Quick now, strip down and I'll help you paint," John said. "What animals or symbols did Sandy tell you to use?"

"Sandy didn't tell me anything!" I was panicking now. She had been totally distracted by the runes, and we hadn't had a conversation about this.

"Well, she always says it is the spirit of it all that counts." John pulled my shirt off over my head. "We'll just go with what makes you happy and hopefully that will be good enough. Quickly now, get out of those clothes and grab a brush."

Before I knew it, I was naked and holding a paintbrush loaded down with red body paint.

"Let's see, you like to pee a lot, so let's go with a stream on your side." John began painting wavy blue lines down my ribs. The paint was cold and the brush tickled. I squirmed, but John was insistent and told me to get painting on what I could reach.

I always liked the cheetah. So I painted a running cat on my chest. John thought I needed grounding, so he did lumps of earth on my feet and legs. I liked the idea of clouds, so I started painting white fluffy shapes on my shoulders.

John was obsessed with not being late and he kept telling me it was the idea that mattered. Sandy would tell me how to do a better job next time, or she could do it herself.

He worked on my back where I couldn't reach, while I was doing green grass on my nether regions. That seemed appropriate to me somehow.

We turned on a fan so I would dry quickly as he got a brush loaded up with blue paint and drew some lines on my face. I guessed I looked like a football player with those lines under their eyes. I wasn't sure how much of a shaman I looked like, but it would have to do.

I occurred to me to ask John why he wasn't getting painted. He said it was because he wasn't magical. He was basically a placeholder for a real mage. He said that was one of the things that really ticked off the Louisville mages. Sandy thought a natural could participate in a circle. Apparently, that was radical thinking bordering on heresy.

The paint wasn't dry yet, but John said we couldn't wait anymore. I'd just have to go like I was. He knew a back way to the circle, though, and I'd be okay.

That's how I came to be running down the hall, naked as the day I was born, and painted within an inch of my life. Once again, I thought that life in the House was strange. Not bad, just strange.

My last naked run had been in the hotel and ended in disaster. Hopefully this would be much better.

John was right behind me. "See that blue door that sparkles? That's the one you want," he said.

The door even looked magical. It had swirls of blue with a hint of a sparkle here and there. I don't know if it was the light or my changing angle of view but the shades of blue seemed to whirl a bit.

I stopped before the door and looked at John for confirmation. He nodded impatiently. I took a deep breath to clear my head even more. That extra pint was working. I was still feeling a bit of a buzz, but in a good way. I touched my magic and it felt good. It felt ready. I was ready. I could do this.

I turned the knob and stepped inside.

The room was dimly lit so it took my eyes a moment to adjust. There was a single light in the center of the room focused on a big gold circle in the middle of the floor. I thought there would be magic symbols or something in it, but it was just a thick line of gold or brass in the wooden floor.

John came in and shut the door behind him. My eyes were adjusting and I could see a couple benches up against the walls and that was it. Clearly this was a single purpose room.

Sandy and Annabeth were sitting on one of the benches. It looked like they had been sitting together talking, now they were staring at us, open mouthed, in shock.

Correction, they were staring at me. Sandy recovered first. She stood up and glared at John.

"What did you do?" she growled.

"Nothing," John said innocently. "I got him ready for the circle." There was a curious catch in his voice.

It occurred to me Sandy and Annabeth were not painted, or naked. They looked casual and normal—t-shirts, jeans, sneakers.

"John!" Sandy snapped. That's when John lost it and started laughing. Once he started, he couldn't stop.

Oh my God. I'd been pranked. John had set me up!

"This is serious!" There was pure ice in Sandy's voice, and she gave him a full-on death stare.

"And you." She rounded on me. "How could you let him do that? You know this is important! I bet he got you drunk too." She sniffed the air. "Yep. His famous lager if I'm not mistaken."

I started stammering while glaring at John myself. I wasn't sure what to do. I felt mortified and stupid. How could I have fallen for this? It had just seemed so natural at the time.

The moment seemed frozen between outrage and humor. Annabeth broke the tie. I heard a snort. I looked over and Annabeth was laughing too. She waved at me as if to say she was sorry and all, but once she started, she couldn't stop.

I looked down at myself. I did look pretty ridiculous. I couldn't help it; I started chuckling too. John and Annabeth's laughter was infectious.

My chuckling turned into a full-on laugh attack. I was laughing so hard I gasped for air and tears ran down my face. I thought the tears were going to ruin my face paint, which got me started laughing all over again.

Somewhere in here, Sandy joined us, and we just let it out. Life had been so serious and overwhelming lately that it felt amazing to just let it all go.

The laughter finally seemed to have died out, until John proudly pointed out his handiwork on my back. He'd written "Sandy is hot" and "crack kills" with an arrow pointed down. It really wasn't that funny, but that set us off again.

John took off his shirt and gave it to me. It was so big it covered me all the way down to my knees. I figured if I got paint on it then that was his problem.

I thought I'd go get cleaned up, but Sandy was serious about the circle. We'd taken time out to have fun, but we really needed to recharge some of their charms.

"Jason, since this your first time in the circle, let's go over what we are trying to do and how you can help," Sandy said.

"First of all, you don't need to get in touch with your inner shaman." She paused to glare at John again. "All you need is to wear comfortable clothing and be in touch with your magic. Speaking of which, can you feel your magic okay? I know John's had you drinking."

I assured her I could feel my magic, and although I was still a bit buzzed, I felt like I could work with her.

"Good," she said. "Let's begin by getting in a circle and holding hands." We gathered around the gold ring and joined hands. If we stepped away from each other and held our arms out, we had enough space for the ring to be in the middle. Going around the circle there was Sandy, John, me, Annabeth, and back to Sandy.

"I'm going to lead the circle and direct the flow of magic. What you are looking to do is have magic energy enter your right hand, flow through your body, and exit your left hand. You want to accept the magic from your partner on the right and give to your partner on the left. Let's begin."

I wasn't sure if I should shut my eyes or chant something or what. Sandy just looked off into the distance, her focus clearly internal. Annabeth's eyes were closed with her head tilted down a bit, also internally focused. I guessed it didn't matter.

I was feeling a bit nervous and distracted so I figured I'd close my eyes and concentrate that way.

"House, some circle music, if you please."

A light flute started playing and was quickly joined by some sort of bass instrument. A cello, maybe. It had a slow beat and a comfortable melody without being distracting.

I touched my magic and started the flow. I'd always been able to feel my magic, but I hadn't started working with how it flowed internally until this afternoon with Sandy. *Had it really only been this afternoon? If felt like forever ago.* The concept of flow was easy for me though, so I felt toward John for energy and pushed it toward Annabeth. I started out with a trickle, though, as this was still so new to me.

John's magic felt very dense, like I was trying to move honey. Honey was a good simile too, as his magic felt very rich and earthy. I wonder what my magic felt like to Annabeth.

"Good," Sandy spoke up. "I can feel the circle starting. What we are doing is spinning our magic. In the process we are influencing the neutral magic in the circle to spin also. If we can spin the magic fast enough, it will create a vortex and compress some of that magic into its denser form. From there the charms will absorb it and be refilled."

I wasn't sure if she was talking to me or everyone. It was helpful to know what we were doing, though, and it made for a great visual.

"We have some flow. Now let's pick up the pace a bit more."

The pace of the music picked up slightly and I felt the power level of the circle jump. John's power was flowing into me much faster and I pushed it out to Annabeth as fast as I could. I felt like we had switched from the flow of a lazy creek to a fast-moving stream. I realized I was breathing quickly, so I smoothed that out and took deeper breaths.

It took several moments, but finally I got my footing and felt comfortable moving at this pace. I had only been in the groove for a few moments when Sandy spoke up again.

"We are doing good. Now it's time for third gear."

The music picked up pace and the speed doubled again. The magic went from a fast-moving regular stream to a flooding torrent of power. I wasn't guiding and pushing the power so much anymore. I was a conduit for the energy, so I just hung on, contributed what I could, and enjoyed the ride.

"Fourth gear. Vortex time."

I heard Annabeth groan as the speed doubled again. I wasn't contributing at all as the power raced through me. This is what I imagined hanging on to a live wire felt like. My muscles shook and twitched, but I didn't let go. The music reached a frantic pace, racing along like the magic.

I opened my eyes. I had to see this. Sandy shone like an angel; full of power and fury. She was the engine of our circle, and she was revved up. Her magic was not only flowing through us but skimming along our circle outside us. Sandy's power created a vortex too. I could see motes of pure magic in the air, like a host of fireflies. They were sucked into our circle and condensed into a bright column.

John looked calm as a mountain, but Annabeth and I were shaking, causing some of the magic to splash into the room. It wasn't anything I could control, though. I was a novice magic user and this was way above my pay grade. I was lucky to just be hanging in there.

Sandy started chanting and the column of light dipped toward the floor. I hadn't noticed this before but there were a few charms already in the center of the circle. The light touched down on the charms, and they began to glow.

All of the power wasn't going into the charms, though. The motes of light bounced off the floor as well as the charms and shot off into the room again. It was like a welder, with a hot flame in the middle and lots of sparks coming off. It was pretty, but the analytical part of me wondered how efficient it was.

The charms glowed yellow and gradually switched to orange. I hoped this meant they were charged up as I couldn't hold on much longer. I had just about hit my limit when Sandy ran out of juice.

I think she meant to let the power down gradually, but Annabeth collapsed, breaking the circle. The power hit me and didn't have anywhere to go, so it flung me across the room. As I bounced off the wall, I noticed it was padded. That was nice.

Sandy sank to the floor, exhausted, leaving John as the only one standing. I tried to stand up, but my head buzzed. I was so dizzy, it felt like the floor was tilting. The floor felt nice, so I decided to just lie there for a while.

"John, take everyone back to their home and make sure they are okay," Sandy said. "Annabeth, Jason, dinner at my place tomorrow night. We can discuss results and see about doing this again." She sounded hoarse and tired.

Annabeth looked the worst, so John picked her up first. He left both Sandy and I resting on the floor. The room had stopped spinning as long as I didn't raise my head up. My whole body tingled and occasionally I felt a muscle twitch. I wondered if this is what it is like being electrocuted. Hopefully I would never find out.

John came back after a while, scooped me up off the floor, and carried me back to my apartment. I don't know if it was the magic talking or the lager, but it sure was nice to be carried by a strong handsome man. I told him that, and he just laughed in his booming voice.

Then I asked if we were still brothers. He said of course, as long as I didn't mind getting painted up every now and then. I said I was fine with that as long as it came with some lager and a nice rug to pass out on.

We got to my apartment and John took me straight to bed. That was probably a good thing as I was still feeling woozy. A few minutes later he came back with the litter box he'd made as well as my clothes and my kitten. He filled up the box with the litter Sandy had given me and plopped the kitten in it. After a promise to see me tomorrow night, he left to get Sandy.

I laid in bed staring at the ceiling, still wearing John's shirt and covered in paint. What a strange day it had been. I probably should have been angrier at John, but I liked the guy and it was hard to stay mad at him. Now that I knew what a circle was like, it probably was a good thing that I hadn't been completely sober.

I heard a little meow, and soon Kitten hopped up onto my pillow. He snuggled up to my face and started purring. I was nose to nose with him, and his beautiful green eyes were half closed in happiness. He was the perfect picture of peace and bliss.

"What am I going to call you? I can't call you Kitten forever," I whispered. I scratched him behind the ears with one finger. I closed my eyes as I started to drift away.

I felt a paw on my cheek. "Bermuda Moses."

I opened my eyes. Had my cat just talked to me?

He was still there, purring away.

"Bermuda Moses." I tried it out. It wasn't a bad name. Kinda had a ring to it. It reminded me of the names of the cats in the play on Broadway. One of the guys I'd stayed with for a few weeks had loved that music and played it all the time. I'd always liked Old Deuteronomy, and Grizabella, who sang the famous song "Memory." Bermuda Moses seemed to fit in with that.

With that last thought I fell asleep.

14

Annabeth's Apartment

I woke up to another perfect morning. The sunlight in the room gently brought me to wakefulness. Tyler was curled up with me, his strong arm around me. I opened my eyes and saw my kitten was on his back, all four legs thrown wide, belly to the sky. It seemed so peaceful. Had yesterday really happened? I ran a finger down his furry belly and caught sight of my hand. It still had paint on it. Yep, last night happened.

I caught Tyler up on what had happened. He had a good laugh when I talked about John's prank. He had been wondering why I was painted up and wearing an oversized t-shirt.

Tyler said he had never been part of a magic circle and had no desire to be part of one. He wasn't sure how his magic would react to the flow. It might be that instead of having a magic circle and charging charms, we could end in a big orgy. I was sure Sandy wouldn't be happy about that at all, so I stopped any efforts to recruit him.

He did say we had good news. The second remnant was now gone. Two down. Two to go, although the strongest one still remained. I'd have to bring that up with Sandy tonight at dinner.

Tyler left soon after, and I played with my kitten a little more. I guessed I should call him Bermuda Moses now. Had that really happened? It seemed like a dream. It was a neat name though, and the little fella seemed to like it.

Showering felt so good. I got all the paint and beer-sweat off me. Bermuda supervised the whole proceedings from the top of the commode after knocking the toilet paper off again. I guessed that was his spot now.

After a breakfast of Raisin Bran and a Netflix show, I felt ready to start working on my magic. I was apprehensive about how I would feel after the previous night. I wasn't tingling or anything and my muscles seemed fine. Hopefully everything was okay now.

I touched my magic, and if anything, it seemed more responsive than before. I swirled it around my body and checked it out with my sight. It was a beautiful emerald green with touches of sapphire blue, just like it was supposed to be. I breathed a sigh of relief. I had been afraid the circle last night had messed with my balance.

I was going to be working with Penny and I didn't want to mess her up more than she already was. I got comfortable on my old couch and started pulling magic from Penny. The core in my left hand was completely gone, so I spun up a new one and added the pure energy from my charm. Then I pushed my emerald and sapphire energy back into her. I used my breathing to keep track of my pushing and pulling, and I soon got into a nice flow. The breathing really helped, and with all the concentration I soon entered a light trance. Bermuda crawled onto my lap and thought this would be a good time for a nap.

I'm not sure how long I did this—at least a few hours—but at the end of that time I felt like I had a better connection with Penny. She wasn't talking to me yet, but I had just gotten started on her recovery.

One thing I really wanted to do today was talk to Annabeth. The last time we had really talked was in the park before the golem attacked. I gave her a call and she said to come on up.

I knocked on her door—which looked normal, unlike John's—and she quickly answered.

"What? No paint?" she said.

I rolled my eyes. "I'm never going to live that down, am I?" I replied.

"Well, it's not every day that a magic circle is graced by a powerful shaman." She laughed and let me inside.

I immediately got why she had been so shocked by my apartment. If my apartment was the simple-generic-one-bedroom-white-walled apartment, hers was the penthouse. The whole place had a Tuscan theme with textured walls, tall ceilings, broad wooden beams, and large tiles on the floor. The openings into other rooms were big arches with some sort of stone all around. There were little murals everywhere and somehow sunlight was coming in from the ceiling, giving the center of the apartment an open courtyard feeling.

It was like something out of *Architectural Digest*, and there was no way this should have been possible in an apartment in Old Louisville. It left me speechless.

Annabeth grabbed my hand and pulled me into the kitchen. She had a freakin' wrought iron chandelier! The countertops were some sort of stone, and she had one of those fancy kitchen islands with a sink and seating and all that. I didn't even know what half of what I was looking at was, but the effect was rustic, casual, elegant, beautiful.

She poured us each a glass of blood orange flavored lemonade, and I finally found the words to rave about her place. We settled onto a comfortable bench loaded with pillows in the 'courtyard' part of the apartment.

"How on earth did you do all this?" I asked. I really wanted to know. It was then I accepted my living space needed an upgrade.

"I've always wanted to visit Italy and tour the countryside," Annabeth explained. "That's something I thought I would do when I retired, but it just never happened. When I moved in here, I was still very sad about leaving my former house. It had so many memories and so much character. This place was a simple white apartment, like yours."

"You turned something like my place into this?" I breathed. "Wow. You really are magical."

"Oh, it wasn't me. It was the House," she said. "I discovered I could make changes quite by accident. I'd be talking out loud to myself and I'd say some of the things I wanted to do to the place, to spruce it up a bit. When I came back later, it was done.

"I found the House likes it when I hum, and I hum when I'm happy. So, the House gradually turned my little white apartment into this place." She gestured around at all the beautiful architecture. "Of course, it didn't all happen at once. Once I found out I could make changes, I created a folder with lots of pictures of places I liked. I'd point out something in the picture I'd like and a place to put it. The House did the rest."

She went on for a while more about her apartment. She showed me around and pointed out things the House had added and the original picture it had come from. She had a great sense of color and how things went together to create a pleasing space. Certainly much more than I did.

I begged her to help me and she said it would be a lot of fun to help me find my style. We agreed to work on it later when we had more time. In the meantime, I wanted to know how she was doing. The last couple times I'd seen her she was either being kicked by a golem or getting overloaded by a magic circle.

"That golem really did a number on me. That kick hurt!" She pulled up her shirt and showed me her middle. It was still a mass of bruises. The bruises were turning those strange green and purple colors which meant they would be going away soon. Still, this was no joke.

"Did it crack any ribs?" I asked. "I saw it hit you. You flew through the air, and I thought for sure some major damage had happened."

"I don't think so," she said. "Don't get me wrong, everything hurt a lot. But it doesn't feel like a broken bone."

"Didn't you go to the hospital? Get some x-rays?" I asked. That would have been one of the first things I did after I woke up. That and get some extra strength painkillers.

She just shook her head. "I would have, but apparently x-rays don't work for us. I guess the magic interferes with it or something."

"Seriously?" I asked.

"It's not just x-rays. Regular medicine doesn't work for us either." She grimaced. "Sandy told me, but I had to try it for myself. I took three Tylenol, but it only helped me for about fifteen minutes. Then my system got rid of it. I took three more, and they did nothing for me."

"That's crazy!" I said.

"I tried everything: aspirin, naproxen, ibuprofen—nothing really worked. I even downed a whole bottle of cold medicine to see if that would help me sleep. It tasted nice, but that was it. I guess it's a good news–bad news sort of thing. We don't get sick, so we don't need medicine, but if we get hurt then medicine doesn't work."

"It is nice we don't get sick," I said. "Or get a headache or anything like that. But not having a pain reliever . . . that sounds kind of harsh. So, is there a magical something that helps?"

"I do have this now." She showed me a tiny four-leaf clover charm on a chain around her neck. "This is one of the charms Sandy had in our circle. She brought it up to me this morning. She said it's only about a quarter full, but it should speed up the healing and help with the pain."

"So, is it working?" I asked.

"Oh yes," she said emphatically. "I sure feel a lot better. That magic circle is rough but having this makes it worth it."

We talked about the magic circle for a bit. She had the same experience I did—that it was like holding onto an electric wire. I hadn't felt any ill effects from it though, and she said she was doing fine too. We both didn't like the experience, and we weren't looking forward to the next time, but it was necessary to get magic into the charms.

We were winding down that conversation when Bermuda showed up. I had no idea how he got in, but he and Little Miss Sunshine hit it off right away. She cooed all over him, and soon he was in her lap, on his back, letting her rub his belly. His eyes were closed and his little paws made squishing motions in the air. He is so freaking cute!

I still wanted to work on transferring magic with Penny and see if I could wake her up. I felt guilty that I'd gotten drunk off my bum yesterday, and I was determined to make up for it.

Annabeth said I could work on it right there in her courtyard. At first, I said no. This was all so new, and I wanted to work on it on my own. That way if I completely messed up nobody could see me. Then Annabeth confessed that it all still felt new to her as well and she'd love to have some company working on it.

I decided to stay, and we ended up sitting on a bunch of cushions and pillows on the ground. Somehow, even though we were indoors, the sun shone into the courtyard and on our impromptu magic session. We both got in touch with our magic and were just moving it around. She didn't have Penny to work with, but she was still working on a core.

I told her about the green water in the vase and the shot glass and what Sandy had suggested for Penny. We also talked about how it felt to move magic around. It was different for Annabeth. She didn't have pure white magic to work with. It was all her magic that she was trying to feel and move. Because it all felt like her magic, it was difficult for her to distinguish it and do something with it.

I had thought of the extra magic in Penny as a problem, and it was to Penny, but it was a bonus to me. Because it had a different look and feel, it was much easier for me to work with. I guess every dark cloud does have a silver lining.

In the process of talking about Annabeth's experience I suggested that a lot of the words, and even the goal we were shooting for, were all visual. We talked about colors and magic swirling, but Annabeth's magic was audio. Maybe she just needed to create a strong pure sound as her core. Maybe her magic would respond better to that.

The response was immediate. Annabeth's eyes flew open and she was so excited.

"I can hear it!" She held out her left hand. "I thought of a tone, like a bell, and thought of my magic condensing around it. It made the sound! Then I poured magic into it and made it stronger and richer. It's incredible. I can feel my hand vibrating!"

I looked at her hand, and sure enough, her left hand was much brighter than her right hand.

We pushed the idea even more and she tried different tones to see if that made a difference. It didn't. It was the richness, clarity, and volume of the tone that seemed to matter.

She tried two tones but that didn't work at all. Still, one tone was a breakthrough.

I also found out that she was left-handed. Sandy had her working on her first core in her dominant hand. That made sense as she wasn't trying to move magic from a charm through her body like I was.

After all the discovery and camaraderie, we got into a groove and worked on our magic for hours. Annabeth's courtyard was beautiful, and it felt natural to work on magic in such a graceful space.

Bermuda napped on the pillows, explored for a while, then napped again. From his perspective we were not very exciting.

The sun was starting to set when he wandered off again; this time, we heard a crash. He ran into the courtyard all fuzzed up. It was time to have supper at Sandy's anyway, so we decided to stop for the time being. I hoped he hadn't knocked over anything important, but Annabeth didn't seem concerned. I picked up my little wild child, took him back to my place, and did a little freshening up.

Supper at Sandy's was awesome as always. We had chicken pot pie, cornbread, and a side salad with homemade honey mustard dressing. I filled up my plate and discovered just how hungry I was. I ate everything on it, filled it up again, and ate all that too. I finished it off with some cornbread and strawberry jam. I was so full but so happy.

Sandy slyly suggested that being a shaman must really be hungry business. John laughed and said it was certainly a thirsty one! Then John went over the story again in great detail about how I'd gotten all painted up and the look on Sandy's face when I'd walked in the room.

We all snorted with laughter like it had happened all over again. John was a good storyteller. He didn't make me sound too much like a buffoon and Sandy didn't sound too mad in the retelling. John started calling me The Shaman and by the end of the evening the nickname had stuck.

We did cover some business. Sandy had me talk about my experience in the magic circle. I told her what I'd seen and felt, how it had been part rollercoaster and part electrocution. Sandy's magic was powering the circle and we were just along for the ride. Sandy said again that a circle is normally at least seven experienced and powerful mages. She didn't know any other way of making our four-person circle work other than pure power and will. Sandy was a prodigy in the power department, so she was able to make up for the missing sups on her own.

It wasn't perfect even then. We'd been able to partially refill seven charms, which wasn't much considering how many charms she had and how many she had given Annabeth. The seven we had charged were only a quarter to a half filled. The whole process was very inefficient, but Sandy wasn't sure how to make it better.

After supper we tried the magic circle again. This time I wore a t-shirt and comfortable shorts and I knew what the process was going to be like. I was both more relaxed because it wasn't my first time, and more tense because I knew some magic overload was headed my way.

This time I kept my eyes open the whole time. Once the magic started flowing, I could see the path it was taking. Since we were four people, we were more of a square than a circle, and the flow reflected that. It kind of wobbled as it moved from person to person. The flow wasn't smooth at all. I could also see the little motes of magic in the air and they were not being influenced by our magic yet.

When Sandy hit third gear the flow was a lot thicker and it smoothed out some of the ripples a bit. I could see some of the magic breaking free and streaming off into the room. The motes of magic in the room were agitated now and starting to spin in the circle. Their spin was interrupted a lot by all the extra magic flaring off from our circle.

Sandy kicked it into fourth gear, vortex time, and I hung on for dear life again. Even though I was shaking and twitching with power, I was still paying attention to what was happening. The flow got even thicker and became the closest to a circle yet. When the magic went from person to person at their hands, though, it threw off sparks. The power transfer wasn't smooth, and the sparks were interfering with the spin of the motes of natural magic. Despite all that, the motes did spin and form a vortex. It was a lurching, twisty sort of thing with a thick funnel on the bottom. It rested on the charms most of the time but what didn't get absorbed just skittered across the floor and outside of the circle. Once they were outside the circle, they rose into the air and get sucked back into the top of the funnel again.

I was still new at all this, but I knew there had to be a better way to do the circle.

Sandy collapsed first this time. I'd been determined that I wouldn't be the first to go down and break the circle. The aftereffect felt even worse than before. My body twitched long after we had ended, and the room was spinning so badly I didn't even try to sit up. I just laid there on the cool floor until John took me back to my room. I thought I would be okay then, but I ended up throwing up for a few hours. Bermuda whined and tried to make me feel better, but there wasn't much he could do.

I spent the whole time going over what I'd seen and felt during both circles, looking for the pattern. I could figure out just about anything, and I wasn't going to go through this night after night for such a low payout. By the time I finally fell asleep, with an anxious Bermuda curled up beside me, I had a plan.

15

Third Time's the Charm

I woke up to sunlight, Tyler, and my kitten again! It was like waking up in heaven. I didn't have an amazing apartment like John or Annabeth, but my mornings were turning out to be pure bliss.

I caught Tyler up on the previous day and what I was planning. He thought it sounded reasonable, but he wasn't a mage so he didn't know if it would actually work or not. He said he was working on my third remnant. The fourth one—Death Experience guy—was staying buried inside and Tyler couldn't touch him yet. I was just glad progress was being made.

Tyler wished me luck and slipped out to go do his stuff. Bermuda yawned and stretched. He looked so cute, I had to kiss him on the head. He put his paw on my face like, "Too close dude. A little too close." Of course, that made me want to kiss him again.

The two of us played a rousing game of Kiss the Cat Before He Gets Away. I got in some good loving and only got scratched a little bit. It's hard to hold onto a squirming cat, and it wasn't long before he was prancing away.

I had a shower, breakfast, and then settled in for some magic work. Bermuda had other ideas, though. He was bursting with young energy and started tearing around the apartment. He needed something to chase so I made one of my little magic creations for him to play with. I was thinking of cats chasing lasers, so I made my creation round, bright red, and glowing. Then I gave it a little hovercraft engine so he could scoot across the floor and up the walls. I called him Dot and gave him free reign over the apartment, except for the TV area. Stay away from the TV.

I filled him with magic and turned him loose. He gave me a big wink then zipped over to Bermuda and began dancing around on the floor in front of him. The kitten was fascinated, and it wasn't long before Dot was zipping around the apartment with Bermuda in close pursuit. Thank goodness I didn't have much in the way of breakables, because they were racing everywhere. At one point, Bermuda was going so fast he raced up the wall and across it like he was defying gravity. His eyes were big and his ears were up. Dot made little zoom-zoom noises and flashed me the thumbs up as he flew by. They were clearly having the time of their lives.

I knew I was supposed to be working on magic, but I took time to just watch them for a while. It's all about the journey after all; take time to smell the roses and all that. I'd never had a pet before, but they sure do make your place a home. I wasn't at the level of Annabeth, but this place felt like mine and it was a happy space.

Finally, I let them do their thing and I settled back in for some magic work with Penny. I needed her to wake up today. She was the centerpiece for my plan tonight. Over and over I pulled in magic from her, mixed it with my magic, and sent it back.

At first, I worked with what felt comfortable. Then I started pushing the boundaries a bit. I gradually took bigger and bigger amounts of magic and pushing back more and more. It was sort of like taking lots of really deep breaths.

Bermuda got tired from all his running and curled up in my lap for a nap. I felt for Dot but couldn't find him. I guessed he ran out of magic. That seemed fast; I'd need to tweak his design a bit when I called him back again. In the meantime, he'd served his purpose and used up some of that kitten energy. I went back to my magic flows. It wasn't until Bermuda woke up again that I realized I'd been at it for hours. I needed a break, so I called up Annabeth and went to her place for a midday sandwich. I told her I was up to something but wouldn't say what. Just that I needed to have Penny's help to make it happen.

After lunch we settled down in her Tuscan courtyard and got to work again. This time I pushed the boundaries a lot. I pulled in Penny's magic until I thought I would burst. Then pushed it back into her until the world turned gray. This was like nothing I had done before, but I thought I was starting to get results.

Since Annabeth had another way of sensing magic, I asked her if she would pay attention to my magic transfer and offer feedback. She thought that was a great idea and listened to what I was doing for a while. She said the pure magic sounded like white noise, or static on a radio. When I moved magic around, she could hear what mine sounded like, and it sounded like bells ringing. Sometimes it seemed like little bells tinkling, and sometimes like big grand bells with volume and vibrancy and lots of tone. I wasn't sure how to use that information, but I tucked it away in my mind for further review.

She listened to Penny and said she could hear a single bell and it sounded huge. Like maybe the biggest bell in Notre Dame. It wasn't loud but it was clear. Penny was in there; I just needed to give her more of my magic.

By the time we were ready to head to Sandy's for supper, I could feel just a touch of Penny again. It was faint, like she was far away or at the end of a tunnel, but it was her.

I was so very glad to hear from her again! Up to this point, we had been working on just a theory that all this exchanging of magic was going to work. Now I had real evidence that she was going to get better and I was on the right track. I headed down to Sandy's with a much lighter heart.

When I got there, Bermuda had already arrived. He seemed to go wherever he wanted in the House. Snowy and Biscuit seemed to have accepted him, or at least decided to tolerate him. Sandy served roast beef and Yorkshire pudding. Apparently, that was a favorite of John's and something he used to eat back in Scotland. I couldn't imagine eating beef with pudding, but John said to wait and see. I was going to love it.

It turns out the pudding was like a fluffy biscuit you poured gravy over. It really was delicious. We had roast beef, Yorkshire pudding, and roast potatoes and carrots. The gravy went over everything and it totally rocked. I had two helpings and started in on a third.

I didn't usually eat this much, but Sandy said using magic is hungry work. John had finished the emerald ring he had been working on. He showed it to us before sending it off to his Etsy buyer. I mostly remembered seeing it earlier, but I'd been wasted. Now that I was sober, it was even more beautiful. The contrast between the white and yellow gold in each tiny leaf was just stunning. The centerpiece of the ring, the flawed emerald, was now finished, and it somehow looked both raw and sparkly all at the same time. Whoever got that ring was going to love it. It was a one-of-a-kind masterpiece.

I was nervous about bringing it up, but when Sandy finally got down to business about tonight's circle, I told everyone that I had something in mind, and I wanted to lead tonight's circle.

Sandy looked shocked and exchanged a look with Annabeth. I wouldn't say more than that and it really got their curiosity going. I told Sandy that if I completely failed then we could always do it the way we had been. I thought she might have an issue with it, but she and Annabeth just looked relieved. I knew that Annabeth didn't enjoy doing the circle, but it had never really occurred to me to consider how this affected Sandy. I'm sure putting out that much power was no picnic either.

We cleaned up from supper and I overheard lots of speculation about what I was up to. I told them it would require them to get in the mindset of a shaman and I was sure John could fetch his body paints.

That was a hard no. I got a glare from both Sandy and Annabeth. Then I suggested that maybe if just *John* got painted it still might work. That was met with an enthusiastic 'yes' from both of them.

John gave a big belly laugh and suggested we could all wrestle him for it. Annabeth agreed and wrapped herself around one leg. Sandy said she always liked wrestling him and wrapped herself around his other leg. Everyone looked at me and said it was my turn to take him down. A seven-foot mountain man was way out of my league, even with two pretty women hanging on to him, but I gave it a try.

I gave a yell, a flying leap, and wrapped myself around his torso. I didn't even rock him when I landed. John walked around the apartment with all three of us hanging onto him. He roared and threatened bad things but was very gentle with us. We were like kids compared to him.

He decided to clean up the dishes with the three of us trying to slow him down. I beat on his back, and Sandy and Annabeth hung onto his legs, digging in for dear life, but we never even slowed him down. It was a lot of fun though, and we soon fell off and helped clear up supper.

We headed to the circle room. That's when I started getting nervous. I knew everything was going to be okay, but I still didn't want to look like a fool in front of my new friends. I took deep breaths and reminded myself that if worse came to worst, we could just do it the way we had done it before.

We got to the circle room and I suddenly had to pee. Come to find out, there was a bathroom attached. Thank goodness. After I did my business, I looked in the bathroom mirror and gave myself a pep talk.

"You can do this. You have a good idea, and this can work. If it works, it will be a major breakthrough and John and Sandy and Annabeth are going to be so happy. This is just like the poker tables. Take the leap. Make it happen. You are good!"

I washed my hands then slapped some water on my face. I felt like it was my first poker tournament. I had been so nervous I'd thrown up for that. Fortunately, I wasn't throwing up this time.

Oh God, I had to pee again! What the heck. Get it together. After the second pee and second hand wash, I was ready.

Once out of the bathroom, Annabeth gave me a big hug. "It's going to be okay," she whispered. I guessed I looked as nervous as I felt.

I got a hug from Sandy too. She could be a bit intimidating at times, but her heart was pure gold. Not to be left out, I got a hug from John as well. Except he picked me up and squeezed me until my eyes popped.

That did the trick. I wasn't nervous anymore. There really wasn't any sort of 'head of the circle' spot so I stepped up to my previous spot in the circle.

"So, I have a theory about how a magic circle works," I said. "And it's based off of what I saw happen in our last circle. We'll go over that, then I'll talk about what's happening with our circle. I have a possible solution to make it better."

I looked around and everyone nodded. They were with me so far.

"First, let's talk about numbers. I think it's better with more mages in a circle because it is closer to an actual circle with more people. We have four people, so we are basically a square. That's not very circle like. Even eight people would make an octagon, like a stop sign, and that's more like a circle. We want magic to spin, so it's all about flow. The less circular we are, the more there is resistance to the flow."

I looked around again and everyone nodded. Sandy looked thoughtful. She had the most experience with magic circles so hopefully this was jiving with what she felt before.

"Now let's talk about flow. I think charging circles normally have the magic flow through the participants because everyone is helping with the spin. The example I'm thinking of is the old grain mills with horses. They would have a giant circular rock to crush the grain and spokes coming off of it. They would hitch horses to the spokes that would then walk in a circle and grind the grain. If you only had one horse, it would still work, but the force would be off balance. If you had two horses, you'd have double the power, and the forces would be balanced on opposite sides of the stone.

"I'm thinking that is the same idea with a charging circle. Magic flows through the mages and they all help get it moving. With the right number of mages, the magic is balanced and it can flow a lot faster. That doesn't work in our situation. John can't help with the magic flow in the traditional sense, I'm brand new to this, and compared to experienced mages, so is Annabeth. So, really, it's you, Sandy, that is making this circle work.

"John said you were a power prodigy and I believe it. If you didn't have the power you did, there is no way four people would work. What is interesting is that, when you really rev up your power, it starts flowing around us as well as through us. That is when it seems to be the most like a circle and that's when the vortex happens."

I looked around the circle again. So far everyone seemed to be following along and in agreement. Annabeth was her usual sunshine self. She beamed at me and sent good energy my way. I really appreciated that. Sandy looked very interested. Clearly, she was enjoying my thoughts and looked relaxed. Looking at her now, I realized how tense she had been before as circle leader. John looked like he was thinking about beer. He probably was wishing he had a pint while he was listening to me talk.

"The final thing I'll bring up is the size of the circle. It makes for a wide vortex and that makes for a wide funnel. When the funnel touches down on the charms, it's much bigger than they are. The excess magic is shooting across the floor and outside of the circle, only to be caught up into the funnel again. It's possible that magic particles are being sucked through the vortex lots of times before being absorbed into a charm. Or, maybe they never end up in a charm at all. That's just a lot of wasted magic. What would solve this is a smaller vortex that spins faster. That would create a tight tip of the funnel, and a very focused magic on the charms."

"That all sounds very logical," Sandy spoke up. "I haven't thought of a charging circle in that way before, but it seems to fit. The only thing is, how do we do it differently? How do we make a better circle? I've tried using placeholders for missing mages before and that didn't seem to work. The House made us some magical dummies, but the flow just wouldn't start. John tried using various metals to see if we could get a good magic conductor, but that didn't work, either."

"This time we have something you haven't tried before." I held up Penny. "This time we have an actual awakened and aware magic conductor. I've been working with her all day, and I think she can do this."

I whispered to her in my mind, "Penny? Are you there?" I heard a distant chime. I sent her the thought of what I needed and felt a small return glow. She had more than enough power to make the transformation, but I wasn't sure if she was awake enough to do it.

There was a pause, then it happened so fast that I almost dropped her. Penny stretched out really thin, like a dinner plate. Then a hole grew in the middle and all the metal went to the edges. She was now a thin ring, about a foot in diameter. She paused for a moment, then started expanding. She had the same amount of metal as always, but she made herself thinner and thinner so she could form a larger circle.

She expanded to about three feet in diameter and stopped. She was so thin and light you could barely see her. It was amazing that there was enough metal in a penny to expand this much.

I held her gently on one side with two fingers of each hand. I let my magic sink into her, making sure she was all right, then wrapped her with my essence. I didn't want anyone else's magic to get into Penny and cause problems. The magic was going to spin outside her, not through her, so she should be okay. I *looked* at her with my magic sight, and she glowed with emerald light.

Once she was wrapped in a layer of my magic I looked to Annabeth on my left. "Touch Penny with the fingers on both of your hands. Be gentle, though. She's really thin and I don't want to hurt her." Annabeth licked her lips nervously and very gently joined the circle with a light touch. Once she held the tiny wire for a moment, and nothing happened, she started to relax.

"Annabeth, have you seen someone wet their fingers and then run them around the surface of a glass to make a tone?" She nodded. "I want you to imagine something like that with this circle. Imagine you are running your magic around the ring and it is making a tone."

Annabeth closed her eyes and settled in. At first, I felt nothing. Then a rich textured magic started flowing around penny. I could see her signature pink color wrapping my emerald magic. Then a faint but distinctive tone filled the room. It sounded meditative and mystical. Annabeth's eyes flew open in surprise. None of us had expected this, and Annabeth was clearly part of the circle in a new way.

I looked to my right and nodded at John. He very gently held the wire like we were.

"John, usually there isn't anything you need to do, but this time I want you to try something for me. This time there is actual metal making the circle of magic. I want you to just sense it and wrap your magic around it. Like you were going to do something with it, only don't actually do anything. I'm not sure what that would do to Penny."

"Sure," John rumbled, and immediately a gray magic raced around the ring. Actually, it wasn't a solid color, it was a mix of just about everything from white to black that blended into a sort of pewter color. It also sparkled a bit, like it had ground diamonds mixed in with it. I sent a mental query to Penny. She replied that she was doing fine. Actually, it sounded like she was having a lot of fun and enjoying the whole process.

"Your turn," I said to Sandy. "At this point just let your magic layer around the circle. We'll spin it in a minute. You're super powerful so be gentle."

"Of course," Sandy said dryly. I'm sure I wasn't telling her anything she didn't already know, but I wanted this to work, and I didn't want anything to happen to Penny.

Sandy gently touched the circle and sent orange magic around the ring. It was the type of orange you see in a candle flame. This suited her. It was gentle and warming at that moment, but I'm sure it could have raged if she needed.

I let the circle rest for a moment, giving the people and the magic time to get comfortable together. Even though three feet in diameter sounds like a lot, it really isn't when there are four people involved. We were standing close together, nearly touching.

Parts of my theory were now proven right. We could make a perfect circle, and we could make it a lot smaller than before. Now I just needed to see if it would spin and create a magic vortex, and if so, then how much energy it would take.

Since I was the base layer, I gave a gentle push and started our magic spinning. I knew immediately this was going to work. The flow was so smooth, like there was no friction at all. It felt like an ice skater gliding around a rink. It could glide for forever.

I checked for sparks or anything that indicated our magic was leaking off into the room. It looked smooth and beautiful. Time to put a little bit more magic into the circle. I started with myself, adding another measure of emerald magic into the base. I asked Annabeth to think about adding more magic to the circle. Maybe adding another tone or making the existing one louder? She tried a second tone but struggled a bit. Making the current tone louder seemed to work much better, and I saw her pink magic strengthen.

John was next and he knew how to add more magic on his own. His pewter gray doubled and then tripled in volume. Sandy was last, and she effortlessly doubled her magic and then doubled it again.

The magic in the circle stayed smooth and easy, although now it was a thick band of power. Magic called to magic, and I could see motes of natural magic starting to spin and cluster in the center.

"The motes are circling," I said excitedly.

"Really?" Sandy was shocked. Annabeth looked so happy.

"We don't have a vortex yet, but we have the beginnings of one. Magic seems to call to magic, and we need a bit more power in our circle. That will exert even more influence on the motes, and then I'll ramp up the speed. Before we do that, is anyone tired?" I asked.

"I hardly feel like I am doing anything," Sandy said, and Annabeth and John agreed.

"We are doing great!" I said. A team leader should always try to be positive. "Let's stick with the safe approach like we have been doing. I'll go first."

I doubled my existing amount of magic in the circle. It still seemed easy to me. I wasn't feeling any of the effects that came with low magic. I could probably double it a few more times if I needed to.

Annabeth went next with no issues. The tone in the room was much more noticeable now. It seemed like such a rich and vibrant sound, like a hundred monks humming in tune. John and Sandy followed with no fuss.

"This is pretty neat. I can actually feel everybody's magic," John said. He did seem pretty tuned in to what we were doing now. I guessed beer thoughts could wait 'til later. "I didn't realize that what you were calling magic is what I feel like when I'm shaping. Now it feels like everyone has their hands on a piece of metal and we are all going to mold it together."

I didn't want to get too distracted from what we were doing, but I mentally filed that away for later. Maybe there was a way to shape with John? He was such an artist. I bet it would be intriguing to feel firsthand what his creative process was.

Our magic ring was very thick now, at least as big around as my arm, maybe even thicker. Our magic melded and flowed easily, and the influence on the natural motes was even more pronounced.

There was a large dense mass of neutral magic in the center of our circuit now. I hadn't planned on this, but it was attracting additional neutral magic. The overall effect of the neutral core and the circle was becoming much greater than the circle on its own.

All that power still needed to get into the charms, though, and for that I needed a funnel. This was where it could all fall apart. I gave another push and our circle spun faster but not by much. It was already spinning pretty quickly.

I thought about it for a sec and realized this was like a merry-go-round. I didn't just need to push, I needed to push faster. Instead of feeling like I was pushing the magic, I gave it a flick. Like a quick rapid tap to the circle. That worked much better.

I flicked several more times and the speed of the circle doubled. Then, what I had been waiting for happened: The neutral magic sped up too, and now it was moving fast enough to make a funnel. It was like the world's smallest magic tornado, and the funnel was small and dense with magic. I very gently increased the speed, until the funnel touched down on the charms.

"We have a funnel!" I said excitedly. "Everybody, keep steady." Excited glances were shared all around. I didn't want to lose our momentum, though, so I mostly ignored them and stayed focused.

The charms in the center of the floor started glowing immediately. They glowed yellow and then orange like with previous circles. This time, the color kept changing, though. It went to a red, then a deeper red, almost a black.

Some of the magic was hitting the floor and shooting outside the circle, but the smaller funnel was keeping that mostly in check. The tighter funnel was a lot more efficient than the last time we had circled.

A few of the charms in the center went from almost black to pure white. They shone like little stars. The charms were in a loose pile, so the funnel wasn't equally touching all of them. Normally that wasn't a problem, but in this case it meant the ones on the edge weren't getting the full funnel treatment.

Still, about half of charms turned white, a quarter were almost black and the rest a dark red, when the funnel ran out.

I'd been so focused on the charms I hadn't been paying attention to the main mass of wild magic that was feeding the funnel. It was now less than half its original size. I looked around our circle room to see if there were any more motes to collect and it looked like we had them all.

This was so exciting. We had never processed anywhere near this amount of magic before. I still wanted to keep going, though. I took a moment to fill everyone in on what I was seeing.

"I want to keep going," I said. "There is still a lot of magic in the center and all the charms are not fully charged yet. Does anyone have any suggestions?"

"We can try making the circle smaller," John said. "If it's a smaller circle, then it will compress the magic in the center and make it spin faster."

Everyone agreed this was a good idea, so we tried it.

It was a disaster.

It turned out that everyone needed to make their magic fit a smaller circle, and we needed to all do it at the same time. That didn't go so well, and the circle started wobbling and slowed down quickly. I was afraid we had completely lost the circle. I had Penny go back to her original circle size and had everyone adjust their magic to match. It took a good fifteen minutes, but we finally got the circle going again. It wasn't as good as the first time. Some of the layers overlapped a bit. Still, it seemed to be spinning well, and I had the speed back up again.

"Any other suggestions?" I asked.

"How about we just lower the circle?" Sandy suggested. "Then the funnel wouldn't need to be as long."

Again, everyone agreed it was worth a shot.

Since everything had gone haywire last time, we were all super cautious. We kept a very slow pace, but gradually we all moved the circle until it was about a foot off the ground. Of course, we were all bent over at this point and nearly bumping heads. Maybe it would be a good idea to try this kneeling next time?

At this distance, I barely needed to make a funnel at all, and the charms continued to charge. That only lasted a few minutes and the central energy shrunk quite a bit more. It was just a bit bigger than a softball, and I decided to try one more thing.

"Let's try one last thing, guys," I said. "Let's take the circle all the way down to about an inch off the floor. Then we don't need a funnel at all and hopefully the charms can get the very last of the energy."

I wasn't sure if everyone was flexible enough to go all the way down. They still needed to be holding onto the wire after all. The person I was really worried about was John. He was so big and tall, but I needn't have worried. Apparently, mountain trolls can be quite flexible, which I'm sure Sandy knew already.

There wasn't very much neutral magic left and the charms sucked in the last of it. One more charm switched over to white and a couple of charms went almost black. All the charms on the edge were still dark red. We were finished.

I had everyone pull out of the circle in reverse order. Sandy went first and took back her orange magic. John pulled back his sparkly gray and then Annabeth pulled in her pink. The tone of her magic faded from the room.

I pulled in my emerald green magic and Penny gradually shrunk back into a penny. She still sounded faint and distant, but she seemed okay. She trilled at me happily, as if to say she had had a great time. Then she switched back to a ring and wrapped herself around my index finger again.

Sandy picked up one of the charms and examined it. "Well I'll be cow-kicked. I haven't seen a charm filled with so much magic in a long time." She was holding one of the dark red charms from the edge. "When I was in Chicago, I got to take part in one charging circle that had a lot of the old timers in it. They were powerful, experienced mages. I was fairly new at the time and they let me be a part of it to see how a real circle worked. The charms we were refilling came out like this, stuffed to the brim. I thought that was just the way it should be, but I've been in lots of circles since then and I've never seen results like that. Until now." She looked at me in awe. Her eyes shining. "Jason, this is amazing! What a breakthrough!" She was so excited she gave a happy twirl.

"Actually, I don't think you have seen everything yet." I told her about the magic colors and that I thought she was holding one of the least charged charms.

She picked up one of the deep red, almost black ones. "Annabeth, check this out!" They started chattering like two magpies over a pile of corn.

"You still haven't seen the best yet," I said, picking up a star-white charm and handing it to Sandy. She almost dropped it. Her mouth opened and closed a few times. She had no words.

She looked at me, Annabeth, and John and started laughing. "You know, what's crazy is that nobody else here knows enough about charms to truly appreciate just how amazing this is. If we were back in Chicago, we'd have the Head of Household herself coming down to check this out. Of course, if we were in Chicago then we would have access to a regular charging circle, and we would never have been forced to experiment like this." She looked at me and I swear she teared up a bit. "This is what I love about magic. There is always something new to learn and discover. It's so exciting, and a bit humbling too. Thank you Jason, for coming up with this. You've made my day. Actually, you've made my decade." She came over and gave me a big hug.

I grinned from ear to ear. It felt so good to be accepted. I'd put my abilities to use on poker, but when I won there, I was taking someone else's money and they were never happy about that. This time, though, my ability to see patterns and figure things out was helping everyone. I was the newest member of this little team and it felt so satisfying to be able to pull my own weight and contribute.

"How many more charms do we have left to charge?" I asked.

"We've been unable to recharge for a long time," Sandy said. "So I'm guessing we have about a hundred and fifty left."

"This room is almost completely out of magic now." I said. "But I do know of a place where I saw a lot of natural magic. I thought they were fireflies at the time but now I'm thinking it was motes of magic."

"I'm guessing the park?" Annabeth said.

"Yep. Right by where we were attacked by the golem. I was going to say something to you at the time, but then we had more important things to deal with. Penny seems to be okay with all this and I have a slight design change I want to try out. Do we want to take this out to the park?" I asked.

"Oh yes!" Sandy said. "I can't wait to get back to full power again. What about you two?"

"Of course. I'm game," Annabeth said.

"Whatever makes you happy," John said diplomatically.

We agreed to meet at Sandy's place fifteen minutes later and head out from there. I suggested we start out sitting down this time so everyone needed to wear something that would be all right in the grass.

I went back to my place to change into long sweatpants. If I wear shorts then the grass tickles me and I think it is bugs crawling on me. I'm a city boy and I hate that. Bermuda was napping so I kissed him and headed out.

Annabeth had one charm bracelet of hand-me-downs from Sandy. Sandy had three bracelets and a sack full of stuff. She wasn't kidding about being out of power.

I couldn't remember exactly which path we were on in the park when the golem attacked, so we had to wander for a bit before we found it. The picnic bench was still there, of course, and the air around it was filled with magic. I'm not sure exactly what it was about this spot, but it looked like someone had set off fireworks. There were some big fat motes too, much bigger than we had in the circle room.

Annabeth made the commonsense suggestion of sitting on the picnic bench rather than on the grass. We could put the charms on the top of the picnic table rather than on the ground, so they were much closer to the circle.

I asked Penny to form into a large ring again. This time we went with a two-foot diameter rather than three. I did change one little thing. I had Penny take a small bit of wire, run it to the center of the circle, then bend and go about a foot down. I was hoping this extra part of Penny would go through the center of the natural magic and guide the funnel so it would be even more precise. It might not work, but then we could just reset and start the circle over without the extra wire.

Penny seemed ready to go again, so I started first and layered her in thick green magic. Annabeth went next and her magic tone filled the air. It didn't bounce back to us like it did in the circle room, but instead wandered through the trees and grass in the park. It was nighttime again so we probably had the park to ourselves. I noticed that her music was attracting the motes already.

John went next, his rocky magic a perfect complement to our new outdoor setting, followed by Sandy. I started the circle spinning at medium speed and let the magic gather. The smaller radius was making a big difference. It spun the core a lot faster, and it seemed like it was taking less magic from the four of us to start the core forming.

Soon the core was dense and seemed to be attracting as much new magic as our circle was. I let it keep building. I was waiting for the right time to kick in the vortex speed, when something surprising happened. The natural magic started peeling off from the core and flowing down the new wire Penny had added. It looked cloudy at the top, then flowed like liquid down the wire, until there was a drop of pure, wild magic on the bottom.

That was crazy cool! Talk about condensing magic! We were using even less effort than before and it was very easy to touch the tip to a charm. The liquid magic must have been very potent, because the first charm went straight to dark red, then almost black, and then to star white in a few seconds.

The only problem was that the magic tip was now so precise we needed to move the circle a bit to touch down on the different charms. It took a lot of communication to make that happen smoothly.

We'd filled up a few charms when Sandy had an idea. She took one hand off the circle. We all held our breath, waiting to see if the circle would collapse.

It didn't.

Sandy was skilled enough to keep her magic flowing with one hand and use the other to move the charms around for us. That way we didn't have to move the circle. After that the recharging started going quickly.

Sandy hadn't been kidding when she said she had more than a hundred and fifty charms to charge. Her sack had all sorts of items in it, including an old set of brass knuckles. I didn't know what they did magically, but they charged just like all the others.

The girls were as happy as kids in a candy store. If I'd been missing my magic and then got it back, I'd be pretty giddy too.

Even with our new method and all the extra magic in the air, it still took a while to charge everything. We were down to our final three charms when I heard a voice.

16

Rumble in the Park

"**W**ell. Well. Well. Look what the cat dragged into the park." I'd been so focused on the magic ring and the whole process that I hadn't paid any attention to the rest of the world.

The voice was behind me, so Sandy and John could see who it was, but Annabeth and I couldn't. They both looked startled and apprehensive, but Sandy kept moving the charms and charging them. Nobody broke the circle, although I could hear the sound of someone approaching.

Actually, I could hear the sound of several someones approaching.

Two charms left, then one charm. Neither Sandy nor John said anything, which was strange. I felt the hair on my neck standing up.

Final charm done! Sandy, John, and Annabeth pulled out of the circle in record time. I pulled my magic and made sure Penny was safe around my index finger before turning around.

What I saw completely shocked me. I'm used to seeing with my magic sight and my natural sight at the same time, and usually they are complimentary. For example, the elephant charm looked like a regular charm to my natural sight, but it glowed with pink light to my magical sight. My magical sight usually just makes things more interesting.

The woman I was looking at was the complete opposite of that. To my natural sight she looked like a real-life version of Lara Croft from Tomb Raider. Long dark hair pulled back in a ponytail, tight fitting shirt with big boobs and slim waist, tight pants with hips and legs for days. Arched eyebrows with perfect skin made her look like a Photoshop version of a real person. She was a walking badass sex kitten.

She was every boy's wet dream, unless they saw the magical side. The only word for what I saw there was abomination—something that should not exist in nature.

Her magic was diseased and rotten. It rolled and billowed around her like a putrid fog. Chunks of it would fall off, like a fruit that had been left so long it was brown, slimy, and falling apart. It would slide down her aura, only to be absorbed again. Her magic looked like it was puking, eating the puke, then puking again.

I thought I saw a face scream at me before fading away. I had never smelled magic before, but she smelled like bodies that had been left in the dark for days. I wanted to run away, wash my hands, something.

Say what you will about the quality of the magic; the quantity of it was enormous. It was thick and powerful, easily the most forceful display of magic I had seen. There was so much it trailed along the ground behind her and towered over her head. I had no doubt that she could hit and hit very hard.

"Annabeth, Jason, get behind me," Sandy said quietly. I was only too happy to do so. I probably looked like a scared rabbit, but I didn't care. I wanted nothing to do with whoever this was. "Annabeth, when I tell you, grab Jason and run toward the House. Protect yourselves as best you can, but do not look back and do not stop for anything." Sandy was talking softly to us, but she never took her eyes off of Miss Tits and Ass.

When the abomination bombshell got about ten feet away, she held up her hand and everyone stopped. I'd been so focused on her that I'd completely missed who she was with. It seemed like a small army was arranged behind her. I did a quick headcount: thirty-six people. So, three full mage circles. They all glowed with various levels of magic, although no one had anywhere near the power of their leader.

They also seemed to share her diseased magic to some degree or another. Most of them still had their original auras shining through with only the occasional pus spot. The ones nearest to her, and obviously her highest ranked cronies, were almost as putrid as she was. There was one person, an older Asian woman, who just had a pure black aura. There wasn't any disease on her that I could see, and she looked calm, even serene. The pure black aura still struck me as sinister and she couldn't be good hanging out with this bunch.

"Sandy," the woman sneered. It was less of a greeting, more a sound of disdain.

"Isobel," Sandy said neutrally.

Ohhhhhh. So, this was the head of the mages in Louisville! No wonder Sandy didn't get along with her. Sandy hadn't mentioned her rotting aura, so maybe she couldn't see it like I could. She had obviously felt it, though, and knew something was amiss.

"Nice circle." Isobel gestured at us dismissively. Now that was some shade. With one comment she managed to point out that Sandy didn't have a full circle and that some of us were complete novices.

"Nice hair," Sandy replied. Isobel looked furious. Oh, that was right! Sandy had set fire to her hair! What had they called her . . . . old burnt and crispy? The tension was getting to me and I laughed. I didn't mean to, but I laugh when I get nervous.

Suddenly their whole crew was looking at me. Not good. I wanted to sink into the ground.

"Run into a golem recently?" Isobel said pointedly to Annabeth.

"Missing a golem recently?" I said sweetly. Two can play that game. She looked at me and hissed. She hissed like a snake! Me and my big mouth. Everyone was looking at me again. One of the guys in the front smacked his hand with a baseball bat.

I looked at everyone again and realized they were here to rumble. I saw baseball bats, tire irons, wands, staffs, a few charms, and even a sword. Oh shit. This was way out of my league.

As far as I knew we had no weapons, and I had no training on how to use them even if we did. Sandy and Annabeth had charm bracelets, but we suddenly seemed pretty underpowered.

I resolved to do the one thing I could do: run very fast.

Like really super-duper fast.

"Nice charms," Isobel said. The bitch fest was still going on. "It's been months since you've had a decent circle. How about you give them to me and I'll make sure they get charged for you?"

She said it so sweetly, but as she looked at our pile of charms her eyes were filled with greed. I'd been looking at charms as something you used for magic but hadn't considered how valuable they might be.

I looked at her crew again. There were a lot more baseball bats and tire irons than magical items. There were easily ten times more charms on the table than they had. This must have been the mother lode for them.

I had a bad feeling about this. They were not going to leave without taking everything we had, and we were going to get hurt in the process.

"My charms are fine," Sandy replied, scooping the loose charms into the bag. Except for the pair of brass knuckles. Those went on her hands. She stuffed the bag into her pants. They were going to have to go through her to get those charms.

"I really must insist," Isobel said. "We will take good care of them. A girl like you shouldn't be playing with them anyway."

Oh, the shade of it all!

"Since I can make my own charms rather than steal them, I would think they are safer with me. Given your age I would have thought you would have learned how to make a few trinkets by now," Sandy said.

Isobel looked furious. That must have been a sore spot for her.

"Some of us don't need charms to work real magic," Isobel spat out. "We are quite capable of defending ourselves when attacked. Just like your friend found out."

Sandy had been pretty cool up to this point, but that last comment got her.

"What do you mean?" she demanded.

"I mean that we can stick up for ourselves, and when your friend attacked us, we attacked back," Isobel said. Sandy looked flabbergasted. "Oh yes, your houseguests think you are so special. That the world revolves around you. That you are all just pretty flowers and that your shit don't stink." She stepped closer. "Well it does, little missy. It does."

"What happened to Jennifer!?" Sandy challenged.

"You're precious Jennifer attacked three of my coven. That arrogant little pisser thought she would teach us a lesson, but I was there. I stopped her. I took that pretentious little urchin and showed her what real power was. And I didn't need any charms to do it!" Isobel was shouting now. Playing to the crowd behind her.

"So, let me get this straight," Sandy said in a quiet, dangerous voice. "Three of your cronies ambushed Jennifer and when she won, you stepped in and beat an already exhausted mage."

Isobel hissed again.

"Did that make you feel like a big girl? Did that make you feel powerful?" Sandy had control of the narrative and it was making Isobel furious.

"Shut up," she screamed.

"Did four-on-one make you proud to be head of your coven that day?" Sandy said louder.

"Shut up!" Isobel was losing it.

"So, what did you do with her? Do you have her locked up in your trophy room? Is she in a cage with a sign that reads, 'Here is the little mage it took four of us to take down.'"

"I ate her." Isobel's eyes bulged and her aura writhed like a nest of angry snakes. "I sucked her magic out one little piece at a time."

Sandy drew back, shocked. I knew they thought Jennifer was dead, but they had never thought of something like this.

"When I was done with her there was nothing but dust. I swept her up and put her out with the trash. But do you know the best part?" Isobel's eyes gleamed with remembered triumph. "Every day she would tell me that her precious housemates would find her. 'Sandy would never leave me,' she said. Every day."

I couldn't see Sandy's face as I was behind her, but the set of her shoulders told me everything. She was so furious and so sad at the same time. I didn't know Jennifer but that sounded like a crappy way to go.

"She had faith in you. All the way until the end. Then you failed her."

"I searched so hard," Sandy whispered.

"Of course you did, dearie. Of course you did. You just aren't powerful enough. You let yourself down. You let her down." Isobel looked at me and Annabeth. "She'll let you down too. The great House is supposed to be all big and wonderful. It's really just a place for freaks and weirdos. A nest of grotesque aberrations that should be cleansed with fire." Isobel was shouting again.

I didn't think she had any room to talk about grotesque aberrations, the way she looked magically. This girl was seriously cray.

I thought she was going to go with a big final line before the battle. Something like, "It's time to burn!" However, she never got that chance.

A mage on the far left got a little trigger happy and shot off a spell at Sandy. The heat shimmer flew through the air, only to die when it met a blue shield that sprung up around our battle mage. With a contemptuous gesture, Sandy shot the heat shimmer back. If Miss Trigger Happy had a shield, it didn't do any good as the spell wrapped around her and she burst into flame.

It all happened so quickly. Isobel barely had time for a furious glare at the unfortunate woman before it was torch time. Everyone froze, almost like we couldn't believe this was happening. Then it was on. Spells flew thick and fast.

Several of them landed on their unfortunate sister, snuffing out the fire. I think they sucked the oxygen out of the air, though, because she was now struggling to breathe.

Most of them shot at Sandy, but she was already moving. She did a diving roll toward one of the mages in the front. She rolled inside his defenses and shot to her feet while throwing an uppercut. She had her whole body and legs behind the hit, and it lifted him off his feet and flung him through the air. She smoothly stepped and punched at the next guy. I think the mage thought her shield would hold as she didn't duck or move at all. Instead, the brass knuckles flared, the mage's shield shattered, and she went flying head over heels too.

John flared his magic and suddenly he was covered in a layer of sparkly gray. Spells bounced off him and didn't seem to bother him at all. He roared and charged.

Annabeth hugged me and a shield of blue shot up around us. Somehow all the spells heading our way either missed or died on the shield. I didn't know who was more surprised, me or Annabeth.

"Run!" she screamed at me, and that is exactly what we did. The park wasn't that big, but we still had to cross most of it to get back to the House.

We ran as fast as we possibly could, which didn't seem that fast at all. There were some spells still aimed at us, but we were farther away and harder to hit now. Annabeth was behind me. Her legs were shorter, so she ran a bit slower, and she was the one with the shield.

I could see the House ahead of me when I heard Annabeth cuss and her footsteps stopped. At the same time, I felt the ground shake. I knew that shake. I still felt it in my nightmares. There was a golem around here. I was about to turn around and see what was up when my feet suddenly stuck to the ground.

My body still had all the forward momentum, but my feet were now flat against the ground. It folded my body in half, and all that pressure landed on my calves, hamstrings, and back. I managed to stay upright, but I felt things stretch and hyperextend the way they shouldn't. Pain flared up all over me and I realized I wasn't going to be running anymore tonight. I might be hobbling or crawling, but sprinting was out of the question.

I looked over my shoulder to see Annabeth was stuck too. I could see what looked like thick swampy magic around her feet. She was glowing in pink light, trying to get herself free.

Then there was a splat, and she was covered in more magic that looked like toxic waste. She kept struggling so she was okay, but it was going to take a long time to get out of the spell that was holding her.

The shaking resolved itself into a golem, but not like the last one. This one had two legs and two arms, but from the shoulders up it was basically a throne. On that throne sat the toxic vixen herself.

She sure knew how to make an entrance. She looked as badass as the White Witch from Narnia, only in all black. I had to admire her style. Just not her smell, or her magic, or really anything else about her. She came right up to me, still sitting on her golem throne.

There is something really intimidating about a hulking stone monster only a foot away, and having to look way, way up to see cruel black eyes looking down on you in judgment. I felt very small at that moment. And very powerless.

Her magic billowed around me, leaving sooty smudges on my aura. I felt like I needed to take a bath. I decided not to look at her. I just stared at the stone shifting in front of me.

Without preamble she demanded, "Where is my golem?"

There was no way she made these golems. They were filled with mystery and magic and their auras were clean. Sandy had said Isobel couldn't even make a charm.

"I don't think that was your golem," I said.

"It's mine by right of bargain. It's mine to command. You have taken something from me, little urchin. Make no mistake, I will get it back. Now, where is my golem?" she demanded again.

"It's in the House," I replied. She was going to figure that out on her own. It occurred to me she had probably lost the ability to track it when my Flying Miners sucked it clean of energy.

"It seems like you are liar, urchin. A lesson is in order," she said.

Without warning, a stone column shot out of the middle of the golem in front of me and rammed me in my face. It was so unexpected that there was no time to dodge.

The beam was big; it covered almost my whole face. I felt things crunch that shouldn't be crunching. It hit me so hard it knocked me right off of the ground.

I flew back several yards, grass and dirt still stuck to my feet. I couldn't see. It was hard to breathe.

I was in shock.

My face was caved in.

My FACE was CAVED IN!

My natural sight was gone but I *saw* the crone leap off the golem and start to come over to me.

Suddenly, a little bundle of pure attitude bounded over the grass and stood in front of me. It was Bermuda, baby fur all fuzzed up, hissing and spitting, doing a little sideways dance. He was the perfect picture of ticked off guardian, even if he was only a few pounds.

I was still in shock at it all, but I wanted to scream, 'Get out of here!' This wasn't a few confused groundhogs. This was a pissed off elder magic user with serious power and a desire to hurt something.

Isobel stopped and regarded the little creature with narrow eyes. She gestured at Bermuda and a thick line of sludge-like magic shot toward him. He clawed at it, and the magic tore apart and faded into the ground.

There was something absurd about the scene. This pocket-sized kitten taking on a magical giant. For a moment I dared to hope. Hope that I would be protected. Hope that I would be safe.

Isobel shot another spell at him, which he clawed apart again. This time, though, she followed it up with a kick. Focused on the spell, my little hero didn't see the kick at all.

She kicked him like a football, and he took it full on his chest. He flew through the air. Up and up until he was out of range of my magic sight.

I felt sick.

I didn't know how anything could survive a kick like that. Not to mention how far he would end up falling.

I wanted to cry but coughed up blood and teeth instead.

"Not so lippy now, are you?" she said.

She kicked me. It wasn't a little kick, either. Her magic made her stronger and she was putting some anger behind it.

"A little more respectful now, aren't you, boy?"

She kicked me again.

"Now, where."

Kick.

"Is."

Kick.

"My."

Kick.

"Golem?"

That last kick actually picked me up off the ground.

I huddled in a ball whimpering. Trying to protect myself. I couldn't believe this was happening.

"That cost me dearly to get. It was loaned to me. Do you know what it will cost me if I don't return it?"

She kicked me again. I felt something snap.

"You had to be a stupid little House boy and muck it up, didn't you? You stupid, stupid, thing."

She stomped on me, then kicked me again.

"Here is what you will do. You will get me the golem back. I don't know where you hid it or what you did with it, but you will get it back."

She stomped on me, and I felt something else snap.

"Then you will serve me, to pay me back for all vexation you have caused. After you serve me, I will eat you. This is your life. What is left of it."

I still had my magic sight up, so I *saw* the stone that smacked into Isobel and sent her flying. It sounded like she had been shot, but she rolled to her feet, surrounded by a thick shield. She favored her left side a bit, but otherwise she looked ticked off and ready to fight.

Another thick stone smacked into her shield. It flew so fast, it looked like it had been launched out of a cannon. I heard a boom when it hit, and her shield cracked, then shattered.

She cast another one just in time as a third stone hit. She yelled something at the golem and it turned to fight. At that moment John dashed into my mage sight.

The golem took a swing at him but was way too slow for John. John might have been a big guy, but he moved like a dancer. He was fluid, fast, precise.

Isobel shot spells at him, but he ducked behind the golem. The golem swung at him but was too slow to touch him. Instead, John reached into the golem and started pulling out thick rocks. He hurled them at Isobel between her spells and fractured her shields.

It was two on one but neither opponent could get an upper hand. Isobel was running through a lot of magic. She couldn't keep this up forever. John couldn't dodge forever either. Someone was going to make a mistake.

Isobel blundered first and hit her own golem. It shrugged it off, but for a long moment it was motionless. John wrapped both hands around one of its arms and I saw his magic cover the limb. A moment later, the arm had been fused into one solid piece of rock.

With a grunt, John wrenched the entire arm off the golem. The strength to do that was just insane.

Isobel screamed in anger; her second golem was getting wrecked. John plucked out two rocks in either hand and hurled them at Isobel. When she ducked behind her shield, he grabbed the solid golem arm and ran at her.

She had enough time to throw one spell, and miss, before John was on her. He swung the rock arm through the air like a sledgehammer and smashed her shield.

She threw up another one and really poured her power into it. This shield was much thicker and glowed with energy.

Undeterred, John swung the massive arm again and again and again. He laid into the shield with a fury, trying to chop his way through.

The shield shivered and shook but managed to hold. Isobel had her feet braced, both arms extended, pouring massive amounts of magic into the shield.

John was winning, though. Isobel was sinking to the ground and the shield was barely covering the top of her. John stepped in close, almost on top of her, and really hammered her.

Suddenly, Isobel extended the shield under John's feet. With a shout, she lifted the mountain man into the air and flipped him behind her. There was now nothing between her and the one-armed golem.

She dropped her shield and sprinted toward her leggy throne. She vaulted into the seat, threw up another shield, and barked a command. With deep booming steps the golem started running away. It ran out of my range, with a furious John chasing after.

I laid on the ground feeling shattered. I felt the numbness and wrongness that comes from broken bones. I was afraid to move. I didn't even know if I *could* move. I was afraid to stay there, though. It was a battlefield and I was helpless to anyone that might come by.

It seemed like forever before someone came into view. It was Annabeth, finally free from the spell. She hauled me to my feet and forced me to get moving. It wasn't a run—it was a shambling walk at best—but we were moving toward safety. Every step was agony, but I didn't dare stop.

We made it across the House boundary and I gratefully sank down onto the ground. Safe at last, I passed out.

17

Recovery

-- Hour 3 --

I was in a burning house and I was on fire. Not the nice on-fire version, where you are just a bit crispy. I'm talking on fire, on fire. I kept running through the burning house, but there wasn't an exit. The fire ate into my flesh, burning me to the bones and then burning them too. I was a running screaming fiery skeleton, but I couldn't die and I couldn't get out. The floor burned out from under me and I fell through. The next floor was on fire too. I looked around in despair. This could not be right.

It was so wrong that I woke up.

I felt relief. It was just a nightmare. It would be morning soon and I would be okay. Tyler would be there with his strong arms again. Bermuda would be napping on the pillow. The sunlight would start shining and my perfect morning would be complete.

I went to open my eyes, but they wouldn't open. In fact, they felt like they weren't there. Instead, it felt like the fire was still burning my face. I heard voices. I took in a breath to cry, and fire filled my lungs. My cracked ribs creaked and rubbed against each other. The intense pain took my breath away.

I didn't cry out. I just whimpered.

"Easy there," John's bass voice said soothingly. "We are just working on bandaging you up."

I tried to ask what happened to my eyes, but my jaw wouldn't move. No words came out. Maybe my dream was real.

Everything hurt. It hurt on a level I hadn't experienced before. When I'd had my Death Experience I'd ended up in some sort of cocoon with the smell of lavender. Recovery had been long, and it had certainly been painful, but it hadn't been this fresh, this immediate, this overpowering.

I went to feel my face and my left arm exploded in agony.

"Try not to move yet," Sandy said. "Wait until we get you bandaged and splinted."

Every breath was agony. Every movement caused pain to flare up in a new spot.

They cut away my clothes. The shirt and pants were covered in blood and removing them normally in my condition was out of the question. My face was already wrapped in bandages, and they wrapped my ribs too. Sandy levitated me so John could wrap all the way around me. My left forearm was broken so they splinted and wrapped that too.

Sandy did a scan with a charm. She said the bones in my face were shattered. That included nose, forehead, cheekbones, and jaw. I had three broken ribs on the right and two on the left. Both of the bones in my left forearm were shattered. I had internal bleeding and more tissue damage than she wanted to list.

Sandy was trying to be clinical and detached, just sticking with the facts. Her voice caught, though, and she almost started crying. She said just knowing what was wrong would help my body start to heal itself.

She put three healing charms on me. One around my neck. One in the bandages around my ribs. One she wrapped around my feet. I was on fire, and the charms felt like ice. Not a soothing cool feeling, but a harsh bitter biting cold.

She said more things, but I was too far gone to hear them.

-- Hour 4 --

I was awake. Fully awake. And I was in hell. Breathing was pure agony. So, I took the smallest breaths possible. Moving was out of the question. Even the slightest movement caused a new cascade of pain. I would tense in agony, and that would cause even more areas to flare up. I tried to relax. To breathe. And that was all.

-- Hour 5 --

You know those pain charts they have at the hospitals? The ones that show a pain level of one with a slightly unhappy face, all the way up to pain level ten. The ten face is red, looking very sad, with a tear running down its face. Ten had nothing on me. Nothing. I was so far beyond that I couldn't even see it in the rearview mirror of my pain index. I wanted to cry and scream in agony.

-- Hour 6 --

The torment I was in was biblical in proportion. This had to be Hell. Demons crawled through my body like maggots. Laughing hysterically and eating me alive. They feasted on my flesh. They swung on my bones. They poked me with red hot pokers and tore at me with pliers.

I endured. That was all I could do. There was no alternative.

-- Hour 10 --

John was sitting with me when Annabeth came in to see him. I think she had slept after the fight, and now she was catching up on what had happened. I listened in. There was nothing else to do, and I desperately wanted something other than the pain to think about.

Other than me, the fight had gone really well. Sandy was a battle mage and she had a lot of frustration and anger built up. Frustration at the challenges of being Head of Household. Especially when the other House heads were feeling jilted that she got the honor. They were not helping Sandy at all. Anger at the Jennifer situation and a good bit of guilt too. She was ready for a good fight and the mages had given it to her.

She'd gone through most of them like a hot knife through butter. The old lady with the pure black aura was powerful, but she didn't seem to be there to really fight. John thought she was there to make sure the others didn't get too hurt. She played defensively in John's opinion.

John fought off Isobel and the last he'd seen, she had been in full retreat on her golem throne. John was very frustrated that he couldn't get to me in time and he was glad that Annabeth had gotten free and taken me to safety.

Sandy had found Bermuda and had taken him to the vet.

Bermuda!! I had completely forgotten him. I felt like such a heel. When Bermuda really needed me, I couldn't be there for him.

The vet had evaluated him and suggested it might be better to put him down. His care was going to cost a lot and he might not make a good recovery.

WTF?! He'd only been in my life a few days, but I couldn't imagine losing him. He filled a part of me I hadn't known was empty. He was the bravest and cutest creature I knew.

Sandy had let the vet know in no uncertain terms what she thought of that suggestion. She would break every bone in his body before he harmed a hair on Bermuda.

I wanted to cry. I couldn't because my eyes were sealed shut, but I wanted to. I loved Sandy in that moment. Standing up for Bermuda for me. Whatever the vet bills were, I would pay. I would pay a hundred times over. I just wanted to bring Bermuda home safe.

Apparently, she was so forceful that the vet turned the case over to another veterinarian. She was a lot more sympathetic to the situation and now Bermuda was in surgery. Sandy was staying there to make sure he got the best care and that the staff was properly motivated.

John left and Annabeth took over for a while. This was feeling like my Death Experience recovery, only a lot more painful. They had sat with me around the clock then, and they were doing it again.

I had good friends. I'd felt alone for so long. But now I had friends that would sit with me in a boring room and make sure I was okay.

-- Hour 11 --

All that emotion had destroyed the little bit of rhythm I'd found in the pain and the breathing. Now I was slowly getting it back.

I was so exhausted. It hurt too much to sleep. So, I just existed in this world of ache. I thought I had a fever too.

I realized Annabeth was humming.

-- Hour 13 --

Annabeth's humming had soothed me enough to get a tiny nap. Apparently, I liked to move when sleeping. That wasn't so good now.

I woke up screaming, but that hurt way too much. I cut that off as soon as I could get control again.

I breathed. Shallow, tiny breaths. Focused on the breath.

-- Hour 20 --

Annabeth had left. Tyler was there. He was still working on my remnants. Even in all this, he was still working on me. He told me he was really worried about them smoking out and attacking again in my weakened state. This was a good time for them to pounce, but that wasn't going to happen. Not while he was there. He tried to tell me more, but I couldn't focus.

My mind was a fog. My body was molten lava. I let it flow. And breathed.

-- Hour 30 --

I thought I was going crazy. The pain was overwhelming. And it didn't stop. It just flowed on and on and on. No end in sight.

I'd raged that I couldn't go to the hospital like a regular person.

I'd raged that meds didn't work for me anymore.

I'd raged that this had happened at all. I hadn't asked for this. I hadn't asked to get in a fight with a two-ton stone beast. Or a cesspool master mage.

Now there was no rage left.

I'd despaired too.

I'd despaired of ever getting better. Maybe this was some new dimension of torment that I'd never escape.

I'd despaired that I would get better but would forever be deformed. I'd be the Quasimodo of Louisville. Living life as a beggar and making children scream when they saw me.

Now there was no despair left.

I felt empty.

Broken.

-- Hour 50 --

Tyler left. Sandy sat with me for a while. Then John. Then Annabeth. Now we were back to Tyler again. Since I couldn't talk, we were communicating via light hand squeezing. My right hand could move a bit without pain. They would hold my hand and ask a question. If yes, then one squeeze. If no, then two squeezes.

There wasn't much to say, of course. I got a tiny bit of water. Didn't want to do too much or I'd have to pee and that would really hurt right now. Otherwise, I didn't move.

Tyler started talking again, and this time I listened. He asked me if I could hear and understand him.

Squeeze.

"Jason, I hope you are finding your balance in this situation. This whole thing sucks. And you are so new to being a supernatural."

What did I say to this? Was I finding my balance? I wasn't sure what that meant. I just left it alone. No answer.

"I do want you to know that I've been through this. I've been through this for longer than you could possibly imagine."

I really doubted that. This was so intense.

"Imagine getting better, then this happening again. Then getting better, then happening again. Imagine it happening over and over again for ten years. That's what I went through after my Waker Moment. There was no one to help me or bandage me up or even tell me what was going on. I had to endure and eventually learn on my own."

Okay. I took it back. That was way worse than what was happening to me. I knew on some level that no matter how bad it was now, it would get better. I thought this was a nightmare.

The picture he was painting was a never-ending horror.

Squeeze.

"Because I've been through this, I'm in a unique position to offer you some advice. Can you listen and understand me? Are you ready to hear me?"

Was I? For the first time I realized it could be worse. Tyler seemed like a good guy. The House relied on him and he seemed to be a force for good in the world. If he had come through this and found a way to survive, even thrive, I wanted to hear it.

Squeeze.

"Let's talk about two things. The first is finding balance. You are going to be in a lot of different situations in your life. Some of them good and happy and wonderful in every way. Some of them will be awful and you will wonder how you will survive. If you live in any situation for long enough, an element of normalcy will start to creep in. No matter how good, or how bad, it will start to feel normal. I call this finding your balance. Are you still with me?"

Squeeze.

"When you find your balance, when you find the normalcy in the situation, then you can start making decisions about what you are going through. You can start thinking about options. You can strategize and find a way to go in the way you want to.

"Through no choice of my own, I ended up in a horrible starting situation after my Waker Moment. It broke me for a long time. I wanted to die, but I couldn't. I thought I would be in this situation forever.

"One day, though, I realized it wasn't as bad as before. It had started to seem normal. The more normal it got, the more I started thinking about how I could get better. I tried a lot of things; most of them failed, but some of them didn't. It took years, but I had nothing but time. I figured out how to master my power and become a much better supernatural.

"I used this power to escape. I found the House and it kept me safe. Now I have a good life of my own. I still practice every day with my power and I still look for more ways to use it. So, lesson number one: Find your balance. Understand?"

I thought I did understand. I hadn't been open to this hours ago. People had been talking but I couldn't hear them.

I was still at a level of pain that made me want to scream over and over again. Somehow, though, I could think now. Maybe this was just a little bit normal. Maybe I was finding my balance.

Squeeze.

"Lesson two: Don't heal. Transform."

Okay, that wasn't cryptic at all.

"You probably have an idea of what healing is. It's something that happens over time. The body gradually generates new cells and goes through healing stages. For example, a cut. First your body bleeds to clean the wound. Then it scabs over to provide protection and a safe place to regrow. Regrowth happens and finally the scab itches and falls off. Then you have a scar that gradually fades over time.

"Next example, a broken bone. First you align the break so it can heal right. Then you immobilize the bone so it can heal without rebreaking. Finally, it heals, but it usually isn't perfect. Maybe you have phantom pains every now and then, or it aches when the weather changes. All of this sound familiar?"

Oh yes it did. That's why I thought I might look like Quasimodo at the end of all this.

Squeeze.

"Now let's talk transformation. Did you ever see any of the Terminator movies where the robot of the future is made of liquid metal?"

Terminator 2 was one of my favorite movies. It was old, but still a classic.

Squeeze.

"When he got shot, the liquid robot in there didn't worry about healing. He just transformed back into the shape he wanted. He was shot, smashed, exploded, lost parts of himself, and still he came back. Just as good as before. He did it by transforming."

I wasn't sure how that applied to me. I wasn't a liquid metal terminator. It sure sounded nice, though.

"Do you have your magic sight turned on? I want to show you something."

Squeeze.

He looked the same to me as he always did. He picked up a small paring knife from the floor, pressed it against his forearm, and cut himself.

It was a long cut, maybe three inches, and it was enough that his skin peeled back a bit. What I *saw* underneath amazed me.

He was filled with magic. Filled with it in a way I had never seen before. Even with Sandy or Isobel. The magic was dense and flowed like lava. The light was intense, but somehow it didn't shine far.

Before my magic eyes, the cut transformed. It didn't stitch itself back together or heal from the ends back to the middle again. The cut didn't even close. It's just that the section of his arm that had the cut transformed back into a perfect arm again.

It looked like the cut never even happened.

"Did you see that?" he asked.

Squeeze.

My mind was blown. I didn't even think something like this was possible. Suddenly I had hope again.

"You don't have anywhere near the magic density to do something like this on a large scale. But on a small scale it might be possible. Sandy has her healing runes working on you and they will help. You are a supernatural now so your body will try to heal perfectly. Most of your recovery will come from healing. But, if even some of it could come from transformation, then you will be well ahead of the game."

I didn't know how to say thank you, so I squeezed his hand a bunch of times.

"I don't know how to teach you to do this. It's just something I've figured out with a lot of trial and error. I can tell you that you will need a lot of your magic, and you'll want it at the place you want to transform. Other than that, you'll have to figure out how it works on your own. Good luck," he said and let me have at it.

-- Hour 51 --

I wasn't having any luck so far. I'd decided to start working on the top right broken rib. I had so many broken bones I could have chosen, but my ribs were the only ones that were moving. I could keep my face and arm still, but I had to breathe. Breathing meant using my chest, and the constant irritation on my broken ribs was driving me insane. If I could just heal my ribs, maybe I could get some sleep and escape from all this for a while.

I'd picked the rib on the right that seemed to be bothering me the most and zoomed in my magic sight to see what I was dealing with. It was a complete break. The bone was cracked at an angle, but the edges were still together. This was good if I could get the transformation going. It was bad right now because every breath caused the two broken parts to rub against each other.

I tried coating the edge of the break with magic, but my magic was like a mist; it just floated away. I tried spiraling my magic and this helped a bit. It created a denser core of magic at the center, but this caused so much turbulence it didn't do me any good.

I tried just squishing the magic together, but the brute force method didn't work. I could make the fog a bit denser, but it wasn't enough to cause any sort of change, and as soon as I let go, the fog just swirled away again.

I'd tried making one of my little cartoon creations, but they couldn't work inside me.

I'd seen it happen. I knew it was possible. I just didn't know how to do it.

-- Hour 52 --

I was so frustrated. I wanted to scream and kick my magic. I'd gone back to spinning my magic, except this time I made it like a cyclone. That was a no go. I'd tried making a sphere of magic and slowly decreasing it down. I didn't really have any way of making the boundary of the sphere and the magic just leaked around my control.

I could feel my magic was eager to help. It wanted to do what I needed. It just didn't know how to compress on its own and I didn't know how to guide it.

Maybe I was being too detailed. Maybe I needed to go bigger picture. I pulled out to a whole body focus and began pulling magic from Penny. I filled up like I normally did when I was cycling my magic with her, but this time I kept going. I just kept pulling and pulling until I was dizzy and felt like I was about to explode.

The dizziness felt good. I couldn't sleep, and my current situation was pure torture. Anything that helped take my mind off of my situation, even a little bit, was welcome. It felt like taking a really deep breath, and then trying to take in even more air. It just didn't feel possible. I held it all in, though, and sip by sip, crammed in even more.

I zoomed back into my rib again. There was a lot more misty magic in the area now. There still wasn't enough for transformation, but there was certainly more magic available. I ran through my bag of tricks again, but still nothing worked.

I needed to condense magic like Penny had when she was filling charms. The final bit of magic that went into the charms was liquid. I needed to get to that.

Penny was an awakened and aware charm, though. I didn't have something like that inside me. Or did I? Maybe I could make one. Maybe I could take a cell, stuff it full of magic, and make it like Penny. If I could awaken a string of cells, I could make a coil that would condense magic inside me.

Nothing else was working, so it was worth a shot.

I zoomed in even more than I had before. I'd been working at the level of the break; now I zoomed in to just one tiny part of that break. Seen this close, the break wasn't smooth; there was all kinds of jagged surfaces. I picked one and zoomed in even more.

I'd never been this deep before. It was like I was looking at myself with a powerful microscope. The jagged piece, zoomed in, had a rough surface to it also. I picked a part that looked even more rough than normal and zoomed in on that.

I wasn't sure what I was looking at. I thought a cell was just a round thing, like a drop of water. It had a center, a wall lining, and that was it. I thought cells were stacked together like a bunch of water bottles and that made up all the tissue we had.

What I was seeing was very different from that. These were more oblong, with all sorts of roots coming off of them. The roots all meshed together, and it was hard to see where a cell stopped and the next one started. Some of them looked squishy and some of them looked solid, like vines growing together.

I felt like I was in some strange fantasy land. What I was seeing with my magic sight was so strange and different. Landing on the moon would have felt more familiar that this.

I took a moment to be amazed at my magic sight. I didn't know what magnification I was at, but I was viewing things at a much more detailed level than I had with the microscopes at high school. That I could see things this small was astonishing.

Everything was so intertwined I wasn't sure I could just isolate a cell like I had originally planned. Instead, I just picked out one of the squishy oblong sacks that was at the surface and decided to pack it with magic and see what happened.

When I looked around for magic, I realized I couldn't see the mist. My magic still had to be here, though. This was my body after all. I called for magic and looked around. Nothing happened. There wasn't the faintest trace of mist that I could see.

I called again and this time held the call. At first, nothing happened. I could feel something, though, getting closer. Then, a huge nebula of lights appeared.

It looked like a dust bunny of lights, the size of a large house. The lights were all jumbled together and scattered around, like a galaxy of stars. The lights weren't spheres, either. They were oblong, and different sizes. It really did look like a giant dust bunny, with all the shapes and sizes of dust tangled in together.

It clearly was my magic, though. It was filled with emerald green and sapphire blue illumination.

I was seeing magic in a whole new way. Just as bone looked so strange and different at this magnification, so did my magic. I'm sure my 'mist' was made up of hundreds of thousands of these magical dust bunnies.

The dust bunny spaceship was beautiful. It was like a Christmas wonderland. Despite the seriousness of the situation, I took a moment to appreciate it. Then I pulled it down toward me and the cell I had picked out. I wasn't sure exactly what to do, other than to try and merge the lights into the cell.

It ended up being much easier than I thought it would.

I picked off some of the lights and pushed them toward the oblong cell. They easily floated inside and mostly stayed there. Some of them floated out again but ended up staying inside the roots of the cell. The cell started glowing from all the magic inside it, then it flashed, and now the lights were a part of it.

I gathered more lights and pushed them into the next oblong cell. It filled, flashed, and then started glowing too. The light went down the roots to where the two cells were connected.

I gathered more lights and soon I had a patch of ten cells and their roots all glowing with magic. I needed more lights, so I sent out the call again. Soon, another house-sized magical Christmas dust bunny showed up and I kept going.

I wasn't sure if this was the right way to heal myself, but I was getting the magic into me at a cellular level. Hopefully, this would result in something good.

I kept working, stuffing my cells with magic and awakening them. It wasn't fast work, but it was steady. I kept the call out all the time and now I had lots of magical Christmas dust bunnies ready for me to work with. They bumped up against each other and merged, forming even bigger dust bunnies. Soon the 'sky' was filled with light and the 'land' was looking like something out of James Cameron's *Avatar* movie.

It was an unearthly supernatural landscape.

I'd filled everything in my view and was getting ready to expand my awareness when the first metamorphosis happened. I was taking a moment to view my handiwork, when I saw a twinkle. It was so fast that I didn't have time to see what happened. Everything was so new to me that it was difficult to see if anything had changed.

I stayed there for a while, keeping my awareness open. Looking for it to happen again.

There! A twinkle. Again, I wasn't sure if anything had changed. This time it almost looked like lightning.

I waited. The lightning twinkles were happening every few moments now. It seemed like they were happening more often.

Then it happened right in front of me. It wasn't so much that lightning came down from the sky. It was more like the ground pulled it down. A cell flashed, and where there was one before, now there were two.

I did a happy dance. My body was fixing itself!

I went to the edge of what I'd awakened and kept going. Soon my garden of awakened cells was double the size of before. It also seemed like the cells were easier to awaken.

I decided to test that theory. Instead of awakening cells that were right next to the mass of already awakened cells, I struck out in a straight line. Very quickly they became harder to transition. I decided to curve the line back toward the mass of awakened cells. That left a group of unawakened cells in the middle.

I was filling in the middle, when I noticed one cell awakened on its own. Most of its neighbors were already awake, and it just flashed and pulled magic itself. That was interesting.

It seemed like I should be able to use that somehow, but I couldn't think of how to make it work to really speed up the transformation. It did allow me to skip some cells, which helped a bit. It wasn't a big time-saver though. Still, every little bit helped.

I made the mistake of zooming out a few levels to see how much I had done.

I didn't know how long I'd been at this, but I'd done a tiny fraction of the break. Like maybe one percent of one percent. At the level where I could see the whole break, there was just a little speck of bright light. It was going to take a long, long time to fix this.

I wanted to cry. But that would hurt too much. This was just one break of many. The whole task seemed overwhelming.

I zoomed back in again, picked a spot on the edge of my cell garden, and kept going. This was a crappy alternative, but it was the only alternative I had.

-- Hour 60 --

It seemed like I had been working on this break for forever. I checked my overall progress. Only about a quarter done.

The sleeplessness and the pain were really getting to me. I had found my balance for a while, but it was slipping away. Working on the break at the micro level helped, but the progress was so slow. It gave me hope, but it also highlighted just how long this recovery was going to take. I didn't know if I could last that long.

I'd found a few other ways to speed up awakening my cells. I brought the 'sky' of magic down closer to the cells. With a shorter distance to channel magic, I could now awaken two cells at once. The closer magic also helped the twinkle lightning to occur more often. That was the real goal, new growth. I needed to bridge the gap between the two sides of the bone.

The sky of magic also slowed me down, though. As the new growth happened, it used up the magic I'd called. I ended up having to pull down more magic, both for myself to use and to cover the parts I'd already awakened. I was now spending almost half my time pulling down more magic dust bunnies over my already awakened area.

I'd realized this meant that the more area I awakened, the slower my expansion would be. It was so frustrating. I didn't think I would be able to awaken the entire area of the break. I'd have to do it in stages.

I'd have quit if there were anything else I could have done. I couldn't talk, move, watch TV, or read. My only option was to just endure the pain and work on my recovery.

I didn't think I'd ever been in a situation like that before. If things got bad enough, I usually just moved on. Or found a solution to what was bothering me. In this case, I couldn't run away and there was nothing else I could think of to improve my progress. It was soul crushing.

-- Hour 65 --

Sandy was here with John, and she was giving him an update. Bermuda had gone through surgery okay and was now recovering. They would release him tomorrow, but he would be in a body cast for a while. There was still a chance for complications, but recovery was looking good for now.

Sandy was still processing what she had found out about Jennifer. John was framing this with the five stages of grief: denial, anger, bargaining, depression, acceptance. She'd been in denial until the rant from Isobel. Then she'd moved to anger pretty quickly. Sandy said she still had a lot more anger to work out next time she saw Isobel.

Right now, she was feeling depressed. She wanted to make a positive difference in the world. The supernatural world was so cruel, and many new sups were exploited for their powers. She wanted to start something new, something safe. The House created a unique haven for new supernaturals, but even then it was filled with politics, secrecy, and hoarding. She wanted to learn everything she could about magic and teach it to others. To create a place for learning and respect, rather than power and exploitation.

She felt like her goals were good, but her results sucked. Jennifer was dead. I was in bad shape, and Annabeth was so different she didn't know how to teach her. The other Heads of House were not supporting her, and now she was in an all-out war with the mages. Being Head of House was a lot harder than she had thought it would be. Life had been much easier when she was just a battle mage. Then, you knew where your enemies were and you went out and stomped them. It was a simple good guys vs. bad guys type of thing. She was thinking that maybe she should have just stayed a fighter.

John let her talk it out and held her in a big hug. After she wound down, they stayed like that for a while. John was a lot like a mountain; big, solid, and somehow peaceful to be with.

I guess Sandy didn't realize I was awake and listening to them. She always seemed so confident and knowledgeable to me. I thought a battle mage was exactly what we needed to deal with these Louisville mages. We needed someone that could kick some ass.

John finally left. Sandy gave me a tiny drink of water. She started reading and I went back to working on awakening my cells again.

-- Hour 70 --

I had completely bridged the gap between half of the break. When the new cells reached the other half of the rib, they had fused seamlessly. Now the break wasn't rubbing against itself anymore. A part of myself wasn't hurting as much. This would have been cause for major celebration if there wasn't so much left to do. I was still working on the rest of the break. The last thing I wanted was for the rib to crack again.

I felt so emotionally exhausted. I hadn't slept or eaten in a long time, and it looked like it was going to be a very long time before that happened again.

Sandy had switched out for Annabeth and she was humming. Her pink magic and positive energy were working on me, trying to give my spirit a boost. I wasn't sure it was working. Or maybe it was. Maybe I'd have felt even more miserable if she weren't here. That was a scary thought.

Annabeth took my hand.

"Are you awake, Jason?" she asked.

Of course I was awake. I couldn't sleep. Didn't she know that? I felt a surge of irritation.

It occurred to me that my face was wrapped in bandages and I was staying very still all the time. They probably didn't know how I was doing at all. I couldn't tell them, and there wasn't anything they could see. They were probably assuming that I was sleeping as much as I could. If only that were true.

She was just trying to be nice. I guessed she wanted to talk. Actually, that sounded nice. It was lonely in my own head.

I gave her hand a squeeze.

"I'm worried about you," she said. "I know there are the obvious issues." She gestured at my bandages. "It's your music that worries me. You normally have a happy beat when I listen to you, like a chorus of bells. When you first got hurt all your bells sounded the alarm, but you still sounded like bells."

I gave her a squeeze. I was listening.

"For a while there, you got your beat and your bells back. I don't know what happened, but I think something gave you hope. Now, though, you sound like breaking glass. There isn't any beat at all. It's just glass shattering at random. It sounds like rows and rows of glass windows are falling out and smashing on the sidewalk."

I gave her a long squeeze. Then just held her hand tightly. That was exactly what I felt like. My sanity was shattering around me. I was focusing as much as I could, but it just felt so hopeless. There was so much to do, and my rate of recovery was so slow. The pain hammered at me in waves, crashing into me over and over again.

Just to know that she was there, that somehow she had an inkling of what I was going through, was enough to break me down. I welled up with emotion. I wanted to sob into her shoulder and have her hold me tight. I desperately wanted to hear that everything was going to be okay.

For a while she just held my hand and hummed. Her good energy washed over me. I wasn't sure what I was sounding like, but eventually I did feel a bit better.

"Jason, I'm not sure exactly what you are going through, and you can't tell me. I'm sure it's horrible in there right now and you are feeling very lonely and scared. I can only imagine how I would feel. There is something I want to tell you and I hope it helps. Can you hear me? Are you able to listen right now?"

Squeeze for yes.

Tyler had given me a path for hope with his talk. It was a very slow solution for me, but at least it was something. Maybe Annabeth had something valuable to tell me also.

"I don't have anything magical to tell you that will help. Sandy and I have been talking and there isn't anything else we can think of that will help magically. You already have three healing charms on you and you are only supposed to have one. If you get too many, they start interfering with each other. In this case, there is enough damage right by the charms that we think they will work in a smaller area and not mess with each other."

I'd completely forgotten about the healing charms. I guessed they were helping. Maybe they were helping me a lot and I would be even worse off without them. That was another scary thought.

I checked them; they were still glowing like little stars. Which hopefully meant they were full of magic and doing their job. I could detect a fine layer of yellow magic coating my injuries around the charms. It looked a bit like someone had sprinkled mustard on them. I guessed they were doing something for me.

I gave Annabeth a squeeze. She hadn't asked a question, but it was a confirmation I was listening.

"I do have something that may help emotionally, and that is where I think you are struggling right now. It's something that a friend told me when I was going through a rough patch with my husband, and it stuck with me over the years. She told me that the way to overcome any situation and make it better is through acceptance.

"That seemed really weird to me at the time. My husband was not doing the things I thought he should be doing. He wasn't treating me right and he wasn't treating himself right. We were in this spiral of arguing and bickering all the time. If I accepted all the crap he was doing, wouldn't that just make it worse? I felt like I would be making him do more crappy things to me. To us. To our relationship.

"My friend and I had a long series of talks, and I finally saw I was putting so much energy into resisting the situation, that there wasn't any energy left over to find another way to deal with the problem. There's another quote I found later: 'Whatever you resist persists.' If you want something to stick around, then resist it. The more you try to make something go away, the more it takes up your time and attention and sucks all the joy out of life.

"Anyway, to make a long story short, I finally accepted my husband just the way he was. He didn't get worse like I feared. He didn't get better either, at least not at first. A few weeks later he asked me what had changed. I wasn't being a complete bitch to him anymore. I was shocked. I thought he was being the asshat but he was reacting to me. We both still loved each other and over time we worked it out.

"I know this may not sound like it applies to you right now, but I'm guessing that you are spending a lot of energy trying to deal with all the injury and trauma. I'm guessing there is a lot of anger about what happened, frustration with what you are going through right now, and worry about how it is going to work out.

"I can only tell you this takes a lot of energy. I can feel you've been working on something. I'm not sure what, but you were doing good there for a while. Trying to make your situation better and being upset about it at the same time is too much. You are going to wear yourself out. I know this sounds crazy to you right now but try fully accepting what happened. Just accept you are in the situation you are, with no judgment about how you got here or how you are handling it. Just accept it. Let the resistance go. Maybe then you can find your strength again."

I gave her a squeeze. I understood what she was saying, but it seemed crazy to just accept it. There was so much that was wrong with my situation. My jaw was broken so I couldn't eat. My nose was crushed so I couldn't breathe normally. My ribs were broken so I was afraid to move. I had real huge problems. Accepting them wouldn't just make them go away.

On the other hand, being upset about the situation wasn't making it any better either. I thought about what Tyler said about finding my balance. This was a lot like that, only it was more proactive. I felt like I had lost my balance a long time ago. Whatever normal I'd found in this situation was gone now. I was just fragmented. Too lost and exhausted to find my way back again.

It seemed like the strangest thing to me, but I decided to embrace her advice. Tyler's advice had really helped and now I had one partially healed rib. Maybe Annabeth was onto something. It sounded bat shit crazy, but I was going crazy anyway, so what did I know?

I centered myself in the middle of my magic and just let myself go. I let go of the fear of moving. I let go of the fear of pain. I let go of the fear of the future and how all this was going to work out.

Instead, I accepted it all. This was what it meant to be a supernatural. I was a supernatural. I accepted that.

I accepted that I was hurt as much as I was. I accepted that I would get better and it would be a rough road to recovery.

I accepted that I hadn't slept at all this whole time.

I accepted that I was weak. I was weak magically, emotionally, physically.

My life was what it was right now. Nothing more and nothing less.

I felt like I was floating in my magic. Arms thrown out, head back. Just gently spinning around in peace. In surrender.

I hadn't realized how much I was resisting things. I was resisting moving. Resisting breathing. Resisting feeling.

Resisting how long this was going to take to recover from.

Once I let it go, I felt a strange sense of peace. I felt power.

Actually, I really did feel power. Like there was a center to my power and I was drifting toward it. I just let it happen. I spun gently in space. Completely yielding to the moment. Letting all the anger and hurt and frustration go.

I moved toward something. And then I was there.

I opened my eyes and touched down. I was in a room. It looked like a throne room that had seen better days.

There were faded banners on the wall. A torn carpet of red led to a throne that was chipped and faded. It had been padded, but now it was just hard black stone. The tiles on the floor were cracked and broken and part of the ceiling was falling down.

It looked like this had been the throne room for a small, poor kingdom, but one that had been abandoned for hundreds of years.

I knew, somehow, this was my seat of power. This was the center of my will. The center of my magic.

The room was in crappy shape, but then again, I was in crappy shape. That was okay. I accepted the room the way it was. I wouldn't be in this shape forever.

I walked up to the throne and sat down on it. It fit me perfectly, of course. It was hard and cold, but it was nice to just sit for a moment.

I couldn't believe how peaceful I felt. I hadn't realized how much energy I'd spent trying to keep it all together.

I looked around my little throne room, and for the first time noticed a cot in the corner. It was one of those cots you use when you're camping, with a simple cross frame and a canvas bed. It had a nice pillow at the head and a blanket folded up beside it.

It wasn't much, but it looked like heaven to me. I hadn't slept in a very long time. Was it possible for me to sleep in here?

It didn't seem like much of a magic thing to do, find the root of your power and then go to sleep.

I went over to the cot and lay down. The pillow was so comfortable, just the right size and firmness. I pulled up the blanket and snuggled in.

The cot was simple and basic, but to me it was the ultimate luxury. I knew this was all make-believe somehow. It couldn't be real.

I wasn't really in a throne room, feeling no pain, but somehow, it was real enough.

I felt relaxed, serene.

I'm sure this wasn't what Annabeth had thought would happen when she told me about acceptance. I was accepting it all, though, and with that final thought, I fell asleep.

18

Matrix

When I woke up, I felt rested. The injuries were still there, they were still sending out the pain so I didn't forget them, but now I felt clear headed.

I wondered if my throne room was real or if I'd just hallucinated it. If it was real, would I be able to get there again? I felt worry and anxiety start to creep in again.

I knew the solution now. I wasn't going to let doubt and pain steal my strength again.

I accepted and celebrated that I'd slept. I accepted that I was now awake and wasn't sure how I would sleep again. When I accepted what I knew was true, the worry just evaporated.

Tyler was with me again. I could feel him plucking at my remnants. There were only two left. Hopefully it would only be one soon.

Waking up with Tyler there made me think of Bermuda. I wished he was there with me. I loved waking up to him all sprawled out on my pillow.

As if he was thinking about me too, I heard a little squeak. I expanded my awareness. Bermuda was here!

He was in a box by my bed. Someone had filled it with towels to make him comfortable.

He was in a body cast, though. It immobilized his front leg and both of his back legs. He only had one paw free.

My heart went out to him. My poor little baby. It hurt like a bitch, but I tried to crawl over to the edge of my bed so I could touch him. I was too weak, so Tyler helped me.

Finally, I could reach out my one good arm and touch his one good paw. He was so soft. Just touching his paw felt like heaven. I stayed that way for a long while. Even that little bit of movement on the bed had exhausted me and all my aches had cranked back up to fifteen on the pain scale again.

I just breathed and accepted it over and over again and loved on Bermuda the little bit I could. He tried to wiggle closer to me. He gave a long pitiful wail. His little mouth was open, and he was panting.

We were both in bad shape. He licked my hand and then rested his head on my fingers. For a while we just existed together.

I tried to scan his injuries, but his aura was strong and it made it difficult. It looks like they had put a pin in both his front leg and his back leg to help the bones heal correctly. He also had some cracked ribs, but there wasn't anything they could do for that other than try to keep him from moving a lot. I knew from present experience that cracked ribs were the worst.

He didn't deserve this. I wished I had been able to protect him. I wished I had been stronger. I wished I was able to help him somehow.

That idea rolled around in my head for a while. It was taking forever for me to mend one bone in my body. I didn't know if I would be able to do anything like this in his body. His aura would stop me.

I saw he had a healing charm on. Hopefully that was helping him too.

He gave another sad little wail. Tyler got up to get Sandy. The vet had sent home some liquid pain medication. It should still work for Bermuda and obviously he needed some.

It occurred to me that healing happened faster with magic. Maybe I could give him some magic and help him out? He was such a little thing that even a small bit of magic would go a long way.

I gently pushed some magic out to him like I would to Penny. To my surprise, his aura didn't resist at all. Instead the magic flowed smoothly and his aura got brighter.

It was my experience that doing magic to other people was very difficult. They were a living creature and their aura always tried to shut me down. Were the rules different now that I was a full supernatural? Or was Bermuda different because he was a cat? Or maybe because I was his human?

That was too much to think about right then, so I filed that thought away in memory for experimentation later. Instead, I pushed more energy to Bermuda. He seemed to like it, so I pushed even more.

Soon, Bermuda was shining with emerald and sapphire light. I stopped pushing magic, but it kept flowing. I started to pull away, but Bermuda held onto my finger with his teeth. He gave a little growl and kept pulling.

He was really sucking it down. I had to start pulling from Penny to make up for what he was taking from me.

He was still pulling from me when his light suddenly dropped. It wasn't shining as much. Instead it looked richer, more solid somehow. What the heck?

I focused on his aura. It wasn't projecting out like before. Instead it looked more like glowing water. It was thicker, richer, more vibrant. It was moving in a pattern too. I focused on that.

Bermuda was folding the magic somehow. He was stretching it out, then folding it up, then stretching it out again. It was almost like he was kneading it like dough. He kept pulling from me and the new magic was getting folded in with the denser magic.

He was up to something, so I just let him have the magic. I pulled from Penny and he pulled from me. He folded and stretched the magic and it got even denser. I had no idea how he was holding so much power. He only weighed about three pounds and he had pulled as much magic as I had in my whole body to start with.

I felt like something should happen. Hopefully he wouldn't blow up or anything. I wasn't sure how that much magic could exist in such a little frame.

Suddenly he shuddered, and the magic rippled. His magic stopped folding and the light faded completely.

I waited for a moment, but he had stopped pulling any magic and nothing more happened. He put his head back on my hand again and closed his eyes.

Sandy and Tyler came back in. I longed to tell them what had just transpired, but I had a broken jaw so that wasn't happening.

Sandy had a little eye dropper of medicine that she gave to Bermuda. He lapped it up and went to sleep right away. She checked on me and I answered her as best as I could using the yes/no squeeze method. I got a bit of water myself. Then she left and Tyler settled back in bed with me again.

It got quiet and I went back to examining Bermuda. His new aura was strong. I poked at it and it just snapped back into place. It seemed stable and powerful. It also seemed much denser than the mist I was working with.

Bermuda's aura had always been emerald, but now it was my exact shade of emerald and there were swirls of sapphire in it. It was certainly my magic with my aura still mixed in it, but he had manipulated it and made it his own.

I was fascinated and looked closer. His aura was much more open to me now. It still wasn't like looking inside myself, but it was much clearer than before. I looked at the break on his leg and zoomed in.

When I zoomed in on myself the magic got thinner and eventually faded. On Bermuda, the magic got thinner and finally turned into a mist. I had to really strain to zoom in that far, but the mist was different. It was like the mist was made up of thousands of water droplets, but they were all organized. Each droplet was about the same size and the same distance from its neighbor. It was a giant organized matrix of magic.

No wonder it was denser and more stable. My magic had bits and pieces everywhere. It was different sizes and just scattered around at random. Somehow, my little kitten had organized my magic and taken it to a whole new level.

What made me most excited was that at maximum zoom I could see lots of little flashes around the break. I couldn't get down to the cellular level on him, but I was guessing that what I was seeing was the twinkle lightning. He was healing!

And he was healing fast. Certainly much faster than I was.

My room was peaceful, and it felt so nice to have Bermuda there. I just relaxed and appreciated him resting on my hand.

I looked at the rib I'd been working on and got a shock. It had healed even more! I'd been about half done when I found my center of power and could finally sleep. Now it was about three quarters finished. I zoomed into the cell level and it looked like the awakened cells at the break were gradually converting their neighbors. When enough of them were converted the twinkle lightning started and new cells got created. It wasn't quick; it was a slow and steady sort of thing.

I was fine with that. It meant my rib had healed enough that I could start working on another one if I wanted. I was very intrigued by what Bermuda had done, though. I didn't just have broken bones, I had lots of tissue damage as well. When Isobel had sealed my feet to the ground I'd been running, and the sudden stop had torn up my legs and back. A denser magic would mean healing faster everywhere, not just at the site I was working on.

I was concerned with how much magic it would take. Bermuda has used a lot and I was many times his size. I didn't know if Penny had enough magic in her for what I needed. I guessed I would find out. The worst that would happen is that it wouldn't work, and I'd go back to my slow healing at the cellular level again.

I picked my next cracked rib, also on the right side, and decided to try folding my magic there. That way, if I failed, at least I'd have a lot of magic in the right area to start my slow healing.

Once again, I pulled in as much magic as I could. I held it for a moment and then pulled even more. I did this several more times until I was as full of magic as I could possibly be. I felt like I was going to burst and rays of light would start shooting out my pores.

I focused on my second break and began folding magic. Or at least that is what I tried to do. My magic didn't fold. It just swirled around like the mist it was.

I tried to compress it into a sheet and then fold it. The sheet didn't hold, and it just floated away.

I tried to fold magic on a small scale, with no luck, so I tried on a large scale. Bermuda had seemed to fold the magic throughout his whole body, so I tried that. It was just too big of a task for me. I couldn't get my magic to fold. Instead it swirled around like crazy and made me feel sick.

I couldn't throw up, not like this, so I stopped.

I played over in my mind what I'd seen with Bermuda. When he started folding, the magic inside him had been thick. It had felt like hot taffy, or thick syrup. My magic, even at full capacity, felt like a dense mist. I finally, sadly, came to the realization that I couldn't fold mist. It just wasn't going to happen.

Since I couldn't duplicate what Bermuda had done, I started working on my second rib. This bone wasn't cracked at an angle; it was more of a clean break. That meant there was less of the bone surface that needed to be awakened. That was the good news. The bad news was the bone had pulled apart slightly so it would take more growth to bridge the gap.

I zoomed in like before, picked a fairly flat spot of cells, and started calling my magic. It wasn't long before my first dust bunny magic cloud showed up and I got to work. It certainly took more magic to get the process started in a brand-new location. I'd gotten used to how easy it was on the other rib. After I'd awakened about fifty cells or so, I started working the edges again and began picking up speed.

My idea of trying to fold magic in this area was paying off. It wasn't long before the 'sky' was thick with dust bunny clouds. I lost myself in the work. It was a simple repetitive task: pull magic from the sky, push it into a cell until it awakened, go to the next cell.

I was doing this for what seemed like hours before I saw my first twinkle lightning. Magic flashed down from the sky, merged with a cell, and now there were two of them. It wasn't happening very often but at least it had finally started.

This seemed like a good moment to pause and celebrate my success. Once again, I was struck by just how different the landscape looked. The land was a dense jungle of cells, all interlocked with each other. There were hills and valleys, just like the hills of Kentucky.

I looked around and drank it all in. I was still in wonder that my magic sight could zoom down this far. I would never have tried something like this if I hadn't been so desperate. I'm not saying this made my broken bones worth it, but it was a tiny silver lining to an otherwise very dark cloud.

I looked up at the sky and admired the magic lights. They were cool to look at. With the green and blue it sort of looked like Christmas. It occurred to me that I'd spent a lot of time examining my cells, but I hadn't really spent much time thinking about the clouds.

I traced a couple of the individual lights to see where they went. They were long and slim, like a hair, with a center part that was a bit thicker and held the bulk of the light. It looked like these hairs had loosely run into each other then stuck together. That was the definition of a hairball or dust bunny and that's why I called these clouds "dust bunny magic."

I knew that when I called them down, they changed shape, though. I called one down to examine it. While I held it in my 'hands' it changed from a hair shape into more of an oblong sphere. It was like one of those healthy pills, like fish oil, only bigger. The magic felt pretty dense and stayed together.

I'd seen a video of astronauts in space playing with water. The surface tension of the water kept it all together in one sphere and it just floated in the air. It looked like a ripply balloon made of water. This unit of magic reminded me of that.

The unit of magic I'd pulled down was green, so I pulled down another one. It turned into an oblong sphere as well. I put the two together to see if they would merge, but they didn't. Instead I had two units of green magic, about the same size, and very close together.

I pulled down more and kept adding them to my layer. I stopped when I had fifteen of them all floating together. The individual units seemed to stick to their neighbors a bit. I could pull them apart easily, but if I left them touching, they stayed together.

How did a piece of magic end up looking like a long hair? I had thought that maybe if a lot of them were together then they would start getting longer and more hair like. That wasn't happening though. Instead it looked like a granny's pill box, filled with green fish oil capsules. A very organized pill box with giant capsules, but still, any granny would be proud.

I started adding a second layer of magic capsules. Once I had fifteen there, I started a third. So far everything was sticking together and everything was keeping its shape. I was done with the third layer and most of the fourth when suddenly there was a pop.

The whole mass of magic turned into one giant green sphere. It wasn't oblong either, it was an actual round sphere.

That was interesting! This was a seriously large chunk of dense magic. Was this what I was looking for?

With any experiment you have to be able to duplicate your results. I was so excited I put my first large ball aside and started calling down more green magic.

Let's see, fifteen units of magic by four layers would be sixty total capsules. I didn't make it all pretty and neat this time. I just pulled down sixty green units of magic and bunched them all together. Nothing happened. I added one more capsule and got the pop. Again, I had a large sphere of green magic.

So, this wasn't a fluke! It looked like I could make large balls of condensed magic. This was a lot more condensed than the loose hairball of magic in the sky. Time to keep experimenting and see if there were other variations of this.

I pulled down sapphire blue magic and tried to combine it. It worked and it only needed about thirty-five units before it merged into a sphere. I made a few of those to see if the ratio held and it was about thirty-five or thirty-six every time.

I made a few more green ones to see if that ratio held, and it did. It was always somewhere between fifty-nine and sixty-three capsules before it condensed.

I didn't have to stack the capsules neatly either. It seemed like I just needed to get the right number of units very close together and the compression happened on its own.

I tried mixing blue and green capsules together, but it would not condense. I stacked more than two hundred mixed colors together before I gave up. It looks like the colors had to be the same. Rather than leave this big stack of mixed colors together, I took the time to break it down into large balls too. I was definitely getting faster at the process.

I tried making a large sphere with more capsules. My hope was to make a giant sphere made up of hundreds of capsules. That would be some dense magic! It didn't work, though. Once it hit that limit of sixty-three green capsules it wouldn't take any more. Instead, it repelled any new magic.

I wondered how many larger balls I had at this point, so I looked over to count them. I had seventeen green spheres and eight smaller blue ones. As I was counting them, I noticed something interesting, they were forming a pattern.

When I'd been making them, I'd just put them to the side. I had expected there to just be a pile of finished spheres. Instead, the spheres seemed to be reacting with each other. It seemed like the spheres couldn't be too close to each other. Maybe I could use this to make a magic matrix?

To test that idea, I made a new green ball, and put it in a spot in front of me. Then I made a second ball and gradually moved it toward the first one. When the second ball got close enough to the first, the first one started moving away.

Interesting! It seemed to me that this was similar to magnets. If you move two magnets together, they will either stick together or repel each other. It seemed like the green ones repelled each other.

I put those two to the side and made two blue ones. The same thing happened. Once the two spheres got close to each other, they started repelling each other.

How about a blue and a green one? I made a green one, made a blue one, and then started moving them together. I expected the green one to start moving away, but it didn't. The spheres were almost touching before the blue one started pushing the green one away.

So, it wasn't just magic pushing against magic. The two magic types had to be identical. It seemed like there was so much to learn. I knew that magic attracted other magic. I'd seen that happen in the park when we had charged the charms. Now it seemed like in some instances it repelled it too. Maybe it was because the magic in the park had been neutral magic? The green and blue were my colors. Maybe that made them similar enough to repel each other? I'd have to ask Sandy about all this when I was healed. Hopefully she'd have some insights for me.

Okay, so I now knew how to condense similar magic from its hair like dust bunny form and turn it into a large ball of magic. I'd figured out that these large balls repelled each other. So maybe it was time to build a matrix!

I called a green sphere to me and put it in my workspace. Then I called a second sphere and move it close until it started repelling. Then I called a third and fourth sphere and completed the square. I made another square on top of the first one and now I had a box.

I needed to work the blue spheres in there somehow. There was a lot more emerald magic than sapphire, maybe I could just put one sapphire in the middle? I wasn't sure if the ratio was right, but it was a place to start.

The blue sphere slipped into the middle of the green box and seemed okay. Now to expand the matrix even more. I took four more green balls and added them to the matrix on the right. I popped a blue one in the center and I now had two boxes. I took six more green spheres and two blue ones and added two more boxes to the top. I now had four boxes total.

I kept adding on boxes. When I ran out of premade spheres, I pulled down more magic capsules and made new ones. It wasn't long before I had what seemed to me to be a pretty large matrix. It was twenty boxes wide by twenty boxes tall by twenty boxes deep.

It was beautiful. I liked patterns and this just looked right to me.

Now that I had such a large structure, I could compare it to the dust bunny clouds above. I didn't have a good way to measure how condensed the magic was, so I thought I would go with brightness.

The dust bunny clouds were pretty, and they had seemed bright to me when I'd first called them. Compared to the new matrix, though, they were pretty dim. It seemed like it took a cloud, which was pretty big, to make four boxes, which were much smaller.

I didn't have anything exact to work with, but it seemed to me that it was a five-to-one ratio. The magic in the matrix took up one-fifth as much space as it would in cloud form. Or, to put it another way, I could pack five times as much magic into the same space in matrix form as I could in cloud form.

That seemed pretty significant.

I went back to making boxes and expanding my matrix. I started to notice that the new spheres I was adding seemed to snap into position. I kept working for a while and decided to test the stability of the structure I was building.

I picked out a green ball that was deep in the matrix and gave it a gentle tug. I didn't want to have the whole thing fall apart so I kept a light touch. The green ball moved slightly toward me, and the matrix distorted a bit, but when I let go it snapped back into place. That was good news. It meant this whole thing wasn't going to get jumbled up easily. It was taking a lot of time to make this matrix, and I didn't want it falling apart.

The next change I noticed was when I was at about one hundred boxes square. The matrix was big enough that it was starting to get close to the clouds and they were reacting to it. Sticking with the idea of magnets, the bigger the magnet, the stronger the magnetic field. My magic matrix was a pretty powerful force now compared to a cloud.

The matrix was causing nearby clouds to compress a bit. One cloud even split apart into its individual magic capsules. That made the whole process a bit faster. I started pulling the clouds closer to the matrix and soon I was showered in hundreds of capsules.

My next speed boost came when I was at three hundred boxes square. The matrix was exerting so much influence on the clouds that it was splitting and compressing them at the same time. Now they were transforming directly into large balls and skipping the capsule stage all together. There were some stray capsules I had to gather and clean up, but overall, it was much faster than doing my own capsule stacking.

When I got to around one thousand boxes square, I started running out of magic. I zoomed out to see how I was doing overall. My mist was now much fainter throughout the rest of my body. The matrix by my rib, though, shone like a thousand LED lights. Those thousand boxes only seemed like a three-inch square when you looked at the total size of my body.

I had originally pulled in so much magic I felt like I would burst. Now I felt empty of magic. This matrix was amazing! I'd thought my magic was compressed five-to-one. Now I was thinking it might be more like ten-to-one. More magic meant more healing. Maybe my road to recovery would be a lot less time than I'd feared.

I'd been so focused on matrix building I'd shut out the rest of the world. Now it all came rushing back. I felt hungry, thirsty, and exhausted. I couldn't eat, not yet. But I could get a bit of water. I twitched my one good hand and John came over with what I needed. A couple questions later, I got a squirt of water. It felt wonderful.

Could a supernatural starve to death? I wasn't sure. I knew regular people can last for a month without food. Hopefully, I wouldn't have to. I really needed to get my mobility back, and then fix my face.

I also really needed to learn how to defend myself so this would never happen again. I didn't know exactly how that was going to happen, but I was surely going to figure it out. This sucked.

The pain was still there, of course, but I was getting used to it. Tyler was right; I was finding my balance. This was my new normal.

I didn't know how long I'd been working on my matrix. Several hours for sure. Maybe longer. I didn't know what day it was or even what time. I was tired, though. It was time to find out if I could get back into my throne room and sleep.

First, though, I wanted to check on Bermuda. He'd moved a bit and was back to sleeping again. I didn't want to wake him up, so I gently stroked his head with my finger. I checked him with my magic sight. It was so much easier to *see* inside him since he had sucked in my magic. The twinkle lightning was still happening and the bones were healing. I couldn't zoom in that much to get a real view, but I thought all of his bones were more than a quarter connected.

That was just amazing. It normally takes weeks to heal a break. Bermuda had multiple breaks and yet they would be healed in only a few more days.

I was so thrilled. I was glad that I had helped him out and he didn't have to suffer anymore than was necessary. I was also so glad he had shown me that I could compress my magic! Maybe I would be up and running again soon too.

In the meantime, I was beat. It was time to sleep.

I was nervous about trying to get back to my throne room. It had just happened before. Hopefully it would just happen again.

I started where I had last time: acceptance. I took time to just accept and relax. I threw out my arms, leaned my head back, and closed my eyes. I just accepted and let it all go again.

I accepted the pain that was still there. I accepted that I'd had success with the matrix. I accepted that there was still so much to do.

Once again, I felt power. This time I'd had much more success than before, but I'd still started resisting everything. Letting my worry and fear evaporate gave me back my strength I didn't know I was missing.

I felt my power, and I felt the power of my throne room. I drifted toward it, and then I was there.

My throne room looked like before except it seemed slightly better. I didn't know if I was just used to how poor it looked, or if it genuinely improved. I went and sat on my throne again.

It was still threadbare and hard, but it didn't look as chipped and faded as before. I looked around again. The throne room was definitely looking better. The ceiling had been a wreck last time; now it just looked moderately dilapidated.

I wasn't sure exactly what to do with the throne and this space. It felt like the throne was some sort of command center. I should be able to do something with it. I wasn't sure how it worked. I was really here for some sleep, though.

The cot was still there, with the perfect pillow and the comfortable blanket neatly folded beside it. I told my throne, 'Thank you.' That just seemed the right thing to do somehow. Then I went over and lay down on the cot. I pulled up the blanket and snuggled in.

It felt perfect. I took a deep breath, gave a long sigh, and fell asleep.

19

Hold the Shields

I woke up to the sound of an air raid siren.

It was so loud I felt the House vibrate. Tyler was with me. He shot up in bed and bolted out of the room.

The wail went on and on and on. I didn't know what was happening, but nobody could be sleeping through this. I wanted to cover up my ears, until I realized the alarm was magical. I was hearing it magically somehow.

Finally, it cut off and all was quiet for a moment. Then, I heard a distant boom. There was a long pause, and then another one. What the heck was happening?

I felt a gentle presence flow over my aura. It was unlike anything I'd felt before. It felt ancient, but friendly. It seemed to interface with me somehow, and my magic vision suddenly expanded.

It was like I was suddenly in the air above the House. I could see the whole House and everything in it, as well as the park and the whole street. The view was amazing, and I quickly caught up on what was happening.

It looked like it was night, and the mages had gathered in the park to attack the House. They were launching giant magical boulders at the House, trying to break through the shields.

I could see inside the House, down in the basement, where our defenders were gathered. There was a room with a giant crystal growing out of the floor. Sandy, Annabeth, and Tyler were gathered around the crystal touching it. It seemed like they were reinforcing and directing the shields somehow.

I looked back out to the park. There were a lot more mages than I'd seen the other night. There must have been more than fifty teams and each team had about ten people. So, five hundred magic users trying to bring us down! That seemed like an awful lot for us to withstand.

Each team was broken down into a couple people to shield the team, and the rest to attack the House. Most of the teams had magic wands that fired bolts of power. A few of the teams had magical catapults that fired large glowing boulders. They arced way up in the air and then came crashing down onto the House shields. These were the hits I was hearing. They made a heavy boom when they landed. If the impact wasn't enough, they also exploded and sent smaller shards of rock everywhere.

The only offense we had was John. He stood on the front lawn throwing baseball sized chunks of rock. He was only one person, but his offense was still pretty awesome.

He was a cannon all by himself. I'd seen what his thrown boulders had done in the park fight with Isobel. They were nothing to sneeze at. What he was throwing now was smaller but much faster. I could see his magic flaring with each throw. He was doing something magically to increase his speed and power.

His shots landed with a boom of their own. Defending shields would crack, and sometimes they would shatter. He kept targeting different groups. I guessed he was trying to find the weaker ones.

I'd originally thought the House shield was solid, but then I realized it was flowing and spinning. Some parts of the shield were thicker than others, and that seemed to be at the direction of the defenders in the crystal room.

I watched one of the big boulders come in. The House shield tripled in size where it was going to land. The rest of the shield got a bit thinner, but it wasn't anything the wands could punch through yet. When the boulder landed and exploded, the shields spun, directing some of the force down and to the side.

The wands didn't have the punch the boulders did, but they weren't ineffective either. Several groups were targeting the same spot, trying to overload the shield in that area. It was easy to redirect the wand fire, forcing the House shield to constantly reinforce itself in a new area.

It felt like Sandy was anticipating the boulders, Tyler was spinning the shield, and Annabeth was reinforcing for concentrated wand attacks. They were a good team.

I sent a query out to the House. What do you need me to do? What I got back was so surprising.

I got back a sense of endless love and patience.

We were in the middle of a war, and the House wanted to let me know it loved me? I was shocked. The House was communicating with me directly and I could feel it on so many levels.

On one hand it was ancient. I felt a sense of age that I couldn't comprehend. It felt like the House had had a presence and a purpose since the earth was formed. That was more than I could wrap my brain around, so I hurriedly let that go.

On the other hand, it felt so very new. Sandy had said this branch of the House had only been around for about a year. It was like the House was a giant tree, and this part of the House in Louisville was a little bud on a branch.

It wasn't old and strong like other Houses. It was still new and weak. I got a sense that if the shield came down and the House burned, then its presence in Louisville would be gone.

If I knew this, it made sense that others knew too. That's why we were having this war. The mages wanted to burn down the House and claim Louisville for their own. It wasn't just the mages either. There was no way Isobel had made those golems. Someone else was helping them in their war.

Aside from the age of the House, I also got a sense of its purpose. It was built to provide safety and acceptance for supernaturals. It wasn't just a house. It was a home. And a home in the best sense of the word.

It was peace, fun, relaxation, happiness, connectedness. It was a place of healing and a place of hope. A place of learning and knowledge.

At the root of it all, it was love.

Not wimpy flighty love. But deep, powerful love, like a force of good in the world. It swept over me and somehow, in the midst of this battle for House survival, I felt joy and happiness.

I'd found a new group of friends. I had a place to belong and I'd been missing that for such a long time. I now had a little magical coin that I felt attached to and missed her when she was gone. I also had a kitten. He seemed to love me and wanted to protect me. Even when he clearly was out of his league.

Now the very House I was in was letting me know it accepted me and wanted me to stay.

I was so lucky. I'd been so hurt and so lonely for years. Sure, there had been some guys I'd connected with. But I hadn't felt loved. Their place hadn't felt like home.

Once I'd found poker, I'd had money to start taking care of myself. I still hadn't had a home, but I'd had enough for a room and a cheap meal. It was still lonely, but I'd had hope. One day I'd have enough money to retire from poker, buy a house, and settle down somewhere. I'd find someone nice and we would make a home together.

I'd thought my Death Experience was the end of all that. In reality, it had been a new beginning. My plans for poker hadn't worked out, but it seemed like I already had the results I wanted. I had friends, a House that wanted to be my home, and a whole new magical life.

I felt blessed. Even with my face smashed in, my ribs cracked, and all my other injuries, I felt like I was home. I felt loved.

Wow, this House was a serious trip. Next thing I knew, I'd be hugging the walls saying, "I love you, man!"

I pulled myself out of my introspective moment and focused on the battle again. Everything that I'd just said I liked about this place was in danger. My friends were in danger. My home was in danger. I was in danger.

There wasn't much I could do about this battle, but I vowed I would find a way to make a difference in future ones.

The mages were not going to win. They were not going to kick the House out of Louisville.

This battle was coming down to who had the most magic and who used it best. The House shield was still strong, but noticeably thinner than it had been before. The enemy was still catapulting magic boulders, but it looked they were almost out of ammunition.

Even the magic wands took magic, and the auras of the casters were much dimmer. They had certainly done some damage, but it didn't look like they were going to make it through.

That's what I thought, until they fired their last boulder. That's when they took the magical catapults apart and reassembled them into one giant battering ram. Oh crap!

The teams with the wands started focusing on the shield right in front of John. The battering ram had room for more than a hundred people, and they lined up and started hitting the same spot.

It wasn't just the weight of the battering ram, either. The ram itself was magical. The mages were not only physically pushing the battering ram; they were also powering it. When it physically slammed into the shield, a pulse of light shot down the ram and exploded against the shield.

This was the serious effort to get through. Everything up to this point had just been to weaken our defenses. Tyler left the crystal room and ran out the back of the House. I could see him circling around the block. He was going to attack them from the back.

He was going to be outside the shield, so I hoped he knew what he was doing. We had to do something, though. The House couldn't take many more hits like this.

It was just Annabeth and Sandy in the crystal room, but they seemed to be doing okay. John was still in front of the House, and he was upping his game too.

His magic flared and a giant rock shape gradually formed out of the ground. It was a stone cylinder, like a giant can of Coke on its side. It was huge—easily eight feet wide and six feet tall. I couldn't imagine how much it weighed. Several tons, at least.

John's magic flared and the cylinder started rolling toward the mages. His magic flared brighter and the rolling rock picked up pace. He kept up the pressure all the way to the shield wall. It was going as fast as a normal person could run when it passed through the shield and smacked into the battering ram.

A battering ram is by default an unwieldy device. It's designed for forward power. It doesn't have any dodge capabilities at all. When you make it big enough for a hundred people, it is even more ponderous, and there was no way it could get out of the way in time.

Rock trumps wood, even a massive wooden device like that. The cylinder smashed the front of the battering ram and threw the whole thing backward. Most of the mages couldn't see what was going on so they were totally unprepared when the battering ram suddenly jumped back. They were all lined up, pushing wooden pegs attached to the main shaft. When the ram jumped backward, the wooden pegs slammed the mages in the chest, knocking them over. Without them holding it up, the whole wooden structure fell to the ground, pinning a lot of mages underneath.

John's rock had so much momentum it kept going. It rolled up over the top of the battering ram and down most of its length. When it finally stopped rolling, the center part of the ram snapped. The weight was too much for it to handle.

All the mages trapped under the battering ram or its handles were crushed. I knew supernatural bodies could recover from a lot, but I didn't know how they could survive this type of damage.

I had totally conflicting feelings running through me. On the one hand, I was shocked by the carnage. I didn't want anyone to die. Even if they meant me harm, I wasn't comfortable with killing people. On the other hand, I wanted to jump up and down with joy. With one bold move, John had taken their battering ram and changed it from massive weapon to massive liability. The enemy was in shambles. Most of them were trying to lift the broken ram and get it off their fallen companions. Lots of the sups were too injured to continue and they were being levitated to the back of the battlefield.

In the midst of all this confusion, shields were dropped, and John took advantage of the distraction. He started power throwing his baseball-sized rocks again, and this time they found unshielded targets. When his rock slammed into a mage you could hear the bones break. The mage would fly through the air and land like a rag doll. They didn't get back up again.

Lots of mages didn't have personal shields, and even when they did, they weren't powerful enough to stop John's projectiles. He threw with both hands and every rock found a target. His accuracy was insane.

All looked lost for the enemy, until stinky Isobel showed up. She was on her golem throne and making a late entrance as usual. I guessed she figured she'd either show up late and be the hero, or all the hard work would already have been done. Either way was a win for her.

With one gesture she threw up a giant shield that John couldn't get through. The remaining mages flocked to her and organized a better defense.

Her magic still looked like maggots on rotten meat. I was glad I wasn't close enough to smell her. She was powerful though. Really powerful.

She'd brought her inner posse with her. Their magic also looked rotten, although not as putrid as Isobel. I took a quick look around. The mages we had been fighting up to this point just had regular-looking magic.

She was good at organization too. Damn it. It didn't take long before she had the teams back together, fully shielded and loaded with wands. She dropped her shield, and with a rallying cry, she led her army back toward the House.

With the battle ram fiasco and John's quick work, he had knocked about half the mages out of the fight. That still left about two hundred fifty to go, not counting Isobel and her inner posse.

Considering John was our only offense, he was a one-man army! He certainly earned battle MVP in my book.

The teams settled back in and started concentrating fire at the front of the House. Isobel and her group started doing some sort of group ritual. I didn't know what it was for exactly, but it looked like they were doing a modified charging circle and gathering neutral magic.

Everyone was focused on either the front of the House, or the ritual with Isobel, and that's when Tyler went to work. He started at the back of the rear-most team of mages and went to town. He had what looked like two stone batons. They weren't that big and they didn't glow or anything, but they sure were effective. He was quickly and efficiently moving through the team and taking them out. In most cases it only took one blow to the head. Sometimes a mage would dodge or duck, and then it would take two hits. It never took three. He didn't seem to exert much energy or make a lot of fuss. Instead, he was smooth, like water, flowing from mage to mage and leaving behind no threats. A few of the spell slingers had personal shields, but the batons went right through them.

John saw what Tyler was up to, so he stepped up his rock missiles to keep the attention on him. Mages were running low on magic and sometimes his rocks would punch right through their group shields, taking someone out.

Tyler took out three teams before anyone noticed what he was up to. By then it was too late. The teams were too tired to defend from both John and Tyler. The remaining mages turned and ran, leaving only Isobel and her final team in front of the House.

John turned his fire on them, but they had a larger shield protecting them. He still managed to crack it and almost got through before it was reinforced. Tyler wasn't idle either. His batons could get through the shield, but he couldn't.

He ran around outside with one hand on the shield. It didn't cover their circle evenly. That was probably because it originated with Isobel. There were several mages at the opposite end from Isobel that were very close to the edge of the shield—so close that Tyler was able to hit them with his batons.

The mages collapsed and so did their magic circle. Isobel started cussing. I'm sure it was difficult to keep up a defense and run a circle at the same time.

Whatever they were working on was stable, though. It didn't collapse with the circle. Instead this blob of energy sat pulsing in the air.

I guessed Isobel just figured she would go with what she had rather than trying to rebuild the circle, because she took the magic blob and hurled it at the House shield.

The blob didn't seem that big or that solid. It was only about the size of the magic boulders they had tried earlier, and they hadn't gotten through.

This wasn't a boulder, though, and it wasn't designed to power its way inside. Instead it hit the shield with a splat and coated it like a ball of hot oil.

My first thought was oil, but then I realized it was some form of magical acid. It started sizzling and eating away at the House's defense.

Sandy left the crystal to Annabeth and sprinted out of the room. It didn't take her long to reach the front door, but in that time the acid had spread and covered a quarter of the shield. I guessed the shields naturally had some spin to them, and that was working against us. The spin was distributing the acid to a wider and wider area. It also seemed like the more the acid ate, the more powerful it got. It hadn't been on there long, but I could see some parts of the shield were very thin and about to break.

As soon as Sandy hit the yard, she yelled at John to get out of the way, and she let loose. Sheets of flame flew from her hands and landed on the hostile magic. It resisted for a moment, but Sandy was persistent, and her fire was powerful.

She burned right through the bulk of the acid, then started on the places where it had spread. Sandy wasn't holding anything back, and about a minute later, the danger was over.

For a moment, there was quiet as both sides stared at each other. The mages had come prepared to do battle. Their magic boulders, the battering ram, the magic acid—any of these were good enough to take down the House shields on their own. Even the mass of mages with their magic wands might have been enough to do it.

We had our own unique talents, though, and somehow we had countered every one of their offenses. I guess Isobel and her crew didn't have anything else to try, because she signaled her gang and they started to retreat.

They kept up a large shield and everyone stayed inside it. There wasn't an opportunity to take any of them out. Tyler stepped back to the front lawn, and he, John, and Sandy watched the mages back away.

The mage with the all black aura made an appearance. She walked out slowly, leaning on her cane, and started levitating the fallen people off the battlefield. She didn't look at the House or acknowledge it in any way. Since she wasn't attacking, our three defenders just watched and left her alone. She moved quickly and soon the battlefield was empty.

The battle was over. We had won.

Except for a massive rock and a battering ram, there wasn't any evidence of the assault that had just happened. Even those were soon gone. Now that it was clear of any hostile forces, John went out and broke the rock apart and sank it back into the earth. It took much longer, but he was able to do the same to the battering ram.

He made the wood decompose and fall apart. Some of it was on the road, so Sandy levitated those pieces into the park. Finally, it sank into the earth just like the stone had. Then the three of them joined Annabeth in Sandy's kitchen and the victory party started.

The House gently floated my awareness back into my body again. I was still on my cot in my throne room. I snuggled down in my blanket in my safe place and tried to process what I had just seen.

This was modern times. Louisville was in the middle of America. Sieges with catapults and acid magic just shouldn't happen. This supernatural world was a whole new ballgame.

Annabeth and I were very lucky that John, Sandy, and Tyler were here to defend us. Without them, the House would be gone, and I'd have been Isobel's slave. The thought chilled me, and I shuddered. I don't know that I had ever seen real evil before, but Isobel was as close as I wanted to get.

I thought about the mages that had been crushed by the battering ram. Were they alive? Would they recover? I certainly knew what it was like to try and recover from lots of physical damage.

This magical world was a lot like the dark ages. Life was cheap, and obviously you could and would get hurt. Being stronger in this world meant being safer. It also seemed to mean that you could use those weaker than yourself.

Isobel had used her crew to try and get the charms in the park. Rather than fighting John and Sandy directly, she'd come after me, the weakest of the bunch.

In this battle she had sent in hundreds of supernaturals to take down our House. They had fought for her and gotten hurt for her goals and ambition. She had only showed up when the shields were weakest. When her magic acid hadn't worked, she'd been quick to retreat and stay out of harm's way.

It was a smart but ruthless way to fight.

I'd seen violence before, but not like this. I'd gotten into fights when I was a kid and some of the poker games over the years had ended up in brawls. You can't take someone's money without them getting ticked off. Add in some alcohol and sometimes it turned into a fight.

Those were simple scuffles, though, with a few punches thrown. Starting with my Death Experience, the new fights I was in were life and death. People got hurt. They got hurt badly.

I'd seen two alley cats fight once. It had been short, vicious, intense. They had wanted to kill each other. There was nothing nice about it. There was only one winner, and even the winner left with scars. These new fights were a lot like that.

I needed to get tougher.

I needed to be stronger.

I needed to recover quickly and find out how to defend myself.

With that final thought, I fell asleep.

20

Penny Is Back

I woke up to the sound of Bermuda crying. I rubbed his head with my one good hand and gave him a quick scan.

He seemed to be doing okay. He was twinkling all over now, not just at the site of the breaks. I zoomed in to check them out. His ribs were completely healed, and his front leg was most of the way there. His back leg was the worst, only about half healed.

It was amazing how fast he was improving. If only I could recover that quickly.

I didn't think he was crying from pain. I thought he was crying because he wanted to get up and move around. Unfortunately for him, the cast was keeping him from going anywhere. That was a good thing, as his bones weren't completely ready for him yet. I didn't want him to rebreak something while he was moving around.

Sandy tried to give him some more pain medication, but he didn't want it. He must have been interesting, though, because both Snowy and Biscuit came into the room. They hopped up on my bed and then sat there looking at him.

They were like, 'Dude, what are you doing in that shell?'

And he was like, 'I don't know. Some stupid human put me in here. Get me out of this!'

Snowy was like, 'Humans. Who knows why they do the stuff they do?'

Biscuit was all like, 'Preach that. Sandy is nice but she cray sometimes.'

Bermuda was like, 'Help! This sucks!'

Snowy was like, 'Your suffering amuses me. I would help, but, you know, effort.'

Biscuit was like, 'Look at my freedom,' and began his tongue bath.

This went on for a while. I couldn't do much to console Bermuda and he was seriously not happy. Sandy laid him on her lap for a while and just talked to him. He finally wore himself out and went back to sleep.

Biscuit finished his bath and then napped too. Now that she wasn't being entertained anymore, Snowy decided it would be fun to get in Bermuda's box and root around.

Since Bermuda was okay—or at least as okay as he could get right now—I switched my focus to the magic matrix. It was still there, still looking as bright as before. I'd been afraid it would drift apart, but it still looked as tight as ever.

It had been affecting my magic a lot while I'd been sleeping. The mist magic near it had been transformed into lots of the larger balls of magic. They weren't in any order yet, but they were there ready for me to start working.

I checked out my ribs. The first one I'd worked on was now completely healed. The break site was still shining with awakened cells. It even looked like the whole awakening process was still happening. It was very slow, but cells next to the awakened ones were coming to life. Was it possible that my entire rib would eventually wake up? Would my whole body?

That would be pretty amazing if my whole body was awake! When I got injured it would start healing itself automatically. It wouldn't be anywhere near a Wolverine ability, but it would certainly be a lot faster than I was currently able to do.

I checked out the second rib. It had just started its twinkle lightning when I had stopped and got caught up in making the matrix. I don't know how long I had been sleeping, but it should have only been healed a little bit. Instead, it was more than half finished. It was the closest to the new matrix, and it was definitely benefiting from the condensed magic. I zoomed in for a closer look. There was a lot of twinkling going on. Each twinkle was a newly formed cell, closing the gap of the break.

I had one more broken rib on my right side, so I decided to start working on that. If I could get it to the twinkle stage, then it could be healing while I was working on the matrix or sleeping.

The third broken rib wasn't a full break. It was cracked, and part of it still held together. I zoomed in, found a good spot, and started awakening cells. I'd done this so much it felt easy now. This was still close to the matrix, so when I pulled magic, I got some clouds, but I got a lot more of the fully formed magic balls. These were the loose ones floating around, not the matrix ones. Working with them was a joy.

I found I could awaken five or six cells at once with one magic sphere. The work went so quickly. It seemed like I'd just gotten started when the first twinkle lightning happened. I grew the awakened area a bit more to make sure it was good, then I decided to check out the two ribs on the left.

They were both bad breaks. One was a diagonal fracture like the first rib I'd started on, but the other was shattered at its break point. It had five pieces of bone, from little chips to a larger fragment.

I decided to start on the diagonal fracture. Since I was on the other side of my body from the matrix, I expected the magic I pulled to be mostly clouds. I was pleasantly surprised that almost half of what I pulled was the magic spheres. I used up all the spheres first and then started working with the clouds. Pulling magic down from the giant cloud dust bunnies was certainly a lot more time consuming, but I felt like I was close. Turned out I was right. The magic started fusing with the cells on its own, and the twinkles started. They weren't firing that fast, but at least the healing had started.

I zoomed out to full body view again and pulled in as much magic as I could hold. I held it for a moment, and then pulled in even more. I went back to the second rib on my left side, the one that was shattered. I picked a small chip of bone and awakened the whole thing. It took a while, but I figured if the awakened part of me had a good foothold, it would just keep healing and eventually fix itself.

I'd been working for hours, but I wanted to grow the matrix too. I topped off my magic and zoomed down to the matrix. It was surprising how many of the spheres had snapped into the right place. I cleaned up all the capsules of magic floating around, turning them into larger balls and then adding them to the matrix. Then I started working on really growing the matrix. It had already converted all of the stray clouds to capsules or spheres, so it was easy to grab the spheres and put them in their place.

It was simple work and I lost myself in the process. I kept running out of magic for the spheres and I'd have to zoom out and pull more from Penny. I was building the matrix in a giant cube, until one side of the matrix hit the edge of my body. When that happened, I zoomed out to evaluate my progress.

I'd started out with a cube about three inches square. Now I was about six inches square. I decided to continue building the matrix but in one direction, across my body. That way it would be close to the ribs of my left side and give them all the support it could.

I worked on that for hours more. I didn't have any idea of the time involved. I wasn't eating and I couldn't see, so any of the normal clues of daytime or nighttime weren't there for me. My sitters switched out as they needed to, but I didn't know what sort of schedule they were on.

I could feel when Annabeth was with me. She would hum to me and the world seemed like a better place. I could also feel when Tyler was there. He would work on my remnants. Whoever was with me would take care of Bermuda. He was healing fast and sleeping a lot.

I built my matrix almost all the way to my left ribs when I realized I just couldn't work anymore. I relaxed, went to my place of power, and slept.

When I woke up Bermuda was snuggled up against my good hand, sleeping. His body cast was gone. I rubbed him and he started purring. The vet had shaved a bunch of his hair, so he felt a bit strange, but I loved having him with me.

I had no idea how he had gotten out of his body cast, but he seemed to be okay. I dipped in for a look and found his bones had healed completely.

His healing flashes were still happening, though. I zoomed in as far as I could. I wasn't certain but it looked like his cells were still awakening. The ones that hadn't been injured were still transforming and becoming magic cells. Would that happen to me also? It seemed like it should.

His magic seemed a bit low, so I pushed some more magic into him. All the cell transformation and healing were using up the magic I'd given him. His magic was still thick and in the matrix form that had inspired my own work. It just seemed a bit less than before. I wasn't sure what would happen if he used up most of the magic, but I didn't want to find out.

He didn't grab me and pull the magic like before. Instead, he just ignored it. He seemed much more interested in getting a good rub and spending some quality time.

Feeling better for my kitten time, I dove into my own body to check my progress. I was very happy to note all the ribs on my right side were healed. It felt wonderful. I hadn't realized just how much it had bothered me until the pain on that side was gone. Now I just needed to finish up the left side. The first rib on the left side was doing well, about half healed. The second rib, the one that was shattered, had done something unexpected.

All the bone fragments were now lined up. Before they had been a bit scattered and I wasn't sure how the healing would happen. Would it grow between the fragments and leave a strange looking rib? Would I end up with a big bump on my side?

It looks like that would NOT happen. Instead, all the bone fragments were lined up perfectly, ready to be healed. The one fragment I had awakened had bonded with two others and was transforming them too. I zoomed down and awakened both sides of the main break. It was so easy with all the magic spheres floating around. Now that the matrix was closer, it had transformed all my dust bunnies to their compact magic form. When I called magic, there were no more clouds in the sky. Instead it looked like the sky was filled with balloons.

I zoomed out for an overall look. Most of the magic in the central part of my body had been converted to spheres. The power of the matrix was much stronger now that it was bigger. It had already pulled many of the spheres into position and there were even some free-floating mini matrices starting.

It was much easier to grow the matrix now. I cleaned up the natural growth and snapped some of the mini matrices into place with the larger one. Before long the matrix had grown from one side of my body to the other and completely filled it from the front to the back. I now had a solid six inches of compact magic in the middle of my body.

With that much influence, the matrix started growing on its own. All I really needed to do was pull in more magic from Penny and clean up any stray capsules. I wasn't sure how much magic Penny had. It had been enough to shut her down and she still hadn't really woken up yet. I could hear her, but it was distant. She didn't seem to be aware of what had happened to me, and I didn't tell her. It was like she could sort of hear me, but not much else.

I thought back to the night of the first golem. There had been thousands and thousands of the miners and Ass Blasters. I didn't know how much magic that would be. I was sure it took a lot to animate a seven-foot tall creature of stone. It occurred to me that one golem had seriously injured me, but another golem was providing the magic needed for my healing. Life is funny like that.

I spent a long time growing the matrix. It was the key to my transformation. With this density of magic, I could heal so much faster. Toward the end I just pulled magic as fast as I could; I'd clean it all up later. Finally, I'd had enough, and I headed to my throne room.

It seemed harder to get there this time. Seeing the matrix grow like this was exciting, and it was hard to just relax and let it all go. Finally, I accepted that the matrix was growing, and I was healing. I was going to be okay. I felt strange accepting good things, but that did the trick. I finally relaxed, entered my throne room, curled up on the cot, and went to sleep.

Bermuda wasn't there when I awoke, but he'd left me a present. There was a metal pin that used to be in his leg lying on the bed by my hand. It seemed clean, like it was brand new, but it was still kinda gross. I pushed it off the bed and it fell to the floor with a clatter.

Sandy was there and we squeeze chatted for a while. She'd been monitoring my progress and she was so excited I was doing better. It felt good to get excited with someone about how I was doing, even if it was through hand squeezes. She said she could see my magic change with her scans, and she was eager to hear all about it when I could talk.

She also said Bermuda was doing great now. He was eating and using the restroom on his own. They had no idea how he had gotten out of his body cast, but he obviously didn't need it anymore. They had found another one of his bone pins lying around. They'd give him a really good checkup, but there wasn't any indication of how it had come out. The skin wasn't broken, and a scan showed the bone was fine. He didn't need it anymore either, so I guessed it was better out than in.

Feeling better after my squeeze chat with Sandy, I dove back into my body to check out the progress. One rib on the left side was healed. The shattered one still needed more time but was almost there.

What should I do next? Starting more bones healing seemed like the best way to go. I just had to get them started and they were fixing themselves.

I checked out my face and just lost my nerve. It was crushed. I didn't want to look too deep, but it was just shattered. I wasn't ready to tackle it yet. I'd finish the matrix first.

There was one other place that needed help: my arm. Both of the bones in my left forearm were shattered. I guessed I'd been trying to protect myself and one of her kicks had snapped it apart.

Once again, I zoomed in, found a good spot, and started waking up my cells. When I called for magic, only magic spheres responded, so the awakening went quickly. I kept working until I ran out of spheres.

I'd done a lot, though. I'd awakened two places on one bone and three on the other one.

I zoomed out to check out my overall matrix. While I'd slept, it had formed all the way to the top of my head and down to my legs. My arms and legs still needed work.

There was nothing to do but get started. I pulled magic and let the matrix do its thing. I finished up the left arm first as that needed the most healing. Then I finished up the right arm and started on my legs.

I hadn't realized how swollen they were. That sudden stop had really done a number on me. I'd been so focused on my bones I hadn't considered what else was wrong with me. It took hours, but eventually the matrix covered my whole body. I didn't stop. There was still so much cleanup to do.

Hours later, I did a final head-to-toe scan and found a last pocket of resistance. I fixed the matrix and suddenly a wave of pure energy flowed through me.

I had felt something like it before. When I took the magic capsules and stacked them together, there had been a point where they transformed into something new. This felt like that.

The magic spheres were still there. The matrix was still there. It was just that now it felt right. It felt solid.

I realized I wasn't shining magic anymore. Before, I'd been glowing magic into the room. Now it was all self-contained. It was brighter. Stronger. But all inside me.

This was like what had happened to Bermuda. There had been a moment of brightness, followed by a wave of energy, and then he'd stopped shining outward.

I paused to just take it all in. My face was still a wreck and it still hurt. However, my ribs no longer bothered me. I could finally breathe without pain. I wasn't holding myself as tightly anymore. Once my arm was healed, I'd actually be able to move around a bit.

I was getting better.

I didn't want to go to sleep yet. Waking up to extra healing was a real treat, and I wanted to plant some more seeds of transformation. Avoiding my face, I did a body scan to find my other pain areas.

It was mainly muscles and tendons. I picked a muscle in my leg and zoomed in. Again, it was a strange world that greeted me. I was used to bones and the cells around them. This was spongier. I hoped my awakening technique would be useful here too.

A break was easy to see, but muscles tears weren't so simple. I wasn't sure what was normal and what wasn't. In the end I just went with my gut and awakened a few spots until the magic twinkles showed up. I touched up the upper and lower parts of my leg and started in my back before I decided I'd had enough.

Sleep was such a luxury. I'd never take it for granted again.

This time, when I arrived in my throne room, there was a noticeable difference. It looked clean! Before it had looked like it had been abandoned for hundreds of years. Now it looked like Mr. Clean had showed up and gone to work. Lots of the damage had been repaired too. The ceiling wasn't falling down anymore and the floor looked good. There were still some cracked tiles, but overall it looked nice. My throne was fixed too. It was now one solid smooth piece of rock. It didn't have any padding yet, but it wasn't chipped either.

My throne room still looked like it was for a small kingdom, but it looked like it was loved now. There were tapestries on the wall, and they didn't look faded and falling apart. One tapestry was dedicated to my fight with the first golem. I was running away, and the golem was chasing me. It was covered in Flying Miners and Ass Blaster 2000s, and a trail of rock was streaming out behind it.

Running away wasn't the most heroic view of the fight, but I'd won in the end and all of its magic was now healing me. The other tapestries were just patterns and colors I liked. Would they fill in with scenes as I progressed? I hoped so. That seemed like a neat idea.

The cot was still there, though. That was all I needed for sleeping and it was already comfortable. I snuggled up and went to sleep.

I woke up what seemed like a long time later. I was so used to checking the clock to see how I was doing. I was very grateful for my magic sight, but it does have some limitations. It's great at seeing shapes and I can see anything magical in color. Anything non-magical, though, I don't get any color at all. Most importantly I can't see screens. I have an alarm clock by my bed, but it uses LEDs to show the time. I can't see color, so it just looks like a blank screen to me. Since I can't see color, I also can't tell if the sun is shining in the window.

Without sight or real communication, I kind of felt like I was in a giant dream. If it wasn't for the pain of my breaks and bruises, I'd have wondered if any of it was real.

Speaking of pain, I was feeling a lot better. I could breathe easily now that my ribs were healed. I checked my left arm and it had almost completely recovered. My legs and back were doing better, but not as much as I'd hoped. I think it was because there was a lot more room to cover. A break is very traumatic, but it's mostly confined to a small area. A muscle and its tendons, on the other hand, cover a lot more real estate.

I knew I should be working on my face, but I was scared to start. I was scared to get a good view of just how bad it was. Instead I procrastinated and worked on my legs and back. I awakened more than fifty new spots in my muscles and tendons before taking a break. It had taken hours, but I still wasn't ready to face my own face.

Instead, I started pulling in more magic from Penny. I was curious to see just how much magic I could store now that I had my new matrix. I had been used to just how much magic it took to fill me up when my magic felt like mist, so I pulled that much in and stopped. I still felt good, so I pulled that amount again. It seemed a bit harder to pull this time but there was still room left.

I zoomed into Penny to get a view of what was happening on the cellular level. I pulled a bit of magic. It appeared thick, like syrup, but white. Once it hit my system, the matrix pulled it apart into spheres. The white color gradually changed into either green or blue. The matrix shifted slightly, and the new magic was integrated. The matrix was stable, but elastic. When the magic twinkled into a new cell the matrix just shifted a bit and kept its general shape.

I did notice the distance between the green spheres was less than when I'd started the matrix. I could feel the pressure there. It was like a bunch of magnets that repelled each other were being pushed together. Or maybe it was like winding up an old watch. The more you wound it, the harder it was to turn.

I pulled more magic and kept on pulling. It was fascinating, watching the matrix form and the balls change color. I pulled some of the new magic deeper inside me and the color changed a lot faster. It was also fascinating by just how much magic I could hold. I had pulled in about ten times as much magic as my max was before.

The matrix was visibly compressed from when I'd started, but it still seemed like I could hold more. More magic meant more healing, so I kept pulling. I was at fifteen times my regular max, and it was getting very hard to pull magic, when something wonderful happened.

Penny woke up.

I was so happy to feel her again. She trilled at me happily and flooded me with images. The last thing she really remembered was accepting all my little creations from the first golem. She was still happy about kicking its rocky ass. After that she felt like she had fallen asleep. She remembered talking to me, but it was like it was all a dream.

I wasn't used to this form of communication, but I sent my own memories back. I told her about the attack of the remnant in the park and how this tiny kitten had scared away the giant groundhogs. I recounted the method we had found to charge the charms and how we had ended up in the park again. She was very interested in how the charms had charged with her help. It all seemed distant to her. I hadn't seen much of the battle, but I showed her what I could. Reliving the beat down Isobel had given me hurt.

Penny wanted more detail, but I told her it was just too fresh. I covered my recovery up to this point: how I'd awakened my cells, transformed my breaks, and created a matrix. I'd finally pulled enough magic from her to get her back to normal, and now here we were.

Penny thought the human body was fascinating. I didn't get any sympathy from her at all. She said metal was crushed and formed naturally, so this all seemed normal to her. I told her that as a living creature we didn't like to get crushed. Too much crushing and we died.

That seemed so strange to her. She asked why I didn't just transform into whatever I wanted, like she did. I said I'd love to do that, but I wasn't at that magic level yet. I was at the level of healing. That took time and patience and involved a lot of pain and recovery. I had some charms that were supposed to help but I wasn't sure they were actually doing any good.

She perked up at that. There was a magic charm that would fix me? She didn't really understand, but she wanted me to be better. She could feel pain and injury from my thoughts, and that wasn't anything she wanted for me.

Penny unwound from my finger and wiggled up my arm like a snake. It felt weird, but she was heading to the charm on my neck, so I just kept still. When she got there, she wrapped around the charm and seemed to talk to it for a while. I could hear her making vibrating whistling noises. I also felt the presence of the House for a moment.

I tried to understand what was going on, but the whole thing was outside my level. Maybe it was a type of charm speak. I wasn't sure.

It took several minutes, and then Penny sent me a feeling of happiness. She'd gotten whatever she was after. She left the charm and wiggled up to my head. Then she stretched around the bandages and covered my whole head, like a helmet.

When she did, the pain stopped.

It just stopped.

My face was seventy percent of my remaining pain, so when it stopped, it was shocking. I'd been living with such agony for so long that it felt normal. I'd learned to think and work and do magic in spite of how raw I felt.

Now that it was gone, I felt so light, so free.

I sent Penny feelings of happiness and joy. I also sent images of me doing a happy dance. She gave me a cheerful trill and said she was working on my face and to go and do something else.

I wasn't sure what that would be. I needed to get my jaw working again. *Would she mind if I helped with that?* I asked and she said she was working on my face. If I could start on my jaw then go for it.

It didn't take much zooming to see my jaw was broken and the place it connected to my skull was all messed up. Again, I was surprised by how my jawbone actually looked. I thought it swiveled like a pair of scissors. It actually looks more like a ladle and connects farther back on the skull than I thought it should.

I knew how to fix bones, so I got started. My jaw had several cracks in it and was completely broken on the right side. I awakened cells in all the cracks and both sides of the break. I wasn't sure how to handle the sockets, so I just awakened as much as I could.

After all that I took a break to have some kitty time with Bermuda. He purred up a storm and licked my fingers a bit. He was growing up so fast. Already he seemed a little less kitten and a little more grown up than he had when he first found me. He wanted to play, but I wasn't ready for that yet. I made my little Dot again, filled him with magic and sent him off zooming around the room. I gave him strict instructions not to come around me, though. I didn't need a cat jumping on my ruined face.

I did give instruction to stay around John, though, who was sitting with me. Those little kitten claws can sting. That was a bit of payback for the whole naked shaman thing. Bermuda went ape shit over the light. He had energy to burn and he climbed John like a tree. John squealed like a little girl and jumped up. That didn't stop Bermuda or Dot at all. My bedroom was a lively place for a while.

In the middle of all that, I went to my throne room and crashed out.

It took two more days until I felt good enough to move. John helped me into the bathroom and showered with me. I was so weak, I could barely stand up. When I got back, Sandy had changed out all my sheets and pillows. I was clean and I slept in a clean bed for the first time in a very long time. It was like heaven.

A few days after that my jaw finally recovered enough for me to say my first words. Not long after that I had a few spoonfuls of chicken broth. It hurt too much to actually chew, but having something with calories and flavor was the best meal in the world.

My face was wrecked even more than I'd feared. Penny moved all the little pieces of bone back into position and I awakened bone cells to fuse it into place. It was like solving a 3D puzzle as we gradually rebuilt my cheekbones and eye sockets.

My teeth were also a big problem. All of my front teeth were missing, both top and bottom and some of my back teeth were cracked. Healing a cracked tooth was just like healing a bone so that wasn't a long-term problem.

The missing teeth were more of an issue until Tyler gave me an unusual gift. He presented me with a little cardboard box. I opened it up, and nesting on a bed of tissue, were my missing teeth. I'd never been gifted my own teeth before. What kind of thank you card do you send for that? So long and thanks for all the teeth? I was feeling long in the tooth until you showed up? I was laughing and sort of crying when he gave them to me. It was so tragic and so sweet at the same time. He said he'd had his teeth knocked out many times before. It's much easier to heal them back into place than to regrow new ones.

Penny made a special grill with some of her metal to hold them in place while I worked on awakening the cells. John made gangster jokes for days. Said he had diamonds for my grill. He made up bad rhymes for my rap album and suggested rapper names. It hurt to laugh but I did it anyway.

Sandy got in on the fun too, but she wasn't as good as John. Annabeth scolded them both, but she was laughing too.

Eight days after my jaw was fixed, Penny left my head and wrapped around my finger again. Sandy unwrapped the bandages around my head and I opened my eyes for the first time since the accident.

I couldn't see.

I thought my vision might be blurry or something like that. I thought maybe I'd be sensitive to the light after so long in the dark. It had never occurred to me at all that I wouldn't be able to see at all.

That was my reality, though. I was pretty sure it didn't mean that I wouldn't be able to see forever; just that I couldn't see right now. At some point I'd be able to transform myself, like Tyler.

Until then, I had my magic sight. My bones were healed. My teeth were back. I wasn't in pain. I was still weak, but some of Sandy's cooking would take care of that.

I wasn't perfect, but life was good. Really good.

21

Celebration

We had a celebration dinner that night. Tyler had cleared out another remnant. Three down and one to go. The last one was going to be the hardest. Still, it was nice to celebrate some progress.

We were also celebrating the fact that I was mostly healed. It felt so good to be up and moving around again. It seemed like everything felt new. Breathing through my nose felt new. Talking felt new. Chewing solid food felt new.

It was a whole new world. I guess you don't appreciate what you have until it's gone.

The only things not healed yet were my eyes. I knew they would heal eventually. At least I had my magic sight, so I wasn't bumping into things.

I still wanted to be careful, though. I'd only been eating solid food for a few days. That's why I took a pass on the large pints of IPA that John started handing out. Instead, I put a little bit of his brew in a cup and sipped on it.

The last thing I needed was to get hammered, fall over, and knock out my teeth again. Or break my arm. I wanted to stay pain- and injury-free for as long as possible.

The party was in Sandy's kitchen/living room, of course, and it featured chicken pot pie, one of my all-time favorites. I tried not to eat too much, but I still ended up with two bowls of it. The pastry was the right amount of flakey and the creamy filling was divine.

After dinner I told my recovery story in full. I'd already told parts of my story to them individually, but this was the first time I covered everything with everyone.

When I got to Tyler's part of the story, I thanked him truly and deeply. His idea to find the balance in any situation really kept me going and helped me keep my sanity. His talk about transforming, not healing, was also pivotal to my recovery. That was what got me to start awakening my cells in the first place.

I was halfway through telling everyone about when he cut his skin and transformed it, when it occurred to me this might be something he wanted to keep quiet. He was already several pints into John's brew, so he was feeling good. He just waved me on and I finished the story. Then everyone wanted a demo, so he cut himself and then transformed it into smooth skin again. It was just as magical to see it the second time.

That was fascinating for Sandy and Annabeth. They wanted to figure out how to flood an area with magic and replicate the effect. John was the most thoughtful, however. He was a natural and he might have enough internal magic to pull it off as well. He didn't say much, but I had a feeling he was going to be experimenting later.

I continued my story with Annabeth's pep talk about acceptance. I thanked her deeply as well. That had been a pivotal moment that allowed me to find my throne room and get some sleep for the first time.

Sandy thought it was hysterical that I'd used my throne room to get some rest. Finding your seat of power was different for everyone and was usually something that took a lot of searching and practice. It was a master level skill that was then used for research or casting high level spells. I'd used it for sleeping.

Sandy said that was like finding the Holy Grail, and then using it as a coffee cup.

Sleep was what I'd really needed, though, and my throne room had come through for me. Sandy said your seat of power appeared differently for everyone. Her center was a tree stump in a vast meadow filled with wildflowers. It had beautiful sunlight, cool breezes, birds that sang, and distant mountains. I thought it sounded wonderful.

John said that even naturals had centers of power. His was a combination cave and forge. He had all kinds of metals and everything he needed to heat and shape them. The cave was well lit and just about every surface was decorated with etching. It was less a damp dark cave and more like the dwarven treasure room from the Lord of the Rings movies. I thought that sounded pretty fantastic too.

I continued my story with Bermuda arriving and pulling my magic. I stopped at that point to thank Sandy for taking care of my kitten. Bermuda had been playing with Snowy, but he came over when we started talking about him. I picked him up and started loving on him in my lap. He purred and looked as cute as a button. I was so grateful that Sandy had taken him to the vet and made sure he got the attention he needed. I didn't want to imagine a life without him.

I wanted to pay her back for her expenses, but she wouldn't hear of it. She said that figuring out how to charge their charms was thanks enough. If I still felt like I owed her anything then I could help her accomplish some of my new discoveries for herself. She was especially interested in my magic matrix. She'd been following my progress as it had grown.

I talked about Bermuda and how he had folded my magic and made it stable and dense. Then how I had figured out how to do it for myself.

Sandy was interested in how the magic matrix compared to her spinning cores. As far as she knew, spinning up magic cores was the only way the House residents knew to progress in magic. It took a lot of attention and constant work. There wasn't anything stable about it.

John and Tyler didn't care about magic cores, so they started telling each other tall tales and getting down to some serious drinking. I think they were trying to see who passed out first. Since they were both powerful naturals with lots of healing, I wasn't sure who was going to win. I did know they were way out of my league. I was perfectly happy to stay mostly sober and talk magic with Sandy and Annabeth.

One thing I did find out was that Tyler had a door to take him home. That's why he wasn't around all the time. I was glad he was helping me, but I was also glad he could go home and be happy too.

I didn't think I could see inside someone else, but Sandy made it happen. It was almost like a formal contract. She took my hand and said, "I swear on my magic to be open to you. You can see my magic like your magic, my body like your body, my power like your power. So long as you do no harm to me, you have this clarity until midnight tonight."

After that, I could see her magic and her cells just like mine. We also got a lecture on swearing on our magic. We could force it to do certain things, but it was binding on us. We should always put a time limit on it, and it should be contingent on the other person doing no harm.

Swearing on my magic sounded awful final to me. I made a note to never do that unless absolutely necessary. In the meantime, I had access to Sandy, so I checked out her cores.

I could see them spinning and the center was pretty dense. It looked like her earliest core was in her right hand. Almost her entire palm had awakened cells. The density tapered off pretty quickly, and the rest of her hand and arm didn't have any awakened cells at all. Outside of the cores, her magic was very thin. It was a mist like I had started with, but the mist was so faint I had to strain to see it. At her most dense, she was close to my matrix.

I realized I was holding a lot more power than her in my body. I had a higher density than her best core and I had it throughout my whole body. She had been practicing magic for a long time, longer than I'd been alive, so it felt a bit awkward to tell her what I was seeing.

It didn't bother Sandy, though. She was just excited for me and excited there was another way to grow in power. The big difference was that in addition to seeing what I was doing, I'd also had a way to store and access a lot of magic. Without the magic of the first golem and Penny being able to store it for me, I wouldn't have had the power I needed to make the matrix.

Sandy and Annabeth both wanted a matrix now. They wanted it badly. I think Annabeth was ready to start making a charm like Penny right away. Sandy suggested a bit of caution. Creating Penny had been an accident. We'd need to go over how I'd done it again, create a safe space, find the right item to awaken, and then make it happen.

I felt like I had almost lost my magic that night, so I was quick to agree. I was sure there was a way for both Annabeth and Sandy to make living charms, but we needed to give it the best chance possible. Running out of magic was no joke.

The talk changed from my recovery to the battle and what that meant for us. Sandy felt like we needed to stay inside the House as much as possible. Maybe only go outside in pairs. She needed to restock her refrigerator, so she would be heading to the store soon. John hated grocery shopping, but it would probably be a good idea if he went with her.

She didn't think the mages would attack in broad daylight, but she also hadn't thought they would mount a full-scale assault on the House either. I figured there wasn't anything that she and John couldn't handle, but I was worried about Annabeth and myself. I was new to magic and I thought any of the mages would probably be able to take me down. The last thing I wanted was to get badly hurt again.

Speaking of protection, I needed to get some charms like Annabeth had. I might not be able to use them like Sandy, but it would be better than nothing.

Sandy agreed and suggested we have our magic assessment tomorrow morning. We needed to see how my magic worked best and then we could start on charm casting.

I was so excited; I wanted tomorrow to be here already. I was like a kid waiting for Christmas morning. My path to becoming a powerful mage couldn't begin soon enough.

On that note, I decided to call it a night. We had talked until late and I realized I was pretty tired. John and Tyler were passed out on the rug. That seemed to be a theme with John. Sandy said they were fine where they were and could wake up on their own. Annabeth said she was ready to head out too and she'd walk me back to my apartment.

It was still strange walking around with just my magic sight. I could see about twenty feet around me, after that, nothing. When I started walking down a hallway, I couldn't see the end of the hall like I normally would. Instead, I could see the walls just leading off into nowhere. As I got down the hall, the end of it would fill in and I could see where I was going. I kinda felt like I was in one of those old RPG games in a dungeon. In the old games you would have a light and you could see a bit of the dungeon around you. Outside of that was darkness.

I thought it was sweet that they were still watching out for me. Since I was more exhausted than I'd realized, I probably still needed it. When we got to my door, Annabeth gave me a big happy hug. I told her again she was the best. Her cheerful humming had been a ray of sunlight in a dark world. I was so grateful and happy for her support.

Bermuda was already waiting for me on my pillow. I shrugged out of my clothes, slipped into bed, and fell asleep to the sound of purrs. It had been a good day.

22

Magic Assessment

I woke up with Tyler's strong arm around me and Bermuda crashed out on my pillow. It felt like old times. I loved on Bermuda and he woke up purring. Loving turned into play and soon I was giving him kisses and he was trying to get away. He jumped off the bed and trotted out of the room. I made Dot, filled him with magic, and sent my little creation after my kitty. Soon the sounds of mad dashing and extreme jumping came from the living room.

"Good morning," Tyler said. He yawned and stretched. Even without my normal sight, he still looked amazing.

"How's your head?" I asked. He'd drunk a lot last night. I'd been pretty sure he'd still be passed out with John, but here he was with me, working on my last remnant.

"That's the nice thing about magic bodies," he said. "No hangovers." I stretched too. I felt good. Really good. I felt rested with energy to burn. Then I remembered. This was the day I got my first amulet!

Even though I wanted to hop out of bed right away, I still spent a few moments awakening my cells. I planned on doing that every morning until my whole body was packed with magic. The next time I got injured, I was going to be ready. I checked and my twinkling lightning was still happening. Come on magic cells!

Tyler must have known what I was doing, because he decided to have some fun with me. He started kissing my neck and running his fingers up my side. His touch was light, sexy, and my body was only too happy to respond. He was trying to break my concentration and it was working.

I couldn't do what I really wanted with him—I still had a remnant left and that one was powerful enough to knock him around—so instead we ended up in a tickling match. Sheets went flying as we rolled off the bed and hit the floor.

He was much better at wrestling than I was. He soon had me in an arm lock and tickled me until I almost peed. It felt good to laugh. It also felt good to horse around and flex a bit. I probably should have been more careful, but I didn't feel any pain. I felt like a live wire, full of energy and sparks.

Tyler stopped just short of an accident. I hadn't been this ticklish before. Now I was so sensitive I was about to explode.

"There is something I wanted to tell you, while I have your undivided attention," Tyler said. He still had me in the armlock so I wasn't going anywhere. I was up for anything he wanted to share. He'd given me great advice before, and as long as he wasn't tickling me, I was all ears.

"Sure, what's up?" I asked.

"You are getting with Sandy today and soon you will be starting on the path of a mage. You'll be learning about how your power works and how to use charms. It will be exciting and your whole world will be taken up with magic."

That sounded about right. I couldn't wait to get my first charms. I knew for sure I needed a shield charm. Protecting myself was my number one priority.

"I've helped out a lot of people and I've seen them start down the path of magic caster. What I've seen is that everything starts to look like a magic problem to them. They forget that there are other ways to get things done. Many times those other ways are faster and better, but they aren't even considered because they aren't magical. It's like the old saying goes, if you're a hammer then everything looks like a nail. Soon, you'll have real magic and your first thought will be which charm to use for every situation.

"There is another way. You are in the unique position of having both mage abilities and natural abilities. You're going to have a magic body soon that is fully awakened. That means you'll be stronger than most people and certainly much faster. You'll recover from injuries a lot quicker and all your senses will be stronger.

"We are in a war with a lot of mages. Most of whom are not that powerful. They have years on you, but they aren't the really old powerhouses. Against these newer mages you have a chance to win in a fight. You learn fast and you're willing to work. They will be thinking of using magic for everything. You can't hope to match them magically as they have years of experience and practice already. However, you might be able to beat them physically."

"That makes sense," I said slowly. He let me go and I wriggled around on the floor to face him. He was right up against me and I almost lost my train of thought. He was so freaking hot. I knew he wasn't using any of his talent on me. I could feel it when he did and so could my remnant. This was all-natural physical attraction. Wow. I needed a cold shower.

"Something just occurred to me," I said. "Did you always look like this?" I ran my fingers over his abs.

"What do you think?" he asked.

"I think you used to look normal," I said. I decided to have fun with him. "You probably had buck teeth and your ears stuck out too far. Your hair never sat right, and you had love handles just like a real person."

He laughed when I talked about his ears. I continued, "I'm thinking this perfect body and perfect face you have now are a defensive mechanism. People will be too caught up in how you look to see what you are really up to. I know you are smart and funny and loyal, but I'm sure most people aren't going to be able to get past the front door of what they see in you."

"You're right," he said. "I am an incubus after all. We don't really have any powers other than sex. John can shape metal, find gems, and move mountains. I just make you feel better. Well, not you," he said playfully. "You still have a remnant. But other people. It's a power just like anything and it's all in how I use it. It's even helped me in fights. If the attraction is there, they don't fight anywhere near as hard as they normally would.

"I'm one of the weaker naturals in the supernatural world, but I've made up for that by creating a kick ass magical body. You have that ability too. I guess what I'm trying to say is that if you combine physical ability with magical ability you are going to be a lot more effective than just using magic alone."

"I like what you're suggesting," I said. "I'll need someone to train me, though. I've been in a few fights, but I've never learned how to do it properly. Is that something you could work with me on?"

"That's what I'm offering," Tyler said. "And I think it is what the House wants too. It has never made a doorway home for me before. I think it would only do that if it wanted me to be here for a longer period of time. The House uses up magic just like everything else. I'm sure the doorway wasn't cheap, so it must want something else from me. The remnants have been an interesting challenge, but it will be over in a few weeks. I think the House expects me to be here longer than that."

"That would be great," I said. I'd seen how Tyler had handled the mages during the siege. He made it look so easy. I'd love to be able to handle them that effortlessly. Plus, any reason to spend time with Tyler was a bonus in my books.

"Good! This is going to be your morning of firsts. A question and your first lesson: What are you most excited about learning magically?"

"That's easy. I want a shield charm," I said.

"Why?" he asked.

"Because I don't want to get hit," I said. "Well, not that I won't ever get hit. I'm sure I'll get hurt. I would just like to minimize it. I don't want to have my face crushed again if I can help it."

"Sounds reasonable to me," he said. He jumped up and pulled me to my feet. "Let's translate that from magical to physical." He threw a very slow punch at my head. "How do you keep from getting hurt?"

I backed away from his punch. "I would think you don't get hit."

"That's exactly right," he said. "Now, for a slightly deeper view of that, how much do you need to dodge before you don't get hit?"

I wasn't sure exactly what he was shooting for. He put me back in position facing him again and threw another slow punch.

"Um, enough so the punch doesn't hit me?" I said.

"Again, exactly right," he said. "It doesn't matter how much an attack misses, just that it does."

He lined us up again. "Moving away from me takes too much time. It's also in the path of the punch. So, if I lean into the punch more, I'll have more reach and may still tag you. This time, try moving to the side."

He threw his slow punch again. This time I moved to the side and his fist passed slowly through the space where my head had been. The movement felt right. It was much faster and easier to dodge this way.

He threw another slow punch and I slowly moved to the side again.

"This is where training and experience come in. You take the time now when you are not in a battle situation to think about the best way to avoid a blow. Then, you practice it over and over again. When someone is really trying to hurt you, you'll just move on instinct."

He threw more slow punches and I dodged them. It felt awkward. My movements felt jerky and wild. Sometimes I dodged so much I went halfway across the room. Sometimes I felt trapped like there was nowhere to go. He just followed me around the room throwing lazy punch after lazy punch.

We were both still naked so I'm sure we looked like a crazy version of the early Olympics. They used to do everything naked back then.

Even though Tyler was moving slowly, I still worked up a sweat. He tagged me a few times, too. It is amazing how much mental concentration it took to stay out of his way. Bermuda came back in and hopped up on the bed to watch us. He got bored of that and started taking a bath.

I had to call a stop before too long. I still needed to get ready and go see Sandy. Tyler had achieved his objective, though. I was now thinking of more than just magic and I was excited to be training with him.

He gave me a naked sweaty hug and a kiss on the cheek before he left. As he walked out, I saw a flash of magic with my sight and he suddenly had shorts on. Tyler clearly still had some tricks up his sleeve.

My shower was colder than normal. Tyler had gotten me all hot and bothered, and I wanted a clear head for my magic assessment. Bermuda sat on the back of the toilet, of course, and supervised—after knocking off the toilet paper.

Soon, I was ready, and I headed down to see Sandy. I was almost to her door when John passed me in the hallway. He seemed extra happy for some reason and he was dressed like a pirate. That seemed strange to me, but I just let it go.

Sandy was also in a good mood, and we grabbed a drink and headed to her workshop. It was huge. I was thinking it would be the size of a bedroom, but it was more the size of a whole house. I couldn't see from one wall to the other with my magic sight, which left me feeling a bit disoriented. She had lots of workbenches. Some of them were overflowing with all kinds of things. Some of them had half-finished projects and one was empty. That's where we were headed.

"Before we begin, let me just set the groundwork for what we are going to be doing," Sandy stated. "We are going to be testing different facets of your magic. Some of it you are going to be good at, some of it you aren't, and that is okay."

She sighed. "I think this has been said by every person who has ever done an assessment, and most times someone is disappointed that they aren't good at one facet of magic. Just keep in mind that no one is good at everything. Even if they were, that still wouldn't be good because then they wouldn't know what to specialize in. They would end up being good at everything but great at nothing. It's much better to be good at a few things and then get creative in using them. Focus and creativity are your best allies. Sound good?" she asked.

I nodded. I knew what she was getting at, but I still found myself wanting to do well at this. I loved the idea of magic and I wanted to be good at it.

She must have seen that I wasn't letting go of being good at this, so she gave it another try. "Remember, this is NOT a test. This is NOT a pass or fail sort of thing. Holding on to those expectations will just make you nervous and skew the test. Now let all that go."

I took a deep breath and let it out. I was nervous. I tapped into acceptance. Whatever results I got was just what works for me. There was nothing to fear. Nothing to succeed at either.

Bermuda took that opportunity to hop up onto the workbench. He walked over and butted me with his head, so I gave him some loving. I was glad he was there. Some of the tension I'd been holding onto melted away.

Sandy gave him some scratching too. "He can stay for most of the tests. One of them is very delicate, though, so he'll need to get off the bench." I was good with that. He'd probably get bored and wander off soon anyway.

"The other thing to cover is that this is YOUR assessment. You can choose to share your results, part of your results, or none of your results. It is however you wish. It's also considered bad manners to ask how others did, although it usually happens anyway. Just be aware that asking the wrong person can make them very defensive."

I nodded again. Don't get nosey. Got it.

"Magic is all about breaking the laws of nature," Sandy said. She was using her lecture voice. "There isn't anything that magic can't do. However, it can take a lot of power to make something happen. The amount of power used depends on two things: how much you are trying to bend nature and if you have an affinity for what you are trying to accomplish.

"The first part is obvious. For example, it takes less magic to lift a grain of sand as opposed to lifting a car. The second part, affinity, is often overlooked, and that is what we are finding out today. An example of that is how John works with metals. He has a powerful connection to any kind of rock, so he can manipulate it much more easily than I can. I can shape rock too, but it would take many orders of magnitude more magic for me and I still wouldn't get the type of results he can."

Sandy opened a big chest on the floor. Inside were stacks of clear boxes, each of which was filled with all kinds of stuff. The first thing she pulled out, though, wasn't a box. Instead it was a big flat charm with lots of little bars in a row.

"This amulet will let us know how much magic you are using. The less magic you use to accomplish your tests, the stronger the affinity you have to whatever you are testing. There are ten rows of bars with five bars each. That's fifty bars. If you light up all fifty bars, then stop immediately. That means you are using a lot of power and we don't want you to run out.

"For these tests we want to test your magic, not your creations. So, don't use any of your little projections to solve these problems."

She pulled out a clear glass container with lots of little cubes in it. "Let's start with solid objects. These cubes are made of different materials, and they are different sizes, but they all weigh the same. It should take the same amount of magic to lift them, unless you have an affinity to a certain material.

"Let's begin."

The cubes were pretty light, so it was easy to move them. I picked them up one by one and all of them registered a five on the power-use amulet. There was a mix of metals, woods, and other stuff I didn't recognize. After I was done Sandy said my results were in the normal range.

Next, she pulled out a cube with lots of tubes in it which were filled with different types of liquid. One of them I think was water and another one I recognized as mercury. Other than that, I wasn't sure what the rest of them were. Again, I just needed to lift them to the top of their tube.

This was harder than the cube challenge. There wasn't anything solid to grab onto. I couldn't use any of my little guys and Sandy wasn't providing any help.

I ended up making a floor of magic at the bottom of the tube and then lifting the liquid that way. My first tube spiked in power usage. That seemed strange as the water couldn't weigh that much. If anything, it should be lighter than the materials in the previous challenge. Then I realized I wasn't letting anything through my floor. I was creating a vacuum and that made it very hard to lift. So I made a little space on the side for the air to get through. Then I could lift the liquid easily. Again, it took about five magic to lift all of them. There wasn't any sort of liquid that I had an affinity for.

Sandy said I did really well. Lots of people couldn't figure out how to lift a liquid as there was nothing solid to grab onto. I didn't have an affinity for liquids, but I didn't have a problem with them either.

She pulled out her next clear cube. It also had lots of tubes in it, but this time they were filled with gas. Sandy told me they were different colors, but I couldn't see colors. The gasses felt different to me, though, so I thought I could work with it.

I wasn't sure how I was going to move gas around. I could zoom in and see the different molecules, but moving the gas around one molecule at a time would take forever. I had an idea, though. I made a floor again, but this time I made it porous. I told it not to let any molecules through that felt a certain way. When I moved the floor, it took all the types of those molecules with it. It wasn't scientific, but it felt right, and it seemed to work.

I told Sandy I couldn't see color with my magic sight, and she'd have to let me know how I was doing. She said I was doing great and I'd separated all the gasses. Sometimes I'd moved the clear gas to the top and the colored gas to the bottom, but the object had been to separate the gasses, so she was counting it as done. I thought moving the gas was easy. It only registered a two on the magic scale.

Sandy said most people could not do this challenge and I clearly had an affinity for gas. I really wanted to make a fart joke at that point, but Sandy had her serious face on.

So, I had my first affinity. I wasn't sure what I was going to do with gas, but it was nice to be good at something. I was creative. I'd figure something out.

Next, Sandy said we would work on distance. She gave me a cube to float above my hand. The cube was small, so it only registered a four on the magic scale. Then she asked me to move my hand away and leave the cube where it was. Magic output jumped to eight. That was the most power I'd used so far.

Sandy asked me to take a step away. I did, and the cube held steady, but the magic output jumped to twenty. Sandy said to take another step away. The magic output jumped to forty-four. We stopped there and I let the cube fall. Clearly I was not a distance person.

"Remember I talked about how the more we break the rules, the more magic it takes?" Sandy asked.

"Sure," I said. I wasn't sure how that applied to this. I hadn't moved the cube around, and it hadn't changed weight or anything like that.

"So, here is a learning example. The question is, how were you keeping the cube in the air?"

"Well, I just pushed it off my hand in the beginning," I said. "When I moved away, I just made it stay in the air. I'm not sure how. I just made sure it stayed there."

"So, would you say that you were making the cube stay in the air relative to you?" Sandy asked.

"Yes, I was. I was thinking of holding it up with my mind. Kind of like what you see in the movies."

"I thought that might be what you are doing. That's what almost everyone does their first time. Let's try it again, but this time let's try a different approach. Hold out your hand and float the cube again." I did that. "What is the cube floating relative to?"

"My hand," I said. The magic output was back to a four again.

"Okay, now take your hand away and, this time, float the cube off of the surface of the table." I did that. The cube dipped before I had the new anchor ready. Once I had it set up, though, I could tell it took less energy. Output had jumped to six instead of eight.

"Now take a step back," Sandy said.

The output jumped to twelve which was way better than twenty. "Let's try another step," Sandy suggested.

The output jumped to twenty-five. We ended the test again. I didn't want to lose too much magic as I wasn't sure how many tests there were still to go.

"That felt so different," I said. "I still don't have an affinity for distance, but the way I anchored the cube was huge. I've never thought about moving objects this way before."

"I'm glad you liked the example," Sandy said. "Anytime you are doing something, and it's not a battle situation, think about all the physics involved and see if there is an easier way to do it. This is where learning and practice come in.

"Just so you know how you did, this is your first weakness. Most people can go the distance of this workshop or even farther before it becomes an issue for them. Even with the new anchor point, you'll still max out in three or four steps."

Well crap. This seemed like a pretty big weakness to me. I wasn't going to be slinging fireballs any time soon. Most of the battle in the park had involved throwing spells at a distance. Not being able to do that was going to be a big disadvantage.

I must have looked upset because Sandy hastened to add, "Now you know about it, though, and you can plan for it. For example, your little cartoon characters you make—where do you start making them?"

"I usually make them in the air right in front of me," I said.

"Since distance is such a big factor for you, try holding out your hand and making them directly on your palm. Or, if you can't do that, try making them as close to you as possible. See if that doesn't make them stronger and easier to fill with magic."

That was a good idea. If I could make my little guys faster and better then that was worth finding out. It still stung that I had such a big weakness, though.

"I'm just curious, what does a distance affinity do for you?" I asked.

"The two biggest things supernaturals do that have a distance affinity is flying and far seeing. Flying is really levitating with speed. Since their magic works well at a distance, they can push off the earth and sail through the air. You still have to have a lot of power to do this, though. After all, you are moving your body weight around."

"Far seeing is being able to see and communicate long distances. This was much more useful before we had phones. Far seers were usually merchants and ended up being very rich. Now, anyone can pick up a phone and call someone in another continent."

Flying would have been cool! I felt really bummed now. Maybe I shouldn't ask about the things I'm not good at.

Focus on the good stuff. Accept this. Move on.

"So, what's next?" I asked.

This time she pulled out a small box with cloudy sides. I couldn't see what was inside it.

"Let's try aura cracking next," she said. "Some supers have the ability to get through magic auras and affect a person directly. This box has aura built into the walls. Just try and see if you can get through and see what is inside."

I already knew I couldn't, but I gave it a shot anyway. I pushed at the walls hard to see if I could part the aura. That didn't work. I tried to narrow my focus and drill through somehow. That didn't work, either.

Sandy did something to the cube and suddenly the walls weren't as cloudy. With a lot of looking I thought there might be a tiny elephant charm inside. Sandy changed the walls again. This time I could clearly see a cat charm. Sandy said my ability to get through aura was in the normal range.

Next, we tested for time distortion. This cube had lots of tiny balls floating around in it. They would flash with magic, but it happened very quickly. My job was to grab the ball when it flashed. Apparently, some supers can manipulate time to become very quick. This would test that.

We started out with slow flashes and I was able to grab the ball every time. Then it sped up and soon I was missing much more than I was catching. At top speed I wasn't catching any of them. Apparently, my reaction time was in the normal range. No super speed for me. I wasn't slow either, so there was that at least.

Next up was a small stick. This would test my magic resistance by trying to change my skin blue. Sandy rubbed it on the inside of my forearm. Nothing happened.

She adjusted something and tried again. Nothing. She adjusted again. Nothing.

"Well, you are certainly resistant to magic!" Sandy said. "I'm going to max this out and see if we get any response at all."

She rubbed my arm. "Still nothing. Not even the slightest bit of color change. You can count yourself very lucky. Even those with a high affinity usually have a slight color change."

I was thrilled! I'd wanted to get some defensive skills. Now I'd found out I was highly magic resistant. This was something I certainly wanted to find out more about.

"So, other than the obvious, how does this affect me?" I asked.

"It means that magic directed at you personally will have a very hard time getting through. So, for example, if someone tried to cast disease on you it won't land. You'll also be very resistant to any sort of mental or physical manipulation. So Tyler, as an incubus, uses magic to make your body ready for sex. Even without your remnant, you are probably still very resistant to his charms."

I wasn't sure how I felt about that. I'd been looking forward to losing my last remnant and then having some good sack time with Tyler. John and Annabeth had felt amazing after their time with him. I wanted that too. I guessed I'd just have to wait and find out if his magic still worked on me.

"Something to keep in mind," Sandy continued. "Magic can still work on something in this world that then works on you. For example, magic can animate a golem and that golem can still punch you in the face."

Oh no she didn't! I stuck my tongue out at her and made a face.

"I am well aware of that. Thank you very much," I said with as much snark as I could muster.

Sandy just laughed and gave me a hug. The moment of levity was a nice break from all this testing.

"Seriously, though, there are other battle magics that can affect you. For example, a heat spell cooks the air around you. Even though it can't raise your temperature directly, it can still cause you to burn and your clothes to catch fire.

"Another example is the spell that Isobel used to stop you running. It stuck your feet to the ground. I'm guessing she did that with either your shoe, or her magic encased your feet and then stuck to the ground. The point is, though, that everyone has some resistance to magic, and lots of spells have already taken that into account. This affinity is really good, but it doesn't solve everything."

"I'm guessing that since you are so good at magic resistance, you are going to be good at the next test." She pulled out a small blank cube. There wasn't anything special that I saw other than that the sides were not clear like most of the others. When she put it in my hand, it lit up.

"This test isn't really an affinity to anything. It just measures how dense your soul is. In your case, it's very dense. The color of your magic is saturated and vivid. That's why you have such a high magic resistance. The soul in other magics can't compete with the density of your soul."

That sounded intriguing.

"This is the first time I'm hearing about soul," I said. "What does that do for me?"

"Your soul is the part of you that mixes with magic and lets you control it. The higher the ratio of soul to magic, the more you can do with your power. When you were talking about being able to direct your magic into your cells, I was pretty sure you had a dense soul.

"Looking at it from a battle perspective, if two magics clash, the magic with more soul wins. That's not a hard and fast rule, because it depends a lot on the situation. If one person has a lot more magic applied than the other person, then they are going to win regardless of soul density.

"Outside of battle, you are probably going to be great at making charms. The more soul you put into the charm, the more powerful it is and the easier it is to use."

"Is that why Isobel can't make charms?" I asked. "She certainly is powerful, but her aura stinks."

"There are a lot of things wrong with Isobel," Sandy said. "But I'm pretty sure that is why her charms are duds. Let's not get off track talking about her, though. Instead, let's test your magic capacity."

She knew I'd have questions, so she kept going. "Magic capacity is how much magic you can hold. It's a theoretical number, as most mages will never realize their full capacity. Being able to make your magic denser is a lifelong journey and takes years of technique and practice. Obviously, the more magic you can hold, the more spells you can cast and the longer they last."

She pulled out a leather case with a zipper. She unzipped it and inside was an array of bars of varying sizes tucked into pockets. It looked like one of those tool cases that hold drill bits, only fancier. They varied in size from something that looked like a pin, all the way up to a thicker bar about the size of a tube of lipstick. She gave me the smallest bar first.

I held it between my thumb and forefinger. It immediately lit up. Sandy put it back in the case and we tried the next size up. It lit up too. We kept going up the sizes, all the way to the biggest thickest one. Even that one lit up like a light bulb with no hesitation.

"There are larger kits in Chicago we can try if we both make it up there," Sandy said. "But in the meantime, I think we can safely say you have a high theoretical capacity. I thought you might, given how you put together your matrix.

"It's great to have lots of power ready to go, but how fast can your magic flow? That's the subject of the next test." She reached back into her trunk and pulled out a cube with a turbine through the middle. "Just let your magic flow into the cube and it will spin the turbine. The faster you can get the magic into the cube, the faster the turbine will spin."

She gave it to me, and I got started. I could make it spin in a lazy fashion, but it sure wasn't whizzing around. Sandy said I was a bit low on my flow, but not by much. She assured me it was fine. It would just take a bit longer to cast spells.

The next test required a steady table. This is the part where Bermuda would need to get down, but I realized he had already left. Cats are like ninjas. He could show up on my lap and I couldn't remember him actually arriving. Or he would be gone, and I couldn't remember him leaving. Sandy just laughed and said it was a cat thing.

The next cube was designed to test how steady I was with my flow. The cube had several metal cubes in it. Each cube was about half as wide as the one before. My job was to stack up as many of them as I could.

I was already pretty sure I could ace this.

I set up the largest cube first, then the next largest on top of that, and so on. Sandy said this cube had almost a perfect vacuum in it so there wasn't any chance of air movement tipping the cubes over. She was also using her power to keep the workbench absolutely still. The only thing that should tip over the stack would be if I messed up.

There were ten cubes total with the last one being long and very, very thin. Like thinner than a needle. This was the ultimate Jenga test.

Placing the first eight was simple. I had to zoom in a bit to place the last two. I still wasn't anywhere near as zoomed in as when I was working with my cells. My magic flowed smoothly and easily. There were no jitters.

Sandy was impressed by how easily I'd completed the task. She said normal was five cubes stacked. She hadn't seen anyone do all ten before. Since I'd done it so quickly, she had a challenge for me. Do it again, but build it upside down! So the whole stack would be balancing on its narrowest point.

If I could get up to five cubes balanced, then I could get supper at her place tonight. I was pretty sure I could get supper anyway, but this sounded like fun.

I took my stack apart and started with the largest cube again. This time I raised that cube in the air and put the next smallest one underneath it. The first four cubes were easy, but then it got tricky. I made it up to seven but I was sweating now. Being top heavy, the stack was super sensitive to the smallest vibration or the tiniest misplacement. When I tried for eight, I realized the table was shaking ever so slightly. It wasn't something I could see normally, but as zoomed in as I was, I could sense it. I wanted to use my magic to keep the stack up, but I let it fall. I was pretty sure I could have done more, but it would have to be in a very stable environment. The workbench, even with Sandy holding it, wasn't going to cut it.

I was really happy with how I'd done, and Sandy was just blown away. She said getting good at magic was a matter of learning how to work with your affinities, and clearly I had some good ones to work with.

I'd come into this hoping I would learn how to throw some fireballs around. That just sounded neat and it would certainly be useful in battle. My results, though, showed I wouldn't be doing that. If anything, I was the opposite of that. My magic was small, precise, and dense. I guess that made sense, because my little cartoon guys were small and dense.

"We have done a bunch of tests, so now let's use what we have learned about your affinities and see how it relates to a real-world example," Sandy said. "Let's start with the most basic of skills, making light.

"This is something mages have been doing since we discovered magic. It's something that has been well researched, and it is a great place to begin. The first thing I want you to do is make a tiny point of light. It doesn't need to be bright. It just needs to be something we can see and measure. We'll build from there."

She looked at me expectantly. "Can I use one of my little guys?" I asked. I'd made light before, but I'd done it using a cartoon light bulb. I wasn't sure if I could just make light on its own.

"For now, let's stick with using pure magic," Sandy said. "Your characters are an unknown we can experiment with later." She gave me the teacher look again.

I took a deep breath and let it out. Where to begin? How do I make light? When I make my cartoon characters, they do all the work and it feels believable to me. Making the light directly seemed strange.

I guess maybe I could make light just like I make a cartoon. I'd just imagine the light and put some magic in it.

I picked my normal spot in front of me where I make my little creations and imagined a tiny sphere that was glowing. Finally, I added a bit of magic, and it worked!

Or I thought it did. I could see a magic glow. I didn't have my normal sight to see how bright it was. Sandy was smiling, so I guessed I was doing it right. "You got that pretty quickly. Sometimes it takes hours for a new mage to find a method that works."

"I just imagined a ball of light, and then put magic into it," I said. "That's how I usually make my characters, so I hope that is in line with what you are thinking."

"Everyone casts magic a bit differently," Sandy said. "That's why it's hard to teach sometimes. I can tell you how to do something, but it might be the wrong way for you to do it. I've found the best way is to let you know what I want and then you figure out how to make it happen. It makes sense that you would cast light the same way you cast a character, so I think we are good to continue.

"Let's take a look at how much magic this uses." It was sixteen. That seemed rather high for something so small.

"Now, using your affinities, how do you bring your magic usage down?" Sandy asked.

What were my affinities again? I need to write them down so I can go through a list. I was paying attention, but I'd done so many tests they were starting to blur together.

Let's see. There was gas. Other than lighting a fart I didn't see how that would help. It was a funny image, though. I'd be a big hit if I ever joined a magical fraternity.

Magic resistance and magic capacity wouldn't help here. Capacity would help me keep the light going for a while, but it wouldn't make it more efficient.

Distance! That's the one I'd been missing. I'd made the light in front of me like I normally did on casting. Closer was better. Time to get close.

I put my hand a few inches under the light, just like I was trying to levitate it. The magic cost dropped to 10. Wow! That had knocked off a third of the power needed. I really needed to start casting much closer.

"Excellent!" Sandy said with a satisfied smile. "I was wondering if you would remember what we had said about casting. Let's test this even more. Since there isn't any heat coming from the light, let's get as close as we can to it and see if that makes a difference."

It felt a bit strange to get this close to a casting, but I moved my hand right up to the light until I was touching it. The magic cost dropped to six!

"Look at that," Sandy said. "Even a couple inches make a difference."

She said it with such a straight face too. My mind went straight to the gutter. As a gay man I was well aware of the difference a couple inches could make.

I bit my lip to keep from laughing. Sandy was in her teacher mode and I didn't want to ruin it. I was learning a lot. This was not the time for that sort of humor.

Being an adult can be so hard sometimes.

Seriously, though, I'd dropped the magic cost from sixteen to six. That was a massive difference. Was there anything else I could do? I thought through what we had tested but couldn't come up with anything.

"I think distance is the main thing," I said. "I can't see how any of my other affinities would help, or how to make this more efficient using physics."

"Are you sure?" Sandy said.

I thought about it, but nothing came to mind.

"Yes. I'm sure," I replied. "Got any ideas?"

"Well, what are you burning to actually make the light?"

"I guess that would be magic?" I said.

"So, you are putting magic into this space and telling it to transform into light," Sandy said. "Does that sound right?"

I could tell she was leading me somewhere, but I didn't know where she was going with this. I hadn't thought of the light source as transformative magic, but that did seem to fit what was happening. I'd just told my power I needed light and it did it.

"Yes. That sounds right."

"How about using your magic to transform something else into light?" Sandy asked. "It would still take magic, but it might not take as much as using it as the power source."

That was a whole new way of thinking. Clearly, I had a lot to learn.

I looked around to see what I could turn into light. The table was littered with cubes, but I thought Sandy would be really upset if I ruined her testing kit. I tried to find something else. There was cat hair on me. Would that work?

"I know someone who has an affinity to gas," Sandy stated. I looked at her blankly. "And the ball of light is floating in the air."

Was she suggesting I convert air to light? That sounded crazy. It also sounded genius.

I turned off the current ball of light. It seemed easier to start over rather than convert an existing process. This time I imagined a tiny sphere filled with air. The air would fill with magic and start glowing. As it was transformed, the air would be used up, so fresh air would flow into the sphere and be transformed into light also.

I set it up in my mind and added a touch of magic. A little round ball of light appeared on my palm. It felt slightly different than before, but not by much. I checked my magic usage. It was a five.

"A five is good," Sandy said. "Although, to be honest, I was expecting a bit more. Using a real-world element and transforming it is usually much more effective than just using magic alone."

She thought about it for a minute. "I guess it does make sense in a way. Your soul is so dense you are already very efficient with magic. It's hard to improve when you are already doing so well. Let's try a few more things with the light. First, change the color to something other than white. Let's go for red."

I shifted my imagery slightly and Sandy confirmed it was now red. Magic output stayed at five. We tried different colors, but it didn't make any difference.

"Keeping the same brightness, let's increase the size of the light. See how big of a sphere you can make it."

That was also simple to do, but I could feel the draw of magic increasing. I found I could increase the globe of light up to about three inches in diameter. Then it just started falling apart. At three inches, the magic draw went up to twelve.

"I thought this might happen," Sandy said. "This is another side of your distance handicap. It seems like there is also a size limitation to your magic as well. Your magic is effective, but only in a small radius"

Well that was a bummer. I really was the opposite style of magic to a fireball. I could probably make a very hot flame right on my palm, but that wasn't any good in battle. Besides, it would burn my hand.

"I do have one more thing to show you before we get into your first charm," Sandy said. She pulled a metal figure out of her chest with a flourish.

"This," she said dramatically, "is a light rune."

It kinda looked like the number four with a few extra squiggles and dots.

"Runes are the secret sauce to magic. Right now, you are working with basic personal magic. Runes take you to the next level. Within a narrow scope, they give you a boost to your magic. Almost like you had a natural affinity for whatever the rune is for.

"They announce to the world what effect you are going to use your magic for. When you add magic inside the design, it's not just you trying to make something happen. The rune helps you bring your intention to life.

"So, this light rune will let you cast light with a lot less effort. It will also allow you to go much brighter than you could on your own. You are already magically effective so I can't wait to see what this rune will do for you."

The rune didn't look like much, but Sandy was clearly excited. I wasn't sure what to expect, but I was getting excited too.

"This is probably going to be easier if you go back to just burning magic. Remember, that was a magic output of six. This time, instead of making a sphere of magic, I want you to incorporate this design into your light. It really doesn't matter how you do it. Just go with something obvious for starters."

I let the magic I had go and started over again. This time I thought of the rune like the filament in a light bulb. I didn't even bother with the sphere. I wasn't used to the rune yet, so I had to keep checking out the metal figure to make sure I was getting it right. All the details in the rune made it hard to duplicate so it took a while. Finally, I was ready. I took a breath, and I added magic.

The magic glow from my hand was powerful. Sandy said the whole workroom had lit up. The light seemed clear and bright too. I'd planned on a low range glow like before. Sandy said this was so bright it was a bit hard to look at. I checked out my magic usage: two!

She did a happy twirl. "I thought that would be something to see! I haven't ever had anyone get their magic down to a two before. And the light is so brilliant. This is just amazing. Good job!"

Sandy really loved talking about magic. It was so neat that she was this happy for me.

"Now let me show you something about runes. Take the light and make it red like you did before."

I did and the effect was obvious. The light was much dimmer and the cost shot up to five. It wasn't six like before, but it was close.

"Runes can be picky things. In this case, the rune is for a white light only. Since you are making red light its effectiveness is reduced. Its potency doesn't go down by just a little bit either, it goes down by a lot."

I tried other colors but it was the same with all of them. This rune wanted white light only.

"Knowing your runes and how to use them is very important. You don't want a rune to fail on you when you're in a tough situation. Well, it won't fail you. Runes work the same way every time. It's more like you would fail it by trying to get it to do something it wasn't designed to do."

"This is so cool!" I was still playing with the light rune. It was pretty picky about its shape too. I changed the rune slightly and it stopped working. I put a sphere around it, and it didn't seem to mind that at all. I made it bigger and smaller and it was still bright as heck. I still ran up against the three-inch size limit. Even a rune couldn't help me with that.

"So where do runes come from?" I asked. I could already think of lots of runes I wanted to learn. There must be a defensive one that powered those shields. I wanted that for sure.

"Apparently runes are everywhere. They make up just about everything we see, touch, and feel. There are abstract runes for things like force and heat. There are runes in everything solid, like this table. If you could see the wood rune it would tell you the color, texture, and all the properties of wood. Some supers have a special affinity to runes and can see them. They have shared some of what they see and that makes up what we use today.

"This is a very rare skill. As far as I know there isn't anyone alive today that can see runes. You can also modify a rune with experimentation. If you knew what you were doing, you could figure out what part of this light rune is for white light. You could then change it to be blue or red. Finding new runes and what they can do is a big deal. Covens hoard the runes they have found and will do just about anything to acquire new ones.

"That's why I was so excited to see the golem core. It has to have new runes for movement, a rune to gather rocks, a rune to hold everything together in a human shape. That's in addition to the runes that give it intention. It needed a way to detect you and know that you were an enemy. Then it needed intelligence to know to run after you and attack you. I don't know any runes like that. The whole core is levels above what I thought was even possible. Someone who is a rune master put that thing together.

"In my experience, though, it's better to have a few runes and know them very well. As you found out, having a rune is only half the puzzle. You also need to know exactly what it does. Using a rune differently than it was intended only gives you a small bonus.

"Now, let's have some fun with this. Crank that thing up and let's see how bright you can make it."

I'd been wondering that myself. I made the rune sit flat on my palm. That way every part of the rune was close to me. Then, I doubled the power.

With my magic sight, I saw it was already a reasonable glow in my hand. When I doubled the power, I expected it to double the light. Instead, it quadrupled it.

Sandy was my best test of how I was doing since she was using regular sight. She started squinting and she wouldn't look at it directly. I doubled the power again. Now it looked like a small sun sat in my hand.

I wished I could see this with my eyes. It must have been something, because Sandy turned completely around and looked at the wall. Then I took off all restraint and gave it everything I had. Even facing the other way, it was too much for Sandy. She closed her eyes and threw up her hands to cover her face.

"Okay! Stop!" she yelled. I let the light go and everything went back to normal. It took her a moment to turn back around again. Her eyes were tearing up and she was holding onto the workbench.

"That was insane!" she said. "I could see the bones in my hand. Even turned around like I was and with my eyes covered, I could still see the light."

"Wow." Sandy looked a bit unsteady. "Are you all right?" I asked. I pulled up a stool for her.

"I will be," she said. "Just give me a sec." She took a deep breath. "I didn't think light could be that powerful. I should have looked away sooner. I'm still seeing spots."

I'd seen the light in my hand get really bright to my magic sight, but it didn't cause me any problems. I needed to keep this in mind. There had to be a way to use this in battle. Of course, I'd end up blinding my own allies too.

Sandy took a few more deep breaths. Then she pulled out something I'd been waiting on; a charm bracelet.

"I think you have certainly earned this," Sandy said solemnly. "I had John make it for you. I do hope you like it."

I could see the bracelet was a lot more than just silver links chained together. He had gone with a vine theme, and they wound around each other forming a complex pattern. I'm sure there were actual links in the chain, but the artistry was so good I couldn't see where one link stopped and the next one started. I could see berries—actually I think those were grapes. Maybe it was grape vines. I'd have to ask John later. Either way, it was a beautiful piece of workmanship.

It had one charm on it: a light bulb.

"It is tradition for a teacher to give her student his first charm bracelet. In this way it shows that he has passed through his assessment and is ready to start down the path of becoming a mage. It shows that the teacher has confidence in her student. Both in the realm of magic and the use to which it will be applied.

"I hope you will wear this charm proudly, as I am proud of you. I hope you will use this one and all future charms as well, in service to yourself, your House, and the world at large. May we all be better for having you as part of our lives.

"I believe in you, Jason. I believe in your goodness as a person. I believe in your ability to grow and learn the magic arts. I believe in your ability to overcome and be a force for good in this world. There will be times in your life where you lose sight of hope, when you wonder if you can do the right thing. In those times I hope you will feel this charm, and my faith in you."

She fastened the bracelet around my left wrist. "Wear it well."

The sincerity of the moment caught me by surprise. This felt like so much more than just a simple gift. This was a statement of faith and belief in me. That I was a good person and worthy of being a supernatural.

I hadn't heard a statement like that in a very long time. It touched me and I got a bit misty-eyed. I wasn't sure what to say, so I settled for giving her a big hug instead.

"Thank you," I offered sincerely. "I'm glad you found me and I'm glad you are my teacher. I can't imagine learning from anyone else." I squeezed her hand and wiped my eyes. "I'm not sentimental, so we'll just leave it at that. Now, how do I use this charm?" I asked.

"I think the light bulb shape gives it away, but that is a light charm," Sandy replied. "It's based on the same rune you just learned. It's one of the charms we charged the other night, so it is full of power and ready to go.

"A basic charm is made up of a power source and a rune. It's up to you to give the result shape and focus. Using this charm as an example, it will be up to you to set where the light appears, how big it is, how bright it is, and how long it lasts.

"As far as how to use it, everyone is a bit different. You will have to find what works for you. I think of it like squeezing. The squeeze lets the charm know I want it to turn on and I cast the magic just like I would my own. Annabeth said she can always hear her charms a little bit and she just imagines turning up the sound. I don't know what it will be for you. You'll just have to try and see how it happens."

Sandy looked at me expectantly. I felt nervous. This was what I had wanted, and now it was here. This was my first charm. The start of my journey. I felt like there should be a drum roll or something.

I touched the charm with my right hand. It felt small but solid. I gave it a small squeeze and imagined light flowing out of it.

Nothing happened.

I tried it again. Still nothing. I was squeezing it physically. Maybe I needed to squeeze it mentally. I released it and let it dangle from its chain. I wrapped my awareness around the charm and squeezed. Nothing. Not even a little flash.

I sunk my awareness into the charm. I could see the rune I'd just learned etched inside it. The rune itself was hollow in the lines. It looked like the edges of the lines were magical. The rune itself connected to a hollow chamber and that was filled with neutral magic. The magic was bright, like a tiny star. This was one of the charms that had been extra filled in the park.

It looked like the charm was primed and ready to go, just like Sandy said. I just had to figure out how to work it.

For the next several minutes I tried just about everything I knew. I squeezed the neutral magic. I tried to pull it through the tubes. I tried to listen to it like Annabeth did. I tried shaking it. I tried just letting it happen naturally.

Nothing. Nada. Zilch.

Big fat zero.

Sandy watched me struggle the whole time and she finally stepped in.

"I think you are going to have to work at this for a bit. Don't get frustrated. You've had so much magic come easily to you. It won't hurt you to take some time to figure this out. What you are going through now is what most beginning mages go through.

"Enjoy the learning process. You'll master it before long, I'm sure, and won't think twice about it anymore. For now, let's stick with just this one charm. Once you know how to activate it, then we can look at adding a few more.

"I'm going to clean up here. I'm heading to the grocery store soon with John, so why don't you meet me later for supper and we can see how you are doing then."

It looked like I was being dismissed. I didn't want to keep trying and failing with her watching, so I was only too glad to head back to my apartment. I'd originally planned on going to Annabeth's and talking about the assessment and my new charms. Since I couldn't actually use my charm, that didn't seem like fun anymore.

When I got back to my apartment Bermuda was waiting for me. He was ready for a snack. I was ready to work on my charm skills. We compromised by giving him a snack.

He was just too darn cute to resist. Post snack time, we curled up on my couch together and I started working on the charm again.

It was so frustrating. Nothing I did was working. There had to be a way for me to make this happen, but I couldn't figure it out.

Bermuda wanted some belly love, so I tickled his soft white tummy as I thought about it. Nothing new occurred to me. Bermuda took a nap. I snuggled him and tried to come up with new ideas. It felt nice lying there so I decided to take a nap too. Maybe my mind just needed time to process it for a while.

I woke up to the sound of someone hammering on my door. I thought it was going to fly off its hinges. Bermuda shot off into the bedroom to hide. I wanted to do that too, but instead I went to the door to see what was up.

It was John, looking frantic.

"Sandy's been kidnapped," he exclaimed.

23

Busting Shields

I was shocked. That was the last thing I thought I would hear.

Sandy was the most powerful person I knew. How on earth had she been kidnapped?

"How did this happen?" I asked.

"I'll tell you on the way. Grab your things. I need you or Annabeth to track her," John said firmly.

I hoped Annabeth knew something about tracking because I didn't. I also didn't know what things I needed to grab. I didn't have any charms or weapons. Well, I had one charm, but I didn't know how to use it. I had on sweatpants and a t-shirt. That seemed good enough to fight in.

I felt very unprepared for whatever we were getting into. John was my friend, though, and Sandy was my teacher. I was going and I'd figure it out as we went.

I hollered at Bermuda to stay put. No more broken bones for him if I could help it. I didn't know if he heard me or if he could understand me in some magical way. He was pretty extraordinary, even for a cat. Then, I left with John.

We went to pick up Annabeth and she had the same reaction I did. Shock followed by disbelief that Sandy could be taken. I told John I needed a weapon and while Annabeth was changing into something more battle appropriate, he ran to his place to get me one.

He returned quickly. He must have run the whole way. Annabeth was dressed like me, sweatpants and a t-shirt. She was putting on her charm bracelet when John handed me the strangest looking club I'd seen.

"What the heck is this?" I asked. It looked like a long wooden hammer, but the hammer part was at an angle.

"It's a shillelagh. They use them in Ireland, near my homeland. This one is made of blackthorn wood, which is very resistant to magic. Most mages won't be able to target this with a spell and rip it out of your hands. The end is capped with silver. That gives it extra heft as well as some additional anti-magic properties. You should be able to crack a fine skull with this thing."

"Why is the end shaped like that? That seems strange," I said. If I was going to use a weapon, I wanted to know what it could do.

"We don't have time for a full discussion on how it works," John said shortly. "Quick version is, it's a club. Swing it and hit someone. The end that curves back toward you forms a hook. You can use that to hook your opponent's weapon and yank it out of his hands. The angle of the club part also makes a bit of a point, so it does extra damage regardless of how you use it. You can lunge with it, like a spear. It doesn't pierce like a sword, but that hurts more than you think it would."

I wasn't sure what to do with it. I couldn't very well walk down the street with a club in my hand. Maybe they did that where John grew up, but that wouldn't work in this city. It was about two feet long, so it wasn't going to fit in my pocket either.

I ended up sticking it down my pants. The shillelagh had a strap to put around your wrist, so I tied that to the string on the waistband. The sweatpants were pretty loose, so it wasn't super obvious. It did sort of look like I had a very long and very thick penis, though. Hopefully not too many people would notice.

"Ready?" he asked Annabeth.

"Ready," she said firmly. We headed out.

There was a grocery store, Kroger, only three blocks away from the House, and that was where we were headed. John filled us in on what happened while we walked quickly. Actually, John walked quickly; Annabeth and I both jogged to keep up. He was both furious and worried at the same time. His hands kept clutching like he was wringing someone's neck.

"We have this routine when we are shopping. Sandy gets the cart and looks for the main items. She is particular about her fruits and vegetables, and I hate waiting around, so I'll go and get some of the easier canned goods. It's a nice system and speeds up the whole grocery shopping process."

John did not look like someone who enjoyed picking up groceries. I was sure anything he could do to make the time shorter was a bonus in his book.

"I'd left her on a second run. It was a longer one and I picked up several items. When I got back, Sandy was gone. I thought maybe she had moved on to another part of the store, so I went looking for her. I couldn't find her easily, so I put my stuff down and did a thorough search. She's not in there, and that could only mean something has happened to her. I ran back to get you two. I'm not a spell-slinger but there has to be some way to track her."

I looked at Annabeth, who looked at me worriedly. I was guessing she had no clue how to track Sandy either.

"I'm sure we can figure something out," I said. John was going so fast I was panting a bit. I didn't have any breath to say anything else. I saved it for the running.

This was the first time I'd been outside the House with just my magic sight. It felt very strange. I could see everything in a twenty-foot sphere around me. It hadn't been too bad inside the House. Most rooms are not bigger than twenty feet, so I had a sense of space. I could see the ceiling and walls. Outside felt very different. I could see part of the road, but not across the street. I could see the air above me, but not the sky. The sidewalk would appear in front of me and disappear behind me.

I felt like I was living in a strange bubble world. It wasn't helping that we were running. Without any sort of perspective, it felt like I we were going so fast.

When we got to Kroger, it was a bit better. There were so many people, though, that it got weird again. I would just see an elbow or half of a person in my vision, then they would disappear. Or someone would walk into my view, pick up something, and walk back out again. Without any visual context it seemed like something out of a creepy movie.

John took us to the produce area. "This is where I last saw Sandy," he said. He looked at us expectantly.

I looked at Annabeth.

She looked at me.

"Do you have any charms that might help?" I asked. I was pretty sure there wasn't one. If there was a good tracking charm, then Sandy would have used it to find Jennifer when she was taken. It never hurt to ask, though. Maybe there was one that could be used in a new creative way to do what we needed.

We went through her charms together. She had one for heat, one for force, one for a shield, one for healing, and of course, one for light. She couldn't think of any new way to use them, and neither could I. John wasn't really participating in our conversation. He was just pacing and looking like he could kill someone. We were getting some strange looks. At least people were leaving us alone.

"You can see all the way down to the cellular level with your sight." Annabeth said. "Maybe Sandy left a cell or a trace of her magic somehow. There had to have been a fight at some point. Maybe you can pick it up where we can't."

"It's worth a shot," I said. This seemed like the only option we had. I had to make it work.

"See if you can get John away from here. He's messing with my vision."

My sight recorded the world in textures and grays. I only saw color if it was magic, and John was throwing off a crazy amount of magic as he paced. John's color was gray, like stone, but it seemed more real than non-magic items.

Annabeth left my side in a swirl of pink and went to John. She talked with him for a moment and then pulled him out of range. I was now alone in my bubble. The only magical creature here.

I relaxed, took a deep breath, and shook out my nerves. I felt like the world was riding on my shoulders. I didn't want to be the lead, but I was there and Sandy was counting on me. I could see in amazing detail. There had to be something I could use.

I stood there and took in all the details around me. My sight really was amazing. I could tell how many oranges were on display, whether they were on the top of the pile or not. There was an endcap of packages of nuts. I could feel every nut in every package if I wanted. I could even see inside the nuts. The problem was one of focus. With so much data, how did I know where to look?

When I looked at something naturally, I usually didn't see everything in my view. My mind filtered out all the normal stuff and I just saw and processed what I wanted to see. This was a lot like that, except that with a view all around me there was so much more information. I was still used to looking at everything like it was my normal line of sight. I wasn't limited to that anymore. I could see everything. I just needed to get better at processing it.

I stood there, just letting it all in. I told myself over and over, "I want to see. I want to see." It was a mantra, focusing me. Gradually the world came into focus in a new way. It was sharper, clearer. I wasn't just seeing it; I was feeling it too. Maybe even tasting it. I could tell one of the packages of nuts had been left in the warehouse too long. The oil in the nuts had gone off. I could taste the difference.

I normally couldn't sense to this degree, but I'd been living with nothing but my magical sight for days now. I'd been relying on it just like I would my regular sight, and my ability to use it had sharpened.

I was annoyed that John had been here. His pacing had messed up the magical spectrum. I could still see traces of his magic floating around in the air. I was looking for something magical, and I kept noting his presence. Annabeth was worse, though. Her pink particles of worry stood out a lot more than John's, even though she hadn't been throwing them off like he had. I tried to ignore them and search for Sandy.

I let my focus go, and just scanned everything. I thought it might be like finding a familiar face in a crowd. Even though there are a lot of people, your mind can still pick out someone you know. I was now processing what felt like a lot of data, but still the only thing magical I could see was that John and Annabeth had been here.

Then it hit me. That was it! John and Annabeth were out of my view, but I could still see they had been here! If I was tracking them, I'd have their trail. I was onto something. They were worried, though, and that must be what was causing them to emit extra magic. Sandy was here according to John, but she hadn't been worried yet. Since she wasn't in the store, she had to have left at some point. Something had to have made her do that and she would have been worried, curious, upset, or something at that point. If I was right, that would mean she had left a magic trail for me to follow.

"Annabeth, you and John stay behind me," I said loudly. "I'm going to circle the store. I think I might be onto something."

"Sure thing," Annabeth said distantly.

I walked forward slowly, processing the new space as it came into view. "Come on, Sandy orange magic," I said to myself. "Give me some orange." I made it to the main aisle that ran around the outside of the store. We were at the front, so I turned and slowly walked toward the back.

I got distracted because one woman noticed my shillelagh and did a double take. It was funny as hell. *"Is that a Shillelagh in your pants or are you just happy to see me?"* I thought. It took me a moment to focus again and move forward.

Then I saw it. A tiny speck of magic orange. It wasn't where I thought it would be, though. It was about ten feet in the air, just sitting there. I guessed all the movement in the aisle had wafted it that high into the air? That was the only thing I could think of. Sandy wasn't ten feet tall or flying through the grocery store.

I examined it in detail. It was certainly Sandy's magic. As I watched, it was fading ever so slowly. A few hours from now it would be gone. John had been smart to get me and Annabeth right away. I couldn't have done this tomorrow.

Now I had hope, and I kept walking the aisle. I made it to the rear of the store and turned to walk along the back. They had all their meats, cheeses, and yogurts here. Sandy would have shopped back here for sure.

Suddenly I walked into a flurry of orange particles. They were everywhere. Stuck in a crack on the floor, on the underside of the display, hovering up in the air. Something had happened right here. Sandy had been alarmed somehow.

"Something happened here," I said loudly. "I can see traces of Sandy's magic. I'm going to follow it." I heard John growl. "Be sure and stay back," I added.

I kept moving forward and saw a shower of dark particles. They were a dark purple in color. Obviously whatever the purple represented had been the cause of Sandy's alarm. I kept moving forward. The purple ended, but Sandy's magic kept going. About halfway down the back of the store I saw the imprint of her hand; it was on the swinging doors leading back to the stockroom.

I made a mental note that touching something left more of an impression. I kept walking along the back aisle a bit more, just to make sure Sandy's trail stopped at the door. For all I knew, she'd touched the door for some reason and kept walking.

She hadn't, though. Her magic clearly led through the doors and back into the warehouse. I wasn't sure what any employees were going to think, but I pushed through the doors and kept going. I had Sandy's trail and I wasn't stopping for anything.

There were metal racks filled with product stretching up to the ceiling. The aisles were wide enough for pallets of stuff to move down them and my trail led down the second aisle. I was almost to the end of that aisle, way on the side of the store, when I saw the purple again. This time it wasn't just a shower of particles. It looked like a purple bomb had gone off. Sandy's orange motes where everywhere, but they ended here.

"This is where it happened," I said. "They lured her back here somehow and then hit her with a trap of some sort. There is purple magic everywhere. They had to have moved her so I'm going to follow the purple trail now."

The purple wasn't personal magic, so it wasn't bonded to her. She was covered in it when they moved her, so it was very easy to follow. I picked up other traces of magic too. Based on the colors, there were three mages involved. Some of the particles had that rotten feel I'd come to associate with Isobel and her crew.

I passed that info along to John and followed the trail to the main loading dock and out of the warehouse. I was afraid they would take a car at this point; I wasn't sure how I would follow a car. It looks like they stayed on foot, though. The alley along the back of Kroger was wide enough for a truck, and they stayed to the middle of it. I guessed they weren't worried about being seen.

Three excited mages and leftover purple bomb particles made this easy to follow, so I picked up the pace. There was another alley leading off of this one. It was much narrower and probably only used by local merchants. I followed their trail down it until it hit Third Street, which was one of the major roads out of the city.

"Annabeth, I need your help. We have to cross the street and I can't see the traffic," I yelled.

Annabeth came up and took my hand. It felt nice to have someone there. I'd felt alone up to this point. She let me know when it was safe, and we sprinted across the road. The alley picked up on the other side. Annabeth fell back, and I kept going. I couldn't see much about the neighborhood, but I passed a lot of large loading doors. We were obviously on the back side of small warehouses or retail stores.

I saw the trail leading through a metal door up ahead, when suddenly a spell flashed into view and hit me. It was angled down, like it came from the roof. With only twenty feet of warning, I didn't have time to dodge.

Sparks danced over my body and I shook and fell to the ground. I heard a boom and a cry. I knew that sound. John had thrown one of his rocks. Based on the cry, he'd scored a hit. One enemy mage down. I'd followed three mages, but that didn't mean there weren't more in the building.

I shook off the spell and stood up. I was surprisingly unharmed. I guessed the spell had targeted me directly and my magic density had protected me. I was about to suggest we proceed slowly and see what we were up against first, when John ran past me.

With a battle roar, he kicked the metal door and it flew off its hinges into the building. So much for going slowly. The mages knew we were here now. He dove into the building with Annabeth right behind him, shield up and ready. I didn't have a shield, but I wasn't staying out of this fight. Sandy needed me. I dove through the door too.

I was in some sort of open space. It looked like it had been a warehouse or storage room at one point. It was empty now, except for steel beams that dotted the space, holding up the ceiling.

I ran over to a beam and got behind it. It would hopefully provide some protection while I figured out what was happening. I could hear John's battle roar. He sounded like a primal force of nature that was pissed off. I was so glad he was on our side. I could also hear Isobel. That was seriously bad news.

It would probably take everything John had to beat Isobel. That means the star players of both teams were out. So, who else were we fighting? Annabeth was in my radius and I could see spells coming at her from two directions. She had ducked behind a steel beam too. They weren't that big, so it wasn't a lot of cover. Her shield was working, so she was okay so far, and she was firing back. Annabeth was short, dumpy, and a grandmother, but she was tough!

I wasn't feeling tough, and there was another mage sprinting toward me. His spell bounced off my beam as I tried to be as skinny as possible. What the heck could I do? I didn't have any offensive spells. I didn't have any defensive ones either. I had my wits and my fists. Oh! And my shillelagh! I hadn't been hauling that around for nothing.

I pulled it out of my pants and the dang wrist strap was still tied to my sweatpants. The knot was tight, and I had to pick it apart. I did not have time for this! They never show stuff like this in the movies.

The mage was circling the beam, trying to get a shot in. I didn't need to look at him to see him, though, so I was circling with him, still trying to unpick the knot. Finally, I got it. I looped the strap around my wrist and gripped it in my right hand. It felt good. It felt solid. It was going to do some damage today.

Now I just needed to close the distance between us without getting spelled.

It occurred to me, I didn't have any offensive magic, but he didn't know that. That gave me an idea.

I cupped my left hand and imagined a firefly in my palm. He had wings, of course, and a glowy butt. I put the rune for light on his chest. Hopefully that would be enough. This was a rush job.

"*I need you to fly toward the enemy,*" I thought, "*shining the whole way. If he dodges, just circle around and come back at him again. If it looks like you are going to get hit by a spell, then just vanish. If you do get hit, I hope it doesn't hurt.*"

I felt bad making a little guy that was probably going to get blasted out of the sky. I didn't know how something like this occurred to them. I didn't want to hurt any of my creations. I liked to think they just vanished and reformed when I needed them again.

"*Thanks bud,*" I thought to my firefly and got a flash in return.

I stepped out from behind the beam and threw him at the mage like I was throwing a spell. He lit up and must have looked threatening enough. I sprinted toward the mage as he threw himself out of the way of the firefly. It wasn't a big distance and I made it to him before he could cast a counter spell.

I swung the shillelagh at his head, and it landed with a hard thunk on his personal shield.

Well crap. Now I was out in the open and it was too far to sprint back to the beam. He could hit me with a spell any time he wanted. The mage looked rattled, though. A club almost landing on your face will do that to you I'm sure.

He went to make a gesture at me, and I hit his hand with my club. Well, I hit the shield around his hand, but it was still enough to jerk his arm around. So, his shield blocked things, but it didn't make him indestructible. I could knock him around and throw off his aim. That was something.

The next few moments were close and very intense. I could swing that shillelagh quickly and I used it to pound him. I also tried to stay to the side or behind him as much as possible. He kept trying to spin around and hit me with a spell. He still wasn't sure about the firefly so he kept trying to dodge that too, which let me hit him even more.

Shields took power, and at some point, his shield would run out. It was a race then. I had to wear his shield down before I eventually slipped up and he tagged me with a spell.

I knew I had to win this. If this mage won our fight, then he was free to join the fight with Annabeth. She couldn't handle three on one so she would go down too. Then it would be Isobel and three more spell-slingers on John. John was good, but I wasn't sure he was that good. If I lost, then we could all end up being Isobel's prisoners. Somehow, I had to own this spell-slinger.

A few moments later he made a mistake. He stumbled and reached out to steady himself. It was an instinctual motion, and he reached out to me. I grabbed his arm to steady him, and I was through his shield! I held on and whacked at his head again. The shield was still there.

This shield was a puzzle I needed to solve now. There had to be a way to get through it, but not by hammering at him. I had his hand so I went up his arm with my other hand. That got through just fine. Our battle quickly turned into a wrestling match.

He was still trying to fire off a spell and I was trying to get him on the ground and put him in some sort of arm lock. I'm not a wrestler, but I was bullied a lot as a kid. I knew the basics. Take an arm, twist it behind the guy, trip him, and keep twisting.

Tyler was right. If you're a mage then everything looks like it needs a spell. If the mage would have just focused on wrestling with me, he might have won. Instead, he focused on trying to cast a spell and I took him down.

He landed hard on his front, and I quickly straddled his back. He was still trying to cast with his other hand, so I needed to finish this off quickly.

It felt cruel to keep twisting while he was hollering in pain. I hated bullies, and this felt just like that. I wanted to stop and let the guy surrender, but I was pretty sure that wouldn't work. He was trying to take me down. If he won, we were all dead. That just could not happen.

I twisted, pulled, and finally felt a pop as his shoulder gave out. He screamed in pain, but he was an immortal. He would heal just like I did. Nothing I was doing to him would kill him.

He could still cast with one hand, so I grabbed his other arm and twisted again. As I was busy wrenching it out of its socket, I noticed my shillelagh was dangling from my wrist and touching him. It was through the shield too.

With both arms out and me on top, I had a moment to test this shield spell. I grabbed the shillelagh, pulled it back and whacked at his head again. It bounced off his shield. I let it sit on his shield. It flared for a moment, then the club fell through. Maybe the shield recognized the force of the blow? Or maybe the speed?

The shield had to let some stuff through, or you wouldn't be able to use the bathroom or touch anything. I swung the club slower and lighter. The shield flared again. I slowed it way down, like I was gently tapping him. This time the shield spell stayed off.

This was some good stuff to know! I could use this to defeat one of the mages Annabeth was fighting.

I wished there was some way to knock him out. I didn't need my hands to cast spells and he might still be dangerous. I needed him out of the fight without killing him.

I didn't know how to do a sleeper hold, so I used the bar part of the shillelagh to choke him until he passed out. Sucked for him, but better than getting punched in the face by a golem. His throat would be sore, but he could recover from that pretty quickly.

I jumped up and ran over to where I'd last seen Annabeth. The fight had shifted, but not that far. The two of them had pinned her down. She couldn't seem to fire through her own shield, so the best she could do was to try and avoid the blasts. Since she wasn't on the offensive, the other two felt safe to chase her down and hammer her with spells.

I looked around for my little firefly. *"Upgrade time little buddy,"* I thought as I absorbed him and started over. This time I made his butt big. He wasn't just going to shine and distract; he was going to go on the offensive.

I made it so his tail was made up of lots of spotlights, then added the light rune to each one. He was going to shine very brightly, in one direction. He was going to be my flasher, so I added a trench coat. It seemed appropriate.

I whispered instructions to him and then he was off. This time there wasn't any light to give him away. He flew slowly and passed right through the mage's shield. He got right in front of the mage's right eye, flared his trench coat, pointed his tail, and let loose.

I'm not sure what it looked like in the natural world, but in the magical one there was a beam of pure magic injected into the mage's eye. The mage screamed and staggered back, holding his right eye. The second mage looked over, concerned, but didn't stop hammering Annabeth. He completely missed me, hiding behind a beam, and my little flasher in the air. The second mage also had some rotten in his aura. This guy was part of Isobel's inner posse.

The second mage went back to focusing completely on Annabeth. The flasher lined up with the first mage's left eye. When he opened it, he got another eyeful.

Meanwhile, I'd come up behind him and pointed my club at his head like a spear. I moved slowly, until part of the head of the shillelagh was through his shield. Then I thrust it at him with everything I had. Since it was already through his defense, his shield couldn't stop me.

Blinded and stunned, he stumbled forward. I followed him, keeping the club head inside his shield, battering him with short thrusts. The head of the shillelagh was weighted and solid. Even without a big windup, getting hit was no joke, and I gave him no time to recover.

I must have hit him more than ten times before he went down. When he did, I grabbed first one arm and then the other and popped them out of their sockets. I was set to choke him out when I saw a flat disk on the ground by his head. It was on a cord around his neck and looked like it had some sort of tribal marking on it. It also had a small glow of power.

I pulled it off over his head. Was this the shield amulet? I swung the shillelagh at his head as an experiment. It hit with a solid thunk and the mage slumped, unconscious.

Annabeth was now up and giving as good as she got. The rotten mage's shield was flashing as much as hers was. Go Annabeth!

The other mage must have been keeping an eye on me because as soon as I got up, he hit me with a force spell. I'd been lucky so far. I'd managed to stay damage free. This time, though, he hit me dead on.

It was powerful enough to pick me up off my feet and fling me through the air. It felt more like a shove, rather than a blow, so it didn't actually damage me too much.

I hit the ground and rolled. It wasn't a graceful roll. It was more like I went ass over tea kettle until I slammed into the wall of the warehouse. I was a little stunned and a little sick. When I'd rolled, my magic sight had rolled with me. It had been like being in a theme park ride that spins you around really fast. Not good.

I staggered to my feet and fell over again. Note to self, more vision meant faster dizziness. I was all set to head back to Annabeth, even if I had to crawl, when I noticed Sandy. She was on the floor, curled up on her side, and she wasn't moving. There was a rune etched on the floor below her and a circle around her. From the circle, a dome of red magic arched up and covered her. There was another rune, a much smaller one, overlaying the circle on one side. Out of that rune I could see Sandy's orange magic heading in a stream somewhere. Based on the battle sounds, it was heading toward Isobel and John's fight.

Isobel was using Sandy for fuel! She had bragged at the park about how she had drained Jennifer until she was dust. She was doing that to Sandy. I had to get her out of there.

I was torn between working on it right away or heading back to Annabeth. If I worked on it now, I could solve it faster. On the other hand, Annabeth might lose. The final mage she was fighting was part of Isobel's group so he must be powerful. If he won, I'd be in a pickle. If Annabeth was free, she could help John or help me. That decided it. Help Annabeth it was.

I staggered back toward her fight, gradually feeling better along the way. I called the flasher to me. He had worked out even better than I'd hoped. I filled him up with more magic and sent him off again. I had just gotten to her fight when I saw the first flash. The mage screamed and flailed around. That light must be seriously bright. Go flasher!

A second flash happened and now the mage was blind. Annabeth stepped in close and really hammered at his shields.

"Try a slow spell," I hollered. She looked at me like I was crazy, but she sent a slow wave of red toward the mage. His shield flared. She could almost touch him now, so she sent a very slow wave. This time it got through.

The result was spectacular as his clothes burst into flames. Annabeth was shocked. I didn't think she had really thought through what would happen if her heat spell actually landed.

Neither one of us wanted him to die so we tackled him, shield and all, and rolled him around on the floor. This got most of the flames out. I ripped off his shield amulet and we stamped on the remaining flames until they died out.

Then I thunked him over the head with my club. No sense in letting the guy suffer. I felt weird popping his shoulder out since he was unconscious, so I settled on clubbing both of his shoulders. Hopefully he wouldn't be able to come after us if he woke up.

I gave Annabeth a quick high five. I wasn't sure how the rest of the battle was going to go, but it felt good to celebrate the success we'd had so far. We had taken down three mages! Annabeth was breathing hard, but she looked okay. I was banged up a bit from my tumble, but it was nothing compared to the broken bones of last time.

I felt strong and full of energy. Thank goodness I had my matrix and had powered through my healing. This fight would have turned out very different if I still had half-healed ribs. One of these days I'd be able to transform my body like Tyler. Until then, I'd take this hybrid of healing and transformation any day.

"I found Sandy," I said. "She's in some sort of rune circle and it's draining her magic. I think it's going to Isobel. She's actually using Sandy's magic to fight John. We need to beat Isobel and stop the fight with John, but we also need to get Sandy out of the circle. What do you think we should do?"

Both options had risk. If we helped John and the fight still went on for a long time, then Sandy might get fully drained. Isobel was tough, so there was no guarantee we could beat her. On the other hand, if we tried to free Sandy, but couldn't do it, then Isobel would be draining her the whole time.

"I'll help John," Annabeth said. "And you work on the circle with Sandy. I can distract Isobel a bit and give John an edge. You are good at unconventional magic so maybe you can defeat the circle like you did the golem."

That sounded like a good plan to me. I'd much rather tackle the circle than try and deal with Isobel. She'd really done a number on me last time. I'm not too proud to say I was scared of her. If Annabeth and John could bring her down, then that would be great. Annabeth dashed off toward the sound of battle and I headed back to Sandy.

When I got to Sandy, I took a good look at what I was dealing with. The circle was actually etched into the concrete floor, as were the runes. I had hoped it was just drawn there. If so, I might have been able to disrupt the drawing.

I tried to get through the bubble and get to Sandy, but it was solid. I even whacked it a few times with my shillelagh to see if a good knock or the silver cap would make any difference. There was no noticeable change. Thinking it might be like the shield charm, I attempted to go through it very slowly. That didn't work either.

There had to be a way to turn the smaller rune on and off. I was sure Isobel planned on drawing this out as long as possible, and that meant she couldn't be pulling from Sandy the whole time. I probed it with my sight and my magic, but nothing jumped out at me. There wasn't any sort of switch that I could see.

I went back to the red dome. It wasn't that thick. There had to be a way to bring it down. I focused on a small section of it and saw something interesting. It wasn't a solid red; there were black jagged lines running through it, and they were moving.

They were moving fast too; I could barely distinguish them before they were gone. I zoomed in and realized they were everywhere. This thing was riddled with some sort of black magic. They were moving quickly, though, spinning around the surface of the dome. I waited for a few moments and finally got a good look at one. The black was strange. It felt empty. It wasn't like the one mage I'd seen with a black aura. This didn't seem to have anything.

Then it hit me. I was looking at this all wrong. The black felt empty because it was. It wasn't black magic; it was cracks in the red magic. That meant it was the red magic that was spinning, not some sort of black magic line.

It was the spin that was giving the red magic its power. It was sort of like throwing something at a ceiling fan. There was a lot of space between the blades, but because the ceiling fan was rotating, it would usually hit anything trying to get through it. I needed to find a way to disrupt the spin.

It would take something small to get through the cracks, yet dense enough it wouldn't break when the red magic came around. Fortunately, I was good at small, dense magics.

What popped into my head was a dam. A beaver dam. Beavers were good at building homes in rushing water. I needed a beaver colony to dam up this circle.

I made my first beaver on my palm. He had a round body, cute face, and wide flat tail. I gave him some nice powerful front teeth for chewing through magic. He was only about a half inch long, but my 'logs' were going to have to be pretty small to get into the cracks. I gave him a duplicator ring. If he could pull extra magic from the circle, then he could duplicate himself and that would speed up the process a lot.

I put him on the floor and started making a few logs. I made them long and skinny with branches so the logs would lock together once they were in place. I stuffed them full of magic as they needed to be strong. The beaver chewed the first log into smaller pieces, then pushed the first piece into the shield. It went in easily. So far, so good.

I zoomed in for a closer view. I could see that even one log had already caused a small disruption to the dome. The force of the spinning magic was pushing on the log, though, so the beaver had to hold it in place. I was going to need more beavers.

I guess my flat tailed friend thought the same thing, because he sucked in some of the circle's magic for his duplicator ring. I guess the circle was powered by Isobel's magic, because putrid power hit his system.

He squealed and tried to run but it was too late. The magic ate into him. He fell to the ground, convulsing. I slapped my hand over him and poured on the magic. Isobel was not going to hurt one of my guys!

My magic was dense and thick, and it quickly pushed out the rotten invader. Her influence went up in smoke. We were both still shaken, though. This is the first time something like this had happened. I wasn't aware you could booby trap spells.

He recovered before I did, squeaking at me to let him go. I did, but first I told him that I'd provide all the magic he needed for duplication. He took me at my word and popped out three more beavers. They went to work right away and soon the dam was under construction again. I gave him as much power as he wanted, and he made ten more copies before heading off to help in the construction himself.

The force of the spinning magic had knocked the first log a few feet across the floor. I recovered it and added it to the pile. The beavers worked quickly and soon they had used up their supply of logs. There was a pronounced ripple in the dome now. It wasn't enough to bring it down yet, but the idea was working. I started making more logs.

For the next few minutes I made the logs and they worked on the dam. As it got higher and higher, the distortion in the dome got more pronounced. What started out as a ripple turned into overlapping waves of turbulence. The whole dome started wavering like it was made of Jello.

Finally, it gave a loud pop and fell apart.

I didn't waste any time. I grabbed Sandy and pulled her out of there. I wasn't sure if the spell could regenerate, but I wasn't going to take that chance.

I didn't want to lose any of my power, so I took a moment to pull the logs back into Penny. Then the beavers waddled up onto my hand, wiggled their whiskers at me and merged with her too. I thanked each one of them personally. I didn't know if it really mattered to them, but they were real to me, and I was grateful for their help. My unique style of magic let me do some pretty amazing things. I wasn't going to take it for granted.

I checked on Sandy. She was breathing but unconscious. She had also lost a lot of magic. She always had a feeling of power about her, and now that was missing. I couldn't see any of her orange light at all, although her aura was still working and keeping me from looking too closely.

She was alive, though. That was what really mattered. Everything else could be fixed. I dragged her over to the edge of the warehouse behind a beam. It wasn't a lot of protection, but hopefully she wouldn't need it. As far as I knew, all the mages had been taken care of except for Isobel, and I could still hear that battle going on.

I felt bad leaving her there, but I needed to help John and Annabeth. I didn't want Sandy any closer to the fight in case she got hit with a stray rock or spell.

John's fight wasn't in my radius, so I didn't know how he was doing. I dodged from support beam to support beam until I was close. I wasn't going to run into battle without knowing what was going on.

What I saw shocked me.

John was transformed. He was already a big guy. Now he had grown even more. He looked like he was changing into an earth elemental. He was eight feet tall and looked like he was made of stone.

If John had changed, so had Isobel. She had brought her A-game this time. She had on what looked like magical armor. It was made of leather and every piece glowed with magic. She was also using two wands in addition to two charm bracelets.

John was huge and powerful, but he was a lot slower than his regular form. Isobel, in contrast, was even faster than before. Maybe she had a charm to speed herself up?

John was attempting to pin her down and crush her. She was dodging like a pro and her blasts were knocking chunks out of his stone. They weren't big chunks, though. It was enough to tick him off, but it wasn't enough to really hurt him.

She was also using force blasts, but it was more to move herself around quickly. John rushed her and almost got her. She jumped to the side and shot a blast of force in the opposite direction. Together it propelled her about ten feet away, out of John's reach. He turned and started stalking her again.

Annabeth was on my side of the fight and doing what she could too. Every time Isobel stopped, Annabeth sent a spell at her. She was using heat and sending out very slow waves of power. They were slow enough to get through her shield but not fast enough to catch her. They were going so slow, it was actually harder to dodge, and one time she almost stepped into one. It was clearly frustrating the hell out of her, but she didn't have time to target Annabeth. John was slow but he wasn't that slow.

I was just starting to figure out how I could help when the House siren went off. What the heck? The House was under attack?

I cussed out loud. Of course it was. This was the perfect time to hit the House shields. All the defenders were away from home.

This whole thing had been about more than just getting revenge on Sandy. This had been a coordinated diversion to get the House undefended.

Annabeth ran up to me. "Can you hear that?" She looked worried.

"Of course I can," I said. "This whole thing was designed to get John and Sandy out of the House and keep them away long enough to break the shields."

I was so angry. We were getting out maneuvered.

"You're going to have to save the House," I said. "With Sandy down, you are the only one that can work the defensive crystal."

"I only worked it once," Annabeth stammered. "And Sandy was there to help. I don't know if I can do this on my own."

"You're going to have to try," I said. "You are all we have left. Hopefully Tyler shows up soon. He's a powerful super too."

I pulled her in for a quick hug. "You can do this, Annabeth. You're smart and you're tough. You can make this happen. I'll help John and we'll be along as soon as we can." I pushed her toward the exit. "Now go!"

She didn't look convinced, but she ran out anyway. I had no idea what she was going to defend against. If it was hundreds of mages again, then we were toast. If it was something else, then maybe we had a chance.

I turned back to John's battle. We had to end this, and we had to do it quickly.

I made another flasher and turned it loose in stealth mode. It flew toward Isobel, but it was moving too slowly. As soon as it got close, she would jump to a different part of the room to avoid an attack from John. What I needed was a bunch of them scattered throughout the space. Then, she might dodge into one of them and we'd get a hit.

I didn't have any other ideas, so I started making flashers and sending them around the room. It took a few moments, but it worked. Sort of. Isobel backed into a flasher and suddenly it was right over her head and inside her shield. It started to fly to her eye and it almost made it before it started falling apart. I watched helplessly as the wings came off my little flasher. He fell into a river of aura that looked like vomit and vanished with a little flash of my magic.

Isobel's aura was large and powerful. The flasher couldn't exist in that environment long enough to get off a shot. I called all the flashers back to me and absorbed them. I didn't want to lose any more of my creations.

Then the worst thing happened. Isobel changed tactics. She had been using force up to this point, both for offense and defense. Now she switched to cold.

This made sense for her. She wasn't injuring John much and her aura had diminished a lot from the level I'd seen in the park. This fight was using up a lot of her reserves and she couldn't use Sandy to recharge anymore. She needed to try something else, and it looked like she had come up with a winner.

The cold was slowing John down. He couldn't rush as fast as before and his swings looked sluggish. Not having to dodge as much gave Isobel more time to cast freeze. This was bad. Really bad.

John knew this too. He reached into a pouch at his side and pulled out what looked like a couple of stones. He popped them into his mouth and started crunching them in his massive jaws.

He swallowed and started growing. Stones popped up out of the floor, and then slid over to him, only to be absorbed into his body.

He gained another foot in height and I don't know how much more mass. He was a nine-foot tall, walking, stone instrument of death. Except, he couldn't catch the object of his rage.

He roared and smashed the ground, but Isobel was too fast. She kept pouring on the cold, and gradually John started slowing down again.

I had to do something. But what? If she couldn't see, she couldn't dodge. I felt like that was the right idea, but how to make it work?

If I made something fast enough to get to her eyes before her aura tore it apart, then it would be too fast and her shield would stop it. If I made it slow enough to get through her shield, then it was too slow to catch her. Even if it did catch her, it would spend too long in her aura and fall apart.

What I needed was something that moved fast, then slow, then fast again. That gave me an idea.

I started hunting on the ground for two tiny stone chips. There was rock everywhere, so they were easy to find. I needed them about the size of a grain of rice.

Once I had them, I sharpened one side to a point, and left fins on the other. Working with rock was not easy. The changes I needed, though, were small, and the rock chips were sitting in my hand. I zoomed in close, made a little door and hollowed out a tiny section inside the rock. I made a little light bulb creation, no bigger than a period at the end of a sentence and filled it with the light rune. I put the light rune inside it and all over the surface. I needed this thing to shine. Then I packed it full of power. I put so much in there that the little bulb started to vibrate. I made a second one and put one inside each little rock missile.

Then I took the rock missiles and built a magic rocket around each one. I poured my magic into them too. I needed them to be as real as possible. I pushed as much soul and magic into them as I could. They had to be the first line of defense against her aura.

"I'm sorry," I said. "This is a one-way mission. You are going up against someone powerful and very strong. I have to save my friends. I have to help the House. This is the only way I know to do that."

I whispered my directions to them, then added, "Once you do your mission, just vanish. Don't stick around or you will get absorbed. Thank you and good luck."

The rockets flared and the light flashed. They were ready to go. Just in time too. John had slowed down even more and now parts of him were covered in ice. This had to work.

"Go," I whispered, and they were off.

The rockets were full of magic fuel, and they were fast. Almost faster than I could follow. They shot across the room and slammed into the shield right in front of Isobel's eyes.

They didn't bounce, though; they hovered in place. Her aura was eating at them but not fast enough. Now that there wasn't anything fast in range, her shield fell, and the next stage launched.

The rocket moved forward slowly so it was inside the shield, then the top opened up and it shot the little rock missiles right into her eyes.

It's very hard for magic to exist in an aura, or for hostile magic to pierce the skin, but rock can do both of those just fine.

I thought the rock would just get stuck in her eyes, or that maybe she would blink at the last minute. Instead, the rock was going so quick that it went through the cornea, through the pupil and into the lens of her eyes. It was two perfect bullseye shots.

That's when stage three happened. The light bulbs shed their rocky housing and exploded in light.

The best I was hoping for was a really bright flash. It ended up being so much more than that.

The light was bright, like it had been back in the workshop, see-through-your-hand bright. It was so magically bright I could see her skull.

Isobel opened her mouth to scream and I could see the back of her throat glowing.

This was all in the magic spectrum. As we'd found out in the workshop, the natural spectrum was even more powerful. I couldn't imagine how bright it must have been in real life.

It was so intense I wanted to look away but couldn't. My magic sight saw everything.

The rockets winked out of existence. They had escaped in time. The little bulbs disappeared too. The rock stayed there, still embedded in her lens. It wasn't a lot of rock, but healing from that was going to be a bitch.

Isobel screamed. She staggered, then screamed again. It was a scream of fear. It was a scream of anger. She was disoriented, unable to see.

And John was coming.

He roared with the fury of the earth. With the fear his love was almost lost. And hit her like a freight train.

He body slammed her.

All nine feet of his rock and power smashed her into the ground.

Somehow, her shield held up. It didn't matter to him. He used one hand to hold her there and the other to pound her. His fury was biblical and even her shield wasn't meant to stop that.

After the fifth hit her shield went out. Now it was just down to her armor.

It flared with magic, then overloaded too.

He smashed her again. And again.

He was going to kill her. Even though she was immortal, there was no way she was coming back from this. I didn't know how to stop him.

Or even if I should stop him.

Suddenly there was wave of force powerful enough to knock John back. Isobel was encased in a blue ball of force. Her crushed body was bloody and limp on the bottom of the sphere. It rose in the air, then smashed through the roof and shot away.

It happened so fast I didn't get a good look at it. The magic had a familiar feel though. It was sort of like the golem magic.

John got to his feet and roared at the sky. I was just glad the battle was over. Isobel scared me. I felt relieved she was gone.

I was scared for John. He didn't seem human anymore. I didn't think he could even talk.

I knew he cared about one thing, though, and that was Sandy.

I yelled to get his attention and kept saying her name over and over again. It finally got through, and he followed me over to Sandy's limp form. He curled up over her and shielded her with his body. After that he didn't move. I got the feeling he was going to stay like that for a long time.

The House alarm kicked up to a whole new level of urgent. Whatever was happening, it needed defenders, and I was the only one that could help.

I didn't want to leave them there like that, but I had to go help the House. I had to help Annabeth.

I turned and left.

24

Fairy Godmothers

I followed the same path back to the store. I knew there was an easier way to get home, but I didn't want to chance getting turned around. I couldn't read street signs with my magic sight and the last thing I wanted to do right now was get lost. From the store it was a straight shot back to the House.

Fifteen minutes later I was almost there, the House alarm urged me along the whole time. I wasn't sure what I was getting into. Hopefully it wasn't catapults, wands, and battering rams again. I couldn't defend like John and he wasn't going to show up to save the day again.

It was unnerving walking into a battle situation and not being able to see what was going on. I slowed down to a cautious walk. I'm not a 'jump in headfirst' type of guy. I like to plan, to have a moment to figure out what I want to do. Plus, slowing down gave me a chance to catch my breath. I couldn't see that far, but I could hear. As I got closer, I could hear a fluttering sound, like a flock of birds.

Nothing showed up in my sight until I was almost to the front yard, then I saw a steady stream of what looked like dusty ghosts slamming into the House shield. They were all sizes, from tiny mouse sized ones all the way up to big people sized. They had solid looking heads, with their bodies trailing behind like sheets in the wind. That was the source of the fluttering sound I was hearing.

They were covered in what looked to be black dust. Actually, dust is too nice a word. Dust just means something is dirty and neglected. This was malignant. Like a parasite. They were black spores that latched onto the spirit, sucking it dry.

The spirits were in torment, their faces wailing and screaming. They took it out on the shield. Slamming into it over and over again. Other than the flutter, it was totally silent. It was the eeriest sight I'd seen yet in the supernatural world.

Sometimes the hits would knock off the black dust, or whatever it was, and the spirit would just hang there, like it was too tired to move. Then it would get dust knocked on it from someone else, and it would go crazy again.

Some of the spirits looked old. Their faces were muddled, and their bodies were tattered and falling apart. Some of them looked fresh, their haunted eyes in full detail. Based on what I was seeing, these were the spirits of animals and even some people. I wasn't sure what an afterlife is like, but I knew I didn't want it to be this.

Whatever this was, it was unnatural, an abomination. We were being attacked by crazy ghost slaves. I had to protect the House, but I also had to do something about the spores. It was not okay that this was happening.

There must have been thousands of spirits. The air was thick with them. One time as a kid, I'd seen a huge flock of birds fly overhead. There had been so many the sky went dark and all you could hear was their wings and their cries. This felt like that. There was so many it felt like they would block out the sun.

I was leery about using my creations, but that was clearly what I needed to do. This wasn't something I could handle myself. However, I didn't want the dust getting on my creations and driving them crazy. I'd just have to be careful and test whatever I came up with to make sure it worked.

I needed something to clean off the dust. What popped into my mind was the granny with the vacuum cleaner that had helped me so much in the training circle. She had such a can-do attitude, and that was what I needed now. I didn't want to make one exactly the same. She had been the final piece in creating Penny and the start of my advanced magic. She was a great place to start, though. I began with a plump figure, gray hair, bun in the back. I changed the color of her dress to pink. Hopefully Annabeth would like that if she was watching. Then I gave her fairy wings and a cute little apron covered with images of apple pies. She needed all the wholesome goodness she could get to combat this evil.

I looked her over and realized she looked like the fairy godmother from the Cinderella cartoon. A granny fairy godmother, that sounded perfect for this job.

I wanted her to be safe too, so I gave her rubber gloves and a white breathing mask to keep out the dust. She needed a weapon, though . . .

I gave her a dust buster. And what's better than one? Two! She was now a dual wielding dust sucking badass.

I added some safety glasses, because, you know, safety first. She needed to be as real and as grounded as possible. I took a moment to go over all the details. Then I stuffed her full of magic. Hopefully the detail and the density of magic would overcome whatever the black spores were going to try to do to her.

I was undecided about adding a duplicator belt, but finally decided to give it a go. Having lots of granny godmothers would save a lot of time and magic. If she could pull in magic and duplicate on her own, then this would go so much faster. I wasn't sure how much damage the spirits were actually doing to the shield, but the quicker they stopped, the more shield would be left.

I didn't add a walkie talkie. It seemed like my new denser creations could communicate with me without it.

I was nervous, but I sent her off. There was a hanging spirit close to us, so I directed her to try that one first. She gave me a happy wave and got to work. It seemed like she had hardly started when she stopped and flew back to me. Her dust busters were full. They weren't very big after all.

Time for an upgrade. At least she hadn't lost her mind to the black spores.

I added two canisters, one on each hip, and included hoses to connect them to the dust busters. I made the canisters so they would spin the dust at a high rate of speed and separate the magic from the black part of the dust. Hopefully, without magic powering it, the black part would just blow away. Actually, I needed a place for the black to go, so I added an exhaust on the back of the canister so it could expel out the back. Just for fun, I made it a dual pipe chrome exhaust. Go big or go home!

I didn't know if it this whole canister thing would work, but the idea was to give her pure neutral magic to duplicate with. In the magic world, intention counted for a lot, so it might be feasible.

She had hardly used any of my power, but I gave her a top up anyway and sent her off again. This time it worked like a charm.

Like a magic charm.

She sucked up the dust and a pure magic glow grew in the canisters. There was a lot of black smoke coming out the back, but it now seemed harmless and dissipated in the air. When she had enough, she backed off, harnessed the new magic, and duplicated.

Now there were two granny godmothers working on the spirit. Soon it was four, then eight, then sixteen. As the spirit got cleaner, it gradually shrunk in size. It stopped having the big head and the weird body. Instead it started turning into an orb of pure light. When the last of the dust was gone, the orb did a little dance in the air. Then it pulsed and just vanished. The granny godmothers went to work on the next one.

There were several hundred cleaners before we ran into the next problem: the grannies themselves were getting dirty. Some of the smoke from the canisters was sticking to them. I wasn't sure if it was still toxic, but I didn't want to chance it.

I got on the sidewalk and made a granny wash. Like a car wash but for grannies. I didn't want them to actually get wet, so I made a series of arches filled with feather dusters. The granny godmothers could fly through the arches and get cleaned up. Just like new.

I let them know, and soon the dirtiest of the godmothers flew over for a tickle and a clean. They loved the feather dusters and soon the air was filled with laughter and happiness.

As they kept multiplying, they couldn't get through the cleaner fast enough, so a line started forming. I made the arches bigger, added more dusters and finally had to make a whole new set of arches so we could run two rows at a time.

That wasn't enough so I added two more rows of arches. I had to stop at that point. It was taking a lot of power to keep them charged and make sure they stayed clean. The lines to the arches got longer, but I was doing the best I could.

I had thousands and thousands of granny godmothers working on spirits, but it seemed like we had hardly made a dent. My happy housekeepers were doing their job: cleaning and duplicating. I just couldn't keep up with getting the smoke off of them. I needed a better way to clean the cleaners.

Then it hit me. I needed a prewash.

I asked for some volunteers and the lots of the grannies that had just been through the feather washer flew over. I modified their canisters so that they were much bigger and no longer had the dual exhaust. Instead, the side of the canister came off for dumping. The idea was for the prewash crew to clean most of the smoke particles off the regular grannies. They would collect the particles in the canister, and it wouldn't escape to get on anyone else. Once the canisters were full, the prewash cleaner would fly down the street and empty their canisters well away from the current action.

The idea worked. Now the cleaner grannies were much less dirty when they went through the feather washer. The lines moved much more quickly, and it took a lot less power from me.

I wasn't sure how long we were at this—it seemed like a good while—but I finally noticed the fluttering sounds had died down. The spirits seemed to know we were helping. Instead of hanging in the air, they actively came over to get cleaned. My vision was filled with spirit orbs doing victory dances and flashing out to wherever they were going. If felt like we had our own fireworks display.

The end came quickly. The granny godmothers had duplicated so much that they vastly outnumbered the remaining spirits. As the last ghost flashed out of existence, I ordered a general cleanup.

"Find any of the remaining black particles and clean them. Clean the House shield, the air, and the ground." I wasn't sure if the black parasites could multiply on their own, but I knew I didn't want that kind of magic anywhere near my home.

The cleaners scattered and it was done. Then I ran everyone through the granny wash, even the prewash crew.

I felt tired and low on magic, but at least the attack was over. Hopefully the House was all right and they hadn't done too much damage.

I felt proud of myself and my crew. I wouldn't have been able to handle this when I first became a supernatural. My creations and I had come a long way.

I was still feeling very satisfied with myself when all the granny godmothers suddenly took to the sky and pulled back toward the shield. Instantly I was on the alert. I couldn't see anything or hear anything, but something had spooked them.

I waited for a long moment. Long enough that I was wondering if I needed to circle the House or something. Maybe there was something going on outside of my range. I was just about ready to move when a mage, dressed in black armor and riding a black saber-toothed tiger padded into view.

I knew I should have focused on the mage first, but the tiger was all I could process. First, it was supposed to be extinct. Second, it was huge. It must have been four feet high and easily 700 pounds. It had powerful shoulders and wide paws. Its teeth were longer than steak knives and looked like they could filet me quite easily. It carried the mage, armor and all, like it didn't even notice the rider on its back.

The mage was no joke either. He was covered in black overlapping scales, and a full helmet sat on his head. It covered up all his features and was intimidating as hell. I say he, but it could have been a powerful woman. The only thing that wasn't black on the both of them was the broadsword strapped to his back. It had an interesting looking handle. It looked like it had some sort of basket weave around the hilt.

I'd been thinking this fight was over. It looked like it had just started.

John could take on something like this, I was sure. He was tough, strong, and his thrown rocks were no joke. They hit with the force of small bombs. I, on the other hand, had no armor, no powerful magic, and no real weapon. I still had my shillelagh, but this was way out of its class.

The saber-toothed tiger got about three feet away and stopped. The mage didn't say anything and neither did the tiger. Not that I expected the tiger to say anything. This had already been a crazy day, though, so anything could have happened.

With the added height of the tiger, the mage towered over me. I was getting flashbacks to Isobel on her golem. This was not good. Not good at all.

I felt scared. Like deep-down, quaking-in-my-shoes scared. I didn't want to get crushed or eaten or cut to pieces. I suddenly felt the overwhelming urge to pee.

I did not want this fight. This was a fight I couldn't win. Give me thousands of tormented spirits any time. That I could handle.

I looked again and it occurred to me that the tiger was made up of the same black spores I'd taken off the spirits. It was just in a dense, solid form. A very scary saber-toothed form.

If the tiger was made of this black material, how about the armor? It looked like it was too, although it was even denser than the tiger.

This mage must have been some sort of necromancer if he could torment spirits and get them to do what he wanted. His magic was versatile too, if it could be used as armor, a mount, and spirit control. I felt a bit jealous. If I could do big magic, then I could do stuff like this too.

We had the brief moment of inspection. The calm before the storm. The moment where we sized each other up, and I was found wanting. And then it started.

The saber-toothed tiger started to lower himself to let the rider off his back, when a black and white fur ball pounced onto the scene.

It was Bermuda. All three pounds of him. Fluffed and hissing and spitting mad. My heart sank. Not again!

He dashed up to the tiger, not intimidated at all by the hundreds of pounds of difference between them, and swatted it across the nose.

The tiger howled and jumped back. A puff of black smoke rose from where Bermuda had scratched him. The mage wasn't expecting this at all. Instead of a nice dignified dismount, he fell on his ass. Legs in the air, flat on his back, arms flailing, on his ass.

I laughed. I couldn't help it. All that tension had to go somewhere.

The tiger roared and went after Bermuda, who took off like a shot.

"Grannies, help him!" I shouted. No prehistoric pile of shit was going to hurt my baby. Hundreds of thousands of granny godmothers heard me. They felt my anger. My fear. And they geared for war.

Their eyes turned red.

Their wings grew longer, slimmer, faster.

Their canisters spun up, and they flew into action.

The air was thick with granny power as they sped after the black tiger.

They were fast, and soon they were gone. Leaving only me and the mage.

He got to his feet, pissed as hell. Or at least he moved that way. I couldn't really tell with the helmet on.

He drew his sword. I drew my shillelagh. And we went at it.

I was very aware that a steel sword beats a wooden shillelagh any day, so I didn't try to block. Instead, I used the club end of the shillelagh against the flat of his sword and tried to bat the sword away.

It mostly worked. It helped that the sword was heavy and the mage was slow. Now that the mage was no longer on his mount, he was actually only a bit taller than me. I'm sure the armor was slowing him down too.

He was strong, though. Really strong. I was doing a lot more dodging than batting. I was able to hit him a few times, but my club didn't even make a dent. I didn't have anything that could actually hurt this guy.

I did find out what that weird handle was for. The woven cage on the hilt protected the sword wielder's hand. I still tried to whack it and see if I could get him to drop the sword. It didn't happen.

I found a brief moment to summon a flasher. He flared his trench coat and blasted the helmet where the mage's eyes should be, but it didn't seem to faze him at all.

I was faster, but he never stopped attacking. At some point I was going to make a mistake. We fought on the sidewalk, in the street, even on grass in the park for a bit. We were back on the sidewalk, and I moved inside his guard instead of backing away, when it happened.

I moved closer to keep the sword from hitting me, but he let go with one hand and backhanded me. It was a solid blow, well timed, and it rattled my cage.

I hit the ground, stunned. He stepped forward, planted his foot on me to keep me from rolling away, and drove his sword into me.

He didn't stop, either; he drove it all the way through me, into the ground, and kept going. Only one thing saved me. I'd dropped the shillelagh at the last moment, grabbed the sword with my bare hands, and tried to shove it out of the way. It hadn't made him miss me, but it had thrown off his aim a bit.

I think he was aiming for my heart. He'd missed. Instead it had gone high and to the left. I had no idea what organs he had gone through, but I was alive. For now.

He went to pull up the sword and have another go, but the sword was stuck. He had slammed it into me almost to the hilt, which meant it had gone through the sidewalk under me and the earth underneath that.

I heard a distant voice. "Ahhhh. Back in stone again."
What the heck?

The mage tugged and wrenched at the sword, trying to get it free from the earth, but it was set. The sword wasn't going anywhere.

Finally, he walked away and began pounding on the House shields with his fists. They were making a booming sound, so he was magically enhancing his blows somehow.

I counted this as a victory. I hadn't gotten eaten by the tiger and I hadn't gotten cut in half. I'd also taken away his sword so he couldn't attack the House with it.

On the other hand, I had a freaking sword through me. Holy crap. Only a few hours ago my worst disaster was that I couldn't get a charm to work. Now I was staked to the ground. I never would have thought in a million years that my day would end up like this.

Being pinned to the ground is a scary experience. I felt trapped. I couldn't move much or I'd just cut myself open even more. If the mage couldn't get the sword out with all his leverage and strength, then there was no use me tugging on the sword. There had to be another way.

"You can do this!" I gave myself a mental pep talk. "You have been punched in the face by a golem. Then got the crap kicked out of you by a powerful mage. This is nothing. This is less than nothing. It's a minor inconvenience." Okay, I didn't really buy that last part, but it helped to talk all brave. It was either that or completely freak out.

Then I thought of my favorite Monty Python movie. "It's just a flesh wound!" That cracked me up and the panic receded a bit. I finally felt brave enough to check out the damage.

The sword had gone in between my ribs. I didn't have any broken or chipped bones. That was a big plus. It had gone in my upper left side and missed my lungs and heart. That was also good.

Of course, you can't have a sword all the way through you without having a lot of damage. I wasn't going to die immediately, though, and it even looked like the sword was sealing the wound a bit. I was bleeding, of course, but it wasn't coming out in buckets.

I had a good day, maybe day and half, before I would bleed out. Plenty of time. I started laughing hysterically, which made everything hurt worse. Okay, maybe I wasn't handling this as well as I thought.

In the movies they never freaked out like this. If this was a movie, I'd get some extra strength from somewhere, pull out the sword, holler a bit to show the audience I was in pain, and then chase after the mage like I wasn't damaged at all.

Unfortunately, this wasn't a movie and that wasn't happening. I felt numb. I felt sick. I still had to pee.

I was gripping the ground with my hands, trying to center myself, when black smoke poured out of the wound.

My final remnant, Thing One, the Death Experience guy, was attacking.

What crappy awful timing. I couldn't run anywhere. Tyler wasn't here to handle him. The House was still under attack and who knew how Bermuda was doing.

This was literally the worst time for Thing One to come out of hiding. I guess from his point of view, that was the point. This last remnant really scared me. He had the soul of an artist with the morals of a serial killer. He was creative and sadistic. That was a frightening combination.

When I think back to that night, my Waker Moment, I think of his face. I know there were three others in the room, and Thing Two was pretty awful, but Thing One is what I remember.

And now he was back to take his vengeance.

I had thought about this moment, about what I would do if he showed up and there was no one else to help me, and I had a plan. I centered myself and dove for my throne room.

I knew I couldn't face him in the real world. He had crazy amounts of power and who knew what he would do to mess me up this time. My throne room, though, was my space. It was the seat of my power. It was my turf. Hopefully the hometown advantage would be enough.

The room looked good. The tiles on the floor were fixed and clean. The ceiling arched overhead, supported by strong wooden beams, and the throne was now padded and decked out with engravings and even a bit of silverwork. It was still the throne room for a small kingdom, but now it was a reasonably prosperous kingdom.

The cot was gone. I didn't need that anymore. Instead, there was a huge steel pillar in the center of the room.

I ran up to the throne and sat on it just as smoke started gathering in the room. I let it come. I needed him here.

It crept in from the walls, the floor, and gathered in front of me. I sat there, gripping the arms of the throne, waiting to receive him. I tried to look regal and haughty. Instead, I probably just looked constipated. It would have to do.

The smoke gathered, formed, and condensed into Thing One. With an effort of will, I sealed the room. Only one of us was walking out of this fight.

"I like this place." Thing One looked around.

"It works for me," I said. I gestured at the big steel beam in the middle of the room. "You came at a bad time. I was just remodeling."

"Well, at least you *staked* your claim," he said. Did he just throw a pun? "I would have come earlier but I had to wait until you were *pinned* down."

"I like to *steel* away and come here when I can," I said. "You'll have to forgive me if I'm a little on *edge*." Two could play that game.

He chuckled. I chuckled. We chuckled together. This was not how I thought this would go. He seemed happy, even cheerful. He was not the vengeful spirit I thought he would be. At least, not yet.

"I confess. I made a mistake," he said. Huh? "I was told you were a mundane, but when I saw you work a little magic, I assumed you were already a supernatural. I didn't realize our little teaching moment would result in you Waking Up."

"By 'teaching moment' you mean when you tortured me and tried to kill me?" I said.

He waved it off. "Supernatural life is tough, as you've found out. You have to be tougher."

"So, all this was to make me tough?" I felt my anger rising. Dad had tried to make me tough too. He'd done everything he could to knock the gay out of me. When he couldn't 'fix' me, he'd kicked me out rather than have to look at his failure.

He didn't realize that being tough is not about being macho. It's about finding a way. A way to survive. A way to thrive. A way to be who you are and have it be okay that others are how they are. That's being tough.

"It's my gift." He shrugged. "I found I was good at hurting people. I liked it. And you know what I found out?"

I shook my head. I wasn't sure I wanted to know.

"I found out I was good at helping people transition. Not everyone with potential has a Waker Moment, you know. They have to have that special few seconds, when their life is at stake, and it's either live or die. That's when they break through, summon their magic, and become a new supernatural. I've seen it a lot and it's a beautiful thing. Of course, I have to end them right after that. Fresh sups are so helpless."

I was flabbergasted. "I don't understand," I said. "Why would you go to the trouble of making a supernatural, someone who is supposed to live forever, only to kill them?"

He shrugged. "That's the job. That's what we did."

"But why?" I said again. This made no kinda sense.

"Who knows?" he said. "Maybe baby sups taste good or something. People eat veal after all. Maybe you guys are nice and tender at the beginning and get tougher with age. That's not something I worried about. We'd just collected the essence and passed it to our contact."

"So, you killed for the money?" I asked. I was having trouble wrapping my head around this. Life had been busy, so I hadn't really thought a lot about why that night had happened.

"Sure," he said. "And why not? It was good money. Really good money. Isn't that the definition of success? To do what you love and get well paid for it? It was the perfect career."

While he talked, he wandered around my throne room, checking out the place and taking in the tapestries. Since he was in a talkative mood, I kept pumping him for information.

"So, who did you work for?" I asked. Someone had sent him after me. I needed to know who that was and why I was in their crosshairs. If they had sent his team after me, they may send another one.

"I really don't know," he said. "We had a contact, but she wasn't the one actually calling the shots. She was just relaying the information. We'd get a token that pointed toward our target, and a general description of who they were and whether they were a supernatural already or needed turning. We'd also get a vial for the essence. After the job was done, we'd turn in the vial and get paid. Pretty simple, really."

So, they'd had a charm that night that led them to me. That was why I couldn't hide. That hotel room had looked just like all the others. It had been a shock when they found me. Now I knew how they had done it.

"What about the Fog of Jonah?" I asked. He was still talking, so I'd keep asking. "Aren't regular people supposed to forget about us?"

"We had a tattoo that took care of that," he said. He showed me his upper arm, but it was just blank. "Ha. I forget I'm a remnant sometimes. Not everything comes with you. If it's not part of your identity, then it doesn't come along for the ride." He shrugged. "Not that I need it now anyway."

He had now walked all the way around my throne room and checked everything out.

"Do you think whoever you worked for will send someone else after me?" I asked. This was the big question. Was I going to have to deal with a hit squad in my future?

"Maybe," he said. "If they do, I'll take care of them. They won't be a problem."

"What do you mean, you'll take care of them?" I said. Was this guy planning on sticking around long term? I didn't think so. I wanted him out of my life.

He threw out his arms and twirled around like a happy little girl.

"This is my lucky day," he sang ignoring me. "I wish there was a recording of this. Some way to share the moment. I feel like we need champagne or something."

He was making me nervous. This did not sound good. Whatever made him happy was bound to make me unhappy.

He stopped twirling and faced me. "I guess since you're here, you'll have to do. See, there was another reason I did this job. There was a rumor—just a rumor mind you—that in some special situations a job would go south, and something would happen to the crew. Something special." He got the biggest grin on his face. "The rumor was that they would become remnants."

"So, you wanted all this?" I said. I knew this guy was crazy. I just didn't know how crazy. "I thought you would be out for vengeance or something. Instead you look happy."

"That's because I am happy," he said. "I hit the lottery. I won the jackpot. Do you know how perfect this has been? I couldn't ask for anything better."

"So, what exactly is your plan?" I asked. I was nervous. I'd sealed off the room, but now I was thinking I'd locked myself in with a maniac.

"They did a test on me, you know. It said I would never be a supernatural. When I died, that was it. No Waker Moment for me. No special powers. No magic spells.

"When I first saw you, I wasn't impressed. You seemed like a whiny skinny little boy who was wasting his life. You did a good job running, though. I'll give you that. When you did a bit of magic, I thought for sure you were already a supernatural. That's why I gave you the deluxe treatment. I wanted you to have a defining moment, one space in time, where you were really truly alive. That is my specialty after all." He bowed. "You're welcome."

I didn't know what to say. I felt like I should say something. He was not finished yet, so I shut up and let him talk.

"Imagine my surprise when I woke up inside you! It was so unexpected. It took me a moment to get myself together and by then Tyler was around. I had always figured I could take care of whoever got sucked in with me, but he made it so easy. I just pushed them out and he destroyed them for me. No more competition." He made like he was dusting off his hands. "I liked my crew. They were almost as good as me, but this is now a solo journey."

"The last part of the plan was to find your center, your place of power, and somehow get inside." He made an expansive gesture at the room. "And here we are! Ta da!"

That didn't sound good at all. I thought this was my home turf. My place. But somehow, he wanted to be here.

"I admit, you aren't the supernatural I'd have chosen. Your powers are a bit too weak for me. I like to have more flair. Maybe throw a fireball or two. Still, you do have some potential. That matrix was genius."

"Wait. You think you're going to become me?" I said. I was flabbergasted. Who did this guy think he was? He couldn't take me over. Could he?

"Of course!" he said. "I can't be a super on my own, so you're the next best thing. You're not perfect, like I said, but beggars can't be choosers as the old saying goes. Or, in this case, mortals can't be choosers." He stopped and looked at me. "I never beg." He suddenly looked very dangerous. "I said that last step was to come here. But, I guess really the last step is to let you go." He started walking toward me with a panther like grace. It felt like he was stalking me.

I suddenly wanted to run.

"I can't have you here, mucking things up." He had almost reached me. I'd brought him here, now what was I going to do with him?

"This is my place," I said as forcefully as I could. "You should be scared of me."

He walked right up to me. Then, faster than I could react, he slapped me.

I always thought a slap was a gentle sort of thing. Much more preferable to being hit by a fist. His slap, though, was hard. It spun my head around and rocked my world.

"I don't think I have too much to fear," he said. Then he grabbed me by my hair and threw me off the throne. "After all, I'm dealing with someone who got punched by a golem."

I got to my feet. He punched me. "Golems are so slow." He punched me again. "How can you not get out of the way of a piece of rock?" I tried to block him, but that wasn't working at all. "It's a rock!" He seemed to be able to hit me at will. "This ain't rocket science. If it's stone and headed your way, duck!" He hit me with an uppercut and my feet left the ground. This guy could really punch.

I hit the ground and tried to shake it off.

"I'm not scared of you," he sneered. I was still blinking my eyes and trying to see when he kicked me.

"You are weak." He kicked me again. It spun me across the floor.

"You are slow." I slammed into the wall.

"You whine." He pinned me down with his knees.

"Your friends are weak." He started raining blows down on me.

"Your House is pathetic." I tried to stop him.

"You are nothing." He was shouting now.

"NOTHING!" He trapped my hands and pounded my face.

"NOTHING!"

I felt so small.

I was a little kid again. My house was a burnt husk. Dad was screaming at me.

I just stood there and cried.

I flashed forward to sixteen. Standing on the steps of my former home, now occupied by strangers. Being told that my dad and my sister were no longer there.

They didn't want me.

They had moved to get away from me. They couldn't get rid of me quick enough.

I felt so small.

I flashed forward. Lying in bed. Face smashed in. Ribs broken.

Annabeth sitting with me. Tyler laying with me.

Showing up for the circle as the naked shaman. John laughing so hard he cried.

Dinner at Sandy's with my friends.

Sandy doing my assessment and getting so excited about my magic.

Penny trilling at me and feeding me her power.

Little Bermuda on my pillow, all four paws in the air, purring as I rubbed his belly.

I was NOT small. I was loved. I was accepted.

This was MY magic.

This was MY place of power.

Thing One was using MY power, and that was going to stop right NOW!

I reached out to Thing One with my magic sight. I could see my emerald green and sapphire blue power inside him, giving him strength.

I reached out and froze it.

Thing One gasped and fell away. Without my power he looked gaunt. Like he hadn't eaten in weeks.

He staggered away. Barely enough energy to stand. My power was still there. Looking like a faceless mannequin. I absorbed it and stood up.

This wasn't real life. I wasn't actually hurt on a physical level, so I healed myself.

No.

I transformed myself.

One moment I was looking like a guy who had taken a beating. The next, I was whole. Perfect in every way.

I looked at Thing One. I didn't want to expel him like this. He still might get up to mischief. I didn't want to keep him here either. That was just asking for trouble. I did have an idea, though.

I created two cylinders in the room. Then I walked up to Thing One. He gaped at me, too shocked to speak.

I grabbed his left arm and ripped it off. It felt spongy and barely solid. I took it over to the first cylinder and stuffed it inside.

The cylinder spun up, separating the little bit of magic remaining from the shadow that was left of Thing One's essence. It ejected the ash into the second cylinder, and I absorbed the pure magic.

I went back to Thing One, ripped off his right arm and did the same thing. He started wailing. I guess he wasn't so tough after all.

I didn't want to underestimate him either. He had been strong and powerful. He was still creative. He might come up with some way to turn this around.

Because of that, I didn't even want his ashes together. I took the tiny bit of his arm essence and sealed it away in a small box.

Then I ripped off both his legs and did the same thing. What was left went in another small box. Finally, I tore him in half, like a piece of paper. I didn't even want all of his head in the same box, so I divided him lengthwise.

Thing One, the genesis of my supernatural journey and my nemesis for weeks now, was nothing but ash in four tiny boxes.

Later I would scatter him to four different parts of the city. For now, it was good enough. My remnants, my personal poltergeists, were now gone.

I dismissed the cylinders and walked over to my throne. I sat down and looked around. This place was mine. All mine. I had fought for it, bled for it, and now conquered for it. There was still so much to do, but taking this moment felt important somehow.

This was my new normal.

I felt a ripple of power flow out from me. The throne room had looked good before, but now it sparkled. It looked beautiful. Brand spanking new.

I'd come a long way from the dusty run-down looking place I'd started with. This was good. Really good.

I wasn't out of the woods yet. While the good vibes were flowing, I decided to tackle the sword sticking through me. My throne room seemed to reflect what was happening in real life, and I was pretty sure my new giant metal pillar was representing the sword. Sandy had said that your place of power was a good area to work powerful magic. I wasn't hurting in here so this was a good time to see what I could do.

I walked over to the steel pillar. It looked good from a distance, but up close it looked worn and faded. It didn't shine; instead it was coated in layers of grime and rust. It looked like steel from a junkyard rather than a shiny powerful sword.

I put my hand on it. I was surprised to find it felt warm. I'd expected it to feel cold and hard.

I was pretty sure I'd heard something when the sword went through me. Was it awake and aware like Penny? Was this a magical sword?

I couldn't tell. There was too much crud on the sword, and I couldn't get a good read. I tried to clean it off, but the grime was thick. I thought it would stick to me too, but it was firmly attached to the steel. Something seemed off about that, so I looked closer.

I thought the film coating the sword was one layer. It was actually lots and lots of layers all stuck together. They were all different colors too, but mashed together, they just looked muddy brown or even black. What I had first taken as rust was actually red layers showing through.

This reminded me of when I'd made Penny. She had been coated with layers of muddy colors too. There was a big difference, though. She'd had maybe a hundred layers. This sword had thousands. Still, the same solution could work here.

I formed a needle of power at the tip of my finger and began to press through the layers. The first ones were pretty easy. They were the newest and not as set in their form. When I punctured a layer it snapped wide open, like it was stretched elastic. It was kind of cool to see all the colors rippling back from the needle.

After I'd gone through about five hundred layers they started changing. They became harder and more brittle. They didn't snap back as far, and they were tougher to get through. To compensate, I made the tip of my power sharper and the needle fatter. Now it was more like a very sharp nail rather than a needle. That worked well for a while but eventually it wasn't enough anymore. The layers had gotten too tough again.

I took a break and peeled off all the layers I'd already pierced. The layers were a bit like the shrink wrap around one of the old DVD cases: It's super tough until you get a little tear. Once you get it started, though, it's easy to peel off.

I also took a moment to check the outside world. I was having some success in my throne room, but was it actually affecting the sword in the real world? Turned out, it was. It probably helped that my blood was coating the sword. That was bringing the outside of the sword under my domain.

I couldn't imagine how old this sword must be to have so many layers. How many people had wielded it? How many people had it run through? All that blood and power creating coating after coating of residue.

It was like rings on a tree stump. The more rings, the older the tree. I felt like I was peeling back history as I tore apart layer after layer. The last few were really tough. They had been there a long time.

I had to change my tactic again from a nail to a drill. I created a spiral in the point and then made it rotate. The last coat was a flat gray, like all the magic had leached out of it many years ago. I cranked up the drill speed to the highest I could manage. It went so fast and the layer was so tough it started smoking. I reinforced the strength of my drill bit, pushed hard, and finally it went through.

I ripped off the last layer. The sword was finally clean, and it was beautiful. There were slight waves in the metal that seemed to ripple a little bit in the light.

I'd come this far. Was the sword alive? Would it hear me?

I put my hand on the bare metal. "Hello?" I sent out a cautious touch of power. It bounced off something.

I felt life. I felt time. Lots and lots of time.

It kind of felt like I was talking to a very old tree. It was alive, but it was asleep. There was so much magic potential, but there wasn't much actual magic left.

I felt something else too. Sadness. And resignation.

I tried again. This time with more power. "Hello?"

My magic was barely a ripple in a small lake. It wasn't going to notice me like that. I pulled back and smacked it hard. This time I let my magic flow.

"Hello!"

"Who disturbs my slumber?" A dry, dusty voice reverberated in my head.

I wanted to say, "It is I, Aladdin," but I'm pretty sure this sword wouldn't catch the Disney reference.

"My name is Jason," I said.

It said nothing back. I waited a few moments. It felt awkward. What does one say to a sword that you are impaled upon?

"So, you like to sit in stone?" I asked. I pushed with more power. I needed to keep his attention.

"It is restful," was the reply. It was more than just words. I got images and feelings. There was a giant blond man covered in furs. He would put the sword in the stone by his house when he wasn't using it. The sun would rise and warm it. The stars would rise and cool it. The stone was solid and quiet. The sword liked that.

It was much better than the times the blond giant wielded it. Then it was all clanging and impacts and screams.

"That sounds nice," I said. "Restful is a good thing to be." Where did I go from here? "The thing is, Mr. Sword, that you are sticking through me at the moment," I said. "For me that's not restful. In fact, that's the opposite of restful." I sent the image of me on the ground with the sword through me.

I felt the weight of its inspection. "Ah. You are but a fledgling. So young. No worry. Soon you will rest." I got the image of my bones in the sun. They had been picked clean by scavengers and bleached by the constant exposure. The sword was still through me. We rested together.

"That's not resting. That's dying." I smacked the sword with magic again. "For me that's bad. I'm a living creature, not stone or metal, so that is the end for me." I attempted to send feelings of just how bad that was. Penny didn't really understand fleshy things, although she tried. It was probably the same with the sword. The sword liked to stay in stone, so it probably figured I was fine laying there for a few decades.

"I'm dying," it said. I knew it was true. The sword was only alive with magic and there wasn't that much left. Well, compared to what I had, it was a huge amount of magic. Compared to what the sword could hold, it was very little.

"You don't have to," I said. I sent images of me powering it up.

"My source is gone," it said with great sadness. I saw a small hairy man of great power. It was the first thing the sword knew, and it loved him. They talked and laughed often. The man shared his life with the sword and the sword held his power. The sword was the man's defense and he was proud of that. They were together, and then they weren't. Now the sword was held by the blond giant and it could no longer feel the hairy man.

The sword didn't have a concept of time. Either something was, or it wasn't. It started dying the day it was taken. The blond giant and many others forced it to use what power it had for them. They also tried to own it, but they were not as strong as its creator. They tried to force their magic in, but the sword would not allow it. Finally, the sword spent most of its time sleeping. It was a magic sword in name only.

The whole revelation gave me pause. Is this what could happen to Penny? If I died would she spend lifetimes just fading away?

I couldn't do that to her. I was determined to live through this day and get this sword to let me go.

"I can be your source," I said. "If you will let me."

It just chuckled. I was far below the small hairy man in power. It was like a candle saying it could take the place of a volcano. That might have been true, but I fought back.

"I am already a source," I said. "I already have an awakened one. I am not powerful enough for you now, but I can be in the future."

It inspected me again. I felt its disbelief. It was looking forward to dying. It wanted to just sleep forever and let all this loneliness go. It also wanted to pulse with magic again and be part of something. The two sides warred for a while.

"No, little one," it said. "You are too small. Too young. Too new." I felt it start to shut down again.

"Penny!" I called desperately, and then she was there. I'd heard her in my head, and I'd seen her assume different shapes as metal, but I'd never seen her as a person before.

She was beautiful. She was about six feet tall and built like an Amazon warrior. Her skin was silver, and her eyes and hair were copper. She flowed and moved with liquid grace and power. Her hair fluttered in an invisible breeze and she smiled at me like the sun rising on a spring morning.

Something about her made music while she walked, like the tinkling of bells. Although she was metal, she exuded warmth and life. She came over and I hugged her. I thought she might be cool, but she was warm too. Maybe awakened creatures were warm?

I realized I was already thinking of the sword as a creature and less as an instrument of death. It was alive and hurting. I hated that.

"Penny, the sword doesn't have a lot of magic left," I said. I wasn't sure how much she already knew. "It's lonely and you know I don't like that. I also need it to let me go. Can you see what you can do?"

She chimed at me and I felt approval and agreement. Penny put her hand on the sword too, and I felt it vibrate. She buzzed at the sword and it buzzed back. This went on for a brief moment. Much sooner than I thought, she looked at me and smiled.

"It is done," she said. I heard it through my link with the sword. "It is done," the sword agreed. I guess we were all communicating together now. Like group Skype, only magical.

"That's nice." I said. "But I'm afraid I don't understand metal talk, or earth, or whatever you were using to communicate with. So, I'm not sure what is done."

"You are a source," the sword said. "That is impressive in one so young. I will not silence you."

"Thanks!" I said. I didn't want to be silenced. What good is being immortal if you only live for a few weeks?

"She has also said you spend time with her. I would like to have that again. I have decided to live." The sword said that as a proclamation. Like it was setting something in stone, which I guess it was sort of.

"We have agreed to share your magic and ownership of you. She will remain your primary, and when you have aged, I will be your secondary."

Well that was interesting. I thought of Penny as my charm. I guess she thought of me as hers, and now she had agreed to share me.

I didn't have the type of power this sword needed, though. I was a trickle; this thing could use a whole river. If it would get me out of this sticky situation, though, I'd give it what I had.

"That sounds good," I said. "There are a couple more things, though. Just stuff for right now." Penny chimed at me questioningly. The sword stayed silent. We'd have to work on its conversational skills. If I made it through this there would be plenty of time for that later.

"I need part of you to stay inside me and seal the wound. If you come out, I'll bleed to death. Us fleshy creatures need liquid to live. If all our liquid runs out, then we dry up and die." I tried to push out images to match what I was saying. I'm sure metal didn't have any frame of reference for blood and what it was to us.

Penny and the Sword buzzed at each other. I'm sure it was something like, "Fleshy things. So strange. Oh well, let's humor him." Then Penny chimed at me that this was okay.

"The other thing is, I still need to take out the necromancer that is attacking the House. I know you are low on magic, but will you fight for me this time?" I knew I was asking a lot, but with a working magic sword I might have a chance.

"Yes," the sword said. "I have something to ask also. I do not want to be a sword anymore."

Say what? A sword that didn't want to be a sword? How was it going to fight for me? I got a series of images with this statement. It didn't like all the screaming and clanging and anger that came with battle. It was a sword, but it did not love battle. Actually, it hated it.

It liked warmth and sunlight and sitting still. I got images of the sword in the forge with the little hairy guy. The guy seemed to have a skill like John's, and he made all kinds of items. He wasn't as good as John, though. John didn't need a forge to work with metal. Most of the items this guy made were normal things for the times, but some of them were magical as well. The sword enjoyed being part of the group.

The sword didn't have a name for it, but in an awakened sort of way, they were friends. They would communicate outside of the hairy guy and they liked being together. When the sword was stolen, it not only lost its source, it lost its circle of friends too. It was lonely. All these years, and it was lonely. I knew what that was like and my heart went out to it. I wasn't much of a source yet, but I could give it a home.

I didn't know how to say that in words, so I just sent it emotions and images. Images of home. Images of belonging. I told it about John and Sandy and how they loved each other even though they said they didn't. I showed it Penny and how much I had missed her when she had taken on too much magic for me. I showed it Bermuda and how I loved waking up to him and Tyler in the morning. As I showed it all this, I got a sense of something. There was something it dreamed about but didn't dare ask for.

"If you aren't a sword, what would you like to be?" I asked. I was pretty sure I was on the right track.

"I want to be round," it said. "And empty. I was near this once. It seemed to have a good life." Of all things, I got the image of a vase. It was old style, with a pot shaped bottom and two handles with a narrower top. It was very ornate, with swirls and flowers and those fat baby angels. I got the impression that this thing had sat in the window, filled with flowers, and been admired and cherished. That was what the sword wanted to be.

"Sure!" I said. "That sounds great to me. I have a window in my bedroom, and it gets the sun in the morning. You can sit there and enjoy your life. You don't have to be a sword for me."

I sent it images of my bedroom window and it seemed happy, even excited. This whole conversation was not turning out like I had expected at all. I got a sense that there was something holding it back.

"Remember, you can't turn into a vase right away," I said. "I'll leak out, and we still have a battle to win."

That's when I got it. This massive magical sword didn't know how to change its shape.

"Oh, that's easy," I said. "Ask Penny. She started out as a flat disk we use for money and now look at her! She's pretty amazing when it comes to transforming." My praise went down well with Penny. All her bells tinkled and soon she was buzzing at the sword. It was surprised at how easy it was, and soon we had a plan.

25

Time for the Claws

I jumped back to real life. On the one hand, nothing had changed. The sword was still sticking through me and stuck into the ground. The necromancer was still beating on the House shields.

On the other hand, everything had changed. My remnants were gone. My body and magic were finally all mine. No more psycho riders trying to take me over. Now I could feel the sword, its power inside me. It wasn't an aggressive battle sword, but it was a defender. That's how it had been made. It had accepted me as its own, and now it was ready. It was time to defend!

It requested magic, and I gave it. The pull was intense. I'd never had anything drain me like that before. I got the impression it was trying to be gentle too. I couldn't imagine what it would be like if it really sucked in my magic. I had a lot of growing to do before that happened.

The sword flowed like liquid, just like it had learned from Penny. The handle fell off; it wasn't enchanted at all. The part of the sword inside me lost its edge. I didn't need it cutting me anymore. The metal flowed around me, like a thin but powerful armor. It also flowed down my arms and I sprouted claws.

This was so badass! I was a liquid metal version of Wolverine.

The sword was still pulling magic, but not as much anymore. I checked the wound. I was bleeding, but the former sword was doing a good job of keeping me sealed up. It was time to kick some mage butt.

I got to my feet. I hurt, but I could move. It was going to be okay. I could work with this.

I started toward the mage just as a horde of red-eyed granny godmothers flew by me and attacked him. The air was so thick with them that I was afraid to move in case I hurt my own people.

For a moment, I thought that would surely be the end of him. There was no way he could stand up to this dense of an assault. As many of them as there were, though, they couldn't get through his armor.

I also saw Bermuda. He was limping, but he was all right. He came up and rubbed against my leg as I watched how the mage was going to fare against the godmothers. I wanted to give him some love, but I didn't want to stick him with my new claws. The sword was slowly draining my magic too; I needed to end this before I ran out.

Once it was apparent that the grannies couldn't get through, I made my move. The mage had gone back to attacking the shield, so it was easy to come up behind him. My creations weren't strong enough to make a dent in his armor, but I had magic claws now. It was time to see what they could do.

I punched the mage hard, right in the center of his back. I felt the sword's magic flare, and the claws pierced his armor and stabbed right through him.

I thought the mage would fall to his knees or scream or something. I expected blood at the very least. Instead, the mage froze. Then he reformed so that he was facing me. He didn't turn around; he morphed like he was made of water.

This wasn't a mage. This was a golem! I was fighting another freaking golem!

When I'd stabbed it in the back, I thought I was being smart. I thought it wouldn't be able to reach me. Now it was like I had stabbed it in the front, and it could reach me just fine.

It swung a blow at my head, and I blocked it with my claws. They cut through part of its fist and a chunk fell off. It hit the ground and flowed like heavy syrup. The grannies pounced.

Now that it wasn't part of the main body, they could handle it, and in a few seconds that part of the necro-golem was gone. The golem's hand reformed, although now it was smaller than before.

So that was my battle plan. Hack this thing apart piece by piece.

The golem hit me with its other hand. It rattled me, but the sword armor stopped most of the impact. I pulled my claws out of its chest and went to town.

It was attacking me with its arms, so I tore them apart first. I found I couldn't take out too big of a chunk or my claws would get stuck. I got battered a few times before I could get away, so I learned quickly. The sword was still using my magic to flow with my movements, so I had a limited amount of time before I ran out and it froze up.

That didn't bear thinking about, so instead I tore into it like a mad man. I hacked at it until it had no arms left. It kept trying to reform them with the mass it had left, so it got smaller and smaller. I didn't want it running away either, so I shredded its legs too.

The last thing I needed was this thing coming back again with fresh spirits and another tiger. It grew most of its arms back, but now I'd managed to completely take off one of its legs. It put its remaining leg in the center and hopped around. Whoever had made this golem was crazy good.

Its new arms were much thinner and easier to get through. I'd gotten the hang of dealing with this necro now. I went after a shoulder and soon its entire arm fell off. That was such a big chunk it took the godmothers a while to clean it up, but they managed just fine.

I hacked off more regrown arms and more legs and soon the necro-golem was down to the size of a sack of potatoes. That was good because I was running out of energy. I was low on magic and low on stamina. I hurt all over, but especially where the sword had gone through me. I wasn't in good shape and I needed this to be over.

I gave a swipe and hit something solid. That had to be the core. I hammered at the spot and finally ripped it out. When I did, the rest of the golem fell apart. I guess the core gave up at that point as thick black liquid leaked out of it.

The granny godmothers did their thing and soon the core was empty. It sat there, a hunk of metal and runes. Whatever life it had was gone. Sandy could add that one to her collection and study it too. I wanted nothing to do with it right now.

I picked it up, walked through the shield, and collapsed on the grass. The former sword withdrew the claws, flowed back down my arms, and started pooling on the grass. The rest of my liquid armor came off, including the part of the sword still inside me. Finally, it formed into an egg shape, just like Penny does when she's resting, and shut down. It was just in time too. It had almost no magic remaining, and I had no more magic to give.

"Thank you so much!" I told it, along with a mental image of a hug. I'd work on giving it magic and turning it into a vase like it wanted. For now, though, I was done.

The House was safe. I was safe. Annabeth was safe.

The danger was past and that was good enough for now.

The front door of the House opened, and Annabeth came out. She looked exhausted but happy, until she saw the blood everywhere. I was covered in it, and now that the sword was out of me, I was bleeding out all over the grass too. She told me to hang on and ran back into the house. Hopefully she was getting some bandages to patch me up.

There was one thing I needed to do. The horde of granny godmothers deserved to rest. They had done an amazing job. They had freed a crap ton of spirits, taken out a saber-toothed tiger, and cleaned up a necro-golem. I'd say my little creations had saved the day.

Now I was thinking about the tiger, it was probably a golem too, which meant there was another core somewhere. Oh well; I'd get it later.

In the meantime, I needed to say goodnight to Penny. She was going to absorb all this magic and go to sleep again. At least I knew what to do to bring her back. This time would be harder, though. This time my creations had absorbed the power of two golems instead of one, as well as the black spores on all those spirits.

"Goodnight, Penny," I said. "I'll work really hard on this and I'll talk to you soon." She gave me a sad little trill. She was going to miss me too.

I held my hand up in the air and my creations swooped in for a final goodbye. Their red eyes were gone, and they were back to the kindly looking, gray haired, dust busting, cheerful godmothers I'd started with. They all gave me a wave as they flew into Penny and went back home.

There were thousands and thousands of them, so it took a while. I made sure they didn't have any black dust on them. I didn't want anything like that near Penny.

Bermuda came over and crawled up by my face. The horde of godmothers didn't bother him at all. He closed his eyes and started purring. Then he started doing the little paw scrunchy thing. He was happy.

It seemed to take forever, but finally it was done. Now that my little flying creations were safe, I pulled in the feather wash and absorbed it too.

I put my arm down and rested. There was so much to do. I'd get to it soon. For now, I was safe.

I was home.

I relaxed—and passed out.

Epilogue

I woke up slowly, which is my favorite way to begin the morning. I had no idea what time it was, and I didn't care. I was just sleepy breathing and feeling the snuggle.

Tyler was there. We were spooning again and he was wrapped around me. His strong arm was snug around my chest and I felt his breath on my neck.

He was my happy blanket and I felt safe.

Bermuda was there too. His kitten breaths were much faster than ours and his paws were twitching. He must have been dreaming about chasing birds or butterflies.

I didn't remember getting there and that was okay. Memories tried to form but I pushed them away. There would be plenty of time for that later. Right then, I just wanted to stay in that peaceful moment.

I breathed. I existed. And finally, I woke up a bit more.

Bermuda rolled over on his back, belly to the sky, and it was finally time for some loving. I shifted to free up my arm from Tyler and pain exploded from my chest. It was so sharp and so fast, it overwhelmed me. I tensed up, which only made it worse.

"Ow! Ow! Ow!" I hissed. I wanted to say a lot more, but I tried to keep at least a little bit of manliness about me. I wanted to holler like I'd been shot, but Tyler was there.

"Easy now." Tyler was awake and helping me roll over on my back.

"Just take it easy," he said soothingly.

My peace was gone. Thank goodness I'd enjoyed it while I could. Instead, everything was shifting and my chest was on fire.

Finally, I got on my back and stopped moving. I breathed through the pain and finally it started settling down. All the memories rushed in—the big fight with Isobel, the necro-golem, and being run through with a sword.

No wonder I was hurting. I'd been impaled by a sword!

Tyler kept talking to me in his soothing voice and I kept breathing. Eventually I relaxed, which helped the pain, so I could relax more.

Finally, we all got settled again. Bermuda wanted to climb up on my chest but that was an immediate veto. Ultimately, he curled up by my head, gave me a couple licks, and then settled into some serious purring.

Tyler was propped up on one arm looking down at me. He looked like an angel. If I hadn't been hurting so badly, I'd have gotten lost in his chocolate eyes.

He ran his fingers through my hair. Then he kissed me. His warmth soothed me, and I finally settled down enough to talk again.

"Well, that certainly brought all the memories back." I tried to sound brave but I'm not sure I succeeded.

"I'm sure it did," he laughed gently. "So, what happened? I can feel your last remnant is gone."

I started with Sandy getting kidnapped and continued to the massive fight in the warehouse, the toxic spirits, facing off against Thing One in my throne room, and ended with the magic sword and the necro-golem. The whole thing seemed fantastical. I almost couldn't believe it had happened.

Reliving it again was traumatic, but Tyler kept calming me down and asking questions which moved the tale along. Finally, I finished up and laid there for a moment, processing it all.

Then Tyler picked up the story and filled in the missing pieces for me. Tyler had arrived while Annabeth was trying to bandage me up on the front lawn. Apparently, there was a lot of blood and I had looked awful. Annabeth was freaking out. Once I was patched up, they had taken me back to my apartment, cleaned me up, and put me to bed. They had found both golem cores and they were now in my dresser drawer, along with the egg-shaped steel of the former sword.

Once I was taken care of, they had gone back to the warehouse for Sandy and John. John wasn't listening to anyone and it had taken everything they had to get him to pick up Sandy and come home. Sandy was now in her bed and she hadn't woken up or moved at all. John, all stony nine foot of him, was just sitting beside her. Annabeth had worn herself out worrying about everyone and had finally gone to bed.

"So, where were you during all this?" I asked. I didn't mean to sound accusing, but it kind of came off that way. "We could have really used you in the warehouse fight."

"The House pulled me away," Tyler said. "I have a unique skill set and there was a houseguest at a different House that needed me. Afterwards, the House sent me home. I hadn't been there in a while and it was nice. Things had been quiet here so I thought a few hours wouldn't hurt. I had no idea all this was going to happen." He gestured at my chest and all the bandages. "I'm so sorry all this happened and that I wasn't here." He cupped my face with his hand and looked at me intently. "I'm really sorry you got hurt again." He kissed me and then started running his fingers through my hair. I wanted to be mad at him, but his touch felt so nice. "I'm not reliable," he said. "Not in the regular houseguest kind of way. I can't just defend one place. I have a home. I have the missions the House sends me on. And I have here." He gave me the intense look again.

Something occurred to me. My remnant was gone, yet Tyler was here in bed with me. Did that mean something?

"So, what does that mean?" I asked. "I like waking up with you. I like the way you hold me. I like the way you look at me." I thought about something else. "I like how easy it is to be naked with you."

I realized it was true. I was comfortable with him in a way I hadn't been before with all my other lovers. I was usually wondering what they were thinking of me and how long I could stay with them. Even when I had my own money, I was still in my head about how I looked and how they were doing.

Tyler was just so perfect that somehow, I was at ease with him. I wasn't competing with him. I couldn't compete with him. Somehow that gave me freedom to just be me. I liked it.

"I'm learning something from all this myself," Tyler said. "I thought I was happy enough. I thought my home and my missions for the House were all I wanted. Now I'm not so sure. This sounds strange, even to me, but I think I was lonely and didn't know it." He gave me a wry smile. "Someday I'll tell you about my Waker Moment. It wasn't pretty and it went on for a long time. When I finally escaped, I was very defensive, and I was determined to make myself as strong as possible."

He paused for a long moment, still playing with my hair.

"Now I think maybe I made myself too strong. Too defended. Spending time here with Sandy, John, and Annabeth has been really nice. I've laughed and connected more than I have in a long time."

"Waking up with you has been the best, though." He smiled and it was like the sun came out. "There is something about you that puts me at ease. I guess you feel comfortable around me and that makes me comfortable around you."

He kissed me again. I really liked where this was heading. This supernatural world was crazy. Just crazy. Having someone to wake up with grounded me. These perfect mornings were pure gold. I loved them.

If my supernatural life kept going like it had the last few weeks, I'd need all the grounding I could get. I wanted to get strong, but I didn't want to get closed off either. Being lonely sucked.

"I was hoping that you wouldn't mind if I slept here sometimes," Tyler said. I went to say, 'hell yes,' but he put his finger on my lips and stopped me.

"Before you say anything, just know that is all I can offer. I have other commitments and you are going to be having more adventures. Life for you and me is not calm right now."

I'd figured that. But I wasn't a home wrecker, so there was one question I needed to get answered.

"I have a question for you before I decide," I said. He cocked his eyebrow in query. "Who do you have at home? I know you said it was complicated . . . or something like that. I just need to know what I'm getting into."

He laughed. Then kissed me again.

"Who I have at home is Mr. Tubbles." I just looked confused. "He's an orange tabby cat. He's only got three legs and one eye, but he's a survivor like me."

Ohhhhhh. He had a cat! Well, that wasn't so bad at all.

"The only thing, though, is that he is very jealous. He doesn't like anyone but me. If I bring anyone home, he cries and glares at them until they leave. It would be funny if it wasn't so tragic."

Now I really wanted to meet him. I wondered if he would like Bermuda? It didn't sound like it.

Tyler kissed me again and this time I gladly kissed him back. If I wasn't hurting so bad, I'd have been more than happy to turn kissing into something else.

"I'll be right back," he said and hopped out of bed. As he headed toward the bathroom, I admired every inch of him. He had the body of an Olympic diver and he wanted to wake up with me. Yes, please!

All that blood loss made me weak and sleepy. I closed my eyes and let my mind drift for a moment. The bathroom was just outside of the range of my magic sight. I listened to the bathroom sounds and waited for Tyler to appear on my radar again. Finally, I heard the door open.

I waited. I heard nothing.

Tyler didn't appear in my magic sight.

"Tyler?" I called.

"Tyler?"

Thank You!

Thank you for reading my book! Not only did you make it to the end, but you're reading all the ending stuff. Clearly you are awesome. :)

I really hope you enjoyed the journey. If you did, please tell others about it! This world only exists when people read it. So the more readers it has, the larger the world can be.

I've wanted to write a book since I was ten years old and I figured I should start small. This whole thing was supposed to just be a writing exercise. Once I made it through the Death Experience, though, the world just kept growing and wouldn't let go. Jason, Sandy, John, Tyler and Annabeth kept whispering in my ear, and finally, four years later, I made it to the end of the first adventure.

The next book is already in the works. It picks up a week later and deals with the fall out of Sandy losing her magic and John having too much magic. We find out what happened to Tyler, Jason starts learning how to fight, and Annabeth gets creative with her sound affinity. I think it's going to be a good time!

Note About Reviews

Reviews are so important! Good reviews let Amazon and Google know you liked the book and they will then suggest it to other readers.

I'm an avid reader, but for the longest time I never posted a review. I didn't know what to say and I felt like the world would judge me. So, for all of you who like the book, want to recommend it, but don't know what to say - here is a simple format to use:

Title: Just say you enjoyed it and how you read it. Example: "This is a fun read. I read it in two days."

Description: Just act like it is a text to me. Just tell me your favorite character and what you liked about them. If you still need more words - just add in your favorite scene.
Example: "John was my favorite character in the book. He seemed like such a fun guy to hang out with. I loved the scene where he gets Jason drunk and they toast everything. That is something I would do!"

More About Author

Before I was a writer, I was a Photoshop artist. I'd ask guys to be my models, shoot them against a neutral background and then Photoshop a scene together. I've attached a few samples below and you can check out my shop on Etsy.

https://www.etsy.com/shop/MichaelTaggartPhoto

Genie

Oxygen

Tryst

Trials of Eros

For all you cat people, Bermuda Moses is real and he's helped me on every step of my journey as an author. He's older now, of course, but I wrote him into the book as a kitten. Here's a picture of him when he was a wee thing.

And here he is with his brother (Memphis Blue Malachi) and my husband Harold

Here is his sister Halo. She's the smallest of the group but she's the boss!